Critically acclaimed Glaswegian crime writer Denise Mina is the author of eleven novels and the two-time winner of the prestigious Theakstons Old Peculier Crime Novel of the Year Award. She also writes short stories and in 2006 wrote her first play. As well as all of this, she is a regular contributor to TV and radio. Find out more about Denise's writing at www.denisemina.co.uk

By Denise Mina

Garnethill
Exile
Resolution
Sanctum
The Field of Blood
The Dead Hour
The Last Breath
Still Midnight
The End of the Wasp Season
Gods and Beasts
The Red Road
Blood, Salt, Water

STILL
MIDNIGHT

Denise Mina

An Orion paperback

First published in Great Britain in 2009
by Orion Books
This paperback edition published in 2014
by Orion Books,
an imprint of The Orion Publishing Group Ltd,
Carmelite House, 50 Victoria Embankment
London EC4Y 0DZ

An Hachette UK company

7 9 10 8 6

A CIP catalogue record for this book
is available from the British Library.

ISBN 978-1-4091-5061-9

Typeset by Input Data Services Ltd, Bridgwater, Somerset

Printed and bound by CPI Group (UK), Croydon, CR0 4YY

The Orion Publishing Group's policy is to use papers that
are natural, renewable and recyclable products and
made from wood grown in sustainable forests. The logging
and manufacturing processes are expected to conform to
the environmental regulations of the country of origin.

www.orionbooks.co.uk

For Gerry, A.K.A. Coffee,
for the story, for shoving me
off walls/bunk beds/sheds and for
introducing me to The Clash.

Acknowledgements

Many thanks to Peter, Jon, Jade and everyone who helped me get this done.

And to Stevo, Mum, Tonia and Ownie and Ferg for their support.

I

An orange Sainsbury's plastic bag in full sail floated along the dark pavement. Belly bowed, handles erect, it sashayed like a Victorian gentleman on a Sunday stroll, passed a garden gate and followed the line of the low rockery wall until a sudden breeze buffeted it, lifting the fat bag off its heels, slamming it into the side of a large white van.

Air knocked from it, the bag crumpled to the floor, settling softly under the van's back wheel.

The van was barely three weeks old, had already been stolen and bore false number plates. It was parked carefully at the kerb, still warm from the heat of the engine, and in six hours' time it would be found smouldering in woodland, all forensic traces of the men inside obliterated.

Three men sat in the cabin, faces turned in chorus, watching the bungalow across the road.

The driver, Malki, leaned over the steering wheel. He was junkie-thin. From deep inside the dark hood of his tracksuit his sunken eyes darted around the street like a cat hunting a fly.

The two men next to him moved as one animal. Eddy in the middle and Pat sitting by the far door. Both in their late twenties, they'd worked for seven years as a two-man door crew on the graveyard shift. They'd watched films together, met and dumped women together, went to the gym together and, in the manner of married couples, their style had harmonised. Both were meaty, dressed identically in brand new black camouflage trousers, high lace boots, flack waistcoats and balaclavas rolled up to their foreheads. All the gear was fresh from the packet, the display creases still discernable.

A longer look would identify the differences between them. Eddy in the middle drank too much since the wife and kids left. He ate greasy takeaways late at night when he got in from work, undoing all the good he'd done himself in the weights room, and had become bloated and bitter. His eye was forever fixed on what he didn't have.

It had long been a bone of contention between them that Pat was handsome. Worse, he looked younger than Eddy. More moderate in his character, he didn't eat or drink as much and fumed less. He was blessed with a head of lush yellow hair, appealingly regular features, and had a stillness about him that made women feel safe. His nose had been broken but even that only served to make his face look vulnerable.

It was Eddy who had come up with the scheme and he had bought the kit. Belligerently, he had bought both sets in the same size, in his size. As they'd dressed together in Eddy's messy bedsit he'd brought out a tin of black camouflage make-up for them to smear on their faces, like they did when they went paintballing. Softly, almost tenderly, Pat said no and made him put it away. They'd be wearing balaclavas; it wasn't necessary and that stuff dried out and made Pat's skin itchy. The glee with which Eddy had produced it worried Pat. It was as if they were putting the final touches to a surprising Halloween costume instead of planning a home invasion that could lead to a twenty-year stretch. Pat had never even done an overnight. Now he fingered the flattened bridge of his nose, covering his face with his hand, hiding his doubt.

He looked down at the gun in his lap. It was heavier than he would have thought, he was worried about being able to hold it up with one hand. He glanced at Eddy and found him glaring at the bungalow as if it had insulted him.

Pat shouldn't be here. He shouldn't have volunteered Malki to be here either. This wasn't about trying to cheer Eddy up any more. This was dangerous, this felt like a mistake. He looked away. Eddy had been through too much recently. Not big stuff but sore stuff, and Pat felt as if a single reproachful glance might snap him in half. Still, he looked up at the neat little garden path, at the quiet glowing house and thought that a twenty-year stretch was an awful lot of sorry-about-your-wife.

It was a nice family bungalow, well proportioned, with a shallow garden stretching all the way around the corner into the next street. The current owner, pragmatic, without thought for aesthetics, had bricked over the lawn and flower beds to create a car park. A blue television tinge flickered in the living-room window and a warm pink shone through the glass front door into the hall.

'See?' Eddy said softly, keeping his eyes on the house. 'Single hostile in living room. Small, possibly female.'

A woman in her own home. Nothing hostile about that. Instead of saying it Pat nodded and said, 'Check.'

'We're going in along the back wall, 'member to stay in the dark, until we get to the front door.'

'Check.' Pat didn't really know the military patter and was wary of straying from that one word. Eddy was enjoying it, the whole special ops thing, and Pat didn't want to spoil it for him.

'Then—' Eddy broke off into quasi-militaristic signs. He pointed at Pat, indicated forwards, touched his own chest and swivelled his head to show he'd be on lookout. He mimed Pat knocking on the front door, his eyes widened with warning as an imaginary hostile opened it, and his hand chopped a Go! Go! Go! through the air. His hand got into the house and then, zig-zagging like a fish through reeds, looked into all the rooms off the hall, circling all the hostiles they had gathered in the hallway.

'*Then* we ask for Bob. Not before. *Not before*. Don't give the cunt warning while he could still be concealed. And no names once we get in. Clear?'

'Check.'

Eddy turned and slapped the jittery driver's arm with the back of his hand. 'When the door opens for the second time, we're coming out. You start the engine, pull up over there.' He pointed to the garden gate. 'Got it?'

Malki stared steadily into the street, his face slack, his eyes glazed over.

'Malki.' Pat leaned across Eddy and touched Malki's forearm gently. 'Hey, Malki-man, d'ye hear Eddy just then?'

Malki came alive. 'Aye, no worries, man, like, soon as I see the light – doof! Up there, right? Straight there, man.' He held the steering wheel tight and nodded adamantly, half affirmation, half wired-junkie tremor. His eyelashes were as ginger as his hair, straight and long as a cow's.

Pat bit his lip and sat back, looking out of the side window. He could feel Eddy's reproachful glance burning his cheek. Malki was there because he was Pat's young cousin. Malki needed the dosh, he always needed dosh, but he wasn't fit for it. Neither was Pat, if he was honest.

For a moment all three looked back at the bungalow, Pat chewing the inside of his cheek, Eddy angry and frowning, Malki nodding and nodding and nodding.

The wind picked up.

Below the van's back wheel the stunned plastic bag was waking up. As the breeze streamed below the car the bag filled up at one corner and began tugging its feet free until it slid out from the undercarriage.

In the wide, still street the bag rose to its feet, performed an elegant cartwheel across the road, towards the house and took flight in a sharp cross draft at the corner. It parasailed ten feet into the air, an orange moon, up and up, drifting out of sight of the van, around the corner to the other side of the bungalow and over the roof of a blue Vauxhall Vectra.

The Vauxhall's headlights were off but two men sat inside, slumped in the front seats, arms folded, waiting.

They were a scant five years younger than the pretend soldiers in the van around the corner but were better fed, better groomed, altogether more shiny and hopeful.

Omar was spindly and awkward, a walking elbow-jab. He still had the sort of ethereal thinness young men have before they fill out; everything about him was elongated: his nose was long, his jaw pointed, his fingers so long and thin they seemed to have extra joints on them. Mo, in the driver's seat, was round faced, with a bulbous end to his nose that would worsen as he aged.

They had been waiting for twenty minutes, talking sometimes to fill the time, but mostly silent. The radio rumbled in the background and the soft yellow light lit their chins. Ramadan AM broadcast locally for only one month a year. It filled its schedules with young Glaswegians clumsily rehashing opinions they'd heard at Mosque or on tapes. Mo and Omar weren't listening for moral instruction; it was a small community and sometimes they knew the speakers and got a laugh when they sounded nervous or said stupid things. The debates were best early in the evening, when everyone was hungry. Mo and Omar would chant over the rancour: 'Give us a biscuit, give us a biscuit.'

Mo sat in the driver's seat resting his eye on a magazine with a double-page spread about Lamborghinis.

'Fuck, man,' he said almost to himself, 'couldn't pay me to take that car.'

Omar didn't answer.

'I mean park that car *anywhere* and it'll get keyed to fucking ribbons.'

'It's not for going messages for your mum.' Omar's voice was surprisingly high. ''S for cruising up the neighbourhood, being seen in.'

Mo looked at him. 'Impressing fit birds and that?'

'Aye.'

Mo looked back at the pictures. 'Aye, well, you'd know, being a noted ladies' man.'

Omar rubbed hard at his right eye with spidery fingers. 'Listen, man women are fighting to get at me. Just, like, when you're there they lay off, because, ye know, might make ye feel inadequate and that.'

'Course they do.' Mo nodded at the magazine. 'You're a good tipper.'

Omar yawned and stretched, drawling when he spoke. 'I'm an international lady magnet.'

Mo jabbed an animated finger at an action photo of a yellow Lamborghini taking a corner on a sunny mountainside. 'It looks like a speed bump. Folk won't know whether to be impressed or slow down, man.'

The pundit on Radio Ramadan gave a time check – 10.23 – and both did the mental calculation.

Mo spoke first. 'Give it five minutes or so.'

'Aye.' Omar yawned luxuriously again, juddering on the comedown, 'Bloody knackered ... Can't have a smoke in here, can I?'

'Nah, man, it'll stink the motor out.'

'Put my window down, then.'

Mo huffed and pressed the button on his door to lower Omar's window. Then he twitched a smile and lowered his own. Tutting, Omar took out his packet, handed a cigarette to Mo and took one himself before lighting them both up.

They sat, puffing shallow breaths, blowing white streams of smoke that flattened over the windscreen. The October breeze outside tugged thin tendrils of smoke out, over the roof of the car and into the quiet street.

Back around the corner, in the front seat of the stolen van, Eddy and Pat were pulling their balaclavas down, adjusting the eyeholes. Eddy picked up his gun and he and Pat looked at it. The barrel was vibrating, amplifying the shakes in his hand. Suddenly angry, Eddy nodded a 'go'.

Pat hesitated for only a moment before loyalty propelled him out of the van. By the time both his feet were on the street he was already rueing it.

Behind him Eddy slithered down, shut the door and thumped Pat on the back, knocking him towards the gate.

Pat turned and squared up to him, ready to say his piece, but Eddy didn't notice. Keeping his gun flush to his side, he ran in a low crouch across the road to the gate and up the dark path.

The wind in the street made Pat's eyes stream and through the tears he watched Eddy running up the path, fast and low, enjoying himself. Pat chased after him, aping him, his head down, back straight, a human battering ram. They took the steep garden path in single file, Eddy heading towards the pink glow at the front door, Pat running after Eddy to say no. Suddenly Eddy veered off the path, standing in the shadow of the fence.

Pat caught up to him. 'Eddy—'

But Eddy swung his gun up parallel to his cheek and flicked the safety catch off. His chest was heaving with excitement as he wrapped both hands around the butt and scampered over to the front door.

7

Pat watched Eddy, noting quietly that he was running too fast across the short space. Eddy arrived before he expected to, spun awkwardly and slammed his back flush against the wall, his head jerking back on his neck, his skull cracking loudly off the brickwork.

Eddy's eyes snapped shut at the pain. He bent forward from the waist slightly, panted, waggled the barrel of his gun at Pat to tell him to move.

Pat wondered suddenly if he could grab Eddy's arm, pull him back to the van. Or just turn and walk himself, get in the van with Malki, refuse to move, but they had shelled out for the van already, bought the guns, and anyway Malki needed to be paid. Malki really needed to be paid.

Pat took a breath and, against his own best counsel, sauntered casually out of the dark, up to the front door.

He pressed the bell.

A cosy three-tone chime rang out in the hallway and a moment later, behind the mottled glass panel, two shadows materialised, one far away down the hall, the other close, coming from the left, just feet away inside the door.

The faraway figure had set his shoulders in a huff, spoke indistinctly, sounded annoyed. The second figure answered him, drawling, insolent. She was close, had come from the living room to the left of the door. It was the hostile they had spotted from the van. Definitely female, she was slim, dressed in jeans and a grey T-shirt with long black hair loose down her back.

Graceful as water she reached for the handle.

The door fell open and a puff of warmth billowed out to meet Pat's nose – the smell of toast.

Pink carpet and walls. To his left was a small black telephone table between the living-room door and another. Above it, on the wall, a cheap-looking black velvet clock ticked loudly, a picture on the back of it, a gold line drawing of a mosque or something. Pat mapped the room: six doors leading off. Paki music coming from a back room, at least one other person in the house.

Pat looked at the hostile who had answered the door. She wasn't obviously beautiful; her nose was long and pointy and she had an angry red spot on her cheek. He could never explain, then or afterwards, why the sight of her struck him so, or why he froze, gun limp by his side, drinking in the flawless 's' of black hair resting on her shoulder. 'Hello Monkey,' said her T-shirt, a green slogan on faded soft grey, the line of the letters cracked and broken from the washing machine.

Aleesha looked back at him, quizzical, eyes snaking across his face as if she was trying to make sense of the black woollen canvas. A strand of blue-black hair slipped softly from her shoulder, coming to rest across her small apple-round breast. She was wearing western clothes and didn't seem to have a bra on under her T-shirt, which was odd because she was definitely the man's daughter; she looked like him, and Pat always thought those old Asian guys had a firm hold over their daughters.

'Who in the hell are you ...' called the man at the back of the hall. He was small, sixty or seventy, had an Amish-looking neat little curtain-hanging of a beard and wore pale blue nylon pyjamas, perfectly ironed, 'coming in here ...' his voice faded, the danger occurring to him, 'so late ... ?'

Ironed pyjamas and warmth and toast. Pat began to salivate. He wanted to walk in, shed his jacket and stay, but a sharp shoulder hit him from behind, shoving him into the house. Eddy barged in, stumbled over the door mat and staggered sideways up the pink hall, his crazy crab dance watched by everyone, until, bandy-legged, he regained his balance. His balaclava had slipped off-centre, blinding him

9

until he tugged at it, remembered his gun, raised it, seemed surprised at the sight of it in his hand.

Watching from the other end of the hall, Pat could sense his embarrassment. Eddy took a deep breath, tipped his head back and shouted through the mouth of the balaclava, 'BOB! *BOB!*'

His entrance, dress and manner were so distracting that no one really heard what he said. The pyjama'd man looked anxiously back at the door to see if anyone else was coming in. The girl next to Pat bristled. Fear settled like smog in the hallway.

Pat looked at the girl again. The colour had drained from her cheeks, her eyes were wide, watchful of Eddy, looking out for her father. He was struck by her again, felt his heart slow and the hairs on his skin rise as if reaching towards her. She saw him look, his pale blue eyes pleading and wondering.

Aleesha was a teenager and therefore only interested in the world as it spoke about her. She saw Pat like her, long for her to like him back and despite her bewilderment and terror, his frank admiration warmed her. Still, she was young and in the presence of her father and felt suddenly terribly embarrassed. Dropping her head forwards so that a curtain of black hair fell across her face, she rolled a shy step back towards the living-room door.

The movement made Eddy jump. He pounced towards her, snatched her arm, yanked her back towards Pat. 'DON'T FUCKING TRY. GET OUT HERE. STAY OUT *HERE.*'

Having thrown her off balance he let go and skipped back down to the pyjama'd man, leaving Aleesha bent over to the side. She glared at the arm Eddy had dared to touch. Ballsy as fuck. Pat smiled beneath his woolly mask. When she stood up straight her face was an inch from Pat's chest and she looked up at him, her plump lips parting, her fear superseded for a moment by anger.

In that moment, when she was no longer terrified, Pat's wool-framed eyes asked her a wordless question. Aleesha arched her back, stood tall, looking down her long nose and answered with a slow, proud blink.

Each smiled and looked away.

The sight of the unfamiliar pink carpet brought Pat to his senses. He raised his heavy gun at the ceiling, half-heartedly, as if he was showing it to her, and Aleesha smothered a panicky giggle.

A sharp click drew every eye to a door across the hall. It opened slowly and a big square man looked out into the hall. Billal took after his uncles, not his wee daddy, and his hugeness was unexpected and alarming.

Though only a few feet away, Eddy screamed at him, 'BOB? Are you Bob?'

Eyes wide, shoulders stiff, Billal stepped out of the room, shutting the door behind him. His hands stayed behind his back, holding the door handle firmly.

'BOB?'

'No,' said Billal quietly. 'I'm not ... no one called Bob here, mate.'

'OPEN IT!' shouted Eddy, jabbing the barrel of the gun at him. 'OPEN THAT DOOR!'

Billal glanced at his feet and swallowed awkwardly. 'Um, no, actually, I won't.'

At this Aleesha snorted, giving Pat an excuse to look at her again. Her hand was over her mouth, fingers glittering prettily with small cheap rings, false nails glued on badly, the index finger nail squinty. She couldn't be over seventeen. He shouldn't think those things about a seventeen-year-old. He had nieces that age.

Eddy stepped purposefully over to Billal, pointing his gun at his nose. 'MOVE IT!'

Hypnotised by the gun barrel, the big man stepped slowly to the side. Eddy raised his foot and kicked at the door with his heel.

The room was dimly lit. Straight across from the door was an old-fashioned double divan bed, high, with a dark wood headboard, much marked. Sitting in the bed was a wild-haired, bloated woman, two fingers of her right hand scissored around a hugely swollen brown nipple. In her other hand she cradled the bald head of a tiny baby.

She stared at the gun barrel and clutched the baby to her breast, covering herself with it.

Eddy was still staring at the place where the exposed nipple had been. 'Out,' he said. 'Get out here.'

Billal stepped between them, his palms forming a wall in front of the gun barrel. 'Careful with that, mate.'

Eddy panicked. 'DONT TOUCH MY GUN! NOB'DY TOUCH MY GUN.'

'OK, OK.' Billal raised his hands high in surrender, 'No worries, no bother.'

'AND YOU,' Eddy stepped aside to shout at the woman in the bed, 'OUT HERE.'

'Oh. But I've not to get up,' she said, looking at the big man for backup. 'I could haemorrhage.'

Eddy glanced at Pat, saw him stealing a lingering look at Aleesha's hair, and screamed across the hall, 'LIFT YOUR FUCKING GUN, PAT.'

Everyone in the hall realised his mistake before Eddy did. He should never have said Pat's name. Billal look away, the daddy flinched and Aleesha snorted and suppressed a panicked laugh.

Eddy bit his lower lip and began to tremble with panic. It wasn't going well. It wasn't going well at all. Feeling himself without an ally in the hall, Eddy spun back to Billal. 'FUCKER! YOU FUCKING FUCK! BOB! WHERE'S BOB?'

Billal raised his hands in surrender. 'Mate, there's no one called Bob here. There's no one else in the house. We've got a wee baby here. Just go.' He gestured to the front door. 'You just go and we'll say nothing, right? Just you go on out and there'll be no problem, eh?'

'*Who's shouting?*' A mother's command. Everyone stiffened and turned to look at the back of the hall.

Sadiqa was wide as she was tall, which wasn't very. She didn't have her glasses on and so peered down at the two black shadows. 'Omar? What are you boys doing?'

With the incongruous grace of a fat boxer, Eddy skipped down the hall, grabbed both her and the old man by the forearm, dragging them up to Billal's side. He stood them in a line, pointing his gun at each in turn, shouting so loud his voice cracked. To Aamir, 'WHO,' to Sadiqa, 'IS,' to Billal, 'BOB?'

Sadiqa was the only one who answered. 'A gun . . . ?'

Eddy's attention was on her now and Aamir stepped forward to distract him. His hands were up, his eyes down, and he wobbled his head, obsequious as an old country boy. 'Son, we's all Indians here. There's no Bobs here. No Bobs, wrong house.'

Sadiqa looked at the back of Aamir's head and sucked her teeth disapprovingly.

But Aamir ignored her and continued to beg. 'No Bobs, mate. Wrong. You go. No problem.'

The black velvet clock ticked loudly.

No one knew what to do. Except Aleesha. Addled with fear and the bold compliment of Pat's gaze, she was sure that the whole thing would be OK, that coming in with a gun was somehow a benign misunderstanding. She wanted it to stop. Looking at the side of Pat's head, she smiled and reached her left hand forward to the woollen rim, intending to whip the balaclava off with a cheerful 'Ta-da', put an end to the awkwardness.

Unexpected fingernails scratching the back of his neck shocked Pat into a spin.

He hadn't meant to pull the trigger.

Omar and Mo jumped when they heard the muffled 'whoomph' coming from the house and saw the flash of white light in Billal and Aleesha's bedroom window.

They turned to each other for confirmation of what they had seen, read the shock on one another's faces and threw their car doors open in unison, dropping their cigarettes in the street, leaving the doors wide as they bolted over the pavement. One after the other they leapt over the low garden wall, scrambling around the corner to the front door. Omar kicked it open.

Malki felt calm now, cool, OK. A flash of pink light caught the corner of his eye as the front door opened. He remembered his instructions and snapped into action.

Crumpling the still warm tinfoil in his hand into a ball, he went to throw it over his shoulder but stopped, thinking to himself that it would be unwise to do so. He smiled at his own lucidity, and brought his hand down, tucking the foil deep into the corner of his hoodie pocket and then, with mechanical precision, twisted the van key, slid the handbrake off, engaged the clutch and drove slowly forwards, straight across the road to the rendezvous point.

He was congratulating himself on having remembered the instructions but forgot to stop and crashed the front of the van into the low garden wall, smashing the left headlight.

Glass tinkled cheerfully on to the pavement. Malki bit his lip.

Omar kicked the door open and found everyone frozen still in the hall. Two strange men were there, dressed in army fatigues. The air smelled odd, smoky, sulphurous. Everyone was staring at Aleesha and for a moment neither Mo nor Omar could work out why.

She was standing with her arm up, as if she was pointing at the wall clock, looking over her shoulder. Omar followed her eyes to her hand. A blur of black red, violent red, fingers jumbled like a scattered jigsaw.

A sudden red snake raced down her arm.

Wild eyed, she turned to face the stranger in front of her. 'My fucking hand!' she said, using both accent and words that were forbidden in the house.

The gunman whimpered a sorry.

A fatter gunman leapt across the hall to Omar and Mo, pointing his gun in each of their faces and back again. 'ONE OF YOU FUCKERS IS BOB.'

Neither spoke.

'YOU.' He poked the gun at Mo's chest. 'You're Bob.'

But Mo had a different nose than the rest of them. Omar had the family features, Aamir's long nose and Sadiqa's narrow jaw. Without waiting for Mo to answer he turned his gun on Omar and said quietly, 'You're Bob.'

Sadiqa couldn't contain herself any longer. She reached for her favourite child and shouted, 'Not Omar! Not my Omar!'

At this Eddy became confused. In the silence, through the open front door, came the sound of shattered glass falling from the lights as Malki backed the van away from the wall's embrace.

'Fuck yees,' said Eddy spitefully. He reached over and

wrapped a hand tight around Aamir's throat. The small man didn't object or raise a hand; he kept his eyes down, implicating no one.

Eddie squeezed, saw that the old man was not going to resist or defend himself and was suddenly calm. 'Yous can tell Bob this: I want two million quid, used notes, by tomorrow night. Call the polis and this fucker dies. Fucking payback. For Afghanistan.'

'Afghanistan?' spat Sadiqa. 'I'm from Coatbridge, what's that ...' She caught her indignation, dropped her chin to her chest, shutting up.

Aleesha's hand was slowly coming down and she watched the blood pulse from the messy end of it. 'My fucking hand,' she whispered.

Letting go of Aamir's throat, Eddy skipped behind him, wrapping his forearm around the old man's chest, holding him along the Empire line.

Everyone in the hall braced themselves for a gun to Aamir's head, more shouting, but Eddy did neither. Instead he tipped his weight back, easily lifting the old man off his feet, and carried him backwards out of the front door like a heavy lamp.

Sheepish, Pat broke eye contact with Aleesha, muttered another sorry and followed him outside.

The hall suddenly came alive: Sadiqa lumbered across the hall to catch Aleesha, whose knees were giving way. Holding her daughter's arm above her head to stem the bleeding, she knocked the phone from its cradle and stabbed 999 on the keypad. Billal blocked the bedroom door with his body as he pulled his mobile from his pocket, punching the number in with his thumb. Even in the bed, the baby thrashing at her breast, Meeshra lunged for the mobile on the side table and called the emergency services.

Omar and Mo chased after the gunmen, out into the street.

The van had one headlight gleaming extra bright from the smashed casing. As it drove off along the street the back door was shutting, a chubby hand pulling at it, and Omar gave a plaintive little cry. 'Nugget . . .'

Mo grabbed his shoulder and tugged him towards the Vauxhall. The boys bolted for the car.

Mo drove as Omar watched for the van. It was a dark road. On the left was a golf course, on the right a dark stretch of balding bushes and shrubs leading up to a blank wall. Though the road was broad and straight, though the streets were quiet, they'd lost a massive white van, the only other car on the fucking road.

They had it at one point, they were sure: Mo had spotted tail lights ahead, high enough off the road to be a van. He saw a glimpse of white door creep cautiously around a corner, defying a red light.

As they came up to the road over the M8 motorway Mo slowed for a red light and Omar suddenly swung his arm over Mo's face, hitting his chin. 'Stop!' he shouted. 'Stop!'

Mo stamped on the brake, bringing the Vauxhall to an abrupt skidding standstill. Beltless, Omar slid like a comedy drunk into the footwell, his cheek smacking off the dashboard.

'Police!' shouted Omar from the footwell, pointing past Mo to the door. ''S police car!'

A squad car was tucked neatly into a small cut-off, lights dark, poised to catch speeding motorists. The two police officers inside had been watching the Vauxhall battering down the empty road towards them, had expected to follow it on to the motorway, pull it over and practise their sarcasm, but the emergency stop surprised them. They watched as Omar jumped out of the car, leaving his door swinging wide as he ran over to them.

'Police! Please . . .' A rude pink bruise was forming on his cheek from the collision with the dashboard.

Wary, the officers unclipped their belts, opened the doors and stepped out to meet him. 'Were you wearing a seat belt just then, sir?'

'Sorry, no, but listen, my dad, my dad's been taken away in a van.'

But they weren't listening to him. The policemen were looking at his clothes.

Both the boys were wearing traditional white baggy trousers and shirts. They had just come from mosque and so appeared to the officers as particularly clean and strange-looking. Omar had a zip-up Adidas hoody over his kameez and trainers, but Mo had a cardigan on and loafers and his scraggy beard was untrimmed.

Suddenly aware of how alien they looked, Mo attempted a friendly smile. 'All right, mate?' he said cheerfully to the nearest policeman but tension and fright distorted his voice and his face. Both officers' hands strayed to their belts. A lorry rumbled along the motorway below them.

'No,' Omar said helplessly. 'Please help us, men took my dad away in a van. They had guns.'

The police examined them in silence. From the open Vauxhall doors the sounds of Radio Ramadan floated out over the still suburban midnight: some guy, young, talking in a phoney Arab accent, arguing about the Qur'an.

Both boys suddenly realised how foreign this whole thing was going to look to the police

Taking this as a cue, the officer standing nearest Omar opened his notebook and spoke slowly. 'Could you tell me your name, sir?'

'Omar Anwar.' He carried on talking as the officer wrote it down. 'Look, men with guns came to our house and stole my dad, took him, they'd guns.'

The officer refused to look up from his notebook. 'How are you spelling that, sir?'

'He's been kidnapped.'

'I see. O – M- A- R, A – N- W- A- R?'

'Yeah, yeah, yeah. Look, we followed the van as far as the last set of lights but we lost them then and I think they're headed for the motorway. They could go anywhere . . .'

The officer taking the notes glanced up at the car, at the voices, at Mo's beard. Omar let out a weak laugh. 'No, look, my dad's just a wee guy that runs a shop, it's not a security matter, it's just guys with guns. They wanted money. Afghanistan, they said it was, something about Afghanistan.'

'Turn around and put your hands on the roof of the car please, sir.'

'They're criminals!'

'Just put your hands on the car please, sir.' He said it more firmly this time. Omar did as he was asked.

The other officer moved round to the other side of the car and motioned for Mo to come and copy Omar's example. With the boys arranged on either side of the car, the officers took a man each, patting them down.

Mo knew he looked the most alien because of his beard and so he started talking quietly to the officers searching him, thickening his accent to its private school best. 'Officer, we really appreciate that you have to do this, really, we do, but my friend's dad is just a very ordinary member of the public. He's Scottish.'

Omar watched across the roof of the car and saw the officer's eyes narrow spitefully at the back of Mo's neck. He knew, suddenly, that sounding posh was not the way to invite sympathy and he tried to signal to Mo, but Mo wasn't looking at him.

'You see,' continued Mo, 'my friend's dad was taken from his home by gunmen, they've injured his sixteen-year-old sister.'

''S that right?'

'Yes. They bundled him into a van and we ran after them, following the van, but we seem to have lost it.'

'Why didn't you call the police, *sir*?'

'Well, we went after them.'

'D'yees not have a mobile? One can drive, one can call.'

'I suppose ... we didn't think ... It's a big white van, possibly a Merc, a panel van, the left light at the front's broken, it's brighter, because they went into the wall near the house—'

'Right? Really?' The officer's pace was slow. He stopped searching Mo, half smirked, pressed the end of his automatic pencil.

Just then, looking over Mo's shoulder at the motorway below, Omar saw the van with one bright light coming out of the empty motorway towards them. He screamed, 'Hoi!' put two hands on the Vauxhall's bonnet and skimmed across it, sprinting to the crash barrier just as the van shot underneath the bridge. Omar hung over the railing, shouted after it, 'Nugget! Nugget!'

A blinding whoosh of pain stabbed his shoulder, swept up his neck and circled his ribcage, making his knees buckle. He twisted as he slid to the ground, trying to turn into the painful hold that the policeman had locked him in.

Holding him by the wrist, the officer lifted Omar to his feet as easily as a hollow stick, guiding him back across the road to the squad car. Omar saw the white van through the far railings, trundling off along the motorway, headed for the city.

2

Alex Morrow bit slowly into her index finger, pressing her teeth until she could hear a small crunch in the skin. She was so angry that the upper lid of her left eye was twitching, blurring the changing view through the rain-splattered car window. If she didn't calm down before they got there she'd blurt something, make a fool of herself in front of him. The thought of meeting Grant Bannerman face to face made her bite her finger again.

Years ago a well-meaning training officer had told her never to question a superior's decision, forget fair, just do the job, ignore the politics and don't take it home. What the hell did he know, she thought now, sinking her teeth a little deeper into the skin. He never rose above sergeant. At her level the whole job was politics, as if she had anything else to think about, as if she had a home.

The tinge of melodrama shamed her to her senses. She released her finger from the grip of her teeth. She had a home. Of course she had a bloody home. She just didn't want to go there.

The car purred quietly, the uniformed driver carefully taking his time, observing every traffic by-law because she was in the car, taking no chances. He pulled on the hand-brake at each set of lights. It was all she could do not to slap him.

She knew her anger was disproportionate and scattered, leaking from her like water through a sock. It was being noticed, remarked upon in her assessments. It's nothing, she said, it's about nothing.

They'd had a quiet night up until now. October was the start of the cold weather, when the drunken street fighters scurried home to beat uncomplaining wives in the warm, when all the really bad men went off to winter in the sun. Start of the academic year, she remembered, a good time for long-term investigations and reviving cold cases.

The streets were empty. Cold rain pattered softly on the glass, swept aside by the rhythmic wipers, revealing and obscuring the Vicky Road. The address they were headed to was familiar from her childhood, so quiet a suburban area that she hadn't been back in decades. The crimes here were burglaries, noisy teenage parties, local stuff.

She saw the driver glance uncertainly at his silent GPS for guidance. 'Take a right at the roundabout,' she said, 'then take a left.'

They were just a few streets away, so she went through the checklist she always followed before a public appearance. Hair tidy, touches of make-up in place, she ran a finger under each of her eyes. She had small eyes and her mascara tended to puddle underneath. Handbag on the floor of the car, nothing personal hanging out of the top, no tampons or photos. She pulled her suit jacket straight, touching the buttons with her fingertips, making sure her armour was secure.

The car pulled up at the mouth of the street, at an unfamiliar no entry sign and the driver hesitated, not knowing whether to break the law or observe it and piss about, circling the address through the back streets.

'Take it,' she snapped.

He turned into the road slowly, as if reluctant. He'd been reprimanded for a high-speed violation, she remembered now, and was showing the boss that all of that was behind him.

The street was smaller than she remembered, the houses

low bungalows rather than the mansions of her memory. She used to cross this street to primary school everyday. Her hand still remembered the warmth of her mother's palm as she led her across the road. She curled her fingers around her palm at the thought. This area seemed hugely wealthy to them back then.

Straight ahead blue and white tape had been strung across the road, blocking the street. A uniformed cop was standing in front of the tape and approached the driver's door as the car slowed to a stop. He was dressed against the cold in reflector jacket and big padded regulation gloves, scissoring the fingers of one hand into the other as he arrived at the window. Not long ago Alex had been in uniform, had worn the ridiculously padded gloves and remembered how uncomfortably they splayed her fingers. Her driver lowered the window.

The cop bent down. 'Road closed.'

'I'm here with a gaffer.' Her driver pointed at Morrow.

'Oh.' The cop blushed, embarrassed that he hadn't noticed her through the windscreen. 'Sorry. Can you park up over there?'

'Aye, keep your eyes open, won't you?' said Morrow.

The driver smirked, trying to side with her as he pulled up the road a little.

She could see all the way down the empty street to the tape at the far end. The house was on her right, taking up the corner, the crime scene forming an awkward T-junction around the house. Straight ahead of her, beyond the second line of tape, squad cars were parked with their siren lights still blinking, bathing the street blue then red, like Cinderella's dress. At Morrow's end of the road a couple of uniforms lingered in front of the tape, backs rod straight, hands clasped behind, formal poses that alerted anyone in the know to the fact that very senior officers were very nearby.

Her driver was pulling a long turn. 'Are you ... um, should I back ...?'

'Just *stop*.'

For a second his lips parted in dismay but then he clamped them shut, staring forwards as he pulled on the handbrake, not reacting. Forget fair. She knew she was wrong to speak to him like that, but she never knew how to fix these things. She opened the door and stepped out into the soft October rain, took a deep breath and leaned back into the cabin. 'Sorry,' she said abruptly, 'for being rude.' The driver looked frightened. 'To you.' The explanation didn't help. She got flustered and slammed the door, cursed herself. She should just be rude; it would be easier.

An older cop with the crime scene log clipboard approached her.

'DS Alex Morrow,' she said and he wrote it down. 'London Road.'

'Thank you, ma'am. DS Bannerman and DCI Mac-Kechnie are over there.' He pointed around the corner to the front of the house. She could see a huddle of heads beyond the low garden wall.

'MacKechnie's here?'

He seemed surprised too. MacKechnie meant it was a big case. A career case, but not her case, she remembered with a grind of her jaw.

'You first here?'

'Aye.'

'Taped off all entrances?'

'Aye. Alerted the Firearms Unit and they're just pulling out now.'

'Gunmen gone then?'

'Aye. They've searched front, back and sides.'

'Shots fired?'

'One, sixteen-year-old girl's hand blown off.'

'Kin hell.'

He hummed in agreement.

'Residents?'

'All over there giving statements.' He gestured straight down the road to the tape where the cars were blinking. Gathered beyond them were a crowd of people dressed in combinations of overcoats and pyjamas, slippers and shoes, and cops with notebooks talking to them one at a time. Everyone who lived inside the taped-off area would have been pulled out of their houses until the FAU had secured the area.

'Well done,' she said. 'Good job,' aware that she was making up for her rudeness to the driver by being nice to him. She knew it wasn't how to develop allies; you have to be nice to the ones you've insulted. He looked pleased anyway.

'Where's the path?'

He used his pencil to point her along the centre of the road and around the corner.

Morrow dipped under the tape and picked her way carefully, keeping her eye on the tarmac for missed evidence. She stopped and looked up. The house was on her right: a small wall on the pavement and then elevated ground, a bit of grass and then bricked over. A series of cars were parked there: a Nissan people carrier, an Audi, a new Mini and a small, dirty white van.

In the road next to her, marked with big white evidence cards, lay two cigarette ends. She bent down and squinted at them: the brand was Silk Cut. They had burnt out where they lay, the log of ash sitting on a strip of tar-yellowed paper. They were five feet apart, as if they had been thrown out of either window of a car. She looked back to the cop who had stopped her car.

'You – why aren't these bagged up?'

'Said to wait until the photographer had a picture, ma'am.'

They should have bagged them. It was raining and any DNA on the stubs would be lost. Bad scene management. Morrow was secretly glad.

She carried on to the corner, could see the residents better now: three Asian men standing together, young, talking to uniformed cops. An elderly white couple were there as well, both in overcoats with pyjamas underneath. A scowling housewife, young, alone, hair a sleepy tangle, stared at her. Morrow glared back: let us apologise for the inconvenience caused by saving you from armed raiders.

Morrow looked over at the house. There were two entrances to the garden: a wide metal gate leading straight up to off-road parking and a small ornamental one, open on to the path up to the front door. She turned the corner and saw a puddle of fresh safety glass on the pavement. Above it on the wall a few bricks were caved in.

Despite herself, her interest was piqued. She could feel it happening: facts, disjointed, irrelevant, being card indexed and filed away in her mind, the familiar private landscape of deduction. All the niceties of politics, personal or professional, eluded her always, but she could do this. It was the one absolute certainty for Alex Morrow. She was good at this.

She looked up and saw them standing just outside the ornamental gate, arms folded, waiting for Firearms to leave the property. DS Grant Bannerman and DCI MacKechnie stood flank to flank, shoulders almost touching, looking back up to the front door as they listened to two animated uniforms brief them on the witnesses' statements. Bannerman was nodding as if he already knew what had happened and was just there to check up on everybody. Next to him MacKechnie watched his prodigy approvingly, a little echo of the nod on his neck.

Bannerman. His sun-bleached hair was too long, hung slightly over his eyes, muscular, suntanned. She thought he aspired to look like a surfer but he looked like a careerist to her, a boy whose dad was in the force and introduced him to senior officers. That's how he got the promotion to DS while still in CID. Morrow had to leave, go back into uniform, do the exams and then transfer back. Friendless, without a sponsor, she'd done it through merit. No one retired and few got promoted in CID; it was a destination and the jobs were few and far. To make DS within CID an officer had to suck up to senior officers, go to the football with them, play golf and let them win.

Morrow and Bannerman had been sharing an office for a month but it wasn't going well. However many coffees he made her, however many KitKats he brought her from the machine, she could see in his eyes that he joked about her behind her back, couldn't take to her, feared her moods. He had already been settled in their office for two months before she arrived, seemed easygoing, was four years younger than her. And she was hard work, she knew that. If Morrow worked with herself she'd try and sit a few desks away.

Bannerman saw her now, walking towards him, and his smile lingered too long, going stale on his lips.

'Sir.' She tipped a nod at MacKechnie but couldn't bring herself to look at Bannerman. 'Grant.'

Grant Bannerman nodded back. 'All right, Morrow? What's happening?'

She could feel the blood draining from her face. 'Hello' wouldn't do for Grant. 'Good evening' wouldn't do. It had to be some cheesy greeting, a bit of a song, a line from Elvis or some fucking thing. He strove to be different because he wasn't. Her ambition was to fit in and she couldn't. Jealousy made her focus on him, notice small vulnerabilities like the occasional sunbed flush to his skin, how he often implied credit to himself for other people's work, and although superficially confident, how lost he sometimes looked in the company of other men.

Heat rose in her cheeks and she knew she had to cover up quickly. 'There's evidence getting wet around there,' she said. 'Two cigarette butts needing bagged up.'

Bannerman was wrong and knew it. 'We're waiting for the photographer.'

'No point proving they came from here if the traces have been washed off, is there?'

MacKechnie blinked indulgently. 'Best to go and get them bagged.'

Bannerman nodded at one of the cops, briefing them to go and do it.

The Firearms Unit were coming out of the house. They crowded out of the front door, looking terrifying. Four big men in black body armour blocking the light of the hallway. They each held intimidatingly large pistols, holding them with two hands as if they were likely to go off of their own volition and blow a hole in something vital.

They were laughing at something as they came down the path towards them, the relief marked in their shoulders and faces. Whenever a gun was used Firearms had to come to either disarm or ensure that no gun-toting nutters were hanging around in cupboards waiting to leap out when the police got there. It was a high-stress, short-life job. They were recruiting all the time, month on month getting more and more calls. A flood of redundant weapons were coming to Glasgow from Ireland, selling for buttons.

As the Unit came past they assumed MacKechnie was the senior and gave him the low-down: no one in there, no guns in the house, one bullet in the wall and a lot of blood. One resident still in the house, a bedridden new mother.

'Bedridden?' asked Morrow.

As if they were seeing her for the first time, all of the men looked at her.

'Well,' their DS answered weakly, 'she's just had a baby. A week ago or something.'

'How's she bedridden?'

'She's not to get up. Said she could haemorrhage.' The sergeant was embarrassed and laughed, 'I'm not qualified to check her stitches, am I?'

She watched as they all giggled together. Even Mac-Kechnie had a titter. Bannerman looked away. The sergeant opened his mouth to add to the joke, say something crude, but he saw the look on Morrow's face and bottled it.

'Anyway, that's us done,' he said, giving Bannerman a sympathetic look about Morrow. 'We're off.'

They watched the gaggle of big men pick their steps carefully down the far stem of the T-junction, tiptoeing until they were carefully beyond the tape and out of the crime scene. They climbed back in their shiny black van.

Morrow wished she was alone and could bite herself again but she took a breath and asked the cop, 'What's the story?'

The plod drew a breath to speak but Bannerman cut him dead. 'Family, at home after Ramadan prayers in the mosque—'

'Which mosque?'

'Central for the kids, Tintagell Road for the daddy.'

Morrow nodded, it made sense. Central was a city-wide mosque, young people from all over the city got to check each other out. Tintagell was smaller, local, had a tighter community feeling about it. If the kids were going to Central then they weren't territorial, weren't gang-marked. Good kids.

'Gathering back at the house,' Bannerman continued, 'doorbell rings, thinking that a family member had forgotten their keys, daughter opens door, father in hall. Two masked gunmen enter shouting threats, looking for someone called Rob. Demanded money and ordered them not to call us—'

'Much?'

'Two million.'

'*Pounds?*'

'Aye.'

They looked back at the house, valued it, MacKechnie said, 'Worth about three hundred K, do you think?'

Morrow and Bannerman nodded in agreement.

'Two million in cash? Did they get it?'

'There was no one called Rob here.'

'What colour were the gunmen? Were they Asian?'

'White. They had balaclavas on but they were white.'

'Who's Rob?'

'Dunno. Everyone's Indian, I mean, has Indian names at least, so ... no one called Rob.'

'No lodgers? No dodgy boyfriends?'

'No one. Money not forthcoming,' continued Bannerman, 'left with father as hostage.'

Morrow was puzzling at the house still. 'Could it just be a matter of the wrong address then?'

'As yet undetermined,' said Bannerman, meaning he didn't know.

'It's not a case of the wrong address,' she spoke to Mac-Kechnie, making him look up the road, 'because Albert Drive's just over there—'

'Millionaires' row,' interrupted Bannerman, leaning between them and nodding as if he'd thought of it.

She ploughed on. 'If they were just looking for a family with money they'd go there and smash a door in.'

'So?' MacKechnie encouraged her to draw a conclusion. Bannerman's nodding became manic.

'So, they came here deliberately, sir. They had intel about someone here that made them think there was money here. Ready money, maybe.'

'Unless …' Bannerman had to get MacKechnie's attention back on him, 'unless, they went to go to another house, set off the alarm or something, and turned back? I mean, we should check it out …' His voice faded halfway through the sentence, his confidence waning.

It was a fucking stupid suggestion.

'If armed men had burst in anywhere else tonight incident room control would have notified FAU, I think.' MacKechnie's voice was softer, correcting.

Morrow looked back at the squad cars littering the street and asked, 'D'ye say they were warned not to call us?'

Bannerman shrugged uncomfortably. He should have thought of that.

The cop answered, holding his witness statements up for support. 'Yeah. "Call the cops and this fu—"' He thought better of a word-for-word recitation. 'Um, threats to the hostage.'

MacKechnie looked at the squad cars and the menacing FAU van pulling out. 'Let's move this visible presence.'

Bannerman sloped off to give orders to that effect.

'If they said not to call us,' Morrow continued the thought, 'they must have been confident that the family would comply. Maybe they're right, maybe there is money here after all.'

MacKechnie checked that Bannerman was out of earshot. 'Morrow, we both know this is your case but I can't give it to you.'

'Sir, you said the next—'

'We've had a lot of trouble here recently, minorities, gangs fighting, the Boyle boy. Don't need any trouble with cultural misunderstandings.'

Morrow ground her jaw and stared at the house as if it had offended her. 'I'm from here, sir, I know the people in this area—'

'DS Bannerman can handle this,' he continued. 'You'll get the next one.'

This case was a career maker and MacKechnie was here guiding Bannerman by the elbow. The decision was made, fair didn't come into it, but her eye began to twitch again and she couldn't even bring herself to look at MacKechnie.

'Why not this one, sir?'

He didn't answer. When she looked back at him she followed his eyes to the Asian guys standing beyond the tape. They had the lost, limp look of victims. The oldest guy was big, and dressed in a plain sweatshirt and cotton trousers, bearded. The two younger ones were tall and thin, wore a shalwar kameez, hoodies and trainers, traditional, religious.

'Personal factors make us suitable for some cases,' he said, 'and not for others. You'll get the next one.'

Typical MacKechnie. Never said anything outright. Delicate situation, he wanted to say, all Asians hate women and anyway, you're a nut case.

Morrow could tell by the size of the boys and the softness of their builds that they were second generation. They had short hair, buzz cut by a barber. One of them had top of the range Nikes on, and they weren't to impress his pious pals at mosque. Those guys didn't care if she was female or male. She was ten years older than them, she might as well have been a man and she knew the South Side. If anyone's personal factors made them suitable it was her. But MacKechnie no longer trusted her, sensed that she was slowly tipping over the edge. It was unfair, but the service was all about unfair and she knew she should let it go.

'Sir, that's . . .' she was regretting it before the word even tumbled past her lips, 'racist.'

They both stood quite still, looking at the house. Cold rain pattered on their heads. A trickle ran down Morrow's cheek, dripping off her chin, soaking into her lapels, marking a ragged bullet hole over her heart. Behind them marked squad cars reversed slowly out of the street. She felt a weight on her chest and realised that she was trying not to breathe.

MacKechnie didn't turn to speak and his voice was less than a murmur. 'Never speak to me like that again.'

He turned sharply and walked away from her, over to Bannerman.

Fuck.

3

They drove the entire distance in silence, as per the plan. Say nothing in front of the hostage. But it wasn't a smug professional silence: Pat was too angry to speak, Eddy was determined to get one part of it right and Malki was so wasted he was incapable of driving and speaking at the same time.

Malki was well used to being the cause of bad atmospheres; he lived with his mother, and assumed the sour mood in the van was his fault, because of the thing with the wall, so he was extra careful and his driving exemplary. He took the slip road to the motorway, drove at legal speeds the whole way into town, came off at Cathedral for a circuit of the Sighthill back road to break the camera tracking and then turned and headed back on to the motorway from a different angle. Flawless.

All the way the old man stayed face down on the rumbling floor of the van, lying in exactly the same position he had landed in after they pulled the pillowcase over his head and shoved his face to the van floor: legs straight out, one arm flat by his side, the other hand by his face, still, as the heavy white plastic petrol cans swam slowly about the floor.

He lay so still that Pat began to worry. He looked back often, concerned that he might have suffered a head injury when they chucked him into the van. Pat'd watched a guy die outside a club once. The guy, mid-thirties, staggered and tripped on the step, toppled backwards, hitting the pavement like a comedy drunk and lay there, out of the way.

Everyone coming out of the club assumed he was pissed and sleeping. They laughed about it.

As they had zipped up the black rubber bag a sad-eyed ambulance guy explained that the skull has limited space in it. A bleed into the brain is like dropping a pickled egg into a full pint of lager, only there's nowhere for the extra volume to go so the brain gets sucked down into the spinal column. That's what kills you.

Remembering that night took Pat back to the door at the Zebra Wine Bar. Ugly drunks and the orange women staggering about on icy pavements in summer shoes. The women all had long hair that winter, he remembered. Nylon hair extensions that looked like bad wigs. 1669, they called the Zebra, because the women there looked sixteen from behind and sixty-nine from the front.

So he worried that the old man was dying under the pillowcase and he thought of the young girl he had shot and the pleasant, toast-smelling house, wishing he had stood up to Eddy and refused to go in. Eddy was a substitute family for Pat, had been for years, but suddenly Pat realised he'd picked the same family again: nasty loser fucking twats.

As though he could hear Pat shifting away from him, Eddy slapped the old man's foot and asked his name. The pillowcase lifted slightly off the floor, said he was called Aamir and Pat knew then that Eddy had been afraid too. It was good because maybe Eddy wasn't totally wrapped up playing soldiers, could still be reasoned with.

Eddy knelt next to the man in the back of the van, his balaclava rolled up around his forehead half an inch above his eyes. He wouldn't look at Pat.

They were at Harthill, the heart of central Scotland, a bleak stretch of high ground littered with TV and mobile phone masts, where the winds were always brutal. Malki took a slip road, a perfect turn at the roundabout, took the sharp turn off the road into a field and rolled the van quietly along the foot of a hill into a coppice of windswept trees. He stopped, pulled on the handbrake and sighed, smacked his lips. He smiled at Pat.

Without a word to either, Eddy stood up, opened the van door and slipped out, closing it after himself.

Eddy stepped out of the tree cover into a vast muddy field.

The ground was frozen solid, the churned mud covered with a fur of sliver frost. A swollen blue moon lit the ground like a harsh strip light. Eddy, arms out for balance, kept his eyes on the uneven ground. The light was so sharp and blue that he could see individual icy fronds as he followed the tracks of the van, heading back towards an opening in the hedge. He stopped and looked around. The fallow field stretched over the horizon. He could hear the hum of cars passing on the distant motorway. No houses in view, no van loads of people camping in the field. No one. Perfect.

He followed the tracks of the van, walking down the churned middle for another two hundred yards, his breath crystalline in front of him. Though he had parked it there himself, Eddy still wanted to rest his tired eyes on the Lexus.

Stopping, he looked up the road at the side of the field and could see the edge of the silver boot, the red tail lights. It was a hire car. As he drove here, trying all the buttons, loving the bucket seat and the steering wheel CD controls, he'd promised himself he'd get one of these, when the money came through. The sight of it now calmed him and slowed his heart from a sprinter's gallop.

Despite everything that had happened it might still be OK. Blinking back tears, Eddy made his way back to the van.

4

It was as a punishment that MacKechnie made her come in here, sitting on a hard chair in the soporific light of the bedroom, interviewing the bed-bound daughter-in-law who was little more than a bystander.

Morrow could hear them behind the door, out there, behind her in the hall, a happy gang, muttering, looking at details, gathering important scraps of information that would flesh out the story while she was in here, being kept busy and out of the way.

Meeshra looked rough, black fuzz grew down the sides of her face and her hair was wild, knotted at the back where she had been sleeping on it.

The door was shut behind them, for the sake of modesty, while Meeshra threatened the baby with her engorged nipple. The two-week-old child bucked and struggled, his gummy, desperate mouth clamping to skin and fingers but failing to meet the breast. It was too full, Alex knew, so heavy with milk that the baby couldn't get his mouth around it. But the advice stuck in her throat. It seemed improper and intimate. It wasn't her job, it was for a health visitor to tell her.

'They were waving the gun and shouting. Looking for a guy called Rob. "Robbie". A right Scottish name, in't it?'

Lancaster lingered in Meeshra's accent but it was fading to Scottish. She had been here for less than a year, she said, moving in with her in-laws after her wedding. They were a happy family, and here she blinked, a prosperous, hard-working family, and she blinked again.

A female officer was standing behind Alex, jotting the lies down, allowing Alex to simply watch. Every individual had a tic that signalled a lie, and the best way to find it was to ask them about their family.

Morrow was sure that Meeshra wasn't lying deliberately. Family myths and fables were more than conscious fibs; they were a form of self-protection, conversational habits, beliefs too embedded to challenge: she loves me, we are happy, he will change. But there was always a tic. It amazed Alex, the craven need of people to tell the truth. During questioning, when inconsistencies started to show in a story, people often broke down, sobbed with the desire to be honest, as if getting caught lying was the very worst that could happen. She'd seen men carve fingernails into the palms of their hands, breaking the skin to relieve the pressure to tell. Adamance was the most common giveaway. She'd never again trust anyone who began a sentence, 'Honestly', or, 'To tell the truth'. These were flags raised high above a statement, drawing the casual viewer's attention; here be dragons.

Professional liars thought out excuses beforehand and stuck to them, but synthetic memories were unwieldy; ask for a colour or a detail and they were too slow to answer. Fluent liars were dangerous, either because they were so malevolent or suggestible.

The skill of spotting lies had given Morrow a jaundiced view of the world. The worst of it was that it denied her the luxury of lying to herself. The cold light of day was no place to live.

So she envied Meeshra's insistence that they were all happy together. Sure, there were tensions but her mother-in-law was basically a good person, a bit educated but still good, and she knew how she wanted the house run and where the furniture should go and she had her own ways of cooking, eh?

That was natural, right? And the baby was such a blessing, a son, first grandchild. She blinked at that and Alex noted it, filed it away. We will be happy, Meeshra said, stopping, surprised to find herself using the future tense.

She pressed the baby towards her tit again. He rolled his bald head back and gave out a dry, thin squeal. Frustrated, Meeshra squeezed her nipple between her fingers and a powerful arc of watery milk jetted across the bed and soaked into the sheet. Tearful with embarrassment, she cursed herself in a language Alex didn't recognise.

'Try again now you've emptied it a bit,' said Alex.

Unsure, Meeshra held the baby to the deflated nipple.

'Nose to nipple,' said Alex. 'He'll find it himself.'

Meeshra touched the baby's milk-spotted nose with her black nipple and he arched his back, finding it with his mouth, clamping on awkwardly, furiously working his tiny jaw, drawing from her so hard she gave a little gasp. The tension left her shoulders as the baby relieved her of the press of milk and she looked gratefully at Alex.

'You've done this, have ya?'

Alex faked a friendly smile. 'Could you tell me what you remember of this evening? Starting from the beginning.'

'Oh.' Meeshra was surprised by the shift of topic but keen to please. 'Um, well, I was lying in bed, with baby. Billal was sitting on the side of the bed, where your knees are,' eyes flicked anxiously to the side, 'helping me. We was having a bit of an argument actually,' she smirked, awkward, 'about feeding and that. We hear shouting in the hall and think Omar's back.'

'Why would there be shouting when Omar's back?'

Meeshra rolled her eyes. 'Well, him and his daddy don't always get on, so, sometimes they do shout at each other, like, but we wasn't listening.'

'What sort of things do they fight about?'

'I dunno, ask him.' She shrugged, not quite of the family but still reluctant to betray. 'Anyway, we wasn't listening, yeah?'

'You were talking to Billal?'

'Yeah, about feeding. So there's shouting and then we realise. Billal's like: "That's not Omar's voice."'

'How would you describe the voice?'

'Scotch. A right Scotch voice. *Rrr*ob,' she rolled her tongue. '"Where's *Rrrr*obbie?"'

She paused there, which Morrow found interesting, and needed prompting. 'What then?'

'Billal went out to see what was going on, because the shouting was getting, well, we knowed it wasn't Omar shouting. So, he opened the door and popped out, keeping it closed because of me, you know.' She looked down at the baby at her breast. 'Me mam-in-law wants the bed here, opposite the door. I want it there.' She looked up over to a private corner. 'Anyway, ne'er mind. So, I hear Billal outside, speaking, saying, like, "No, man," and then suddenly the door's kicked wide open and me with my nightie all open and the baby here.' She blushed at the memory, running her fingers over the baby's down hair.

'What could you see through the door?'

'Little man, well not little, but he was standing next to Billal, who's about six foot three and wide.'

'How far up Billal did he come?'

'Top of his head come up to Billal's jaw, little bit past his jaw.'

'So he was about ...?'

'About five eight, ten, summat like that.'

'And build?'

'"Bout, dunno, wide, a bit fat. Had them shoulders, you know, where the neck's gone slopey and the shoulders just go straight up to their ears?'

'Like a weightlifter?'

'Exactly. A weightlifter. But fat belly, like.'

'And you didn't see his face?'

'He had a woolly mask on with eyeholes.'

'A balaclava?'

'Yeah. And he says, like, "You come out here," or summat, and I'm like, "I can't, I've just had a baby," 'cause ye know how you're not meant to get up, yeah?' Alex remembered quite the opposite. She also remembered envying the gall of women who treated having a baby like full body polio, making visitors get them this, hand them that, though they usually staged miraculous recoveries the minute visiting was over. 'So he's like, "Get up," right? I'm like, "No." And then Billal stepped in front of us and says, "Come on, mate, that's enough," but then the gun fella says to the other bloke who's wi' him, shouts at him, really angry, "Lift your gun, Pat."'

'*Pat?*'

'Yeah, that were his name, Pat, and they both froze then, like they'd shit themselves 'cause he'd said it.'

Alex had heard Billal's accent as she came through the hall. Unless she missed her guess he had been educated at St Al's, the private Catholic school in the city centre, an expensive highly academic institution. He had that confident public-school charm and a particular turn in his 'r's. Meeshra was common, used swear words without a thought, had bad grammar, reported speech as if she was telling another girl on a street corner about a fight at school.

'Just out of interest, how did you meet Billal?'

'Come up with my family.'

'To live in Glasgow?'

'Nah, nah, it were a set-up. Arranged marriage. We only met four times before we got married.'

'Oh, I see.'

Defensive, Meeshra turned back to the baby. 'Yous don't

42

understand about it, think it's all forced and that—'

Alex cut her off. 'I don't.'

Meeshra looked at her.

'I'm all for it. Especially if you're moving in with the in-laws. You're not just picking a husband, are you?' Alex had thought about it often, who her mother would have picked for her, how differently her life would have gone. That was the thing about arranged marriages, she thought, no one got the right to choose an unexpected future for themselves.

Meeshra gave her a soft smile. 'Exactly.'

'You're picking the whole family. You need to know you're compatible in lots of ways.'

She nodded. 'Exactly, exactly,' and tipped her head at Alex, wondering if she was being played. She seemed to realise Alex was genuine and smiled softly, almost grateful.

Alex blinked, resuming her questions. 'Back to before, so the gunman says "Pat" and they both freeze. Then what?'

'Yeah, so, he's like "Pat" and they both freeze and then, suddenly, me mam-in-law's like, "What's doing out here?" and the fat one run down the hall, I seen him skip past my door here,' she pointed past the door to the back of the house, 'and he brung me mam-in-law and Dada back up. Then they was quiet for a bit. And then Pat shot Aleesha's hand off.'

'Just out of the blue?'

'Yeah.'

'No threats or demands?'

'Nah.'

'Did you see him shoot the gun?'

'Naw. I heard a, like, a big "whump" noise and seen a light and then Aleesha says, like, "You've shot me fucking hand off!"'

'How did you know it was Pat who did it?'

43

''Cause the other one was there at the door and I could see him.'

'You heard the shot?'

'Yeah. And light, like white light, a flash and everyone looked over there and I seen blood on the wall and I thought Aleesha had been shot but then I heard her go, "You've shot me fucking hand off."' Meeshra didn't seem very sad that Aleesha had been shot. She actually smiled a little.

'She swore?'

'Aleesha's ...' Meeshra looked away quickly, snorted a joyless laugh. 'Well, a *teenager*.' Received opinion, repeated comments. Meeshra wasn't far off her teens herself.

'Were you like that?'

That hollow laugh again. 'Me dad would have battered me.'

'Is Aamir not like that?'

She shook her head. 'Even if he were I don't think she'd be any better. Jeans and T-shirts. Nail varnish. Won't observe religious practice *at all*.'

'A rebel?'

'No. Stubborn.' She was angry about it but not really with Aleesha, seemed slightly removed from it, as if her belonging to family was contingent on her joining in a campaign against the girl.

'Did she stop wearing traditional clothing?'

Meeshra became embarrassed. 'Never done. Dunno. I just ... Dunno.'

'She hasn't ever worn them?'

'Nah. I dunno.' She wouldn't look at Morrow.

'Are the family converts?'

'Naw, just not always that, ye know, religious.'

'Oh, I see, just recently become more observant?'

'Aye, yeah.'

44

Morrow noted it but let it pass. 'What happened after the shot?'

'Then, well, then, Mo and Omar come in the front door.'

'At the sound of the shot?'

'Yeah, I heard them come past outside the window there,' she pointed to the window at the side of the bed, 'running there, round.' Her finger traced their passage along the blank wall. 'And then they burst in through the door. The fat one, not Pat, the other one, he started shouting at them, "You're Robbie, no, you're Robbie," and then he grabbed Dada and went. I's in the bed the whole time, so I only seen little bits.'

The baby's head slumped drowsily on his tiny neck. Meeshra looked down at him, calmer now, her fingers curling around the perfect sphere of his skull.

'So,' Morrow prompted, 'Omar and Mo had been waiting outside in the car?'

'Is it?' Meeshra looked up.

'Well,' said Morrow, 'they're unlikely to have just pulled up at that moment, aren't they?'

'Dunno.'

'What did he say as he left, the fat one?'

'Two million quid by tomorrow night. Did he not see the house? *Two million?* He's mad.'

'Anything else?'

'Not to call police and it were payback for Afghanistan. Mental case.' She nodded out to the hall. 'They're from Uganda and I'm from bloody Lancaster. You wouldn't believe the shit we have to put up with now, 'cause of all them fucking Arabs.'

'D'you think that's what it was? Just a case of misplaced bigotry?'

'Well, what else could it be? 'S like kidnapping a African because of the slave trade.'

Alex wrestled with the analogy for a moment before realising that it didn't quite fit. 'Right.' She stood up. 'Thanks very much for your help, Meeshra, I'm sure we'll need to talk to you again later but now we'll leave you and the baby to get a sleep.'

Meeshra leaned back on the pillows, pleased with herself. 'Robbie, he says. *Rr*robbie, right Scotch, like.'

It was a final statement, a goodbye, not requiring a response, but Alex couldn't resist showing her cards. 'Is that right?' she said pointedly.

Disconcerted by the steely edge to her voice, Meeshra blinked.

5

Pat felt a whoosh of cold hit the back of his neck and knew Eddy had opened both doors.

'Help me,' said Eddy sullenly, taking hold of the old man's foot and tugging.

Pat climbed out of the van and walked around to the back doors.

The old man shivered in his pyjamas as he shuffled back on all fours, awkward because Eddy was keeping hold of his bare ankle, guiding his foot down to the ground.

The spongy sole of his slippers made it hard for him to stay upright on the uneven ground. Pat watched him totter, looking at the pillowcase where his face might be, searching for signs of humanity and finding nothing. The pillowcase wasn't unusually big, but it covered the small man to his waist.

Once he found his footing, the pillowcase stood perfectly still, waiting until Pat and Eddy each took a firm grip of his elbows and guided him along the path. He didn't resist or try to get away but accepted what was happening, as if the situation couldn't be helped and none of them had decided any of it. He stumbled, his ankle buckling on the lumpy mud, and gave out a little cry, like a field mouse being stepped on.

Over the head of the pillowcase, Pat felt Eddy's eyes burning into his cheek, begging him to look back at him. He kept his eyes forward, refusing to look at him, refusing to make it OK. The sheer effort of resisting Eddy made him sweat.

At the edge of the field Eddy reached into his pocket, pressed the car key and the Lexus lights flashed twice. They led the pillowcase over to it, opened the door and bundled the old man in, shoving him along to the middle of the back seat. Eddy shut the car door, reached into his pocket again. The car winked and chirped. They were alone.

Pat and Eddy stood close, so close the white of their breath mingled, not looking at each other. It was a habit developed from cold night after cold night standing on the door of shitty little nightclubs.

'OK,' said Eddy, 'it didn't go ...' He couldn't think of a neutral word.

Pat caught his breath to speak but words failed him.

Eddy looked at his gun and spoke calmly. 'If you never shot the girl—'

'*If I never shot the girl?* Are you *mental?*'

'You pulled the trigger.'

'You shouted "Bob" soon as we got in the door and then bawled my fucking name. And what's that "Afghanistan" shit about?'

'Just – throw them off the scent. Something ye say—'

'Something ye say when you're paintballing. *You* grabbed the wrong fucking guy. This isn't who he said to get. This is some old Asian bloke. He's sixty, seventy fucking years old.'

They looked into the car. The upturned pillowcase was staring straight ahead, sitting in the middle of the seat with a hand calmly on each knee, blank as a packet of crisps, waiting to go a place.

Eddy's face convulsed in an abrupt pulse. Pat fell back from him, thinking he'd been shot or, worse, was going to cry, but Eddy blurted a loud panicky laugh. Surprised at himself, Pat laughed too.

The wind was picking up over the field, carrying the

rotting smell of cow shit, and it seemed suddenly funny to be out here, with Malki off his tits and Eddy so jittery he shouted Pat's name. The pillowcase heard someone outside. It twitched a ridiculous swivel round and back, comical. Pat and Eddy laughed, falling into each other, snorting like boys at a dirty joke.

Eddy calmed down first. 'Oh, fucking hell, honestly.' He pinched his nose, and smiled warmly off at the far hills. 'Will we just shoot it in the head and leave it here?'

Pat's smile evaporated.

'You know, near the van,' Eddy suggested with a smile. 'Drive off and leave it?'

'Um, nah.' Pat was sweating again, really quite afraid now. 'Nah, let's . . . not do that.'

'But, um, look, every minute we're with him is a chance to get caught.'

'Aye,' Pat tried to sound calm and reasoned, 'but the old guy could, you know, might do just as well as Bob. Might be better, even.'

'How so?' said Eddy and tittered at his own phrasing.

'Well, Bob'll pay up to see him again. I mean, if we took Bob, how would he get to the money? We'd have to take him to it and if it's in a lock-up or something we'd maybe get caught going there, eh?'

Eddy frowned, only half understanding.

'I mean think about it, really, this way Bob can get the money and give it to us without us going with him, eh? So, with the old guy, it's *less* chance to get done.'

'Oh, I see. I see . . .'

'Yeah? We don't need to shoot the old guy.'

'Nah.' Eddy looked far away and his smile faded. 'Just . . . you got to fire yours and, you know . . . shoot someone.'

Pat didn't know what to say to that. 'Hey . . . um, let's get back, and . . . and phone the boss.'

'He's not the boss,' corrected Eddy sullenly. '*I'm* the boss. He subcontracted us. It's more of a contractor–contractee relationship than a boss–employee relationship.'

'OK,' said Pat carefully. 'But maybe it's best not to leave Malki too long . . .'

'You go.' Eddy was stroking the barrel of his gun with his fingertips. 'I'll just . . . I'll wait and mind him.'

'Aye, aye,' but Pat didn't move, 'you're just going to mind him . . .'

Eddy smiled. 'I'm going to *mind* him. What?'

'Nothing, just . . .' Pat cleared his throat. 'Just . . . I'll get Malki started.'

'Aye. See he does it right.'

Aamir could hear them talking outside the window. The white light of the night flooded in through the pillowcase, a new-smelling pillowcase. He sat, small and still, listening as they laughed and one of them said he wanted to shoot him. One of the men walked away, he didn't know which one.

In passing, a hand brushed against the door handle and Aamir's stomach turned to stone. The door didn't open, the hand left the door, but suddenly, like the memory of a migraine, Aamir felt the heat in the car and the red dust rise from the road.

Time began to melt.

The heat of the Kampala road rose in the car until he felt himself engulfed.

A taxi with his mother. They should have got out sooner but she was an optimist. In the back seat with his mother, heading for the airport and, afraid, she reached for his hand along the hot plastic seat. He withdrew his hand, did not want to admit that he was afraid himself.

A jolt beneath the car, a former person on the road. No

one felt safe enough to stop and care for the ragged mess of skin and bone, shirt ripped into rags, buffeted by passing cars and coaches.

He smelled the jasmine oil his long dead mother put in her hair. He withdrew and refused her hand and then he saw what she was afraid of. Up ahead: another road block. The brightly coloured contents of suitcases scattered across the dusty red road, the soldiers looked crazy, army shirts unbuttoned, rifles slung over shoulders, a hostile tribe. His mother made a sound he had never heard from her before, a sharp sound that came from her throat, like a long-ago contented sigh snatched back from the world.

Now, in the bubble before, as the brakes on the taxi squealed, Aamir knew he should have reached over and taken her hand. He should have comforted his mother because now he understood the noise and knew how afraid she had been. He had remembered her only vaguely in the decade since she died in hospital in Glasgow of a weak heart, but found himself now muttering soft words under the pillowcase, telling her not to worry, that all would be well, his voice strangled by the knot of terror throbbing in his throat.

The hand brushed against the door again and the heat, the smells were gone, his mother, the hot wet blood blooming through the seat of her yellow sari, was gone.

Aamir was alone, in the dark, in bloody Scotland.

6

Alex Morrow stopped outside the bedroom door, pulling it closed, feeling for the click. The white-suited Forensics team moved like ghosts through the hall and living room. They worked in a studied calm silence, gathering and measuring, face masks giving them an air of graceful anonymity.

The wall opposite the bedroom was splattered with blood. A short guy was worrying holes in the plaster with tweezers, another picking up fibres from the carpet, both kneeling on small stools that matched their outfits.

Morrow picked her steps through the hall to the door shadowed by the woman officer who had been taking notes. Outside the darkness was deeper, turning bitter. They took the path down to the gate, faces closed against the chill, and Morrow made her way across the road to the witnesses behind the tape.

The neighbours had gone back indoors leaving just two of the three Asian boys clustered together; the younger, thinner ones.

They were silent now, smoking, standing as if they were in a line-up, shifty and shocked. The passive weight of guilt.

She was surprised, doubted her impression, but she knew that her first thought was often her best and she recognised the stance, the head hanging, the exhausted slope of the shoulders, eyes flicking about the floor. They weren't just running through the night, she felt; it was deeper, they were mapping the shift in their world. CID saw it all the time, the aftermath of lives taking violent turns and the turmoil of victims re-engaging with a changed world: I was a wife, now a widow, I was a child, now an orphan. The young were better at it, their identities not yet fixed, but she saw the boys struggling hard and sensed that there was more to it than lucky/unlucky. The shift in their world view was more fundamental.

She stopped and looked again: the boys looked straight, they seemed to be from good, moderate homes. Hair cuts, straight teeth, well nourished, no big flash cars or clothes. And yet they were standing as if they had done something very bad indeed. She found herself salivating with the desire to know.

Turning to the officer who had been taking notes during her questioning with Meeshra, Morrow spoke quietly, asking her opinion about Meeshra but not listening to the response, using the opportunity to examine the two boys. Not brothers, but very alike. They must be friends, close friends, shared values. They were smoking. The one bearing a family resemblance was wearing Nikes. The other: same age, same dress, more traditional though. The son held his cigarette between finger and thumb, cupped against the wind like an outdoor worker. It didn't look like an affectation either, it looked working class but his family weren't.

She watched him bring his cigarette to his lips and draw hard, puffing out his chest to hold the breath. Blow. Definitely. She guessed blow was forbidden by Islam. It wasn't exactly a gin or a ham sandwich but Islam didn't encourage people to use mood-altering chemicals. She looked at their beards and salwar kameez and smiled to herself. Ostentatious show of faith but they were Glasgow boys underneath.

Taking out her mobile phone, she pretended to fumble for a number, calling up the camera and taking a picture of each of the boys over the officer's shoulder.

'Could you get yourself back to the station?'

'Yes, ma'am.'

Absentmindedly she said, 'Thanks very much.' She didn't mean it and the uniform looked puzzled. 'For the notes.' Morrow thumbed back to the house but she hadn't even seen the fucking notes, they might be crap.

'Sure.' The officer still seemed unsure but turned and left.

Morrow felt foolish as she looked around. Bannerman and MacKechnie were off somewhere, probably scheming Bannerman's golden future.

But she was here, on the ground, fitting facts and impressions together to make her own picture, making sense of the fractured night, godlike, forming order from chaos. She loved the process, but tonight, with the dread of home weighing on her, it felt more like a compulsion.

The first taste of a hard winter was in the air. She pulled her jacket tight around her. The moment Bannerman knew the boys were involved he wouldn't let her near them. As conscious of the threat of interception as a gazelle on a grassy plain, Morrow stepped across the empty road towards them.

7

Pat could hear nothing but his own shallow breath as he stepped back along the path to the field. His skin was anxious-clammy, his face veiled in a thin layer of greasy sweat. They had battered guys, hurt women sometimes, but always for a reason, never just so they could get a shot of a gun. The shit-smelling wind chilled his skin, the electric blue moonlight lit the shards of frost crunching under his every step. At the end of the path he turned into the field and chanced a glance back at the Lexus.

Eddy had his back to him, his head dropped forward, looking at his gun. Pat broke into a trot, stumbling gracelessly over the lumpy ground, running from him.

It was age that had brought them to this. Age and coke.

Seven good years sharing doors all over the city. They were liberal with their hands, known for it, good at the job, until Eddy's missus left. Then came the fights and restraining orders and the drinking. He was drinking that night, now that Pat thought about it.

It must have been cut with something, the coke. The boy was thin, too young for that bar really, granny grabbing, but his pupils were pins and he was twitching when he stumbled out and into Eddy, his mouth staggering to keep up with the words drenching his chin – fucking old fuck fat fucking old.

Afterwards, Eddy said he was off balance, the boy was lucky, the night was wrong. He was probably right; on another night, at a different angle the boy's first punch wouldn't have got him down. The boy never went for Pat, just Eddy, the one who had nothing left to be but hard. He kicked Eddy's face in.

Pat rallied when Eddy's wife left, when they lost jobs over arguments with managers, but the bruises of that fight never left Eddy. He didn't know what was wrong with him. A bird, he said he needed a bird, so Pat set him up but she wasn't right and he gave her a slap and her brother came over and it got messy. New job, so Pat got them an indoor, but Eddy said the money was shit and they weren't allowed to drink. Now he needed money, if only Eddy had money. One big job. Pat was losing faith, wouldn't use his contacts, so Eddy'd done it himself, set it up and got the guns, the van, the address. And now what was wrong was an old toast-smelling man who didn't have a hole in his head.

Walking along the sea of frozen mud Pat realised that soon he would be what was wrong with Eddy.

Up ahead, in among the trees, Pat saw an orange eye widen in welcome. Malki was smoking a fag, casual, standing next to the two large white plastic drums of petrol. Pat bolted over to him, slapping the cigarette from his mouth, scattering flecks of red all over the ground and stamping on them.

Malki had been enjoying that cigarette. He looked down at it sadly. 'Aw, man!' he droned, 'I havenae opened the petrol, calm the fuck down.'

Pat grabbed him by the hoodie zip, held him up on his tiptoes, and spat in his face. 'You calm *fucking* down, Malki. *You* fucking calm down.'

Flecks of Pat's spit freckled Malki's forehead. It was so obvious neither of them said it: Malki was medically, chemically, technically perfectly calm. Despite the freezing cold of the night, despite smoking a fag next to two giant cans of petrol while being threatened by a man twice his weight, even then Malki's physiology couldn't summon up enough adrenalin to redden his cheeks.

A bead of sweat trickled down Pat's forehead and Malki watched as the urgent trail disappeared into his eyebrow and dripped from his slightly overhanging brow.

'Not being funny, Pat, man, but have yous twos been doing steroids or something?'

Pat let his wee cousin drop back onto his feet. 'Malki—'

'Yees are awful fucking jumpy.'

'Just shut it, Malki.'

Indignant at the insult, Maki straightened the front of his hoodie and unseen, the tiny ball of foil tumbled gracefully out, bouncing on the grass, falling between the blades. Malki muttered, ' . . . need tae be fucking rude, man.'

Sulking, they took a petrol can each and unscrewed the caps, Malki in charge now because he had been burning out stolen cars since he was twelve and knew what he was about. It was surprisingly easy to get it wrong.

While Pat soaked the seats, Malki opened up the tank and threaded in a line of tubing, sucking the petrol out. They didn't want an explosion or a fire ball drawing anyone's attention; just a good, thorough job. The longer it took the police to find the van, the longer they had to muddy their trail.

By the time Pat had finished, the fumes were prickling at the skin inside his nose, making him dizzy. His mind was on the Lexus, listening, the hairs on his neck on standby, alert for the muffled 'pop' of the gun.

He found Malki round the back, blowing into the petrol tank through the tube.

'Disperse the fumes, man,' explained Malki between puffs. He smiled as he blew, eyes wide, excited.

Pat watched. Malki came from a family of arseholes but he himself was a good wee guy. He smiled again, puffing his cheeks out like a trumpeter. How did that happen, Pat wondered, a good guy from that family, a moral guy, with standards.

'Eddy's lost it a bit,' he said quietly.

Malki puffed and raised his eyebrows.

Pat kicked at the ground, looking away because he felt disloyal. 'His wife ...' he said, backtracking, excusing.

Malki took the tube from his mouth. 'Three nice wee kids.' He pulled the tube out carefully. 'She's well out of it. Did the right thing fucking off to Manchester.'

Pat couldn't look at him because Malki was right.

He pulled the tube out and laid it flat on the ground, pointing away from the van and into the dark woods. He motioned to Pat to drop the cans underneath the van and stepped back, guiding Pat away, checking the ground they were stepping away from for oily smears of petrol.

Malki was taking no chances. He made Pat stand a good distance away along the tyre tracks because he'd been in the van and would be all fumed up. Malki went back himself, crouching at the end of the tube, his lighter sparking twice before the flame caught. He held it to the end of the tube and got up quickly, backing off to Pat's side.

A warm glow shot along the tubing, spilling a sudden sheet of light into the grass. The flames took, licking up at the surrounding air, racing into the petrol tank until a 'thwump' and a spluttered belch of fire came from the petrol tank, spilling onto the grass, lighting every drip and smear of petrol. The inside of the van was on fire, the back windows bright. The fire spread to the front seats and a wave of warm and smoke hit their faces. Pat blanched at the heat but Malki didn't even blink. His mouth had fallen open a little, his small teeth white against the dark.

''Mon,' said Pat, anxious to get back. He hurried out of the trees, following his path to the Lexus. Eddy's head was no longer visible over the scraggy hedge around the field. Pat sped up, keeping his eyes on the place Eddy had been standing, imagining him crouched over the old man's body, rolling him into the ditch. Malki trotted after him, almost bumping into him at the mouth of the field when Pat stopped in his tracks.

Eddy was gone.

Pat ran towards the car, looking over the roof, in the ditch by the car, but Eddy was gone.

'Where the fuck . . .?'

Malki was behind him, staring hard at him, worried. With a limp hand he pointed at the car, at the driver's seat. Eddy was sitting in it.

'Oh,' said Pat.

'. . . the fucking motor,' mumbled Malki, shaking his head.

Pat looked at Malki. The harsh moonlight cut lines deep into his face, he looked forty and he was only twenty-three. And yet he was looking pityingly at Pat.

'Fucking junkie twat,' said Pat.

Malki turned square to him and raised a warning finger. 'Patrick, my friend, I have to say: you're being a bit ignorant there.'

'Get in the fucking motor.'

'No need for rudeness, my friend. We've all got our troubles.'

Pat rolled his eyes. 'Malki—'

Malki raised both hands. '*Polite*. That's all I'm saying . . . Us and the animals, man.' He opened the back door and slipped his skinny hips in next to the pillowcase, shutting the door before Pat had the chance to tell him off again.

Heavily, his head throbbing slightly from the fumes, Pat made his way around to the other rear door and got in. The pillowcase was slight as well as small: Pat's hips didn't even touch him. It was like sitting next to a child.

Eddy started the engine and his eyes met Pat's in the rear-view mirror. Pat blinked and looked away.

When they hit the motorway, Pat looked back to where the van was burning. A calm smoke plume drifted up into the clear night, it could pass for insignificant, unless a local was passing and knew there was no house over the shoulder of the hill.

They drove on in silence as before but now Malki was content, having had the release of setting fire to something, on his way to a midnight assignation with his beloved scag. And Eddy was happy at the wheel of the Lexus, imagining a future where he owned such a car and could look at himself in the mirror.

But the pillowcase was rigid with fright and Pat looked out at the dark fields and wished himself someone else, somewhere else. He should have refused to get out of the van.

8

Rain fell softly in the dark street, regular and rhythmic, like a comforting pat on the back. Beyond the tape the boys watched Morrow's feet as she came towards them, their cigarettes were polka-dotted with drizzle. Neither could bring their eyes up further than her knees.

Young, slim and handsome, their clothes were expensive and well laundered, ironed.

She stopped in front of them. 'Are you ...?'

For a moment neither spoke until the friend said, 'I'm, eh, I'm Mo. This is Omar. He lives, eh, it's his house.'

'Right?'

They sagged like sacks, brought their cigarettes to their mouths. Omar opened his mouth to speak but shut it again, stunned. He struggled to look up at her and seemed very young.

'You've had quite a night,' she said.

Mo told the tarmac, 'Aye, then we got almost arrested for asking the police for help.'

The hope that Bannerman had fucked up made her ask, 'What happened?'

'We drove off after the van,' said Omar, 'and lost it and then when we saw a police car we stopped them and they arrested us.' His words were slurred, bizarrely languid, as if he was already stoned. After-effect of shock: massive slump in blood sugar after an adrenalin rush.

'They arrested you?'

'Yeah,' Omar smirked at Mo, 'for a BB offence.'

She didn't understand. 'You had a BB gun with you?'

'No, BB offence: Being Brown.' Omar became embarrassed, as if he was growing out of the adolescent sentiment while he was saying it.

'I'm very sorry,' she said formally, feeling defensive. 'I sincerely hope you don't feel that race has been an issue in the investigation. We really are trying our very best to help.'

'No, sorry, no.' Mo looked shamefaced too. 'Sorry, it's just a daft thing they say, you know, see, they looked at our clothes and, you know, think stuff about you ...'

'Well,' she said softly, 'if *anyone* here has given you the impression that race was any kind of an issue for them I do hope you'd feel free to tell us. We certainly wouldn't want politics like that interfering with an investigation like this.'

They were mortified now, caught out in an unsupportable myth between them and Morrow leaned in and went kindly for the kill. 'You know, you weren't arrested. If you'd been arrested you wouldn't be here now, you'd be in a station somewhere being questioned. It creates a lot of paperwork, they don't just do it for a laugh.'

'You know what?' Omar's knee buckled and he looked at her. 'We're being stupid. It was my fault, we did an emergency stop, leapt out at them. I forgot, you know, what we'd look like to ...' he scratched his head hard and sighed, 'and I said a series of key words ... that would alarm anyone really, I suppose.'

'Like what?'

'Guns. Van. Took my daddy.'

'Afghanistan!' interjected Mo, as if it was a guessing game.

'Why did you say Afghanistan?'

'Well, they said it, the gunmen, as they were leaving: "This is for Afghanistan," but it didn't sound right.'

Mo nodded. 'Yeah, it didn't sound kosh.'

'Sounded like some bullshit Steven Seagal tagline. Like someone who watches a lot of action movies and is in a fuckin' – sorry – is like in a dream or something.'

They were talking to each other, not her, and their speech speeded up, took on colour and motion.

'Aye, yeah, but shit action movies,' confirmed Mo and affected a Schwarzenegger accent: '*This-is-pay-back,*' but his joke was half hearted, addressed to no one but the pavement.

Omar smiled dutifully and echoed, '*Pay-back.* Anyway, we jumped out and they were just asking questions and then I saw the van going under the bridge and I forgot and I ran off towards it. They must have got a fright and they grabbed me in a hold. Hurt my shoulder a bit, actually.'

Mo reached out and patted his pal's back. They were close, she liked that, and Omar had an insight and honesty rare in a young man.

'You saw the van?'

'We were on the bridge over the motorway and we saw it going underneath and I ran over to it but they stopped me.'

'On the bridge?'

'At Haggs Castle.'

'Great,' She pulled out her notebook and wrote it down. 'We can get the CCTV footage and trace it.'

'They hurt my shoulder ...'

'Well, I can only apologise for that.'

'Yeah and we were shitting ourselves anyway, buzzing because of the blood and Aleesha and that anyway.'

'She's been taken to hospital.'

'I know.'

'I'm sure she's fine.' She didn't actually know how Aleesha was doing, she'd heard someone else say it but hadn't spoken to the hospital herself. 'In the right place ...' She was

63

slipping into hollow clichés as a barrier to empathising. Bitter night streamed down the road, chilling their ankles. 'Were you in the hall when the men came in?'

'No.'

'Where were you?'

'In the car outside.'

'Where?'

They pointed up to the evidence markers for the cigarette butts. She looked and saw that the cigarettes they had in their hands now were brand matches for the stubs she had seen in the road and she was pleased, found she wanted to trust them, whatever the story.

'What sort of car?'

'This car.' Omar pointed to a blue Vauxhall parked behind him. 'The Vauxhall. His Vauxhall.'

'What were you doing out there?'

'Chatting.'

'Where had you been?'

'Mosque.'

Morrow read Omar's face. What she had taken for guilt could have been shock and tiredness. He looked drained and spent, but there was something else there too, a reticence. 'Did you see the van waiting in the road?'

'No.'

'Why not?'

'Were around the corner. Couldn't see it.'

'It's a one-way street. You must have passed it when you drove up.'

'We'd been there for twenty minutes. Must have arrived after us.'

'What were you doing there for twenty minutes?'

Omar drew himself up, straightening his back, looking at her properly for the first time. She felt plain. The suit made her look tidy but not attractive. No elegant details,

64

no statement stitching or anything that would draw the eye, make a casual viewer wonder about her as a person. Bland was the look she was going for.

'Shouldn't you wait until there's another officer here before we speak to you?'

Morrow was surprised. 'Why – what makes you say that?'

'For corroboration, for if the case comes to court.'

She gave an unconvincing half-laugh. 'What would you know about that?'

'I'm a law graduate,' he said, looking unaccountably sad about it.

'Oh.' She nodded for a minute, only vaguely aware of the car drawing up behind the boys. 'Oh. When was your ... When did you ...?'

'June,' he said.

'Morrow!' Bannerman was out of the car almost before it stopped. The bigger brother climbed out of the back and strode over to them, almost overtaking Bannerman in his eagerness to get to his brother's side. They'd been on their way to the station for a formal interview, she realised, and both wanted to break up the conversation she was having, for different reasons.

'Morrow?' asked Omar.

'I'm Morrow,' she said. 'Who's the big guy?'

'My brother, Billal.' Omar dropped his chin to his chest and when she looked back she found the brother was glaring at him.

'Morrow,' Bannerman scowled, 'could I have a word?'

She blushed high on her cheeks, and turned away, stepping over to him with her head down.

Bannerman turned her away from the boys and muttered reprovingly, 'What are you doing?'

'Just talking to the boys ...' She sounded flat, as if she'd done a bad thing herself. She looked for something to attach the feeling of guilt to: 'Any word from the hospital?'

'Yeah.' Bannerman took her elbow and moved her out of earshot of the boys. 'Fine. Going in for emergency surgery but should be OK. Hand's mangled. She's only sixteen.'

'Her mother with her?'

'Yeah, we've left some cops there. We'll get a proper statement off her when she comes out of it.'

'Something funny about the family,' she murmured. 'I grew up on the Southside. I know dead religious families and this one isn't right.'

'How do you mean?'

'Omar, the son? Smokes fags like he's smoking a joint. Aleesha wears jeans and T-shirts, Meeshra's embarrassed about it, but kind of suggested that they've only recently become very observant. They're from Uganda origin-ally, traditionally that's a pretty assimilated pro-British community.'

'Are they recent converts?'

He wasn't listening to her. 'No. They're not converts, just become more observant.'

Now he wasn't even looking at her. 'Yeah, great, Morrow: local knowledge. Let's get them to the station.'

Omar couldn't look back at Billal. He seemed to be shrinking under his brother's gaze.

'We're *all* going to the station,' Bannerman called to him.

'The boys saw the van,' she said. 'They tried to get a squad—'

'Yeah,' he cut her off and called Billal over to his side. 'Let's get the boys into a car. We're going to the police station, right?'

'Have I to come too?' Mo was asking Billal.

'We're *all* going,' Billal said sternly.

Bannerman waved the boys to a car door and they trotted obediently over. As Omar came past Billal reached out a

66

meaty hand and grabbed his arm, with unnecessary force. 'Just tell the truth,' he said loudly. Omar didn't look at him.

Bannerman watched approvingly, as if he had located the biggest boy in the class and made friends with him.

'Tell them the truth.' But Billal was talking in exclamations, so loud he wasn't really talking to Omar.

The two boys got into the back seat of the squad car and Billal shut the door on them.

Morrow sidled over to him, touching his elbow gently, guiding him away for a moment. 'Billal, I'm DS Alex Morrow. Can I just ask you quickly: why were they waiting outside the house while it all went on?'

Billal looked at her as if he had misheard. 'What?'

'The guys,' said Morrow, pointing back to Mo and Omar, 'they were waiting in the car for twenty minutes before they came in.'

Billal looked shocked. 'Really?'

Bannerman hurried, came back around the car, possessive of the brother, slipping in almost between them.

'Yeah,' said Morrow.

Billal looked at the police tape, along the road, to the open front door of his house, frowning as he tried to answer the question. 'Where?'

Morrow pointed up the road. 'There, where those markers are.'

Billal imagined it for a moment. 'But the gunmen were parked down there.' He pointed around the corner to the garden path.

'That's right.'

Billal frowned. 'So, they might not have seen them?'

'They said they didn't see anything.'

'And that's possible?' Billal looked at Bannerman, asking him if his younger brother could be telling the truth.

'Yeah,' said Bannerman, trying not to smile, 'it is perfectly possible.'

Billal looked angrily at the window of the squad car. 'Good. Good.'

He turned back to look at Morrow and nodded back at the house. 'Meeshra help you?'

'Yes, thanks, she was very helpful.'

Billal arched his back slightly at that. 'She didn't see very much. She was in the bed the whole time,' and he nodded, a strange pecking nod, slightly out of time. Morrow didn't know what it meant. He looked at Morrow's shoes, curled his lip and turned away, walking away without saying goodbye.

Bannerman backed up to Morrow's side as they watched him fold his big frame into the backseat next to Mo. 'Yeah,' he said as if Morrow had expressed her reservations out loud. 'What did the daughter-in-law say?'

'Not much. Do you still think they got the wrong house?'

'Dunno. They rang 999. Neighbours put the shot thirty seconds or so before all the calls so, they rang immediately . . .'

Innocents call for the police, generally. It meant they didn't feel responsible for the attack. Or else they were criminal but had a grotesque sense of entitlement. There were families who knew whole shifts by their first names. When they weren't getting lifted they were calling cops in to resolve family arguments. Morrow dismissed that option though: they'd have heard of them if that was the case.

Bannerman sighed heavily. 'Look,' he said, 'I'm sorry about this, just . . . MacKechnie's idea. I'll be working for you next time.'

Morrow froze slightly. The skin on her finger was throbbing. 'Yeah, well it looks complicated. Time consuming. I know your mum's not well.'

'Oh, no, no, no,' he said quickly. 'She'll be fine.' Bannerman's mother had pneumonia, both lungs, not good when a woman was in her late seventies. He'd been milking it for sympathy in the office for a week but now he squinted at her, guessing at her motive for bringing it up. 'You'll cooperate on this, won't you?'

'I'm not a child, Grant,' she said coldy.

He flinched at that and she regretted saying it. His mother wasn't well and she was being mean.

'Sorry.' She said the word so quietly she saw him glance at her mouth for confirmation.

He brightened. 'Yeah, can't get a handle on this at all.' His bewilderment seemed feigned. 'They seem as straight as anything, no crims in the family, no enemies, nothing. They haven't even got a big telly.'

He was at it. She'd seen Bannerman do his wide-eyed fishing act before, letting people explain things to him and damn themselves.

'Could be a wrong address . . . ?' she said weakly.

Bannerman looked angry, knowing she had more than that. 'Oh, thanks for that, Morrow. Really insightful. You want me to chisel it out of you?'

Morrow bit the corner of her mouth hard, watching Billal. Fury tinged with shame. Her emotional staples. 'What do you want me for when we get back?'

He looked at her, his mouth twitching down at the corners. 'What do you want to do?'

'I could talk to the young guys . . .'

'You think they're it?'

'Dunno. They were hanging about outside . . .'

He read her face. She could feel him realising that she did think they were it. He wouldn't let her near them.

'No, I think I'll talk to them. Could you do me a favour and listen to the tapes of the emergency calls? See what you can get off them?' He smiled, pleased to have thought of a punishment job that was out of the way, time consuming and menial. 'That would be really helpful, Morrow, thanks.'

He pressed his lips together to stop himself smiling and sloped off to the car.

9

Pat watched the Lexus headlights sweep across Malki's face, bleaching him. It was a narrow road and Malki had to stand flat against the chapel wall to let the car turn in the street.

Pat could see the quiet content on Malki's face, a soft smile. He had a pocket full of dough, rare enough, and he was going home excited, off to his bedroom to see his powdery white darling. She never failed Malki, never bored or annoyed him. Malki's only problem was getting enough of her. True love, thought Pat, and he envied Malki that certainty. He had never gone out with a woman he didn't have reservations about. He thought about the girl in the hall, jeans and T-shirt and everyone else in Muslim gear, and found himself warm at the thought of her.

Eddy drove on, sticking to the big roads. A car as smart as a Lexus would only ever pass through streets like these, never stop. It would draw the eye of anyone who saw it, stick in the mind.

Back on the motorway they took a cut-off for Cambuslang and drove along empty roads, through green light after green light, straight through sleepy Rutherglen to the broad winding road that cut straight through the south.

Eddy pulled off unexpectedly, took two turns into increasingly dilapidated streets. He slowed and cut the lights as they drew up into a dead end of boarded-up houses. Bushes grew wild over the pavements and roads. Not a single other car was parked anywhere and all of the windows were dark.

Pat'd assumed he'd know the hideout when they got to it

but he'd never been here before. 'Who's . . . ?' He broke off, realising Eddy couldn't say in front of the pillowcase.

Eddy steered a wide swing at a break in a bushy hedge, bumped up a steep concrete drive with a tectonically deep crack across it.

The sight of the house made Pat flinch. Stucco peeled off the front wall, window frames were splintered and peeling, the front door shored up with rotting leaves and litter. Between the house and the hedge was a knee-high sea of grass. In every dark window curtains were yanked shut, hanging heavy with grime and time.

Watching Eddy's eyes in the strip of mirror, Pat saw him glancing resentfully at the house as he eased the car to the left, flattening the vegetation lapping at the side of the building. He stopped when the car was around the side of the house out of sight of the street, pulled on the handbrake and sighed angrily.

As if he thought Pat hadn't noticed, Eddy turned to Pat and made that face, the face that said someone had let him down and someone was going to pay. Pat raised both eyebrows, keeping his face neutral, and looked away. Eddy had organised the hideout. If there was a fuck-up it wasn't anything to do with Pat.

On balance, if Eddy was determined to shoot anyone, Pat would prefer that it wasn't the pillowcase. Pillowcase had a family, a clean house, a daughter. Be better if it was the person who never washed their curtains.

Eddy opened the car door, stepping out next to the windowless side of the house and Pat climbed out on his side. They looked around. Down the short drive the other houses in the street were all sagging and rotting too, windows peeling and cracked. Straight across the road conjoined houses were boarded up with fibreglass. From their promontory they could see the roofs of houses and flats, street lamps in the distance throbbing orange into the night sky. Far to the left, a bus or a lorry cast its lights over the fronts of houses, cutting a road through the quiet dark.

'Whose place ...?'

Eddy ground his jaw towards the back seat. 'Get this fucker out.'

Opening the door, Pat reached in and pulled the pillow-case out by the arm. It followed every direction passively, stepping out next to him. In the nervous excitement of getting away Pat hadn't really noticed how small the man was. He only came up to Pat's chest and he realised suddenly that this was why Eddy took him.

Pat let go of the arm. Free from touch, unsure what to do, the old man raised his hands to his shoulders, as if he was being held up by cowboys. His liver-spotted hands were swollen; Pat's papa had hands like that.

From behind, Eddy jabbed a mean knuckle in the pillow-case's back, between the shoulder blades, making him arch his back. Then he shoved, made it stumble through the vegetation, heading towards the back of the house. Eddy went after him and grabbed his elbow, swinging him roughly around the corner to the back door.

The back door was unlocked and opened with a yowl into a kitchen that reeked of mould. Eddy shoved the pillowcase in ahead of them, through a narrow corridor between stacked bags of weeping rubbish.

Pat thought the house was abandoned but noticed that the doorless units were strewn with fresh empty beer cans and full ashtrays, one of them still smoking lazily.

'Smell.' The pillowcase had spoken quietly, inadvertently, to no one. Pat smiled at that. It did smell.

Eddy glared at the pillowcase, as if it had insulted his house. Spitefully, he poked an index finger into its shoulder, making it think he had his gun out, bullying him through an open doorway into a living room.

A stone-cladding fireplace covered most of the facing wall, each plastic brick covered in its own layer of dust. A broken chair lay on its side. A settee was set against the wall and a thin, tinny whistle was coming from the sleeping figure on it.

Pat recognised him. It was Shugie. 'Oh fuck me . . .'

Eddy glared at Pat, so angry that his top lip was white with tension.

Shugie had a shock of white hair, yellowed from ardent smoking. His swollen eyes were framed by wild white eyebrows. Legs and arms, skinny from lack of exercise, were attached to a beer-bloated barrel body.

Eddy had a fondness for Shugie that Pat never understood: the guy was a wreck, a mess and a bore. He had drunk so much for so long that even his stories sounded drunk. Tales about the old day bank jobs and getaways crashed out in mid-flow. But Eddy called him old school, saw a glamour in his wild past that Pat was blind to.

Eddy raised his leg and kicked Shugie in the side. The eyebrows came down but the old man didn't stir. Eddy kicked him again, hard this time, right in the soft flesh below his ribs. Shugie frowned, let out a little groan, but still he didn't move.

And then, as they stood watching him, a dark stain spread from his groin, a circle creeping outwards across his jeans.

'God almighty,' said Pat, averting his eyes.

Eddy shook his head. He took his embarrassment out on the pillowcase, shoving him off guard, making him stumble towards the hall and the front door.

'Take it upstairs,' ordered Eddy.

Pat raised an eyebrow and hissed a warning through his

front teeth. Eddy had the good manners to drop his gaze. 'Just so I can make the call ...' he muttered.

Pat let him stew, staring at Eddy who shuffled uncomfortably from foot to foot. "F you don't mind.'

Pat nodded and walked after the pillowcase, pinching his sleeve, pulling him across the path of the front door.

Covered in uncollected post, the carpet was shiny with trampled-in dirt. Pat didn't want to touch anything. He kept his hands to himself as they walked up the stairs, wary of the sticky banister. Hands out, blind man's bluffing, the pillowcase tentatively touched each step with his toe before taking it.

On the landing Pat opened a door. Bathroom, stench of piss and mildew. He tried the next door and found a dirty bedroom full of boxes and crap. Too many chances to find a weapon. He looked in the third door. A bare bed and scattered magazines.

'In here,' he said, softly guiding the pillowcase to the door.

'You want me to go ...?' the pillowcase answered Pat's whispered tone, as if they were the conspirators instead of Pat and Eddy. Pat liked that. 'Aye, pal, you go in here.'

At the word of kindness he could feel the tension release from the old man's arm, felt the give in his footsteps. Touched, Pat led him gently over to the side of the bed and turned him by the shoulders so that his back was to it. 'There's a bed right behind you. Sit down on it, put your feet on it and I want ye to stay there, OK?'

'But, I have shoes on.'

Pat looked at the stained yellow sheet, at the creases on the linen. 'I wouldn't worry about that too much, faither.'

Blind, the old man reached his hands behind for the bed and lowered himself slowly. Pat helped him. 'There ye are. Swing your feet up, that's it. Shuffle over into the middle.'

The old man did as he was ordered. 'That's it,' said Pat. 'Now listen, don't move from there.'

'What if I need to . . . use a bathroom?' The pillowcase's face looked up at him from the bed, like a child afraid to sleep.

'Um.' Pat wanted to say just do it in here, because Shugie had probably pissed the bed often enough but he liked the association with order, wanted to distance himself from the mess of the place. 'Bang your shoe on the floor and I'll come and take ye.'

'OK.' The pillowcase crossed his hands in his lap. 'OK.'

Pat stepped away, out the hallway and shut the door on the neat white figure sitting upright in the filthy bed.

He stopped outside the door, reluctant to go downstairs. If he wanted to go anywhere in the house it was back into the bedroom with the neat little man.

Outwardly his composure was still intact: Aamir sat still, his hands carefully crossed in his lap as orderly alone as he had been in the full glare of his captors. He wasn't moving because he couldn't move, his muscles were frozen, his throat felt as if it had been punched, as if a scream was strangling his Adam's apple. He didn't actually know if he would be able to move without being ordered to.

Testing his motor skills, he tapped a finger and found that he was shaking slightly but could move. He took a breath and opened his eyes. Through the pillowcase he could see a slight light from the left, perhaps a window, at waist height. They had been driving for two hours, perhaps one and a half, allowing for his fear, which made time go slower. In two hours they could have gone from Glasgow to Dundee, to Edinburgh and anywhere over in the east, to Perth perhaps, Stirling certainly.

Aamir had an acute sense of time, from working the shop for so long.

He tapped his finger again and suddenly saw Aleesha's hand come apart, fingers hit the wall behind her, the newly bought Madinah clock, and the violent red spill down her forearm. And then he saw himself begging them, wobbling his head like a TV Asian, talking in broken English when he was fluent: please sir, me be good boy, let me go by, let me go by, British passport, sorry, sorry.

The red dust of the Kampala road was choking his throat. He saw again that arrogant swagger of the soldiers, their rifles slung across their peasant shoulders, their grins, their black features lost in the glare of their white teeth. And beyond them, his mother. She staggered out from behind the army van, not even crying, not even looking at where she was going, just falling forward and catching her weight on one foot then the other, her eyes were glazed, her mouth slack. She was clutching the hem of her yellow sari, holding it up so that the mud and dust didn't mark it. On her seat, from her backside, wet, scarlet blood soaked into the material, blooming into a giant verdant flower as Aamir watched through the dirty glass of the taxi window. Aamir and his mother had British passports. It was a licence for the soldiers to do whatever they wanted to them.

Aamir survived. That was his skill. He took a breath. At the cost of his mother's dignity, they escaped, and she never mentioned it again. For the rest of her life, in Scotland, Aamir had pitied and despised her for letting them, for buying his freedom with her dignity. Now it was his turn.

She knew he could never touch her again after that. In the dark, he reached across the hot plastic of the taxi's back seat and took his long dead mother's hand. In the filthy bedroom, on the piss-stained bed, he lifted her hand to his mouth and kissed her fingers.

Pat stepped into the living room and found Eddy gone. Shugie was snoring, frowning an unconscious protest at the piss prickling into his skin. From the kitchen came the tiny tones of a phone number being tapped into a key pad.

Eddy was standing in the dark, next to the sink, his phone blue-lighting one side of his face. He flared his nostrils at Pat, showing that he was disappointed at the mess as well. The phone was answered at the other end by an ominous silence.

'Um, hello,' said Eddy, nervous but hopeful. 'Eh, it's me.'

The house was so quiet Pat could hear the answer: 'Say it's done.' The strangulated Belfast accent was crystal clear in the stillness of the kitchen.

'It's done,' said Eddy, trying to copy his professional manner. 'Got one guy. Old guy.'

A pause. 'Old?'

'Not actually the target. But another one, an old guy.'

Another pause. Not friendly. 'Why not the target?'

'Eh, he wasn't there.'

'Not *there*?'

Eddy was sweating now, looking to Pat for backup. 'Eh, well no. But we got an old guy.'

'How old?'

'Um, sixties?'

An angry sigh fluttered into the receiver. 'You said you were fit for this.'

'We did, we got … Um … this old guy.'

'*I told you twenties*.'

'Well, he wasn't there so … we got an old one.'

'Not twenties?'

Eddy's face tightened. 'Um, we've got the old man.'

'Any shots fired off?'

'One. Pat. A hand injury. Nothing much.'

A sound from the other end, a groan or a huff or something, a muffled exclamation.

'Sorry? I didn't catch—'

'*Yees are fucking amateurs.*'

Eddy found himself listening to a dead tone. He sucked his teeth, flipped the phone shut and looked to Pat for comfort.

Pat pointed at the festering bin bags. 'I am not fucking staying here.'

IO

London Road Police Station was down the road from Bridgeton Cross. Bridgeton was pretty, near the vast expanse of Glasgow Green, had a couple of listed buildings and a museum. For years it had been mooted as an up and coming area but Bridgeton stubbornly neither upped nor came. Drunken fights were vicious and hourly, streets were graffiti-declared Free States, and the children's language would have made a porn star blush.

The station itself was relatively new. From outside it looked like a cross between a three-storey office building and a fortress. Built of shit-brown bricks, the front was shored up with supporting pillars, the windows sunk defensively into the facade. It was set back from the main road by overgrown bushes in massive concrete pots that served as bollards to stop nutters driving into the reception area.

The door was always open to the public, welcoming them into an empty lobby with free-standing poster displays of friendly policemen and women chortling happily. For safety reasons the front bar wasn't manned. The duty sergeant could see the lobby through a one-way mirror and CCTV. He came out in his shirt sleeves if the member of the public didn't look tooled up or mad with the drink, but if they had as much as an air of melancholy about them he brought his deputy and a night stick.

Morrow's driver took a street up the side and a sharp right into the police yard. A high wall topped with broken glass was arranged around a windowless block of cells. He cruised around to the back side of the cell block and found a space next to the police vans.

'You better lock up,' said Morrow as they got out.

Most officers didn't bother locking their vehicles but the yard gate had been broken for a fortnight and spite-theft from a police station wasn't much deterred by cameras.

Morrow walked up the ramp to the door, stopped outside, looked straight into the camera, and punched in the door code. John was behind the processing bar, always immaculately uniformed, leaning his weight on a tall stool preserving the creases in his trousers.

He bid her good morning and she gave him a smile. She pushed through the door to the duty sergeant's lair and saw Omar and Billal through the striped window, sitting on the visitor's chairs by the front door, waiting. Their postures didn't match: Billal was upright, his arm around the back of the chair, his expression hurt. Omar was slumped over his knees, his mouth pressed hard into his hand, holding in a scream.

The senior duty sergeant, Gerry, grunted an acknowledgement at her and went back to filling out some time sheets. Morrow had been on at weekends when fights broke out in the waiting room and had seen Gerry plough into a crowd, peeling the drunks off one another like a surgeon easing skin back, never breaking a sweat. Gerry's hair seemed whiter every time she saw him. They kept starting new trainees but it would be a rare copper who could follow Gerry. The blend of meticulous form-filling and sudden violence took a particular kind of man.

She grunted back and opened the door into the lobby. Omar and Billal recognised her. Omar stood up, hopeful she would take him away from his growling brother.

'No,' she raised a hand, 'I'm not here to get you guys, I'm

not doing the questioning, just going in here.'

She backed off to the CID corridor on her left. She punched in the security code and opened the door, glad to get into the long green corridor. MacKechnie's office was at the far end, so he could stand at his door and look down at all of them. He never did.

The clarity of rank structure was one of Morrow's favourite things about the force. She knew who she had to take shit from and who she could give it to. It made sense to her. MacKechnie was not comfortable being in charge, she felt, and apologised for his status by pretending to listen. He had a leadership style that would be described with a lot of bullshit buzzwords: inclusive, facilitative, enabling.

Even at half three in the morning the corridor was relatively busy. MacKechnie's lights were on, his door open, his office empty. An incident room was being set up next to the tea room. She could see two uniforms moving a table through, negotiating the legs around the door frame.

She walked into her own office, flicked on the light and dropped her handbag. Bannerman's computer was on, his screen saver a photoshopped picture of himself on a body builder's body. Hilarious. His mouse had purple lights on the underside that distracted her eye when she was working. He kept chewing gum and healthy snack bars in his desk drawer, afraid of getting fat, she thought.

Everything on Morrow's desk was new and ordered and anonymous. A drawer of neat pens, a sharpener and spare jotters, always three, for making notes. She liked them new, threw them away once they had been used. She liked to think the desk could have been anyone's anywhere, devoid of history, that she kept her personality out of it, bland as beige, how she liked it.

She was hanging her jacket up by the door when she saw

Harris standing outside. DC Harris was small and coarse-featured, as if he'd grown up outdoors. He was likeable, had a flat Ayrshire accent and a perpetual look of surprise on his face: eyebrows raised, mouth in an open 'O'.

'Ma'am?' He seemed excited. 'Great, eh?'

'Is it?'

'Aye.' He had probably been expecting a routine night but found himself confronted with an actual genuine mystery instead of depressing, go-nowhere domestics and drunks clubbing each other for the price of a packet of fags. 'My piece break. Coming to watch?'

'Watch what?'

'Bannerman thinks the youngest son's it. He's getting him into Three.'

Bannerman had clocked her interest in Omar and she rolled her eyes without thinking, annoyed at herself for being so obvious. Harris saw her and misunderstood, remembered that it was supposed to be her case and felt bad about it. As a consolation he said, 'Coming anyway?'

She chewed her cheek, tried to change her face from huffy to neutral, said, 'Aye, fuck it,' and followed him out of the door, past Billal and through the far door to the stairs.

They trotted up to the second floor, into a room that always smelled of vegetable soup.

Everyone on CID was on their piece break apparently. Orange plastic chairs were laid out in two ramshackle rows of four but they were full already. MacKechnie must have given them permission. A short DC stood up to give Morrow his seat in the front row and everyone else in the room lifted their arses off the chairs as she sat down, respecting the rank.

'Yeah, yeah,' she flapped a hand at them, 'calm down, it's not a parade.'

She could see them from the corner of her eye, sloping down in the chairs, not as they had been but relaxing within regulation stipulations, wary. It made her feel powerful. She kept her eyes on the boxy black television against the wall.

CID recorded their interviews and the cameras could be used as a feed to keep everyone briefed. Not everyone liked being watched though and it wasn't always because they were bashful: some preferred to do an interview themselves and highlight lines of questioning themselves. It took a lot of balls to let other officers watch.

Morrow felt that being watched had forced a strange, strained quality on interview technique. Questioning was different now; guarded and formal and questioning officers were routinely respectful of even the lowest scrote. They spoke in a bizarre police-ese, as if they were giving evidence in court.

It never used to be this way. When she was younger Morrow remembered questioning as a drunken polka, officers and suspects swinging each other wildly around the facts, faster and faster, until something got broken. Now it was a strained quadrille where the rules of the dance stood hard and fast until one capitulated or the tension of the moves strangled the breath out of one of the participants.

Morrow thought people's responses to being watched said a lot about their view of themselves: some enjoyed it, assumed a positive response from a viewer. Some couldn't cope, froze, glanced at the camera and had to hand over to a colleague. Morrow felt she looked shifty on camera, guiltier than the crims she was interviewing.

The shot of the room was badly set up. It wasn't there to capture the nuances of the suspect's facial expressions but to prove that no one had been throwing punches. Because the camera was mounted high up on the wall the room looked narrower on camera than it seemed when she was in there, more claustrophobic. And the image was grainy, the colour drained from the room into a palate of grey and blue and yellow. A table with a wooden top, four chairs, a light switch and the door which had been left open slightly, the dusty top of it visible.

The door opened suddenly and Omar Anwar walked in. A muted cheer rose from the officers in the viewing room, muted because she was there, but it was as close to camaraderie as she had felt since her promotion and she found herself not exactly joining in but smiling along.

They liked that.

Omar sloped into the room as if he had extra vertebrae, hips first, bending like a question mark as he put his plastic tumbler of water on the table. Bannerman came into the room after him and some of his fans gave another cheer. Morrow didn't concur with that one and felt them clock it.

A fat officer nicknamed 'Gobby' came in after them. Gobby rarely spoke. Bannerman had chosen him over her, she realised, so he could shine.

Someone at the back muttered to themselves, 'The Banner-Man'll nail him.' The nickname brought a sting of bile to the back of her throat.

At Bannerman's invitation Omar sat down facing the camera, sitting well back from the table to make room for the splay of his legs. They couldn't quite see his face but his body was expressive enough. He was jittery, reached for his water, withdrew his hands, wriggled in the seat as Bannerman took off his suit jacket and hung it carefully on the back of his chair.

He took his time, sitting down, rolling his shirt sleeves up, assessing the tall, anxious boy without addressing him.

Gobby handed him one of the tapes and they turned away in their seats to the tape recorder, noisily pulling the cellophane off two cassette tapes which they slipped into the tape recorder behind them. Omar watched, frightened, as the policemen looked at each other, nodded and shut the cassette cases, pressing record. A high-pitched yowl filled the room as they turned back to the table. Reverently they waited until it had finished.

Omar looked quizzically at Gobby.

'Blank bit o' tape,' said Gobby quietly.

Pathetically grateful for the explanation, Omar smiled and leaned towards him, clutching at the implied kindness, pleading with Gobby to be his ally.

Gobby looked away.

Bannerman opened the play with a lingering explanation of what had brought them all here today, the rules, telling Omar that he was being watched by third parties, slowing his speech to a languorous drawl as if to counter Omar's frantic interjections of yes, thank you, thank you, he understood, his face twitching into micro-frowns and frights, his leg vibrating up and down under the table.

Bannerman looked straight at the boy suddenly. 'Omar,' he flashed a smile that even looked cold from behind, 'what do you do for a living?'

Omar looked at both of them. 'Living?'

'A job. What do you do for a job?'

'I've just graduated.'

'From uni?'

'Glasgow Uni, yeah, law school.'

'Law school?' He was building to something but Omar interjected.

'Got a first.'

'Good, good. Have you got a job to go to?'

'No, still looking around, ye know . . .'

86

'Had interviews and so on?'

'Well, no, not really, not sure if Law's for me really.'

At the back of the viewing room someone made a joke about one less of 'em. No one laughed. Jokes about lawyers were fine but the guy was Asian and the racist connotations were uncomfortable.

'I want you to talk us through what happened tonight.'

'OK, OK.' Omar took a sip of water.

'Whenever you're ready,' said Bannerman, meaning hurry up.

'OK, well me and Mo—'

Bannerman read from his notes, 'Mohammed Al Salawe?'

'Yeah, Mo. Me and Mo were sitting in the car—'

'The Vauxhall?'

'I was outside with Mo, in the Vauxhall, round the corner, smoking actually, and had the radio on, just chatting and, and we heard a loud sort of "pop" like a "pwomf" sort of noise, never heard anything like that, and there's this light, sort of white light in Meeshra's window...' The story got faster and faster, the words splattering into the room. 'And we never even said anything to each other just, like, ran—'

'What did you think it was?'

Omar looked confused.

'The noise,' explained Bannerman. 'What did you think made it?'

'Honestly?' Omar tipped his head sincerely.

Bannerman nodded.

'I thought it was a gas canister on a stove cooker. It's stupid because we don't use a stove cooker but in Pakistan you often hear of honour killings where a mother kills a daughter-in-law if she's had an affair or something and the way they do it is tamper with the gas canister on the stove.

Stupid,' he shrugged, 'but that's what came to my mind ...'

'Are your family from Pakistan?'

'No.'

'Why would you think that then?'

'Dunno.'

Bannerman tipped his head to the side, as if Omar had said something significant, wrong-footing him. 'And so you ran to the house, which way did you go?'

Omar shook his head and blinked, bringing himself back to the memory. 'Um, I was on the passenger side, the road side. I opened the door, stepped out into the street,' he flicked his hand to the side, as if he was throwing a cigarette butt away, 'ran around the bonnet of the car—'

'Mohammed's car?'

'Yeah, yeah, Mo's car ...' He had lost his thread.

'To the house?'

'Yeah, jumped onto the wee garden wall there, ran over, slipped at the corner a bit, caught myself, didn't fall, ran to the door—'

'Was the front door open or shut?'

'Um, shut.'

Morrow felt sure he was telling the truth, from his short sentences, the distant look in his eyes, the way he glanced downwards to see the road, the garden wall and the reflexive flattening of his hand in front as he stopped himself from falling.

'The door was shut—'

'And you opened it?'

Bannerman should stop interrupting, Morrow observed, he was breaking up the memory. It was easier to spot the lie in a long flow, the break in style was more obvious. It was the intrusion of the camera, Bannerman was determined to be seen. She envied his confidence but she could see that it was a handicap sometimes.

'Yeah, I opened it.' Omar looked at Bannerman for a prompt.

'And?'

'And.' He stopped, glanced into the camera and froze a moment as he realised that the eye was judging him. His forehead wrinkled suddenly, a child giving an excuse, and he looked away. 'And what?'

'What did you see when you opened the door?'

Omar looked at the camera again but his brow had straightened defensively. 'Saw my folks standing in the hall, on the right.' He put his hand out to indicate their position. 'Saw my brother Billal there too, near the door, standing in front of his room. The door was open behind him. Saw my wee sister, Aleesha,' his throat caught when he said her name, 'standing to the left, with her hand up.' He raised his left hand, twisting the wrist like the Statue of Liberty. 'Everyone was looking at her hand . . .' His chin buckled at the memory and he lost his breath.

'What about the men?' said Bannerman briskly. He was busy looking at his notes, he was missing all of it.

'The men.' Omar shook himself. 'The men were standing in the hall, yes. One with my folks, between me and my folks, the other in front of Aleesha, looking at her. His gun was down there.' Omar slung his hand down, at ninety degrees to his thigh.

Morrow sat forward.

Omar was pointing two fingers at the floor, his hand wide, out of kilter to his body. 'The gun had smoke on it. I looked at his face and I thought he had a really long jaw because he was wearing a balaclava and I only saw him from the side. But then he shut his mouth . . .'

'There were two men?'

'Two men—'

'What did the other one do?'

89

Bannerman was missing it. Morrow wanted to jump into the screen and make him look at the angle of Omar's hand, at the gestures of his jaw. The gunman's mouth had been hanging open in surprise; the recoil from the shot had thrown his hand to the side. He hadn't been ready for it, didn't have his elbow at the proper angle or his muscles relaxed. He'd been shocked by the force of the recoil, which meant either the gun had gone off by accident, or he had never fired a shot before.

Anxiously she looked at the officers sitting next to her and noted which were straining towards the screen along with her, who was willing Bannerman to shut up. Three out of eight. Sitting two seats down in the front row, Harris was one of them: he caught her eye, the 'O' of his mouth tightened.

Back on the television Omar carried on. 'He shouts "*Rob*", "*Where is Rob?*" He came running up to Mo and goes, "You're Rob," and then they grabbed my dad and took him away.'

'Did they ask if you were Rob?'

'Me?' Omar touched his chest and looked surprised. 'Me? Well, he sort of looked around and said, "Who is Rob? One of you is Rob."'

'But did he ever say, "*You* are Rob"?'

'To me?' His eyebrows rose indignantly to his hairline.

'Yeah, to you.'

'Um, yeah, I suppose he did but my mum said, "Oh no, not my Omar," and then he just sort of backed off because, obviously, then, he knew I was Omar, that I wasn't Bob.'

Bannerman, looking at his notes, failed to see the twitch on Omar's neck, head flicking back a little, but Morrow noted it. Something had happened there but Morrow didn't know what. She looked at Harris. He was straining forward on his chair, alert, looking for clues as to what had just happened.

They both watched as Omar leaned across the table, his hand under Bannerman's eye, drawing him back up. 'And then, and then, the other one, the fat one, he grabbed my dad, like around the neck with his hand.' Then Omar did a strange thing: he wrapped his own hands around his neck to illustrate the hold but somehow he pressed a little too tight, too adamant about it, as if he was actually trying to hurt himself. 'And I thought he was going to kill him!' He let go and stopped for breath. 'I did! And then he said he wanted two million quid by tomorrow night and not to call the police or he'd kill my dad. And then he's like: "This is payback for Afghanistan."'

He stopped talking, watching Bannerman to see if the dissemble had worked.

Bannerman had noted the change in tone, the excitement. He spoke calmly, 'Do you know anyone in Afghanistan?'

Omar was bewildered. 'No!'

'Have you ever been there?'

'Never.'

'Does your dad have any dealings with Afghanistan, any family there or anything?'

A hand swept the table top. 'No connection with Afghanistan whatsoever.'

'OK. And then what?'

'Then he grabbed dad there,' he laid his forearm over the bottom of his ribcage, like the Queen carrying a heavy handbag, 'and lifted him up,' he tipped back in his chair, 'and took him out the house.' Omar's arms flailed expressively at the door, making Morrow think of a stage magician diverting an audience's eye.

'Me and Mo ran after them, saw a big white van, like a

Merc panel van, pull away. So we ran to Mo's car and got in and followed them but we lost them at the motorway. They weren't driving fast, just within the law, didn't want to get caught, I suppose, and we shouldn't have lost them but we were panicking and driving fast and following tail lights in the dark and they didn't go the most obvious way, down the main roads.

'Then we saw a police car and stopped and I said to them that my dad had been taken by men in a van and about Afghanistan and that, but they tried to arrest us.'

Morrow saw the boy on the screen stop waving his hands and the hurt in his voice. To be treated with suspicion at a moment of grief. She knew the deep stinging cut of that feeling. That was why he looked like that in the road, he and Mo, because they knew they were not among friends, that they were other.

She sat back and glanced at the officers in the viewing room. Smart men, top of their game, all staring at the screen, willing him to be it. He must sense that.

When she stood up to leave someone called 'Down in front'. Their voice tailed off when they realised it was her.

The officer who had given up his seat was leaning against the wall, tipped his forehead out of respect, 'He's good, isn't he?' He meant Bannerman, wrongly supposing they were friends.

'Aye.' She leaned over to Harris and tapped his shoulder. 'Have a word?'

Out in the corridor they dropped their voices. 'What happened, just before he started rambling?'

Harris shrugged. 'I was trying to remember myself.'

'Get the disk would you? As soon as ...'

Still frowning Harris looked back into the room. 'His mum said, "Not my Omar."'

She turned her computer on, waited for what felt like ten minutes, signed herself in and called up her email. The digi recordings had already been forwarded to her. The transcript would take a few days to weave its way through form-filling and desk-landing but the digi recording was immediate.

Opening her bottom desk drawer she took out a brand new pad of cheap paper, a sharp new pencil from a box and a plastic container with a set of earphones in it. Plugging them into the hard drive stack, she clicked on the attachment.

The first file was numbered and she jotted it down in the pad before starting the recording. A caller panted loudly and a bored operator asked them: 'Which service do you require?'

Barely contained sobs demanded, 'Ambulance! Please! Tell them to come, please come! She's bleeding all over the place!'

'Who's bleeding please?'

'My daughter has been shot by ... men, they came into our home and threatened—' The mother, Sadiqa, had an English accent, a crisp fifties accent, and made the operator sound coarse.

'Can ye give us your address?'

Sadiqa gave it, becoming calm in the familiar recitation, but she was interrupted by a girl crying out in the background and began panting again, 'Oh dear, my God, my husband has been taken, my Aamir—'

The operator's voice was nasal and bland, told her to calm down, the ambulance was on its way. No, there wasnae any point in her getting off the line because the ambulance was on its way right now. She made Sadiqa spell her name, her husband's name, what sort of guns were they?

'I have no idea. Black guns? Big—'

'Are they still in the actual house?'

'Gone! Left! I've told you that.'

'Did they leave on foot or in a car?'

'I'm afraid no, I didn't see. But my son, my Omar ran out into the street.'

'Has your son come back in? Could he come to the phone and tell me if it was on foot or in a vehicle, maybe?'

But Sadiqa wasn't listening to her any more. 'Aleesha, oh Lord, Aleesha is bleeding. Please, please come quickly.' She dropped the receiver noisily and spoke urgently to someone. A thump sounded like a body falling. Someone picked up the receiver and hung it up.

The call lasted one minute fourteen seconds. The second call started ten seconds later than Sadiqa's.

Billal was calling from a mobile so the line was less clear. In the background she could hear Sadiqa's voice repeating one side of the conversation she had just listened to. Shock made Billal shout a series of exclamations: 'Police! Police! And an ambulance!'

'And what is your call concerning, sir?'

'Two men! Two men!'

'Two men what, sir?'

'Two men came in our house! They took my daddy away!'

'So, they're not there now?'

'They shot my wee sister. In her hand!'

'*They* shot *her* hand, sir?'

'Yes! Yes! She's bleeding really … God … badly! It's all … blood—'

'Did you see them shoot her?'

'Yeah, with guns! Big guns, real guns.'

The female controller tried to get him to spell his name and the address but Billal could barely hear her he was so shocked.

94

'Please come and help us, help us, please come.'

'We are on our way, sir, right now, but—'

'We've got a baby here, a new baby! They pointed the gun at a baby!'

'Did they say what they wanted, sir?'

'Ob.'

Billal had moved his face, his chin was slightly over the receiver, so it wasn't very clear. Morrow had to use the mouse to listen to the portion of speech again.

'. . . what they wanted, sir?'

'Hob. Were after someone called Bob.'

It was clearer the second time he said it, the puff of air from his lips popping gently on the receiver as he said the 'b's.

Morrow wrote 'Bob' on the pad and put a question mark next to it.

'Mum! She's falling—' He hung up. The conversation had lasted less than a minute.

The last call was from Meeshra, sobbing loudly, wailing about Aamir and Aleesha. She sounded calmer than the other two, even a little excited but much more upset, the way a distant acquaintance sobs at a funeral of a child while the family hold tight, afraid the force of grief will rip the earth from under their feet.

'They've taken my dad-in-law, just lifted the poor man up and went off wi' him—'

'Could you tell me your—'

'Lifted him off—' She broke off to sob theatrically and ask Dear God to help them.

'Could I have your name and address, please? Madam, are you there? Can I have your name, please?'

'Meeshra Anwar. They've took 'im.'

They were talking at the same time, the controller and Meeshra, and their voices coiled around one another:

'... wanted 'im ...'

'... spell that ...'

'... shouting, looking for ...'

'... out for me?'

'... some bloke called ...'

'... spell that name?'

Both voices stopped dead for half a second of dead air, and then Meeshra spoke: 'Aye, they was shouting for some bloke but they couldn't find him and just took Aamir instead.'

Morrow looked at the pad. Meeshra was avoiding saying the name. She looked at her writing: small and regular, the word less than half a centimetre long but pressed so hard into the paper that the free edges at the bottom of the page curled up to meet it. *Bob?* She touched it tenderly with her fingertip. *Bob?*

Reluctantly she pulled the sheet of paper out of the pad and stood up, stopping by the door, nodding a con-gratulations to herself for being honourable and giving up the information so quickly. She opened the door and stepped out into the hallway. Outside a uniformed copper was chatting lightly to a plain-clothed DC showing him something in the paper. Night shift. Hard graft but there was a kindness about it. Everyone moaned about it but they missed it when they were promoted and went days only. There was a closeness in being sleepy together, in minding the drowsy city.

MacKechnie was still in, the light from his office spilling into the corridor. Morrow stood at the door and nodded politely. 'Sir?'

'Come!' He always said that, not knowing it had another meaning and that they laughed at him. Morrow looked in and found him squinting at something on his computer. 'Yes?'

96

'Sir, I was listening to the 999 calls just now.'

MacKechnie frowned at her, one eyebrow arched accusingly. 'Why?'

'In case there was something on them.'

MacKechnie sighed at his clasped hands and sucked his teeth. 'Sergeant *Mor*row.' He had a way of pronouncing her name that made her flinch. 'I have asked you to work with Bannerman on this.'

'Bannerman told me to listen to the tapes, sir.'

'*Bannerman* told you to listen to the tapes?'

She stepped into his office and held up a hand to fend him off. 'OK, that aside, they've all said the gunmen were asking for "Rob". On the 999s they're avoiding it but I think the son said "Bob".'

'OK.' He looked confused.

'He's interviewing Omar now, shall I send him up a note? Get him to ask about it?'

Confusion gave way to certainty. 'Yes.'

She withdrew and stood in the corridor a moment. She'd expected a bit more of a reaction. It was something concrete after all, and she'd discovered it. Disappointed, she went back to her office and wrote out the details, marked that the note was from her and caught a DC lingering by the board in the incident room.

'DC ...?'

'Wilder.' He stood to attention and she appreciated that he knew who she was.

'Wilder, take this up to Bannerman in Three right away.'

He took it from her and set off quickly, leaving the door to slam shut behind him. At least someone was taking it seriously.

Deflated, she went back to her office, dragging her eye and her pen across incident forms. The warm glow of her discovery was fading, swamped with tiredness and the mundane job. She broke off from the admin task to listen to the section of Meeshra and Billal's emergency calls several times, her certainty paling a little each time.

She was about to do it again when Bannerman opened the door and leaned against the door jamb like a louche lover coming back from the bathroom. 'All right, Morrow?'

'Fine.'

'How are you getting on?'

Morrow blinked hard, her eyes were burning. 'Just ... paperwork.' He slouched into the room. 'Did you get my note?'

He had to think about it. 'The note? About *Bob*. Yeah, the note. God, great, thanks for that. Great.' He dropped into his seat and unlocked his drawer, pulling out a grain bar and ripping the wrapper open with his teeth.

'And?'

He shrugged without looking at her.

She wanted to get up and go over and kick his shins. 'What did Omar say about it?'

'Well, I'd actually finished interviewing him by that point, so we'll ask him next time.'

They looked at each other across the office and Bannerman smiled. He hadn't asked Omar about it because it came from her. He'd been unprofessional and she should let it go, win some, lose some, but the point wasn't about her and Bannerman: a small man was sitting in a cold van somewhere, surrounded by armed malevolent strangers and the information could be material.

'You didn't ask?'

Bannerman refreshed his smile.

'Look, come over here.' She held up the headphones.

Bannerman looked wary, didn't budge from his seat

and instead swung his feet up on the edge of his desk, crossing them, stubbornly chewing his health bar. The interview had been a disappointment, viewed by the entire squad. She understood how foolish he would have felt if the only significant question was on a note from her but she was sure she was right. She called up the audio file of Meeshra's phone call, a tiny box on her screen with a jagged visual of her speech. She pulled the earphones out of the hard drive, double clicked and Meeshra's voice burst into the office, weaving through the crackle of switchboard operators.

'She's dodging the question,' she said. 'And Billal said "Bob" instead of "Rob".'

Bannerman didn't react.

Morrow tutted and held her hands up. 'Well, I've told you. MacKechnie knows I did, Wilder's a witness I sent the note, so if it goes tits up because of you it's nothing to do with me.'

He narrowed his eyes at her.

'OK?' She leaned across the desk towards him. 'You can't say I haven't told ye.'

'OK,' he said slowly, as if trying to calm her down. 'Thanks.'

'If you want to fuck it all up, that's up to you.'

Bannerman smiled condescendingly at his health bar, peeling the wrapper off the end and popping it in his mouth. He would tell MacKechnie that she'd said that, tell it as a funny story about what a character she was, knowing MacKechnie would hear it as confirmation that she was impossible, mad, no team-player.

'This animosity,' he was muttering, 'you and me, professional jealousy, you know, I'm sure we can work around it.' He was turning it around, making it about her and him, not Aamir Anwar's safety.

99

'Not if you're going to act like a cunt, we can't.'

She was too angry, almost dizzy and the words fell out of her before she could catch them. A hot blush ran up her neck. MacKechnie would hear that comment too.

A perfunctory rap at the door was followed by Harris looking in. 'Ma'am?'

'What!'

He paused, looked frightened and addressed himself to Bannerman. 'Just looked the DVD of the interview over. Omar says they were looking for Bob, not Rob.'

Without a word Bannerman swung his feet to the floor, stood up and left the office, shutting the door behind him, leaving her alone in the rancorous silence. Outside some guys were talking in another room, having a laugh and she listened jealously for his voice, suspecting, as always, that everyone had more allies than her.

She was filling out the forms, cooling down to a cold rage, when she heard excited footsteps in the corridor, an exclamation and a scurry.

Bannerman threw her door open. 'Found the van.'

They took a car from the yard and Bannerman drove. All the cars in good condition were out and they had an old Ford with an engine so noisy that idle chat was impossible.

Bannerman concentrated on the road, uncomfortable at the silence, but Morrow was glad to be let alone, her face slack as the warm orange lights of the motorway clicked past on the quiet road. The drive was long and effortless, all the way to Harthill on a smooth and empty road.

Bannerman didn't know the area they were going to and made a big production of looking for road signs, muttering inaudibly to himself about turns and directions, winding himself up. Morrow said nothing. They took a roundabout, a side road and finally a rough road down the side of open fields with intermittent hedgerows. It had been tarmacked at one time, but a decade or so of harsh winters and tractors had churned the ground uneven. They pulled up outside the perimeter tape.

Blue and white was strung up between some of the hedges, blocking the roadway, and a fat copper was standing next to it, a local plod, warming his hands by rubbing them together and stamping his feet. He wasn't acting it either; his nose was red and his top lip looked damp.

Bannerman cut the engine. 'Noisiest bloody car I've ever fucking been in,' he said to himself.

'Saved us having to talk to each other for forty minutes though.'

Bannerman swung to her aggressively, ready to take it out on her, but found her smiling pleasantly. Despite himself he smiled, swinging away from her so she wouldn't see him concur. He opened the door and stepped out. She liked him better away from their gaffers.

Opening her own door she stepped out into the bristling cold. Harthill was on higher ground than the city and the air was thinner here, the skies often brutally clear. Tonight a giant white moon lit it. The tarmac on the road had snapped like a slab of toffee. The motorway was hidden behind a hill, the lights glowing over the low horizon. Whoever brought the van here knew the area. Looking to the foot of the hill she saw a clump of wind-gnarled trees gathered around a smouldering white van, well lit by the Forensic Fire team.

The Scene of Crime Forensic team would not be here for a few hours, not until it got light. There wouldn't be any point in the dark. Unless Osama Bin Laden personally organised a massacre in the Glasgow city centre over the next few hours theirs would be the first crime scene they came to. In the meantime a crew of two were trying to pat out the dying fire, preserving what little trace evidence they could.

It was hard to put out a fire in a vehicle that would serve as evidence. Smother it in foam and you might as well wash it under a tap. Throw water at it and any accelerants would disperse and start an ancillary fire elsewhere. In the morning they'd do a fingertip search of the surround and lift the van without opening it, take it to a sterile environment for analysis.

'Harthill,' she said. 'On their way to Edinburgh?'

Bannerman shrugged a shoulder. 'Not an obvious place is it?'

'Maybe they knew it from somewhere.'

'Can't exactly make that the basis of a search though, can we?' Bannerman pointed to the ground. 'No marks.'

She was desperate to know but embarrassed to ask. 'What else did Omar say?'

Bannerman looked at her curiously, surprised by the tone in her voice, not knowing what it meant. 'Not much. I thought he was it, but ...'

She shrugged and looked off towards the van. 'I thought he was too.'

Mistaking consensus for intimacy Bannerman leaned into her, quite close, and drew a breath. Suddenly panicked by his proximity she scurried away, over to the fat copper guarding the tape.

He was freezing but still nervous, asked their names and rank and where they were from, jotting it longhand in his notebook, as if he was doing an exam. He probably didn't have much crime scene experience. He must have been the same age as them, Morrow thought, early thirties, but his ruddy face and fatness made him look much older. People got old quicker in the country.

Sensing Bannerman coming up behind her Morrow ducked under the tape and walked over to the mouth of the field, staying on the far side, away from the obvious path anyone leaving the field would be likely to have taken. A farmer was standing there with a copper but she didn't look at them. She was looking at the ground.

The moonlight was so bright she could see the shadow of marks in the frost: tyres from a car were picked out in the tarmac, a parked car had sheltered a rectangle from the ground frost and then driven away. She looked up the road, squinted, crouched.

Indistinct footsteps trailing back and forth to the car from the field, muddying one another, some deep zigzagged treads, like army boots, size eightish, some flat soled, like slippers, another pair of trainers. Disappointing: frost was a useless medium for prints.

Bannerman saw her looking at them and shouted back to the plod by the tape, 'Get the photographer out here and get them before they disappear.'

The plod looked shocked and hurt, as if he had been reprimanded, and swung away to talk into his radio.

She looked away from the footprints and saw the press of tyre tracks. New wheels, clear zigzags and deep lines, which was bad. It was easier to match worn tyres to track marks, chips and wear in the rubber could be as effective as a fingerprint, but factory fresh all looked the same and there were only a few manufacturers.

Bannerman was behind her and nodded at her thought. They traced the movements wordlessly, pointing and tutting and humming, keeping their eyes on the ground. They traced the footsteps to the break in the hedge and looked into the long stretch of churned mud in the field. The footsteps broke up here, the ground was too lumpy, but some of the partial impressions were clearer, a toe, a heel, the side of a sole.

Morrow took what she could from it: three sets of feet coming towards her, muddied by steps that were there already, perhaps meeting others who had been waiting. She looked back, sorting the impressions in her eye: two sets coming towards her, a scuffle of overlaps, but they looked like the same treads on the soles.

Finally Bannerman asked, 'What ye seeing?'

He was good at this, she knew that, but was either trying to be friendly or intending to steal her ideas for his own. She almost hoped it was the latter. 'Two gunmen,' she said. 'Same boots on. Thought for a minute they were met here but unlikely. Two big men, a driver and a hostage. They wouldn't all fit in a car unless they were met by just one other guy. Only the army boots go to the driver's door.' She pointed back up to the large patch left bare of frost by the car. 'They must have left a car here to pick up. We can check the CCTV at Harthill, see what pulls off earlier and match it with what pulls out later.'

Bannerman was still looking back at the rectangle. 'How do you know that's the driver's door?'

She drew her finger along the tyre marks. 'They didn't reverse out, did they?'

Bannerman looked pleasantly surprised. 'Hm.'

He was going to steal that, she fucking knew it, he was known for it below ranks. Gaffers thought he was a genius.

'That's the third one this year, burnt-out cars on my land.' The farmer standing opposite her was wearing a Barbour coat and had a pissed-off, sleep-puffed face. His accent was almost impenetrable and Morrow found herself watching his lips for clues.

'Is this your land, sir?' she said.

'It is my land, aye, aye, mine, yeah.'

'Would you mind standing behind that tape over there? We've got frosty feet marks here and we're trying to keep them good until the photographer gets here.'

'But it's my land.'

'Ye can see my point though, eh?' She gave the copper a look, tipped her head to the side to get the farmer out of the crime scene.

'It's my land,' mumbled the farmer, unsure if he'd been reprimanded, but proactively annoyed anyway. 'I'm staying here if I want to stay here. And why did you not bother before and now you're bothering about this one? They've burnt out cars before this one and ye did nothing at all. Had to shove the cars out mysel'.'

He was almost unintelligible. Too long Bannerman's eyes stayed on his mouth and when he finally broke off it was to nod, bewildered, and frown at his feet. He turned to the uniform. 'Officer, were you the first here?'

The uniform nodded at Bannerman as if he was meeting a film star. He had a red farmer's face and round body, not flattered by the double-breasted plastic police issue jacket buttoned tight across his belly.

'Find anything? A passport or a home address? No letters with photo ID on the path up here?'

'Nothing like that so far, sir, no, as far as I know, like.' Same accent, voice quiet because he was intimidated by the specialist from the town, almost as hard to understand as the farmer.

Bannerman snorted, looking to Morrow to laugh along with him: a bonding moment between colleagues.

'Have you actually done a search?' she pointed towards the van.

'Not yet, ma'am, no.'

'How do you know, then? Get that man out beyond the

tape.' She walked off into the field, leaving Bannerman to stand with the two men he had been ridiculing a moment ago.

Even she was starting to wonder if she was an arsehole.

II

'I am not sitting down *anywhere* here.' Pat crossed his arms and looked around the living room. There was not a surface on floor, walls or ceiling without a suspicious stain nearby.

Sitting in the least damp corner of the balding brown corduroy settee, Shugie looked up at him, tipping his head back to compensate for the puff on his eyes, and whispered, 'OK then.' His smoke-fucked voice was barely a rasp.

'Because,' Pat, leaned in to provoke him, 'it's fucking *ginking*.'

Shugie blinked, sanguine about the charge. 'OK.'

Foiled, determined that Shugie would be as upset as he was, Pat looked around the floor, at the settee, through the door to the kitchen. '*You live like a dirty fucking animal.*'

But Shugie was unperturbed, distracted, perhaps by the profundity of his hangover. He shut his rheumy eyes to sniff, the violent action disturbing the delicate balance of forces behind his eyes, and he cringed with pain. 'Oooh.'

'Did you hear me?'

'Oh aye. OK.' He kept his eyes shut, awaiting equilibrium. 'You're saying it's dirty and that's fair enough.'

'*Look at that.*'

With supernatural effort Shugie peeled one swollen eye open and followed Pat's finger to a distant meeting of floor and wall. He squinted at it: something small and brown had grown its own white fur coat.

'*Wit the fuck is that?*'

Shugie shrugged at the distant object. 'An orange?'

'*An orange?*'

'Or a tangerine?'

'*It's a shit.*'

Dropping his feet heavily on the stairs they heard Eddy coming downstairs from keeping guard outside the old man's room.

'There's a fucking dog shit in your living room.' Pat raised his voice, restating his case so that Eddy could hear.

'Naw,' Shugie sighed with the effort of talking, 'there hasnae been a dug in here for three month, man.'

'Then it's been here for three month. Look at the bloom on it.'

Shugie did as instructed. 'Nah,' he said unconvincingly, 'that's just an old tangerine or something.'

Pat looked accusingly at Eddy but didn't get the chance to speak.

'Your watch,' said Eddy, thumbing over his shoulder to the stairs.

'This place ...' Pat found himself lost for words. He pointed at the furry white intruder by the wall.

Shugie threw his hands up and rasped an appeal to Eddy. 'He's going mad over an old orange or something.'

In a gesture of solidarity Eddy flopped on to the settee next to Shugie. He sat suddenly straight, his eyes widened. He jumped to his feet again, turning to look at the damp seat of his trousers, moving his hand to brush the urine off and then thought better of it, flapping his hand at it instead. 'Oh, ya dirty fucking ...'

Pat grabbed his arm and pulled him roughly into the kitchen. 'Come in here.'

The kitchen looked even worse in the weak morning

light. The window above the sink was broken, a triangle of glass missing from the bottom corner, the rest of it documenting every splash of dirty water that had ever hit it, a thick layer of grey dots emanating from behind the mixer tap. Beyond the lace of dirt the very tip of the Lexus's silver bonnet shone in the sun.

The wall of bin bags blocking the passage to the back door were not just leaking sticky mess on to the floor, the ones on the bottom were stuck in a pool of white.

'I can't stay here,' said Pat.

Eddy was standing too close to him, chewing his bottom lip.

'It's not . . .' Pat looked around the floor, 'healthy.'

'Pat—'

Pat pointed into the living room. '*There's a shit with mould on it in there.*'

Eddy pinched his nose, paused, and shut his eyes. When he spoke it was with forced patience. 'The trouble I had to find this place—'

'*Trouble?*' shouted Pat. 'The cunt drinks in your fucking local. All ye did was buy a pint and turn around.'

Eddy's eyes were still shut. 'I looked at a number of places as possible—'

'Oh, "A pint o'eighty",' shouted Pat, flailing his hands about indignantly, '"Aye, you, you seem to smell of pish, have ye a house? Can I hold a hostage there? Would that have a shit in the corner?"'

Pat looked up for a response and found the barrel of Eddy's gun pointing at his eye. Eddy spoke quietly to the tip of his gun. 'Patrick,' he told it, 'I've went to a lot of trouble and you're not really appreciating that.'

Pat was hypnotised by the circle of deep blackness.

'I have tried reasoning with you,' whispered Eddy, a tremor in his voice as the enormity of what he was doing sunk in. He was looking at Pat's mouth, quite close, as if afraid to look at the eye he was about to shoot. They were wet again, the eyes, the bastard fucking eyes brimming with panic.

'I've tried so *fucking* hard ...'

'Edward.'

'*I've really fucking tried.*'

'Get the gun away from my face or I will kill you.'

'Oh, *you'll* kill *me*,' and Eddy waggled the end of the barrel in Pat's face, afraid to drop it now, in case Pat did kill him. 'I've got a gun on you and you're threatening to kill me, is it? You're threatening me? Who are you tae fucking threaten me?'

They both knew who Pat was. Pat was a Tait, and he didn't need to threaten Eddy. Being a Tait, even an estranged Tait, meant that he was a walking threat. The barrel was pointing at Pat's ear now. 'Point the gun at the floor,' he said carefully.

Eddy didn't know what else to do. He lowered the barrel, spluttering a sob of relief.

Calmly, Pat reached over and, hand over hand, took the pistol from him. He held it away from Eddy and flicked the safety on, took a deep breath and spoke: 'This is a fuck-up from start to finish. We both know it.'

'Aye,' whispered Eddy urgently, tears rolling down his face. 'Aye, I know it's a fucking mess, I don't know what to ... *I just sat in that old cunt's pish.*' He rubbed his eyes with the ball of his palm, smearing tears into his hairline.

Pat reached out and touched Eddy's back with his finger-tips and Eddy covered his face like a girl and cried, high pitched, helpless. Beyond the kitchen door Shugie crossed his legs and Pat saw that he was wearing trainers with the wrong laces, brown laces from brogues. I don't belong here, he said to himself, knowing that he really meant that he didn't want to belong here.

'If she hadn't taken the fucking kids, man,' squeaked Eddy. 'If she'd only let me see my fucking weans ...'

It wasn't the wife stopping him from seeing the kids. This lie had developed slowly, like a lot of other lies in Eddy's life. Pat went along with it but now, abruptly, he looked at Eddy and saw a man refused access to his children by the courts because he was an unreliable moody arsehole, a man who brought Shugie in so that people in their local would know he was up to something big, a man who, over the course of today, would misremember last night, rewrite events so that Pat was the nervous one who fucked up. He looked at Eddy, self-pity seeping out of him. Eddy wasn't capable of being honest. I do belong here, Pat admitted, I do belong, but I don't want to.

As Eddy bubbled, Pat calmly took himself away, back to the pink hall of the toast-smelling house. He wasn't in this kitchen, wasn't in the house with a disputed mouldy shit in the living room and fossilised bin bags in the kitchen. He was back in the pink hall, watching a lock of perfect silky black slide over a young shoulder. He was back in the clean, where bad smells elicited disgust and a shit on the floor wouldn't even get the chance to get mouldy. That's what he wanted.

She had just brushed her hair before they came in, he realised. Sat in front of the telly and brushed her long hair. The image made him smile, made him warm, until Eddy's shrill sob shattered the image.

Pat reached out to still him. 'Don't ...'

'That Irish cunt ... I don't know what to do ...'

'Let's go and get some toast or something.' Pat's voice was expressionless.

'We can't leave that pishy cunt to mind him,' said Eddy looking out to the living room.

'OK. We need to get moving.' Aleesha's hand came up and touched his face, the hand that was no more, but he wrote that part out. Her fingertips touched his face, her pretty gold rings glinting in the corner of his eye. 'I'll call Malki, get him over here to mind Shugie.'

'How are we, how are we gonnae do that? I mean, we can't move now, that fucker'll go and get pissed and tell everyone.'

'Malki'll come, I'll get him to bring bevy for Shugie, get him to stay in the house, say we'll be back any minute. You and me, we'll go get some toast or something—'

'*Toast?* What ye on about *toast* for?'

'And we'll phone the family.' Pat imagined himself arriving at the door of the Anwar family home, being greeted by the brothers as a long-lost friend, being offered tea as he slipped his jacket off in the pink hall. 'Ask about the money. I'll sort it out, man, don't worry.' He pointed to Eddy's pocket. 'I'll speak to the Irish.'

Eddy took his phone out and selected a number, pressed call and handed the phone over.

Irish had been asleep. His voice was an angry, startled bark. '*Whit?*'

'We've got the father and we're calling them this morning.'

'Who's this?'

'The other one.'

Pat could hear the Irish consider the angles. 'I don't know you.'

'I'll call you after,' said Pat and hung up.

Eddy took the phone back, dropping his chin so he was looking up, puppyish, 'Pal . . .' he said, meaning thank you, meaning to express affection, hinting at words he would never say.

Pat was thinking words he would never say too.

Pat was thinking that the world would be better off if a cunt like Eddy wasn't in it.

12

Morrow sat in her car as the sun came up over the young trees in Blair Avenue. It had been a warm autumn, plenty of rain and the gardens were bursting with life. Balding branches of well-tended trees shadowed the road and the hedges, verdant, waxy leaved, littered the pavement below. A smattering of rain had cleared the sky to an uninterrupted solid blue.

Her bum was numb. She had been sitting there for forty minutes, tiredness and indecision pinning her to the seat. In every fraction of a second she was poised to reach for the car key, pull it out and open the door. The muscles on her forearm twitched in rehearsal, her mind focused on the plastic casing around the key, the crunch of the lock as she pulled the key out, the warm mottled plastic of the door handle, but still she didn't move.

She had been there so long that the blood had drained from her hands resting on the steering wheel. Several times she had thought about turning the radio on for company, but that would have meant admitting that she wasn't going to get out of the car.

She could go back to the station. Bannerman was giving a briefing but she could still hide in her office. She had the day off. She could go into the office and say she couldn't stay away – never mind that she wouldn't get overtime – show willing, instead of going indoors and dealing with Brian.

She looked up at the brand new house. All the lights were off, the curtains still drawn in the living room.

This had been her dream once, when she was little, to live in a clean, bland house with a clean, bland husband. A man who would never raise his voice or say anything alarming. A man who never shouted 'fire' into her sleeping face in the middle of the night because he was pissed and wanted attention. A man who would never get taken away by the police at 6.15 in the morning and spit saliva streaked with blood on his own hall carpet as they dragged him away.

The Blair Avenue house was new, they were the first people ever to live in it and she savoured the absence of history. They chose it because it was quiet and there were so many children in the neighbourhood.

The front door was painted red, the brass letter box polished, glinting a chirpy answer to the early morning sunlight. She'd liked that door when they bought the house. Most of the new-builds had white plastic doors. It was the first thing she'd liked about it, at the viewing.

'Look at this, Brian.' She ran her fingers down the watered sheen of red paint and looked up to find him smiling at her hand. She had looked at his lips and known precisely the words they were going to form.

'That's a lovely colour, isn't it?'

She glared at the door now, her mouth moved soundlessly, reforming the words – *that's a lovely colour.*

The straightness of the man was gone, the steadiness she had fallen in love with. Brian had become the chaos she was running from.

The postman's back suddenly obscured her view. He opened the gate and left it wide as he stepped up the path, looking through a bundle of letters, pulling their junk mail and bills out and shoving them through the door. He didn't look up as he came back down towards her, already sorting the mail for the next house. Birds twittered in trees. A commuter with a briefcase and grey suit crossed the road to his car. People were beginning to stir. She had to go in or be spotted spying on her own home.

A sudden longing struck her, to see Danny, speak to him, be back in that familiar set of tracks. She knew Danny, understood him, could predict him. He was never a straight line and a sudden curve. Danny was always the same and not sorry about it either.

Somehow in her head the thought of Danny became entangled with the Anwar case because of the area, because they were both at school there. She had never asked for his help before, always kept those worlds as far apart as possible, but she was so angry with Bannerman she was prepared to consider it.

Brian was in there, awake possibly, wondering where she was, why she hadn't come home, why her phone was switched off.

Reaching for the car key her hand lingered for a moment. She turned it, starting the engine and pulling out into the street, heading back into the vibrant, screaming city.

13

It was only a twenty-minute drive from her house at this time of the morning but the brand new block of luxury flats was a world away.

Morrow looked up at the verandas as she pulled on the handbrake. Thrown up during the housing boom they were already beginning to disintegrate. A number of them had been bought with dirty cash, at a time when all property was a good investment. But the gangsters wouldn't pay the exorbitant maintenance fees and now the flats were coming apart.

They dumped bags of rubbish in the lifts and left police cones in the best parking spots. The factor wasn't attending to the building any more and lights were out all over the halls, dents in communal walls were being left. One lift in the block was always well maintained though, no one would have dared piss in it or use a lighter to melt the plastic buttons: it was the lift that went to Danny's penthouse.

She had passed the entrance to the underground car park and pulled up in the street. Going down to the underground car park was safer but buzzing up to Danny would give him advance warning that she was coming up. If he had the chance he'd hide anything incriminating, and they'd have to go through the embarrassing pretence of talking about his security firm and the problems of book keeping and managing men. He was on the cusp of legal, running a string of security firms that ring-fenced a territory and won the contracts in it through threats and sabotage. Anyone who didn't use Danny's firm would find their site subject to a spate of fires or assaults on staff until they capitulated. Danny had even made the papers once, a full page stop-this-evil-man. Ambushing him in the early morning was brutal, but at least it was honest.

She took a long breath and looked out at the street. Ahead of her the motorway was choking up with morning traffic. Behind, the road running along by the river was getting busy too, but this street was broad and empty. Bad place to park, she knew. Exactly the sort of spot cars got stolen from.

This used to be the dockside, wild sailors' bars and flop houses, huge warehouses full of goods from all over the world, waiting to be lifted by light-fingered dockers. No longer. For decades the riverside had been an empty series of sheds until it was cleared to become an industrial estate: carpet warehouses and furniture sheds struggled there for a while until recently, when the housing boom cleared them away to make room for luxury riverside apartments. Twelve storeys of plasterboard and gimmicks, wet rooms, wall-mounted coffee makers, all with verandas looking over the water to one of the most deprived boroughs in Scotland. House buyers had camped overnight for the privilege of buying the first phase of the development. The market changed so quickly the builders could hardly give away the final phase.

Weak with tiredness Morrow climbed out of the car, pulling her coat closed against the wind coming off the river, and opened the boot. The presentation bottle of single malt had been in there for two weeks. She picked it up, cradling it like a puppy under one arm, locked the car and went around to the front entrance. Dan's buzzer: 12.1.

'What?'

'Danny, it's me.'

She sensed him hesitate, then the entrance door clicked

and hummed and she pushed it open. The clip-clop of her modest heels ricocheted off the stone floor as she walked over to the steel lifts and pressed the button. Plastic plants were placed on either side of the doorway, improbably green palms that were dusty, cigarette butts scattered around the gravel at their feet. Canvases were screwed tight to the wall: slashes of green and red.

The lift came to a stop in front of her, the doors opened and two hoodies and a businesswoman in a trouser suit stepped out, the hoodies shifty and smirking, the woman newly coiffed for the day, looking alarmed.

Morrow stepped back to let them pass, got in and pressed the button for the twelfth floor. The button lit up pink but still she stared at it, wondering. Because it opened straight into the flat the button for the penthouse suite only worked if a key was used or someone in the flat pressed a button to allow it. She always wondered if Danny would refuse her, not because he ever had, but just because he could. The doors slid shut, the metal box giving a little jolt downwards before setting off for the roof. Her stomach tightened at the thought of seeing him.

Softly, the lift came to a standstill and the doors slid open into the bright daylight. Crystyl was standing fifteen feet away in full make-up, blond hair brushed down her back, wearing skinny jeans over four-inch heels, a pink sequinned T-shirt stretched tight over the tennis balls she'd paid someone to surgically implant on her chest. Disconcerted at the sight of Morrow glaring out at her, Crystyl raised her hand to her waist and gave her a little wave, whispering her hellos in a child's breathy voice.

Morrow stepped out on to the stone floor. 'Right, Crystyl?'

'Aye, brilliant, how are ye, yourself?'

Even though Alex forced social pleasantries out of her

mouth she knew her face twisted with annoyance when she spoke to Crystyl. It wasn't Crystyl herself so much as the type: glam, fluffy, sentimental, but underneath the glitter nail varnish she was hard enough to live off a man who broke legs in the course of his business. Crystyl pretended she didn't know, that the business existed in some parallel universe, but she used notes greasy with grief and sweat and terror to buy thoughtful greetings cards and angel key rings. Alex wanted to slap the woman and tell her to get a fucking job.

'Yeah. Dan about?'

'Be down in a wee tiny minute.' Crystyl giggled at this, a nervous titter that sounded like a high heel grinding glass into a dirty pavement. 'Um, could ye go a coffee at all?'

On the basis that they could either stand here and try to talk to each other, or busy themselves with the rigmarole of making a drink, Alex nodded and followed Crystyl through the living room, heading for the kitchen.

The living space in the flat was gorgeous: warm yellow sandstone two storeys high with a wall of glass looking down the river towards the Irish sea. A big L-shaped sofa faced the view. Throughout the flat all the fittings were either yellow or stone, all the furniture show-flat tasteful, included in the price. Alex had been in Crystyl's own flat years ago, when she and Danny first got together. Decorated exclusively in pink it felt vaguely obscene to Alex, like walking into an instructive model of a vagina.

Crystyl led her across the living room and into the kitchen. The lowered ceiling had dazzling halogen lights punched into it. Glassy black granite worktops shone around the room meeting at a massive double-door fridge with a wooden pediment built over it, like a mausoleum to food.

'I'll make ye a real coffee, in the coffee machine. I *love* real coffee. Do you like it?'

Alex shrugged.

Running out of things to say about coffee Crystyl hummed tunelessly to fill the awful, prickly quiet. Silence was the most basic interview technique; Alex knew most normal, innocent people would try to fill the conversational void. Glaswegians would give up their own mother rather than sit quietly with a stranger. She didn't want Crystyl to talk but couldn't think of anything to say herself.

Crystyl went to a cupboard and took out an unopened silver tin of Illy coffee, took the plastic lid off and peeled back the metal, looking into the tin, bewildered. 'Oh,' she said.

'What?'

'It's wrong,' said Crystyl.

Alex went over and looked in. Beans. 'Can't you grind them up?'

She looked at the food processor. 'In that?'

'Haven't you got a coffee grinder?'

Crystyl looked at the wall-mounted coffee maker. 'Is there one on that?'

It had a button for pushing warm water through coffee grinds and a nozzle for frothing milk. Crystyl pressed buttons, trying to decipher the symbols. Getting nervous she opened a small door in the machine and took out the water tub, yellowed because it had never been used. 'Do the beans go in here?'

As Alex watched Crystyl a burst of compassion for the silly woman came from nowhere. 'Look, never mind coffee, I'll have a cup of tea if you're having one.'

'But I'm not.' Crystyl looked up, over Alex's shoulder and her face brightened. 'Hi, darlin'.'

Alex hadn't heard Danny coming in. He had his jacket

on already and was pointedly twirling his car keys around his index finger. The jacket was down-quilted for warmth and bulked him up, made him look as if he'd spent a two stretch lifting weights in prison. His shaved head and the long scar on his cheek didn't contradict the impression.

'What you doing here?' he said, trying not to smile.

'Visiting,' she replied, chewing her cheek so that she didn't either.

'At seven thirty in the morning?'

'I'm on nights, on my way home. Wanted to see you before ye set off for the day.'

He pursed his mouth. 'Easy to miss each other.'

'It is.' They nodded away from each other, both wishing in their separate ways that this was easier.

'Baby?' he asked.

'Not recently,' she answered quickly, making a joke to deflect the question. She reminded herself to breathe in. They smiled away from each other. 'Nah, he's fine. Good. Brought ye this.'

She set the bottle of single malt on the kitchen counter and he sniggered at it, touching the lid lightly with a finger. 'Thoughtful.'

Confused, Crystyl looked from one to the other. Danny didn't drink.

Alex smiled away from him. 'I'm always that. Happy birthday, Danny.'

'I missed yours.'

'Don't care,' she said honestly.

Crystyl gasped and brushed past Alex to Danny's side, wrapping her arms around his middle and pressing her tits into his side. She gave him a weak mock punch. 'Your wee sister's birthday! What a bastard – pardon my French – you're a bad bastard, Danny.' She smiled. 'Total.'

Danny straightened his face. 'Right, doll,' he said,

wrapping a hand around Crystyl's tiny waist and giving her a squeeze. 'I'm off then, I'll get Alex here downstairs,' and to Alex, 'did ye park on the street?'

'Aye.'

He understood why and it hurt him a little, she could tell.

Crystyl trotted out to the lift door on her tiptoes, ponytail swishing ahead as they followed her. She stopped in the same place she had been in when Alex had arrived, and let them pass her. She must think she was well lit there, that whoever was looking out from the lift would get the best view of her from this angle and would perhaps remember her fondly while he was shutting a car door on someone's fingers during the day.

'Bye, da'lin'.' She blew a kiss.

Seeming rather tired Danny raised his hand to catch it in his fist. The doors shut.

Mirrors on all four walls threw their reflections back at them: both tall, blonde, both thirty-four, both with their father's baby dimpled cheeks. They looked sweet on both of them now, babyish, but they knew from their father that ageing dimples sagged into gashes. Their father looked as if he'd been in a fight with a knifeman plagued by a need for symmetry. Apart from that they didn't look alike: Alex took after her mother's side for eyes and chin, and Danny had his own mother's mouth, tight, mean.

Three months between them. Their father was a charmer in his day, and had all of his many families concurrently. Alex's mother was naive and loved him with a passion that congealed when the baby arrived. Danny's mother was younger but already inured to disappointment. Danny didn't grow up with shame and anger, just in a household governed by a series of bad men and drink.

Alex and Danny met on their first day at school. They

looked like twins, everyone said so, it was an innocent joke. They were sweethearts for their first term of school but it all ended abruptly when their mothers met at the gates. The most vivid memory of Alex's early life was walking home through a park, blood dripping from her sobbing mother's mouth on to the grey path. She'd ripped her blouse in the fight and everyone could see her bra strap.

People didn't move schools in those days. Danny and Alex went all the way through primary school together, and secondary. And all the time there was the ever present threat of their mothers fighting, of the other boot falling.

She was glad when Danny's mum died of the drink in second year and no doubt he was glad when they were sixteen and hers died, but she never knew: he was long gone from school by then.

She was lucky never to have had the McGrath name, she realised later. Her mother always wanted it for her but her father wouldn't admit she was his. Somehow that mattered then. If she'd had his name the police admissions board might have worked out where she was from, who she belonged to and not let her into the force.

Neither spoke until they were three floors down.

'I came to ask ye about someone,' said Alex, taking out her mobile. She flicked through the pictures until she reached the photo she had taken in the road the night before. Standing behind police tape was Omar Anwar, as clear as she could get him, smoking and looking sorry. She showed it to Danny, 'Know him?'

Danny narrowed his eyes. 'Nut,' and handed her back the phone. 'Seen anyone?'

'No.'

'Lan Gallagher go' married last month.'

Morrow smiled. 'Who in the name of God'd marry her?'

'Well, ye know,' he shrugged, 'for every ugly there's a bugly.'

She smiled. Charm that sagged into gashes. That's how the McGrath men got you.

Before the doors were open properly Danny nipped through them, stepped quickly across the lobby and through a side door marked 'car park'. Alex went after him.

The door led into a bare concrete corridor radiating damp with cold, brutal strip lights. She turned the corner and found Danny standing still, waiting for her. He was pressed up tight into a corner at a turn in the corridor. 'We've put up hundreds of cameras.' He circled his finger to the ceiling. 'Trouble in the halls. I know where they are so ... never say nothing ...'

Disappointed at having to acknowledge who Danny really was, Alex slumped her shoulders, but Danny ignored the reproach and reached for her, pinching the elbow of her coat and pulling her into the corner with him. He took the phone from her hand, called up the photo of Omar and examined it.

Alex found it strange, standing so close together but not touching. She could feel Danny's breath on her neck. It was like being young together again, like when he tried to teach her how to smoke hash in a cupboard in Bosco Walker's bedroom during a party and she vomited on his new trainers. She remembered being glad about it because the trainers had been nicked. Bosco and Lan and all of them inhabited a place in her life that was long ago, a network of memories she never accessed so that when she did it all seemed so crisp and immediate that it was more real than the grey now.

Danny held up her phone and handed it back. 'This boy's a southsider.'

'I know. Is he ... you know ...' To another policeman

she'd say 'dirty' but she could hardly say that to Danny.

He helped her out. 'Into anything?'

'Yeah.'

'Nut, good family, Daddy runs a twenty-four-hour shop. Two boys went to St Als, both done degrees I think.'

'Yeah,' she said. 'The young one did law.'

'Right?'

Watching him make a mental note, she wished she hadn't been so specific. Danny could retain information for decades before he used it. 'How do you know him?'

'Used tae run with the Young Shields when he was a wee guy. Got out of it, haven't seen him about for years.'

Most Asian guys ran with a gang at some point in their lives, usually for protection from other gangs of Asian guys. It didn't mean Omar was good or bad, all it confirmed was that he had once been young and frightened. From Alex's recollection they were the same thing.

''Member his brother?'

Danny cast his mind back. 'Bill?'

'Yeah.'

'Big soft boy, never got in tow with anyone.'

They heard the door from the lobby open, steps and a trendy young guy turned the corner, started with surprise when he saw them standing so close together in an otherwise empty corridor. He averted his eyes and slipped past.

Alex scowled at Danny for scratching his nose as the guy came past. He was hiding, obscuring his face with his hand. He always did that when anyone looked at him. It was one of his many giveaways, like thinking before he admitted to being anywhere, or mapping the doors when he entered a room.

'Does this make me an informant?'

'Naw.'

When Morrow abandoned her family ties she did so

completely. It was out of character for her to ask for anyone's help, Danny's help especially, and she knew it would excite his interest, that he would wonder about it until he understood why she had come to him. She didn't understand it herself.

'Da's dying,' he said abruptly.

'Is he?'

'Moved him from Gen Pop to the infirmary block. Cancer. Said it'll be a couple of months.'

She nodded at her feet. 'Right?' she said, noticing how tight her lips had suddenly become. 'Asking for us?'

'No. Dunno.' Danny was muttering too. 'Why? Have ye heard he was asking for ye?'

She smirked. 'No.'

Danny laughed too. 'Well, why did ye ask, then?'

'Dunno, just something ye say, isn't it?'

'Suppose. If he's only got a couple of months he won't have time to see his kids.'

'How many of us are there, do ye think?'

'Dunno.'

'D'you ever see people and wonder if they're his?'

He smirked. 'Nut. D'you?'

'Nah.' He knew she was lying too and they smiled warmly at each other.

'You OK?' He said it so fast it sounded like a burp, as if he couldn't wait to get the concern out of him.

'Fine!' She sounded shocked when she'd meant to sound breezy, and corrected herself. 'Fine.'

'The boy.' Her heart tightened until she saw him looking at her phone. 'You asking . . .'

She shrugged and found she was breathless. 'Just thought you could help, 'cause it's near the old house . . . old stomping . . .' She couldn't bring herself to look at him, afraid he would see the spark of loss in her eye.

'I need to go,' he said, but stood still.

'Me too,' said Alex but she didn't move either.

Finally, they couldn't drag it out any longer. She stepped away from him. 'Happy birthday, Danny.'

'Aye.' Danny stayed where he was, watching her walk away until she was out of sight around the concrete corner. His voice came after her. 'Phone me.'

'Nah,' she wrinkled her nose and reached for the handle on the lobby door, 'haven't anything to say to ye.'

'Phone and tell me what happens with Bob.'

Alex dropped her hand and backed up to the corner. Danny was still pressed into the cramped corner where she had left him. 'Bob?'

'Bob.' Dan flicked a finger at the phone in her hand. 'The wee guy . . .'

'Omar?'

'Aye, Bob's his street name.'

14

It was daytime. Aamir could tell that for certain. Bright day outside.

The previous night had been so frightening, his muscles so tense for so long that he fell asleep mid-thought, exhausted, holding his mother's hand. When he awoke he was drooling into the pillowcase and it was stuck to his face. He sat up, straightened the pillowcase, and realised that he could no longer remember the night very clearly.

They had driven for a very long time, changed from the van to a car, driven a long way again and he knew that home was hours away. He could be in the highlands or Manchester or even London. And out there, somewhere beyond the cheap weave of the pillowcase over his head, were his children and his wife, his brand new grandson and Aleesha, bleeding, dead for all he knew.

Aleesha. A bad daughter: rotten, opinionated, disobedient. He adored her. She got all that from Sadiqa, all of that anger and energy was why he had fallen in love with her mother. His mouth said a prayer that she was well but his heart was shut to God.

Omar had betrayed him. A second son himself, Aamir had always loved Omar best. Aamir sighed, turned to his mother and asked her: why would Omar do this to him?

Maybe he was on drugs. Of all his three children Aamir could imagine Omar as a junkie. A lot of junkies came in his shop, looking for things to steal, buying sweeties. They loved their sugar. He had decided long ago that there were as many nice junkies as there were people, most were pleasant unless they were withdrawing or desperate, but you could say that about all people. Anyway, there was an off-sales on the next side and a supermarket up the road. Much easier to steal from. Aamir liked the junkies better than the alkis.

Omar stood by and let them take his father in his place. Only Billal stood firm. The one child he didn't really like. Aamir wasn't just making excuses for Omar the way he always did, he genuinely understood. He had done the same to his mother, let them take her as payment for his safe passage and, like Aamir now, she did not mind. Aamir did not mind.

She was frightened too. He clutched his mother's finger for courage and told her not to worry. He understood her now, giving herself for his safety. As a young man he thought she should have fought to the death, but he understood now.

Aamir did not find family life comfortable. He held resentments against his children, but all the day-to-day animosity of normal family life had evaporated in the night. At a distance, with an impassable sea of longing between them, he could see that they were good, that the values he was trying to drum into them by checking up, shepherding, shouting, those values were there already. If he could see them right now, just once more in his life, he'd kiss his grandson's head, rub his nose in the baby's downy hair and tell Omar he wasn't really angry, smile at Aleesha and tell her that her wildness was beautiful. He would lie in the dark next to Sadiqa and not think about how fat she was, how she was bending the bed to herself and smelled of cooking oil. He would lie there in peace and enjoy the peaceful dark, the sheets, savour the pulsing green light from the radio alarm smeared across the ceiling.

The thought of his own bed raised a sob to his throat, but the bruising on his ribs choked it.

There were two men, one whose voice was strangled with rage. The other one was less interested, kind sometimes when his friend was out of the room. Strangle voice had come back into the room last night and punched a vicious jab in his side, sniggering malevolently as Aamir struggled to breathe. He had ordered Aamir to stay on the bed, like a childhood game of crocodiles, and not to take the pillowcase off. Aamir did as he was ordered. He had a CCTV camera in the shop and knew how cheap they were: they might have one in here.

He imagined himself seen from up high: a small grey man, cross-legged on a vast grey bed. A pillowcase over his head, neat, tidy, and next to him a fat woman with a blood bloom flowering at her seat, holding her sari to her face to dry her tears on, sobbing, but only out of habit, not because she was sad.

He saw her looking around, far, far into the distance, as if they were on an open-top bus and she was anxious to see the sights. His mother reached over to his hand and squeezed it tight, not with fear, not that, no soldiers with rifles and an eye for a British passport here, but squeezed it with excitement because they were seeing things together, finally. He had taken her hand, finally. She pointed at the window, smiled a grey smile and the CCTV cut out.

There was a window; she was right. He could see through the weave of the linen. And there was a door at the bottom of the bed, closed, the men went through there, he remembered now. When he coughed he heard the noise bounce back off the walls and knew it was a small room. A man's bedroom. A woman would not allow that smell of dirty hair and feet to build up like that. She'd know to open a window, change the bedding once in a while.

He pulled the bottom of the pillowcase out a little so he could see the bedding. He pulled the edge in, covering it up again. Disgusting. He didn't want to see it. Yellowed where a man's body had lain, creased into sharp edges, a faint tinge of urine. Hadn't been changed in months.

Disgust made him panic, dirt made him panic, but it was essential to stay calm. A clever man in a mundane profession, Aamir was used to altering his mood through force of will, doing sums and mental inventories to stay alert. He started now to think his way through a day of regulars at the shop, beginning when the doors opened at half past six and working his way through the shift, telling his mother about them. He thought through the odours of people who came into his shop, cataloguing their smells, their various problems: drink, drugs, mental illness, laziness, incontinent animals running about the house.

It was 9.30 a.m., give or take four to six minutes. He didn't have a watch on but had spent that last thirty-five years sitting in shops, his uncle's and then his own, waiting for people to come in, and had developed an acute sense of the rhythm of time. The shop would be getting quiet. Johnny usually made them a cup of tea about now, getting ready for the rush of school children in for chocolate and crisps. He couldn't remember Johnny's face, just his presence. Calm, shoulder to shoulder, a set of eyes seeing what he did, hearing what he did, sharing his day.

Aamir stiffened as the door at the foot of the bed opened softly and a grey shape leaned into the room.

'Hungry?' Not the strangled voice, the other one. 'Are you hung-ary?' repeated the guy, as if he thought Aamir couldn't speak English.

'Yes,' said Aamir clearly. 'Thank you. Something to eat would be most welcome.' He meant to sound articulate but instead, he realised, sounded as if English was his second language. Actually it was his third.

'OK, faither.' The man held something out towards him.

'Here's um, not toast but bread, anyway. And a can of ginger.'

He came down the right side of the bed and bent down, putting something on the floor, giving a little 'there ye go!' as he stood up again. Aamir had reached for the edge of the pillowcase, lifting it a little.

'Not being funny.' Gently, the guy stopped his hand. 'Sorry, but can ye not take that off until I get out of the room?'

'Sure.'

'Not being funny.' He stood straight up and dropped his voice. 'D'ye sleep OK?'

Aamir matched his tone, whispering, 'Aye, son, no bad.'

'Sorry it's smelly in here, eh? Sorry. Bit stinky. Soon as your family stump up ye'll be home, eh? D' ye need the loo?'

'Not yet. Is my wee girl OK? Her hand ...'

The man hesitated. 'Don't know,' he said when he finally did speak. 'But I'll find out and let you know.'

Aamir nodded.

'Drink your juice now, OK?'

The guy turned and left, shuffling his feet on the carpet.

He listened until he heard the door close firmly and footsteps trailing down the stairs. Tentative, he lifted the edge of the pillowcase, looking down over the edge of the bed. An open can of Irn-Bru and two slices of plain white loaf stacked on top of each other, not cut in half, sitting on top of a page of newspaper. Prepared by a man. He reached out and touched the can with his fingertips. Warm. He shouldn't break his Ramadan fast but didn't know if they would bring him anything later. He could make up the days, he might be saving his life and Aamir was seventy, old enough not to fast. Anyway there was no one here to set an example for.

He picked up the can and pulled the pillowcase down

again, enclosing himself in his little white tent. The drink was sugary and tangy. Nice. He finished it and reached down for the bread, lifting the edge of the pillowcase higher than he meant to, seeing the wall next to the bed. Wallpaper had been pulled off from the skirting board, the effort given up halfway up the wall, the edges tattered, showing the lining paper.

Kneeling behind him his mother lifted the pillowcase gently with two hands, resting it on his forehead. A filthy room. There were crumpled magazines on the floor, *Loaded*, *FHM*, and pornos too, *Escort*, *Fiesta*. Very old editions, Aamir knew, from the covers. He stocked them, fewer now because they hardly sold any more, since the Internet. The window had curtains on it but they looked greasy and weren't shut properly, just yanked together and separated at the top so that the white day streamed in, a spotlight for the dust.

His mother's hand touched his back, fingertips making one of her irresistible suggestions: Go, Ammy, she said, go look for me, see where we are.

Aamir looked at the door to the room, back to the window, back to the door. He pulled the pillowcase off and stopped still, waiting for them to run in and beat him. If they had CCTV in the room they would know. He waited for a moment but no one came.

Go on, Ammy.

He looked at her, skin slack on her jaw, the impossibly silken skin on her underarms, her long lashes. Aleesha had her lashes.

Keeping his eyes on the door, he swung his legs to the left side of the bed, stood up swiftly and found his nose an inch from the grey curtain. He could see out into the street. His heart was thumping in his chest, his neck stiff with fright.

'A street,' he told her.

Badly overgrown, the garden had huge hedges, once cared for, now bursting up and out, over a broken-up concrete driveway and wind-flattened grass. It was a short garden, council probably, and steep. The dark green grass was littered with rubbish: bits of plastic, sun-faded Tennant's cans, cardboard boxes melting in the rain. Straight across the street were houses that he supposed matched this one, double-storey council houses with black slate roofs and picture windows on the ground floor. One of those dying council estates like they had in Glasgow.

Looking beyond the roofs of the neighbourhood houses he was surprised to see hills. Neither Manchester nor London had great big proud hills like that. Those were Scottish hills and he recognised them. He blinked and looked again. Castlemilk. The high flats, the water tower, Cathkin Brae. He shut his eyes and tried to remember, then opened them again and saw that he was right. He was on the south side of Glasgow, half a mile from home. His uncle lived near here when they first arrived, in a prefab in Prospecthill. He used to stand in his kitchen and look at this view. Heart racing, Aamir realised that he could walk home from here, or catch a ninety bus. At a push he could walk to his own shop from here.

'Near!' he said triumphantly.

On the bed his mother covered her mouth and laughed softly, happy because he was happy.

Aamir smiled. If they came in now and shot him, if they both came in and beat him all over he would care less, fear less, hurt less, because the shop, the shelves full of things he had chosen, priced and catalogued, the little prayer area in the back room, the stickers on the door, the sweet rack he had stacked, the world of order he had created, refined, savoured over the decades, it was all close by.

'My shop,' he told his mother, 'is here.'

The street was quiet, but they must be near the main road because he could hear traffic. Buses, possibly even number nineties, were passing by, taking people to the town, to Langside, to Rutherglen and the Asda.

Movement in the street: a thin figure in a white tracksuit and cap scurried around the hedge, hurrying up the steep drive. He was carrying a heavy blue plastic bag, clutching it tight to his chest. From the outline Aamir guessed it contained lager cans. The skip of the cap made it impossible for the man to see up but Aamir stepped back from the window anyway, watching as the figure approached the front of the house. He listened for the door opening, but heard nothing. The man must be going around the side.

He stood back from the window, listening for movement in the house. If they drank a bag load of cans between them they might get sleepy; Aamir could leave without a fuss, he could walk home to the shop.

Thinking these things he only gradually became aware of the purr of the engine. The road was empty and for a moment he thought that the wind was changing, carrying sounds, but then he saw the car stop in the road at the bottom of the driveway.

'Maman!' he whispered urgently. 'Maman!'

She looked over his shoulder, standing close but not touching him, she looked out and she saw the police car too.

'Marvellous, Ammy,' she said, and was suddenly back on the bed.

Aamir watched the car brace itself as the handbrake was pulled on. The driver's door opened and a leg stepped out on to the street.

Aamir turned around and scrambled back onto the bed

next to his mother. He pulled the pillowcase down over both their heads, pulled his knees up to his chest, and held his breath: the police were coming to save them.

All they had to do was wait.

15

Morrow sat in the slowly cooling car, staring at the blank wall in the yard at London Road. She couldn't cite Danny as a source. She couldn't let it be known that he was her half-brother. Police liked the absolute value of 'them and us' and she and Danny looked so alike, the slightest suspicion would prove the relationship. But Bannerman was determined to ignore the lead and, even if it did pan out, he wouldn't credit her with it. She had to tell MacKechnie without looking underhand.

Stepping out of the car she locked it and walked up the ramp to the security door, feeling her heart rate slow as she reached for the security pad. She always felt calm before she entered the station, the balm of order. Behind the door she knew which desks would be manned, who was responsible for which job, who to look up to, who to piss down on. Sometimes when she was lying awake in bed at home she put herself here, outside the door.

She punched the code in, the door buzzed in front of her and fell open. Through the processing bar and the lobby she reminded herself Danny had given her important information and ambition wasn't met by giving leg-ups to rivals. She needed to stop, make a plan.

The disabled toilet in the lobby was empty and she sloped in and locked it, lowering the toilet lid and sitting down. She needed to give the information at a time and in such a way that she would be acknowledged as the source. Couldn't mention Danny but needed to give the information in front of MacKechnie, while Bannerman was there. She needed them together.

Shutting her eyes she saw the Blair Avenue red front door again. She snapped her eyes open and stood up, stepped over to the low sink and glared at herself in the mirror. Red eyes, blue shadows under them, bitterness twitching around her mouth. She was starting to look as sour as her mother.

Avoiding eye contact with the mirror she made herself tidy, smoothed her hair back. Now wash your hands. Turning the tap on she was ambushed by the image of chubby fingers under clear running water, fingers flexing curiously, savouring the new feel of it. She shut her eyes, threw her head back, opened them. Scrawled in biro, in tiny writing at the side of the mirror, someone had graffitied 'TJF'.

Morrow snorted furiously, scooped water from the running tap and threw it at the wall. She snatched green paper towels from the dispenser, spilling them on the floor, and scrubbed at the writing. The fury passed and she took her hand away. The letters were slightly fainter, not by much. TJF. A catchphrase officers used to denote the death of morale, an excuse for shoddy work and buck-passing, the death of order. TJF: The Job is Fucked.

She squeezed hand soap from the dispenser and rubbed it on the letters, scrubbing again, using wet towels this time. Even fainter. She wiped the blue soap off the wall and ran her hands under the water to get the residue off, keeping her eyes on the letters, directing all her anger and focus on them.

Picking up the scattered green paper towels, she dried her hands, unlocked the door and threw it open so it bounced off the wall, striding across the lobby to the front bar. She pressed the doorbell strapped to the desk, staring at herself in the mirrored wall, knowing they were back there looking at her.

The duty sergeant must have sent him: a young copper came out with a pained expression on his face. She pointed back to the toilet. 'Have you been in there recently?'

He had been relaxed back there, and it took him a moment to adjust his mood. 'Sorry?'

Morrow glared at him.

'Sorry, ma'am, been in where?'

'Disabled toilet. On the wall.'

He frowned over at the toilet. 'The wall?'

'In the toilet. Graffiti on the wall. Was it you?'

He looked picked on, and Morrow felt that this was the problem with the job now, not that it was fucked, but that no one wanted to take shit from anyone else, as if it was any other job, as if it was selling computer equipment or something and everyone had rights and no responsibilities. The job was all she had. If it was fucked, so was she.

'Why would I?' he said simply.

She had no answer for that. Of course he didn't do it, he might be dumb and new and young but he wasn't going to vandalise a toilet when he was the first person they'd ask about it.

'Ridiculous,' she said, looking him up and down, knowing she was being unreasonable. She turned on her heels and stabbed at the security pad on the CID door, turning, opening the door with her back so she turned back to the desk. She pointed at the toilet. '*Get it cleaned off.*'

The desk copper nodded, muttering after her, 'Yes, ma'am.'

The door slammed behind her and she found herself looking down the CID corridor. MacKechnie's office was dark at the far end, door shut. He wasn't in his office, might not even be in the building. To her right she saw that her own office lights were on, the door hanging open. Shit. She put her head down and walked over to it.

There he was at his desk, hair carefully waxed and tousled, suited, looking tired but professional. His Elvis mug was sitting on the desk, by his elbow lay an empty health bar wrapper: Apples!Apples!Apples!

'Bannerman,' she said, notifying him of her presence.

His eyes narrowed with spite when he saw her. 'Morrow. You missed my briefing.'

'Um, well,' she said uncertainly, 'I had—'

'You will not miss briefings under my command. We've got a million calls to make this morning. You cannot swan in and out.'

It was an order, a call to tow the line, inappropriate coming from someone of equal rank. 'Bannerman, it's supposed to be my day off.'

He held up a hand to stop her, shutting his eyes and turning his head away. 'MacKechnie suspended days off. You got the email.'

Stunned, she watched him stand up and walk out to the incident room, keeping the staying hand up at her. It was always the soft ones who came down hard, she thought, the bastards who left the chain of command vague to make themselves feel like one of the troops. Then they had to enforce it by humiliating people. TJF.

The incident room desks had been arranged in a horseshoe. Five DCs were sitting, working phones, reading files and every single one of them had laptops. Three of them weren't even part of this division; they must have been called in from somewhere else, which meant the case was having resources thrown at it. High profile, well resourced, every DS's dream.

It took her a minute to spot MacKechnie. He was standing at the side of the room, glaring at her. Morrow brightened at the sight of him but he didn't smile back. He kept his head down as he came over, as if he was walking through driving hail, across the lobby and into the office, Grant following in his wake.

Grant shut the door carefully behind himself. She could imagine the giggle of excitement in the briefing room, the looks passing between the DCs, mouthing her name to anyone whose view of her had been blocked, all speculating as to why MacKechnie, Mr Inclusivity, needed the door shut to speak to her.

Bannerman stayed out of his chair, leaving it to Mac-Kechnie to sit. They were moving as a single animal, they had talked about her, the two of them, wound each other up over her absence, reading things into it that weren't there. MacKechnie sat down heavily in Bannerman's chair, pursing his lips, letting off a martyred sigh. It must be a struggle, she imagined, to blend his vegetarian management style with honest aggression. She stood at ease in front of the desk, her head tilted insolently.

'DS Morrow, I am aware that you are unhappy with my choice of lead on this case,' MacKechnie narrowed his eyes for emphasis, 'but I *never* expected you to usurp the management of his investigation.'

'Sir, I've—'

'If you compromise these proceedings through sheer bloody-mindedness because you feel picked on . . .'

He caught her off guard. She expected them to say she was an arse, an idiot, malevolent but not that, not to accuse her of claiming to be a victim. 'Sir—'

'I will remind you that a man's life is at stake here.'

'I'm cooperating,' she said. 'I've done nothing that I know of. I didn't mean to miss the brief this morning.'

MacKechnie shut his eyes and rubbed the bridge of his nose. He was too old to be up all night, she thought, too old to do anything other than desk work. He should fuck off to admin and leave the real coppers in peace. These small insults, never uttered, were what kept her head up and her gaze steady.

'Sir, I didn't receive the email about time off, or if I did—'

'*Bannerman*,' he cut across her. 'DS Bannerman has done his *utmost* to make you feel welcome here, hasn't he?'

She kept her face neutral.

'Hasn't he?'

'Yes, sir,' she hissed slightly. 'He has.'

'Can we agree that you will work with him to resolve this case as a matter of the utmost urgency? Let's remember – a member of *our* community has been taken hostage.'

She kept her face straight, not even blinking at the emphasis that signalled the lie. When she looked at him his mouth twitched at the corner, a micro-expression, saying what he was really thinking: how kind he was to include a small Asian man with a beard in his definition of community.

'Sir,' she said to the back wall, 'I haven't been in my kip. I've been up all night, talking to informal contacts and I've uncovered information that materially affects our investigations.'

MacKechnie cleared his throat and dropped his voice as if he was disappointed. 'Go on.'

'The family lied about the gunmen asking for Rob. On the 999 calls Billal said "Bob", Meeshra fluffed the question from the operator and Omar said Bob in Grant's interview. It's on the DVD. Harris spotted it as well.'

'Harris?'

'Yes, sir, Harris. And this morning an informant told me that Omar Anwar was in the Young Shields and his street name was Bob.'

In the pause that followed she could feel each calculating the likelihood of her having fabricated information like that. Would she make up a mystery informant to confirm the Bob allegation, just so she could be right? Was she mad enough to make a play that wild? Someone laughed loudly at the far end of the corridor and a door slammed. She was asking MacKechnie to referee between them and she knew that even if she won the argument he would hate her for it.

MacKechnie tried to claw back the high ground. 'And Bannerman, what did Omar say about this?'

Bannerman became flustered. 'We, um, I didn't get the note . . .'

MacKechnie looked at him. When he spoke his voice was horribly quiet: 'Do you mean Wilder didn't give you the note?'

Wilder would get his books if Bannerman suggested he'd wandered off with her note. 'No, sir.' Bannerman's mouth sounded dry. 'Wilder did give me the note—'

'It was a matter of minutes,' Morrow burst in, appearing magnanimous, while winning the competition and not competing. 'Between Wilder getting there and the inter-view ending, sir. We didn't get the question in . . .'

United front. MacKechnie couldn't afford to discipline both of them in the middle of an investigation. He cleared his throat. 'Can we confirm that he uses the name Bob? Is this informant on the books?'

'No, it's an informal contact.'

It sounded weak. MacKechnie blinked and asked her straight, 'How far are you prepared to go with this?'

'Sir, I can play you the audio files right now to confirm that they said Bob. The other part I can't confirm right here and now.'

MacKechnie looked accusingly at Bannerman. 'When

did you get the note from Wilder? Bear in mind that I can check the DVD.'

Bannerman cleared his throat. 'I got the note but didn't ask.'

'Why?'

Bannerman looked trapped. Morrow pitched in, 'There was a lot going on last night but it's better this way because we can blindside him with it.'

'Yeah,' nodded Bannerman, 'do our research.'

'Yeah, research it properly.'

In a dizzying switch of loyalties MacKechnie was suddenly furious with both of them. 'You two – Bannerman, leaving aside what made you think that the best use of a DS in a major case was listening to emergency calls—'

Bannerman blushed. 'Sir, I genuinely thought there might be something important on the tapes.' He looked at Morrow pleadingly.

'Yes, sir, Bannerman was right,' she said. 'His instincts were right; there was something important.'

Bannerman nodded. 'The inconsistency in the names, if they agreed to say Rob and not Bob, it must have been after the calls. Aleesha was unconscious. We should interview her this morning.'

'Yes,' said Morrow, struggling not to smile. 'Yes, we should.'

MacKechnie looked away. 'DS Morrow, how do you explain your absence this morning?'

Morrow stole a look at Grant. 'I'm sorry, I didn't check my email before I left.'

'You *must* check your emails.'

'I will, sir, sorry, sir. Are the family dodgy, then?'

'Don't know.' Bannerman was eager to move the conversation on. 'If they have that kind of money or anything approaching that kind of money, where is it going? Who do we know in the community we could ask about the family?'

'Mahmood Khan?' suggested MacKechnie.

'Nah,' said Morrow, 'he'll just give us the party line.'

'Yeah,' said Bannerman, 'he'll be checking party contributions before he tells you anything about the family.'

She had kept her distance for twenty years, but now, like asking Danny, she was surprised to find herself willing to reach back for help, 'Ibby Ibrahim.'

They both looked at her curiously.

'Ibby Ibrahim?' repeated MacKechnie. 'What on earth makes you think he'll talk to us?'

She cleared her throat. 'I know ... Ibby. But I'd need to talk to him alone.'

They were both impressed, glanced at each other, back at her. 'How do you know him?' asked MacKechnie.

She saw Ibby, ten years old, sobbing in a playground and the bad children standing around watching him in an awed circle, herself among them. 'From a case,' she lied. 'A few years back.'

'What case?' MacKechnie was impressed.

'Ah,' she said, 'kind of hard to say ...'

If they had any kind of connection to her, any level of intimacy, they would have pressed her to unofficially tell. They'd have gathered around, pressed and teased, guessed until they had some idea. Instead, they slid glances across the desktop to each other, referencing a conversation had elsewhere, away from her.

'Right.' MacKechnie moved the conversation back to a safe area and stood up, coming around the desk to her, forgetting how angry he had been only a moment before. 'Get the background before we ask him about it. We've got officers assigned to the door-to-doors but I want you two to take a look at the shop and the shop helper, find out if there's anything going on there, betting, drugs, anything that would generate big revenue. Bannerman, make the Rob/Bob thing the focus now, *yes*?'

'Sir, I'd like to drive Morrow to meet Ibrahim,' said Bannerman, quietly. 'I can brief her on the way.'

'I need to speak to Ibby alone though,' she said, reluctant to spend longer with Bannerman than she needed to.

'Yeah, but I'd like to see him in the flesh. Just for future ...'

For future what he didn't say. It wasn't an efficient use of two DSs but MacKechnie nodded. 'Bonding. Good. DCs busy?'

'Sir.' Bannerman handed him a duty sheet. 'We're checking the CCTV from the M8 for cars going to and from the van site. Lab reports on the way. Fingerprints on their way. Researching all family members for Afghani visas. Two DCs are doing door to door around the house and processing the witness statements. Morrow and I could go to the hospital for a follow-up and take a look at the shop as well.'

'OK,' said MacKechnie, and turned to Morrow. 'Check your emails from now on.'

She nodded, hoping she looked sorry.

He stood with his back to the door, addressing the troops: 'If this is right then it's not the wrong address. The gunmen were after the Anwars, Omar specifically. What we need to know is why anyone thought they had two million to hand over.' He put his hand on the door to the corridor and stopped. 'Well done, Morrow,' he said, opened it and left.

Grant was a little red in his cheeks. 'Yeah, well done,' he said, with more grace than she would have.

147

16

Shugie was in the living room, sitting defiantly on the piss-damp settee, casually reading a newspaper from July.

In the kitchen Eddy sat on a stool, Pat crouching on a rickety wooden box with 'FRAGILE' stamped on the side. They sat away from each other, each marooned like boats lost on a dead sea. Dumb with tiredness they were both struggling to keep awake. Someone, not Shugie, had put down laminate flooring but a long-ago flood had warped the boards. They were curving up at the sides making the floor choppy and uneven. Under the dirt Pat could see that each board was a photograph of the next, the same knot in the wood repeating like a greasy dinner.

Eddy held a loaf in a waxy wrapper, opened out like a bag of sweeties. He had been eating dry bread all night because that was the only foodstuff Shugie had remembered to buy with the forty quid Eddy had given him in advance. He'd invested the rest of it in superlager.

Pat breathed heavily through his nose as a precursor to speaking but Eddy looked away. 'Man,' said Pat regardless. 'We *need* to move.'

'Leave it,' Eddy warned through his teeth.

'We need to move him.'

Eddy didn't answer. He held out the bread wrapper as if it was a solution. Pat shook his head. He couldn't eat in here. He felt as if particles of Shugie's piss would be getting in his mouth and into his stomach when he ate. Had to be. That's what smell was, particles.

He brought his elbows and knees in, shuddered a little,

thinking about dead skin. Then he remembered the girl and wondered how she was. But Shugie didn't have a radio, never mind a telly. They didn't know if they were in the news or not. If it was in the paper there might be a photo of her. The chances were that she'd been taken to the Victoria Infirmary. Less than a mile away, in a clean bed.

Desperate to relive the warm glow he felt when he first saw her, Pat imagined her lying in a hospital bed with her hair fanned out over the pillow, smelling nice, peachy or flowery, clean, thinking about him perhaps. Pat shook his head softly. No. He had shot her fucking hand off: if she was thinking about him it wasn't fondly. A girl like that wouldn't go with someone like him. The father was annoyed that the door was chapped at night. The house was clean and pink, nice. She was from a good family. Even if he hadn't shot her by accident she'd never go with him. Her father wouldn't allow it.

He imagined himself walking into the ward with a big bunch of flowers, dressed smart, looking sharp, but her face was horrified when she saw him again. Disappointed with the fantasy, he took himself back to the hallway to see her there. Her waist was tiny, the waistband of her denims hanging off her hip bones. He realised suddenly that the bridge of his nose felt hot when he was in the hall. Looking at her waist he could see the black woollen edge of the eyeholes. He had a balaclava on. She didn't know what he looked like.

Pat sat upright, smiled, almost laughed. She had no idea what he looked like.

Back at the Victoria Infirmary Pat walked into a ward that didn't exist and smiled at a girl who didn't remember him. Shy, she looked away but he gave her an impossibly glorious bunch of flowers and she suddenly loved him back.

He had been in the Vicky once, to see someone, he thought, a niece with tonsils or someone. Smiling at the dirty laminate he walked through the lobby, took a lift, sauntered into the ward. He could pretend to visit someone else and just look at her. It would be reckless, stupid.

If he did go, which he wouldn't, he'd sit far away and just look at her. Then he'd go over and say something nice, you've got beautiful eyes or something, something to make her feel good even though she was missing a hand.

Surrounded by swirling particles of Shugie's urine, Pat's thoughts went off on their own, to a romantic, wordless conversation between himself and Aleesha at her bedside, to cups of tea in the hospital cafe, shortbread, smiles. He picked her up in a car he didn't own, went to places he'd never been, places in the country, sunny places.

A girl like that, a girl who smelled of toast and warm, she wouldn't go with someone like him. Her father would never allow it. She'd only go with him if she wasn't living with her father, like if he was dead or something.

A rap on the glass above the sink made them both sit up. Malki's skinny face looked back at them, smiling and Pat grinned back. Malki disappeared and then the door opened. He stood in the doorway, wearing a new white tracksuit with twin blue strips up the leg and a matching cap.

'Been shoplifting?' Eddy thought buying clothes was womanly.

Malki didn't answer but curled his lip at the bin bags piled up by the door. "Kin hell.' He held the knees of his pristine trackies away from the bags as he sidled by. 'Been in some dives, man . . .'

Pat was on his feet, unreasonably happy to see Malki. 'Thanks for coming.'

Malki held out a thin blue polythene bag. 'Call me with offers o' money and I'm there, man.' He gave the rubbish a sidelong look. 'Only, eh, the job doesn't involve touching stuff in here, does it?'

Pat looked into the bag of lager cans. 'Four's not enough to keep Shugie in all day.'

Eddy stood up and looked into it. 'It'll need to be.'

'He'll go out for more. And he'll be pissed when he goes. He could tell someone.'

Eddy looked at him. 'So what ye saying, tie him up or something?'

Pat and Malki looked at each other. 'Hm,' Malki smirked, played it as if he was thinking really hard. 'There may be another way ...'

But Eddy was in at him. 'Don't you take the piss out of me, you junkie fuck.'

Malki fell back. 'Yous are on steroids.'

'Eddy, I think Malki means we can just buy Shugie more bev.' Pat the peacemaker.

'OK.'

Malki was embarrassed. 'Anyway, it's *Mr* Junkie Fuck to you.'

No one laughed. It was an old joke. Feeling he had the high ground again Eddy handed Malki a gun. 'Take this and stand outside the door of the bedroom.'

Malki held the gun between his forefinger and thumb, looking at it as if it was a used condom. 'Eh ... Eddy, man, no guns, man.'

'How are ye going to threaten him if he tries to get away?'

Malki held the gun out to Pat. 'Is it the old guy from last night?'

Eddy took the gun back. 'Aye.'

'Well, he's not gonnae try to get away though, is he?'

'Well, we don't know, do we?' said Eddy, goading. 'That's the raison d'être for having the guns, isn't it?'

'No.' Malki held firm. 'No guns, man.'

'Take the fucking gun.' Eddy shoved it back at his hand.

Malki dodged him. 'Man, I'm a lover not a fighter.'

Eddy was furious. 'What if he tries to get away? What ye gonnae do? Fuck him back into the room?'

'Keep your money, man.'

Eddy and Pat looked at Malki. He was not going to change his mind. He took a step to leave but Pat blocked his way and looked at Eddy. 'Come on.'

Eddy was bewildered, unable to understand anyone passing up the opportunity to threaten a man with a gun.

'We need to phone,' said Pat reasonably.

Doing his laugh that wasn't a laugh Eddy turned his back on them, sliding the gun into his trouser pocket.

Pat nodded Malki through to the living room, where he was treated to the sight of Shugie sitting on the edge of the settee looking at the racing pages of meets long past. Shugie looked the junkie boy up and down, huffed at the obvious inadequacies of his replacement. But Malki minded his manners. 'Right?'

Shugie didn't answer.

Pat brought him to the bottom of the stairs. 'Go up and watch the door til we get back, OK?'

'It's the old guy, yeah?'

'Yeah,' said Pat, keen to get away.

'Has he eaten anything?'

'Bit of bread, can of juice.'

Malki whipped a family bag of wine gums out of his trackie pocket. 'Grub's up!'

'Aye, very good.' Pat smiled, glad Malki was here to lighten the mood, glad he found the place as disgusting as Pat did. 'Get your arse up there.'

Malki stopped on the second stair and turned back. 'Same rate as last night?'

Pat nodded. 'Aye.'

Malki grinned and jogged up five stairs.

A knock at the front door made them both freeze. They looked at each other. In a flurry of silent motion Malki ran to the top of the stairs and Pat bolted through the living room to the kitchen door, stopping when he was flat against it. Eddy followed him, cowering in next to the stack of bin bags.

'Fuck!' Pat whispered.

'Malki?' hissed Eddy.

Pat nodded and pointed at the ceiling as Shugie looked in through the kitchen door. The knock came again, three formal raps on the front door. Shugie raised his eyebrows.

'Answer it and get them the fuck away frae here,' ordered Eddy.

Shugie looked confused. 'What if it's someone who wants to come in?'

'Don't fuckin' let them.'

Shugie nodded and shuffled off to the door.

They listened, breathless, as the door creaked open on unaccustomed hinges in the distant hallway. A low rumble addressed a question to Shugie which he answered in the affirmative. The voice, an official voice, told him something. After a pause Shugie said 'No'.

The door creaked loudly and Eddy and Pat both breathed out, realising too late that the door had not shut but had been opened wider, that steps were coming into the hallway, into the house, towards them.

Eddy opened the kitchen door and they shuffled gracelessly into the garden, crouching down under the kitchen window, praying the Lexus was low enough not to be seen through the window. They held their knees tight to their chests, listening to the long grass hissing spitefully around them, hearing through the broken window as footsteps came all the way into the kitchen. Three sets.

'And does anyone live here with yourself, Mr Parry?'

Eddy and Pat looked at each other. Polis voice. Shugie had the fucking polis in his kitchen. Pat buried his head in his knees, looking down at the grass flattened below him. He shut his eyes and saw the sunshine die on the girl in the hospital bed, her hair slid across the pillow into ash.

It was a young polis, high voice, just new to it: '... regarding an incident at Brian's Bar on the weekend of the fourth?'

'Nah, nah.' Shugie's rumbling smoker's voice. 'I wiz out of it, and ah, I cannae just remember.'

'Well, Mr Parry,' said the polis. 'Judging from the overwhelming and pungent stench of urine in your domicile, it is my firm conclusion that you do indeed have fuck all recollection of that particular incident.' The second polis was laughing softly, repeating the line: 'stench of urine'.

'And so, Mr Parry we will be getting the fuck out of this disgusting abode pronto.' He stopped for a titter himself. 'Thanking you, but offers of tea and biscuits will be declined.'

'And biscuits!' echoed the giggly second polis.

Shugie said nothing. He stood and took the abuse until a sudden thump came from the kitchen ceiling.

The polis shifted their feet. 'Is there someone else in this house?' It was the other one talking. Shugie didn't answer him.

'Mr Parry?'

Shugie mumbled, 'Cheeking my fucking ...'

The giggler was suddenly stern. 'Is there someone else in the fucking house, Parry?'

'... disrespectful and that, talking about smells and that, whit's your fucking house like, then?'

'Come on, we'll just go and see, Paul.' It was the first polis again, the comedian.

Shugie spoke up. 'My mate – he's ... sleeping it off.'

'Right, answer us when we fucking speak tae ye, well.'

''S get the fuck out of here before we catch something.'

'Too fucking right ... disgusting.'

They were walking away, Shugie grumbling behind them. Finally the front door slammed shut.

Pat raised his head from his knees and whispered, 'I can't ... my fucking nerves are shredded here,' he reasoned. 'Eddy, I know you're the contact, but I'm facing the same time as you and I can't fucking take it.'

Eddy raised a hand, Pat expected him to get angry but he looked frightened too. 'Let's go and phone and then we'll come back and move him.'

'Where to?'

'Well, you fucking decide.' Here was the spite. 'You fucking come up with somewhere better if you're so much fucking smarter than me.'

'Breslin's.'

Eddy blinked, his bottom lip flapped as he thought of things to say. He licked his lips, disappointed that Pat had come up with somewhere so much better. 'Let's phone.'

The roll shop was tiny, little more than a dirty-looking door with a chalkboard outside announcing the availability of tea and full breakfast butties. Pat made Eddy stop here because he knew it sold newspapers too.

He stepped across the pavement, alive with the urgent tenderness of a lover orchestrating a chance encounter. Workmen in dusty jeans stood by the counter. The heavy aroma of spitting fat filled the narrow room with sticky air. Trying to act calm Pat turned to the newspaper stand. She was looking out at him.

A bad photo, grainy head and shoulders, taken by a mobile phone, but it was clear enough for him to see what he wanted. Long black hair parted in the middle, a large nose, hooked like a finger curling come hither. White perfect smile and hooded eyes that spoke only to him. She was injured but not dead. The first paragraph said that they were a respectable family. Shows what they know, thought Pat.

She was making a face in the picture, puffing up her cheekbones and pouting a little, not tarty, just sweet. Pat reached out to pick up a copy and felt the texture of the rough paper kiss his fingertips, smelled the hot fat as sweet, the daylight glinting on the greasy wall as a sparkle. That she existed made the tawdry present bearable. He folded the paper and tucked it under his arm, smiling, as happy as if it was her arm, and went over to the counter, ordered two egg and bacon rolls and two cans of ginger, handing over the money to the beautifully hungover fat man behind the counter.

He read on as the rolls were made. Her name was Aleesha, she was sixteen, a pupil at Shawlands Academy, loved by all her classmates. Pat knew she would be popular, he'd known it. She had lost several fingers and was in intensive care in the Victoria Infirmary. At that he slowly dropped the paper, his mouth hanging open in amazement. He *knew* she would be in the Vicky. He just knew that she would be there. It was as if they were connected somehow, as if he had picked the place they would meet again.

He read about the terrible damage to her hand and empathised with her pain, with the awful disfigurement she would have to live with, but deep inside he was pleased that he had shot her, because now she wouldn't be perfect and a hundred miles above him, because he had caused her photo to be on the front of the paper and he could look at her whenever he wanted.

The rolls arrived and he carried them, fat seeping through

the paper bag out to the car. Eddy told him to be careful not to get grease everywhere; it was a hire car and they'd have to pay extra if they got stains on the seats and that. Use the newspaper on your lap, he said.

But Pat folded the paper carefully and tucked it into the pocket on the door, letting the fat get on his jeans instead.

'What's it saying?' Eddy nodded at the paper.

Pat filtered through the story to find the facts. 'She's stable,' he said. 'In the hospital. Intensive care.'

Eddy stopped chewing and stared at him. 'Who's stable?'

'The girl.'

'Oh, the one you shot?'

That stung, him saying that so lightly, as if it was a detail. Pat looked out of the window. 'They've clues anyway.'

Eddy took another bite and asked through a mouthful, 'Can I see?' He held his hand out to the paper but Pat hesitated. He didn't want Eddy to touch his paper. He braced himself and handed it over casually.

They finished their rolls in silence, Pat holding a secret vigil over the paper until Eddy handed it back, and licked his fingers before accepting. He folded it nicely so that her face was visible and tucked her into the car door pocket. They drove on, looking for a phone box that didn't have a camera right nearby. Cameras were all over the city like rats.

Finally Eddy stopped the car in a quiet street, a few spaces away from the phone box in case they were being watched, and they looked around, keeping their eyes up, looking for cameras on the sides of buildings and on street lights. It was a residential area, a quiet street with big trees and bushes in front of the tenements.

'Right.' Eddy pulled on the handbrake, and snapped his belt off.

'No.' Pat touched his arm with a staying hand. 'No, I'll do the phoning.'

Eddy looked at him. 'Why?'

''Cause you've been under a lot of pressure ...'

Eddy liked that characterisation. He nodded at the windscreen. 'Well, be threatening. And tell them two million by tonight.'

'And we'll call back with a drop place?' Pat knew that was what they had to do, they'd talked about it enough, but he wanted to make Eddy feel as if he was deciding.

'Aye, that's right, that's ... a drop point. We'll call back later.'

'When they've got the money?'

Eddy nodded again. 'When they've got the money.'

Pat got out and took the newspaper with him.

17

The street of tenements was tall and narrow but surrounded by fields, like a lone passenger crammed into the corner of an empty lift. The pink sandstone was stained to blood red over the years by the black belching from the backsides of cars and buses passing through the stone valley. It was part of a city now gone, the buildings running along either bank of a road that once snaked through other tall streets. All its neighbours had been knocked down before they crumbled away, the families of mine and dock and factory workers decanted to the schemes and new towns.

The Anwars' shop would never have excited the interest of an avaricious passer-by. It was a poor corner shop. The shop front was painted with what looked like navy blue undercoat, matt and dusty from the street, with 'News-agents' hand painted in red, weathered to pink, above the window. The window was frosted with dirt, the counter inside abutting glass obscured with adverts for newspapers and magazines and comics. A blue plastic ice-cream selection board sagged drunkenly in the window, too far in to be read, too old to be true.

The close was straight across the road and the outside door didn't give a good account of the neighbourhood. Wired glass scarred with poorly drafted graffiti in felt tip. Names on the intercom were messy, biroed on to stickers, stuck over the outside of the perspex. Something dark yellow, possibly paint, had been spilled on the red floor tiles and scrubbed into the grout.

Nestled in among the messy names 'J. Lander' was

typewriter-written in an old-fashioned font, the plastic over his name was clean, as if he had tended it carefully over the years. Morrow pressed the button.

'Hello?'

'Is this Mr Lander?'

'It is indeed.' His voice was high but steady, neat, like his name plate. 'Who is this?'

'Mr Lander, we're from Strathclyde CID. We'd like to speak to you concerning Mr Anwar.'

'Of course.' The door clicked open in front of them and Lander came back on the intercom. 'Two up, first on the left.'

Morrow thanked him and he hung up.

The inside of the close was clear, no piles of rubbish bags or discarded furniture, well tended but the building was in bad shape: a white plastic mobility handrail had come loose from its shorings at one end and was resting forlornly on the floor, as spent as the tenant who had requested it. The walls above the skirting board were damp-bubbled, crumbling but held together with thick burgundy gloss paint. The imprint of a heel in the skin of paint had burst a bubble and white plaster powder had been walked up and down the steps.

Above in the echoing stairwell a door opened. Footsteps clip-clopped out on to the landing and a man called over the balcony, 'Hello?'

'Hello?' Morrow led Bannerman up the stairs. 'Mr Lander?'

'Aye, that's you, come on,' he said, guiding them, as if there was any way of getting lost in a close. 'Up this way.'

Morrow looked up and saw a small man in his sixties leaning over the rail, big hands clutching the banister. Brown cardigan, grey slacks with stay-press seams down the front, a neat white moustache no wider than his mouth, grey hair that had been tidied with a watered comb.

'Good morning, officers,' he said, withdrawing as soon as he was sure they had seen him and knew where to go.

Morrow reached the top of the stairs first and followed him through the brown front door. His front step was dust free, the 'welcome' mat clean and square to the door.

She stepped into a moss-green hallway and found Lander standing patiently at the door to the living room, watching behind her for Bannerman. When Grant stepped into the hallway behind her and shut the door Lander nodded, muttered a little orderly, 'Uh huh' to himself and went into the living room, ready to receive them.

The hall had a single shelf above the radiator with a bowl for keys on it. On the back of the door was a single peg for a scarf. No coats chucked on chairs, no bags dumped on the floor, no shopping bag of rubbish left hanging on a handle ready to be taken out when someone remembered.

Morrow followed Bannerman into the living room.

An old-fashioned box television sat on a low table. A small settee in orange velvet and matching armchair, both old but well preserved. Hanging on the arm of the chair was a cloth pocket for TV remotes and a booklet of the weekly television listings inside. There was nothing in the living room that was not functional or essential, no display cabinet of half-loved ornaments or better-day mementoes, no unread newspapers. It was more than bachelor-flat tidy. It was institutional tidy. Morrow made a mental note to check for a prison record.

They stood in front of the settee in a perfect equilateral triangle. Bannerman looked at Morrow expectantly, telling her to take charge of the questioning, as if he was saving his own moves for the more important interviews.

'Please,' said Mr Lander, taking the prompt for himself, opening his hand to the settee. 'Sit down.'

Against his orders Morrow sat in the armchair, and saw Lander's eye twitch. He would have to sit next to Bannerman on the settee, sandwiched between them. He pulled his trousers up at the knees with an irritated flick of the wrist and sat down.

Morrow looked around. The electric bar fire was surrounded by framed photographs. She expected to see a wife, grandchildren, perhaps a mother in a formal pose, but instead found photographs of Lander in military uniform, standing among friends in uniform.

'A military man?' she said, apropos of nothing. Bannerman looked up, suddenly interested.

'Yes.' His tone was clipped. 'Twenty years in the Argyll and Sutherland Highlanders. Ten served in the First Battalion and then a further ten years in E Company.' As if he sensed her reservations he said, 'E Company is the TA.'

The intense attraction of order had a pull over her too. She had considered the army herself. 'Dedicated,' she said.

'Yes,' he said and thought about it. 'Yes.' Patting his knees with his open hands he turned to Bannerman. 'So, tell me about Mr Anwar. Do you know who took him?'

They weren't supposed to give away any information, but a stonewall was often cold news to an interviewee so Bannerman tempered it. 'Well, Mr Lander, I'm sure you've seen the papers. We really can't say anything other than what's in there—'

'He was taken by gunmen demanding a ransom?'

'Yes—'

'And Aleesha was shot in the hand?'

'—But what I can tell you is that Mr Anwar was kidnapped last night for a money ransom. Do you know anything about that?'

'Other than what was on the radio,' Lander breathed heavily through his nose, as if he was holding back a strong

162

emotion, 'all I know is I got a call this morning from his *cousin*,' he said the word disapprovingly, 'telling me that I was not required this morning because Mr Anwar had been indisposed last night. I had to dig for information. He's over there.' He nodded out the window. 'Now. Working the shop for him.'

Bannerman carried on. 'Is Mr Anwar a popular man? With locals?'

'Popular?' Lander's eyes searched the carpet. 'Well, people come into the shop a lot.'

'The same people?'

He nodded. 'Often the same people. There's a bus stop outside so people on their way to town often come in for a paper but after rush hour in the morning and the afternoon our customers are mostly locals, yes.'

'How long have you worked there?'

'About fourteen years. Nearly fourteen years.'

'And what shifts do you do?'

'Ooh.' He rolled his eyes up. 'Well, I start at six thirty a.m. and finish at twelve thirty. But I often stay on or go back in for the afternoon shift, help with the lunchtime rush and stocking up and so on. Sometimes I go back in to listen to the cricket with Mr Anwar.'

Morrow chimed in, 'So, he's a friend?'

'Very much so,' said Lander seriously. 'Very much a friend.'

'Are you paid for those extra hours?'

He seemed offended at the suggestion. 'In the afternoon?' 'Yes.'

He gave a small cheerless laugh. 'Paid for listening to cricket matches?'

Morrow blinked slowly. 'When you work extra hours are you paid for them?'

Lander's expression hardened towards her. 'No. I'm paid

for my shift in the morning. Anything else I can do for Mr Anwar is a gesture of friendship.'

'You do it out of loyalty?' She meant it as a compliment but he seemed to have taken against her.

The lip beneath his moustache tightened. 'And friendship.'

'I am just asking ye questions, Mr Lander.' Her voice was soft. 'It's my job to find Mr Anwar and bring him back safe and sound. I take it very seriously.'

'Good,' he said and blinked. She realised suddenly that he was terrified for his friend.

'How much are you paid an hour?'

Lander was a little embarrassed. 'I'm paid two hundred pounds a week, flat, whatever hours I do.'

'I see.' She jotted it down. 'Not that much for a thirty-hour week.'

'Thirty-six. Sometimes forty-two if I work the full week but it suits me,' he said simply.

'In what way?'

'The hours, the location and the company.'

'You get on well, then?'

He spoke as if it was a pre-prepared speech, looking over her shoulder to another audience. 'Mr Anwar and I have been friends for fourteen years. Over that time we have become as brothers.' His hand chopped the air a little for emphasis. '*He is as a brother to me.*'

Having finished, he coughed, embarrassed. Morrow recognised his discomfort, his inability to Oprah-sob on demand. Like him, she didn't believe sincerity was marked by incessant emotional revelation. She yearned for a time when it was enough to tell a man you loved him on your wedding day and expect him still to know ten years later.

Lander was controlled and would be hard to wrong-foot.

She slouched in the chair and sucked her teeth sarcastically. 'Yeah, I see, kind of, what you're on about.'

'Do you see?' He was suddenly angry. 'Do you?'

'Oh, aye, yeah, see whit ye mean.'

'What do you see?' He seemed furious, at both her belittling tone and scattered grammar.

She slapped the air carelessly. 'You work together, you enjoy cricket together?'

'Correct.' He pointed a finger at her nose and his rage subsided. 'Correct.'

Morrow stared at him, letting him stew for a moment. 'In the days and weeks running up to the kidnap, did you see anyone hanging around the shop?'

'Many people hang around the shop.'

'Anyone unusual? Anyone take a special interest?'

'In what?'

'In Mr Anwar? In the shop's income, anyone ask about the takings, for example?'

He thought about it for a moment. 'No,' he said finally. 'No, not that I can think of. We get a lot of odd types. Alcoholics, junkies, odd types, but they're all locals, if you don't know who they are you'll know who they belong to.'

'Belong to?' asked Bannerman.

'Who their family are, their mother's name or granny's name.'

'No unusual phone calls?' asked Morrow.

'No.'

'Can you think of anyone Mr Anwar owes money to?'

'No.'

The answer came a little too fast; he hadn't considered the question. Even if there had been someone Morrow felt sure that Johnny Lander would not tell her. He wouldn't say anything harmful to Aamir. His loyalty ran too deep.

'What do you think happened?'

165

'Wrong address.' He sounded certain.

'Why?'

'They're a modest family. Religious. They give a lot of money to charity, on the quiet, the way it should be.'

'What charities?'

'Earthquake appeal, important things.'

'Humanitarian appeals?'

'Yes.'

'Afghanistan?'

'Never mentioned it specifically. Pakistan I think . . .'

'Any connection with Afghanistan? Do they have family there?'

'Not that I know of, they're both from Uganda.'

'How about yourself, did you serve there, ever?'

'No. After my time.'

She tried a blank card. 'Would you say that you are a loyal person?'

'Yes.' No flinch or hesitation, not a moment's doubt or a glimmer of shame.

'But you don't have a family of your own?'

'No.'

'Are you friends with Mr Anwar's family?'

'No. Just Mr Anwar.'

'But you must know the family?'

'A little. Billal and Omar both worked Saturdays in the shop when they were at school, but I don't really know them.'

'You worked every Saturday with them for years but you don't know them?'

'No. I didn't work with them. Their daddy worked with them. I didn't go in then, when they were on. There isn't really room behind the counter for three and I used to fish, so . . .' Small shrug. 'I was glad.'

'You must hear a lot though, know about them?'

'No. Mr Anwar doesn't really talk about his family.'

'Does that seem odd to you?'

'No. Why?'

'Most parents like to talk about their children. But Mr Anwar doesn't?'

'He doesn't talk about anything but the shop.'

'Doesn't that get tedious?'

'And cricket. We talk about cricket too.'

'Now,' she sat forward, '*that* must get tedious.'

Lander warmed to that a little, allowed himself a small, crisp smile.

Bannerman interrupted, 'Are you still involved with the TA?'

'No.'

'Can you tell me when you left the TA?'

'I can: in April 1993.'

'Quite a while ago, then?'

'Yes.'

'Do you still know people in the TA?'

Morrow could tell where he was heading with it, the military connection, the guns and gear the gunmen had could have indicated a TA connection, but the gunmen weren't trained, they made mistakes so fundamental no one with any army training would have made.

'No. I know people who *were* in the TA at the same time as me but I am not in contact with them on a regular basis.'

'How about an irregular basis? Who has seen you in the shop?'

He thought hard. 'No one.'

'Not one single person from the TA has ever come into the shop?'

'Why would they? Sure, most of them live in Stirling. If you don't believe me you could contact the HQ and ask for addresses. I'll give you the number.'

He was very exact, his military mindset letting him answer without questioning their authority. Most interviewees struggled to understand the reasoning behind a train of questioning, attempted to connect with their questioner. It was refreshing.

She took over. 'Do you get arms training in the TA?' Bannerman's eyes widened in warning, as if she was giving too much away. When she looked back Johnny Lander's back was straighter than before.

'Of course. There wouldn't be much point in having an army if they can't use arms.'

The damage was done now so she went for it. 'Hand guns?'

'Certainly. But if you're thinking I had anything to do with Mr Anwar's kidnap you are very wrong indeed. He is a good personal friend of mine and I most certainly would never do anything to harm him in any way.'

He was panting a little at the end, looked upset and she reached over to him, touching the air above his knee. 'There's no suggestion of that at all, Mr Lander, but the men used guns and we have to explore every possible connection with Mr Anwar.'

'I see.' He still looked nervous.

'It's our job to get him back and we are trying our hardest.'

'Good.' He pursed his lips tight. 'Good. He's ... a good man. If there's anything I can do ...' He thought they were going and leaned forward to stand up but Morrow stayed him with a hand.

'The TA. What sort does it attract?'

He sat back down. 'Ex military, who can't quite give it up.' He twitched his mouth, touched his chest indicating himself. 'Poor men with families, in it for the money. Others ...' he shrugged and wondered about it, 'seen too many action movies. They don't last.'

'How come?'

'They want to be heroes. Not what the job is. Discipline. Can't take it. Not about being popular. Not about being nice.' He smiled knowingly at Morrow.

'What happens to them, then?' asked Bannerman.

'Leave or get put out. It's hard to do things right.' He nodded at Morrow and dropped his voice. 'You were doing something hard there, before, weren't ye? Noising me up, trying to shake a monkey out of the tree?'

She smiled and he leaned forward, his face close to hers. 'When you get old,' he whispered, 'it's very hard to find people you can stand the sight of.'

Morrow whispered back, 'I have that trouble now.'

He smiled and sat back. 'D'you think you'll find him alive?' he said, his voice cracking a little.

She gave an honest shrug. 'The gunmen came in asking for someone called Bob,' She watched him for a reaction.

'There ye are, then,' Johnny Lander said certainly. 'It *was* the wrong address.'

He led them out to the hall, opened the door and saw them out formally, shook their hands in turn and gave all the formal pleasantries a gentleman would, nice to meet you, anything I can do. He watched them take the stairs, looking over the banister again, lifting a hand to wave when they looked up to see if he was still there.

Morrow found herself leaving the neat world of Mr Lander reluctantly, dragging her feet as she tripped after Bannerman down to the bubbling damp and noisy street. He was a soldier, had that capacity to form ferocious, blind attachments, lived in a world of moral absolutes. She envied it. He probably never had to call into question the army; it must have served him well. Her own experience of joining the force was her father and the rest of the family turning from her, thinking themselves betrayed. It was twelve years ago and she still wondered if the desire to shed them was the reason she joined. She saw herself as an old woman in a personality-free house, sitting in a desolate silence as a bus rumbled past the window.

Outside the close the day had descended into cold drizzle.

'You shouldn't have said that about the guns.' Bannerman squinted out into the road.

Morrow pulled her coat closed. 'Those guys last night, they aren't firearms trained.'

'How do you know?'

'Omar did that, didn't he?' She threw her hand to the side, the way Omar had during questioning the night before, at a low ninety-degree angle. 'I was watching on the remote.'

'Yeah.'

'Doesn't that look like recoil put it there?'

Bannerman looked at her hand, reluctant to admit she was right.

'And he said he thought the guy had a long face under the balaclava. He said that, "a long face", until he shut his mouth.' She dropped her jaw in shock and shut it again. 'Just after he fired the shot.'

Bannerman shrugged. 'It's an idea.'

'Plus, think about the order of things: the girl was shot at an irrelevant point in the negotiations. It wasn't a ploy to up the ante, wasn't to move the threat forward. It was just a stupid mistake.'

Bannerman wouldn't look at her.

'Well, it's a theory anyway.' She shrugged. 'Don't like being wrong, do you?' She dropped from the step into the street. Buses passed noisily in front of her. Cars edged impatiently around them and drew back at the stream of traffic coming the other way.

Bannerman was at her side. 'No, but, it's ... that's much

worse, isn't it? If they aren't used to firearms. They could shoot anyone at any time.'

The traffic in front of them came to a standstill as a bus let its passengers off and the lights changed on the other side.

'On the upside,' she stepped out between the back of a bus and a car, 'they might shoot each other.'

The shop door was sticky and needed a shove. It chimed as Bannerman opened it and stepped in. It was a small room, smelled of dust and stale body odour. On the right the wall was lined with newspapers and magazine racks, with the porn high up and children's comics. Near the back sat a rack of glass bottles of fizzy juice, laid out on their sides like wine, with an upright crate of empty returns next to them. A central stand displayed household absolute essentials: shampoo next to tea bags and washing powder and nappies. Expensive items like peanut butter were arranged to face the shopkeeper, close enough to lean over and slap any shoplifters who tried their arm. The counter ran half the length of the shop, which wasn't much. Behind it cigarettes and cheap drink and coffee were kept beyond grabbing distance.

Twenty years of small change had eroded the white plastic counter through to the brown chipboard beneath. Behind it sat two high stools, still angled into one another, as if duettists had just left the stage. On one of the low shelves she saw a little silver short wave radio. It would be a comfy perch to watch the world from.

The shop was being manned by a man who was too young for his beard and old-fashioned manners, as if he was acting a part. He looked at her expectantly but didn't speak.

'Hello, are you Mr Anwar's cousin?'

'Yes,' he said, heavily accented, nodding his head passively.

'DS Morrow.' She held out her hand. 'I'm one of the police officers investigating your cousin's kidnapping.'

He didn't take her hand. 'Yes,' he said again, trying, she thought, to process the words she had said individually.

'This is DS Bannerman.' She gestured behind her. 'What's your name?'

'Ahmed Johany.' When he saw her confusion he added kindly, 'John.'

'John?' She laughed.

'You call me ... John.' But he wasn't smiling now, at least his eyes weren't smiling, they were sad, as if he was mourning Ahmed Johany and wished he had a place in the shop too.

Bannerman leaned over her shoulder. 'Mr Johany?' He pointed to a high corner behind the counter and they all looked up together. A video camera, a small red light next to it. 'Is that ... ?'

'Camera, yes.'

'Do you keep the tapes?'

He shook his head. 'For one, two weeks only ...'

'Then ... ?'

'Tape over.' Apologetic, he smiled, rolling one forearm over the other. 'Save on tapes.'

'Can we have the ones you've got from last week?'

He indicated that they could but was worried about leaving them while he went through to the back shop. Bannerman took out his warrant card and showed it to him but Ahmed shook his head, embarrassed at having doubted them. He scuttled off quickly though, glancing back a couple of times as he made it to a door at the back. He took barely twenty seconds to bring out a stack of dusty video cartridges to them. He hurried back behind the counter, not happy until he got there, and found a thin blue plastic bag to put the tapes in. He tried to fit them all in one bag, but they wouldn't go and he had to get another bag out from under the counter.

Morrow watched him put them in, careful as eggs, trying not to rip the thin skin of the bag. 'Have you worked here long?'

'Hmm.' Worried at the question, he handed the bags to Bannerman by the handles. 'I come here just ... *now*.' He added quickly, 'Not Scotland. Here many years, but shop, I just come now.'

The distrust, the soft passive smile, all reflected poorly either on the neighbourhood they were in or else the one Johany had come from. Morrow felt ashamed, remembered racist graffiti on a shop front when she was small, thought of a shop in Partick that had a felt-tipped sign in the window: '*This Shop is Run by Scottish People.*'

The door opened behind them, a puff of noise and dust from the street, and an elderly woman with a severe white perm stood in the doorway. She looked from Bannerman to Johany. 'Where's he?' she said indignantly.

'Who?' asked Morrow because Johany didn't say anything.

'The wee man.' She pointed at the counter. 'Is he sick or something?'

'How?' asked Morrow sharply.

The woman scowled at her. 'Who are yous? Have you bought the shop or something?'

'No. Who are you?'

'Who am I?' She couldn't quite believe she was being asked. 'I'm in here every day. I come in here every day. Where's the wee man?'

'Which wee man?'

'The fella, the wee black fella.'

'Mr Anwar?' corrected Morrow.

'Is that his name?' The woman hung out of the door,

173

looking down the road for her bus and ducked back in to ask, 'Is he sick, then? Is he in hospital?'

'Mr Anwar isn't able to come to work today. How long have you been coming in here?'

'Twenty-odd year. How?'

'And you don't know his name?'

'He doesn't know mine either.' She scowled at Morrow. 'Tell him, anyway, say that the twenty Kensitas and four rolls lady hopes he feels better soon. And my granddaughter's out of hospital. She'd a boy.' She looked uncertain. 'Just saying 'cause ... eh ... he'll be wondering.' And she left.

18

Omar Anwar was at home, sitting in the peach living room, frightened and watching the rain patter on the window when the phone rang out in the hall, a soft unfamiliar trilling. He heard Billal's bedroom door fly open and a heavy gallop across the hall.

'Omar! Get the fuck out here!'

Omar sprang to his feet and hurried out to the hall. The brothers stood away from each other, staring at the strange green phone. It wasn't their phone. The police had given it to them. It was old and slightly dirty, the rubbery cord on the receiver coated with a layer of grey that came off under the nail. The receiver was so loud it had to be held away from the ear. When they spoke into it they could hear an echo of their own voice. The recording device was a tape recorder plugged into the back. They expected something more high tech and the rudimentary nature of the equipment made them feel dismissed, as if the police didn't really care too much about their dad.

Billal bent down abruptly, pressed the record button on the tape, checked it was turning and lifted the receiver, carefully holding it to his ear as if he had never used a phone before and was uncertain of it. He listened for a moment, nodded and offered it to Omar, his arm straight, staring at the mouthpiece as if afraid.

Omar took it and listened.

'Who is this?' The voice was familiar from last night.

'It's eh, Omar. Who's this? Are you the guy from last night?'

175

'Put Bob on.'

Omar looked awkwardly at the recorder. 'It's, em, Omar.'

'We've got your dad.'

'Right? Look, mate, was it yourself who was here last night?'

'We've got him. We want two mill, in used notes, we want it today.'

'I know, mate, right, there's no need for this to go on any longer, OK? How is my dad, is he OK?' Omar was surprised at his own mannerliness, being so polite to a man who had threatened his family, shot his sister and kidnapped his dad, but Sadiqa had drummed social grace into him and, at a loss for protocol, he found it was his default position.

'Listen, pal, your dad's fine, fine. Don't worry.' He was being polite too. In the background Omar could hear a bus or a car pass: he was calling from a street. 'Is your sister OK?'

'My sister?' asked Omar.

'Aleesha, that got shot, is she OK?'

'She's fine, she's in hospital.'

'Is her hand OK?'

Bewildered, Omar looked up and found Billal glaring at him and he was suddenly tearful. 'No, mate, it's a mess, to be honest with ye.' He stopped for breath. 'She's lost a thumb and her forefinger and a bit of the next one. They said they can sew her big toe on as a thumb. Mum thinks it'll look weird. But you need opposable digits for your hand to be any use, y'know ...?'

'Aye, well, OK. Don't worry.'

'It'll look weird though.'

'Um ... couldn't she wear gloves?'

Omar frowned at the phone, it seemed an odd thing to say. 'Maybe ...'

'Nice gloves, I mean, different colours on each hand ...?'

'Different colours?'

'Just a thought, anyway, um, tell her ... say we're sorry about that.'

Billal saw Omar's confusion and poked him in the arm, shaking his head at him, asking what was going on. Omar ignored him. 'We'll tell her,' he said, 'that you're sorry.'

'OK. OK then ...' The kidnapper's voice sounded as if it was retreating from the phone and Omar had the feeling the conversation was coming to an end, as if he had forgotten about the ransom.

'Mate, didn't you want to ask us about something?'

'Oh, aye, yeah, listen, right: we want two million in used notes by tonight.'

'Look, mate, I want to do whatever you want, right? I want to help you, make this OK, get my dad back safe and sound. Thing is, yeah?' He took a desperately needed breath. 'Um, are you still there?'

'Aye, I'm here.'

'Thing is, we don't have *anything* like that kind of money.'

'You don't have that ... ?'

'We don't, but listen, I'm going to the bank right now, mate, yeah? I'll get whatever I can out and give it to you tonight, happily give it to you tonight, I'll give you anything we can get, right? For my dad.'

'Well ... how much is that gonnae ... ?'

'I've no idea, mate, right? I can get a loan. But I can definitely get, like forty K right away.' He said it like that, *forty K*, instead of forty thousand because he thought it sounded like a bit more. 'But whatever I can get I'll give it all to ye really happily, right? Will ye phone back later? Say at five o'clock and we'll arrange to meet?'

'Forty K's not enough, mate.' He breathed loudly into the receiver, this almost friend, held it close to his mouth so the sound was breathy and distorted. 'OK, listen to me now: *we know about you.*'

Omar looked at the tape recorder. 'What?'

'*We know about you,*' he said carefully. 'See what I'm saying here? We know about *you.*'

Omar was watching the tape turn, 'OK, mate, honestly, I don't know what you're on about, right? Genuinely. But listen, right? If you call back in two hours I'll have been to the bank and I'll see what I can do for ye, right?'

'*We know all about ye.*' And he hung up.

Pat could see Eddy sitting in the Lexus, stroking the leather of the steering wheel, and smiling smugly to himself.

He drawled as Pat got back in. 'What did he say?' His blink was too long, the smile too fixed for it to be real and Pat knew that Eddy was off again, gangster tripping, imagining himself more than a fat divorcee in a hire car.

'Well,' Pat pulled the seat belt over himself, 'spoke to Bob and he said he'll get out what he can. He's got forty K already but he'll get more. We've to phone back at five to arrange a drop. This should be over pretty soon, I think.'

Eddy nodded slowly and blinked again. He was so caught up in the role play he almost seemed drunk. 'Good one, man, good work,' as if Pat was working for him and he'd pleased him. 'Was he niggaring about it?'

Pat flinched. 'What?'

'Niggaring, ye know, havvering about the money.' Eddy started the car and pulled out smoothly, driving to the end of the road.

Pat didn't know what to say to him, didn't want to implicate himself in the general air of ignorant madness by responding to the term. He wished Malki were in the car to say something. 'He said he doesn't know how much more he can get, but he'll try his best.'

'Yeah.' God almighty, he was even doing an American accent now. 'Yeah, niggaring it.'

That's not really a word, Pat thought of saying. He licked his lips, drew a breath, but by the time he had his courage up the moment had passed. He held his newspaper to his chest with two hands, like a woman clutching an evening bag in a dark alley.

'Aye, wait an' see, those fucker's'll pay up, right enough ...' Eddy gabbled on, still doing the accent, confident again now that the arrangement had been made. Pat answered in grunts, trying not to engage but keeping Eddy going, studying him.

The realisation was slow but profound: whatever amount the family offered tonight Pat would accept it to get away from Eddy. All the years of listening to him, coaxing him, rearranging facts to suit him, smiling away from him, it was over. Pat had other things to do, other matters to take care of.

They had driven around quiet streets for half a mile before they hit the main road. Mid-morning traffic was building up and they joined a queue of cars trying to dodge through the traffic. Eddy saw the lights changing up ahead and squeezed the brake on, bringing the big car to a stop. A brand new Mini was next to him, blue, shiny, and the woman driver saw the Lexus's silver bonnet and turned to look into the car. Her eyes were obscured by the Mini's roof. All that was visible was a lipstick-tackity mouth hanging open, looking at them. She smiled and Eddy drank it in, smiling at his steering wheel.

'Check this cunt checking me, eh?'

Pat didn't answer.

'Pat, man, check this bird checking the car.'

Pat wasn't looking at him.

'Man ...'

Eddy followed Pat's eyeline, over the dash, over the bonnet, past the lights to a green and white tiled rotunda in a traffic island. It was a strange wee building, like something from a garden but in the middle of a sea of traffic. A hand-painted sign on the window read 'The Battlefield Rest'. Eddy looked back at him.

'Had your dinner in there?' he asked.

But Pat didn't answer. A horn tooted behind them, the lights had changed. Eddy cursed the driver and took off.

Pat wasn't looking at the rotunda, he was looking over the road again, to a small wall around a visitors' car park and a tall Victorian building. Built in a comma around the cars it was the Victoria Infirmary.

'Pat, man, you're miles away.'

Eddy was right. Pat stared at the building and his mind took him out of the car, away from the racial slights and the bad role play and the hint of Shugie's piss on Eddy's trousers.

Pat and his beloved newspaper were in the lift in the Victoria Infirmary. Pat was holding a bunch of flowers, yellow flowers, he could feel the cold damp from the stems creeping through the tissue paper in his hands. And he had a suit on.

19

Perhaps because Bannerman had believed her when she pretended to stand up for him over the 999 call detail, or because they were both tired and bored of fighting, for whatever reason peace broke out unexpectedly as Bannerman drove them to the Victoria Infirmary. He took the drive slow, hardly talking except to fill in the spaces in the briefing as they occurred to him. His delivery was thoughtful and Morrow found him beating her to conclusions a couple of times. More astute than she had given him credit for.

'Why burn it out in Harthill, is the question. Either they went to Edinburgh or pass there often, knew it and sensed it would throw us off the scent.'

'Serial number trace on the van's origins?'

'Nicked from a dealers in Cathcart. Nothing unusual about the theft.' He slowed for the lights at Gorbals Cross.

'Could explain them burning it out there, if one of them was an experienced car thief. The farmer said he'd had nicked cars there before.'

'Yeah. Could be a known place to leave cars. Tried and tested, they'd know it would take a good few hours before anyone would find it.'

'What'd the burnt-out look like?'

'Professional. You know that fire ball effect you get sometimes?' He waved his hand flat over his head, skimming the roof of the car.

She did. 'When they leave the tank full and it explodes and burns itself out?'

'Exactly.' He smiled a little, pleased that she knew what he was talking about. 'Well, no sign of that. They doused the inside thoroughly and it burned nice and steady so there's no fibre or hair traces or anything.'

'Did the family have any Afghanistan visas?'

'Nah, no connection. Doesn't seem to be one. Mum and dad are both refugees from Uganda. Any extended family they have is from there as well. Couple of cousins from Pakistan, distant, Ugandan émigrés.'

'I think Mo and Omar were right, it's just the thing an idiot would say to Asian people. If they are unprofessional enough to use a gun they've never fired before ... You'd think they'd try it out.'

'I know.' The lights changed to green and he eased the car through the junction and down the Vicky Road. 'They did make one big mistake: tin foil wrap found in among the trees.'

'No!' She grinned at him. 'No!'

'Yeah.' He was smiling too. 'Heroin. But let's not get too excited because even if it was from the kidnappers and not the van thieves, it's so hard to trace anything from a wrap.'

'The gunmen weren't mellow.'

'Yeah, well, it was just one wrap, there's tar on the inside.'

'Maybe the others didn't notice he'd been smoking. High functioning, you know?'

'Long habit then?'

'Yeah, not mixing or out of control.'

'Yeah, I think you could be right.'

'Yeah.'

'Yeah.'

Sensing that they were getting on, Bannerman bit his lip. 'You all right with me?'

Morrow cleared her throat and shrugged. 'Sorry I called you a cunt. I's tired . . .'

He flinched at that. 'You *didn't*. What you said was that we wouldn't get on if I was *going* to be a cunt about it, but you didn't *call* me a cunt.'

This semantic difference seemed to matter to him. 'Yeah,' she said. 'No, that's right.'

'We've been kind of put in an awkward situation here, you know? Kind of competing when we could be working together. Bad management.'

The implied slur on MacKechnie was meant to be a bonding move, or trap. Queasy with sleep deprivation and tired of having to guess what the fuck was going on with Bannerman, she could feel the anger building behind her eyes. 'Grant, I feel that you're very into your career . . .' She stopped, took a breath, stopped again. He waited for her to get it together. '. . . Less about the service . . . you know.' She gestured outwards with both hands, as if she was opening a book, meaninglessly. 'I feel I'm more about the case . . . expending energy, y'know?'

Bannerman took it in good part. 'My dad was a copper, you know.'

'Hmm.'

'Grew up with the service.'

'Yeah.' Morrow scratched her face, a little too hard. Just because his father was in the force didn't mean she was less committed.

'If you grow up in it,' he frowned at the windscreen, 'you know it, a bit more maybe. Know what it's really like, what's likely to happen at the end of a career. New recruits, they're idealistic, yet to lose faith with it.' He was talking about her.

'I'm not a new recruit,' said Morrow.

'No, but you're not old police family, are you? I mean, in

some ways you're lucky because you'll have to find those things out yourself. Just ... it can be a bit of a shocker when you do.'

'TJF,' she said sullenly.

He nodded. 'TJF. But me, I know what to take on and when to make my moves, I know the limits of the job. You don't have that killer instinct ...'

She suddenly found herself confused. 'Killer instinct?'

'How to work the system to get the job done right.'

She didn't understand but had a bad feeling about the way it was going.

'Anyway,' he said, as if that had cleared all that up, 'if Omar is Bob, why does anyone think he's got two mill kicking about? He's twenty-one, he's been studying since leaving school, doesn't have a job. Why would they think he has millions of pounds?'

'Oh, I dunno.' She looked at Bannerman, saw him concentrating on the road and realised that the conversation hadn't bothered him at all. Killer instinct. Somehow she felt he was telling her that he was indeed, as she suspected, a complete self-serving arsehole.

He looked out at the road. 'This junction's a pain in the arse.'

'Go right,' she said quickly, keen to maintain the forward momentum in the conversation. 'Round the side there to the left.'

Bannerman followed her directions into the visitors' car park in front of the infirmary, found a spot near the far wall and stopped. He took the key out and stepped out of the car into the wind coming off the bare junction in front of them.

Still suspicious, she opened her door, climbed out and shut it, watching him carefully over the roof of the car. He was squinting at the Battlefield Rest, a restaurant in a converted Edwardian tram depot. 'Looks like a seaside ice-cream parlour or something. Why's it called the Battlefield Rest?'

'You don't know this area?'

'No.'

'Mary Queen of Scots fought her last battle here. Against her son's army. She lost.'

'What were they fighting about?'

'Religion.' She stopped to frown. 'I think.'

He pointed to the little rotunda. 'And she rested in there?'

The tram stop was built during the Great War, over three hundred years after Queen Mary was executed. Morrow looked for a note of humour on his face but found nothing. 'No,' she said, 'she just sent in for a lasagne.'

Bannerman didn't react. He turned and walked into the hospital. Morrow wished she had a pal at work to tell the story to.

The lobby was busy but the lifts were efficient, sucking in groups gathering in front of them and spiriting them off to different floors. Bannerman checked his notes as they stepped into a lift. They were crammed in next to a woman and her very fat toddler in a pushchair. The fair-haired girl was three, sleeping, her head dropped forward onto her chest, dressed in clothes that didn't quiet fit her. A roll of belly peeked out from under her T-shirt. Morrow noticed the back of the pram was littered with sweetie wrappers and empty juice bottles.

The mother herself looked nippy, a skinny strip of anxious annoyance, hair yanked up into a ponytail, smelling of stale cigarette smoke and perfume.

Morrow saw Bannerman looking at the wrappers and frown a reproach at the mother. The doors opened on the second floor and the woman shoved the pram out, spitefully bumping it over the metal ridges, jerking the fat sleeping child around in her chair.

Bannerman tutted when the doors shut and muttered, 'Feed your kids shit like that . . .'

Morrow didn't join in the cosy sanctimony. Bannerman didn't have kids. He knew fuck all about it. 'Have you got the statements there?'

Bannerman opened the folder and pulled out three sheets. One was Aleesha's statement. She had been out of it and said nothing. The second one was Sadiqa's, taken at the hospital, probably while Aleesha was in the operating theatre. Sadiqa had been in the kitchen, heard a noise, went to see what it was. The lift doors opened on floor five but Morrow continued to read, stepping out into the lobby, standing to the side as she quickly scanned the notes. Men with guns threatened them, pulled her up the hall. Aleesha was shot. Then Omar came in and she screamed and then they took Aamir.

When Morrow looked up she was smiling. 'She says they were asking for Bob.'

Bannerman sighed and conceded, 'I know. I only got it this morning. Feel like an arse now.'

She gave him back the statement as they approached the ward doors, walking slightly behind him, a disingenuous gesture of companionship. She wanted him to trust her. When she reached forward to press the security buzzer on the door she saw that he was smiling quietly to himself. It worried her. A wash of exhaustion swept over her, shift change from night to day was always painful.

A voice on the intercom interrupted her train of thought; 'Yes?' A young nurse in glasses was looking out at them from an office a hundred yards down the corridor.

'DS Bannerman and DS Morrow from Strathclyde Police. We're here to talk to Aleesha Anwar.'

'OK.' The nurse reached back into the door and pressed a button to release the lock, walking down to meet them as they entered.

Two coppers had been ordered to stay outside Aleesha's room and were stationed in the corridor, one sitting on a chair in the corridor, the other leaning against the wall facing the door, watching the nurse's arse as she passed him.

Morrow and Bannerman walked into the ward corridor, getting out their warrant cards. The nurse gave them a brief glance. 'Anwar's in IC.' Without a word of explanation she turned on her white heels and led them to the room opposite the nurse's station.

A large window looked into the room from the corridor. A tangle of wires was threaded through a hole in the wall, plugged into monitors sitting on a metal trolley in the corridor, where the nurses could watch the numbers. The DCs standing outside stood upright when they approached. Bannerman told them to go and take a ten-minute piece break. They thanked him and shuffled off out the doors.

Through the glass they could see Aleesha was asleep, propped upright against puffed-up pillows. Her left hand was heavily bandaged but the shape still discernibly distorted: three of her fingers were missing, only the index finger still clearly outlined, the others stubs after the first knuckle. The dressings on the stubs of her two middle fingers were discoloured with a translucent yellow fluid.

She was terribly pretty, Morrow thought, young and vulnerable, with the perfect skin and effortless grace that no one ever appreciates until they've lost them.

They stepped into the room. The lights were calmingly low but vicious strip lighting outside the room kept it bright and clinical. On the nearside of the bed, between the window and the patient, Sadiqa was dozing in a big purple recliner armchair, covered to her neck in a pink cellular blanket. She was very overweight, a heavy wattle of fat pooling around her chin, her massive round stomach splayed to the sides.

The chair was upholstered in waterproof plastic and reclined so that the footrest rose and the back dropped down. Morrow had slept on those chairs and knew how fantastically uncomfortable they were.

Sadiqa half opened her eyes, saw their feet, realised they weren't hospital staff and looked up.

'Mrs Anwar, I'm DS Bannerman and this is DS Morrow from CID. We were at your house last night.'

Befuddled with sleep Sadiqa's hand rose to her chest under the blanket. Morrow stepped forward and reached out to shake. 'I don't think I met you last night, Mrs Anwar, I'm Alex Morrow.'

Sadiqa reached her hand out from under the cover. She was still wearing her nightie. 'Nice to meet you ...' said Sadiqa, lost for forms of address in the strange circumstance.

'We wondered if we could have a word with you?'

She tried to sit up suddenly, as if she had just remembered. 'Aamir?'

'No.' Alex held her hand up. 'We haven't come with any news. We just wanted to ask you about a couple of details that might help us find him.'

'OK, let me get ...' Sadiqa struggled to get out of the chair. She kicked her heels at the footrest but her weight pinned her to the chair. She had to use her arms to hoist her bottom off the chair and haul the chair into the upright position. She was embarrassed, gestured to her stomach, blaming it as if it was a separate entity. 'Fat,' she said and stood up.

The blanket fell to the floor revealing her pink nightie, still splattered with dried blood. She slipped her feet into her shoes.

'Wouldn't you like to change, Mrs Anwar?' said Morrow.

'Into what?' Sadiqa wasn't pleased by that. 'I haven't anything to change into.'

'Couldn't your sons bring you something?'

It was impertinent, a reproach to those only Sadiqa had the right to reproach. She gave Morrow a steely stare and muttered something about the baby.

'I'm sure it's been a huge shock for all of you,' said Bannerman, making it all right.

'Yes.' She looked at him. 'Yes, it has.'

She glanced at her sleeping daughter and ushered them both out ahead of her into the corridor, pulling the door closed behind her. They stood outside the window, Sadiqa tugging them around by the elbows so that their backs were to the window and she could keep her eye on her daughter.

Bannerman looked around for a chair. 'Couldn't we go and sit down somewhere?'

'No,' she crossed her arms over her chest, 'I'm not leaving. We'll stay where I can see her. You can ask me questions here, can't you?' It was the accent from the emergency call: prim, proper, like a fifties movie siren.

'Well,' Bannerman looked back at Aleesha sleeping in the bed, 'we'd really prefer to speak to you so that you can concentrate, maybe somewhere private. We could get the nurses—'

'No.' Sadiqa had her hand up to his face, as if she was ordering a child to sit down again. She saw the expressions on their faces and her knee buckled in dismay. 'Please excuse me, my manners . . .' She covered her mouth with a hand, drew a shuddering breath in, nodded as if she had decided something. 'OK. OK.' She dropped her hand, stood straight and looked at them. 'Sorry. I'll concentrate. Ask me anything.'

Bannerman looked at his notebook. 'Just going over what you said last night . . . who were the men asking for?'

She nodded, as if affirming a decision she had already made. 'Yes. They asked for *Bob*.'

Morrow was surprised. 'You sure?'

'Yes.' It was hard for her to say that and she blinked as she did, nodding significantly. '*Bob*.'

Morrow was impressed. Sadiqa seemed to understand the significance of what she was saying, knew there was an alternative to telling the truth and implicating her son, but she was doing the right thing anyway. She clasped her hands over her bulging stomach and nodded at them to ask her another.

'OK.' Morrow looked at Bannerman but he was pretending to look at the statement again. 'Can you tell us the course of what happened?'

Sadiqa hesitated, still staring at her daughter. 'What happened chronologically?'

'Yes.'

Sadiqa took a breath and stepped back. 'We were in the house, I was in the kitchen. I hear shouting and go out into the hall to see what it is. There are two men there, I didn't . . . I wear reading glasses, I was reading in the kitchen, and I took my glasses off, didn't have my other ones, when I went out to the hall I couldn't see properly, just shapes by the door. One of them,' she circled her wrist indignantly with her hand, 'he grabbed me and dragged me back up the hall. 'They were asking for Bob. Shouting. The shot went off . . .' She looked up to where the wall would have been, reliving the shock. 'Then Omar comes in, one of them shouts, "You're Bob," and to Mohammed, "You're Bob."' Sadiqa came out of her trance and her eyes focused on them. 'Then he grabbed Aamir and left. The other one followed him out.'

'What were you reading?' asked Morrow. She seemed confused. 'In the kitchen,' said Morrow. 'You said you were reading, what was it?'

'Oh, a test: it was a poetry collection. *The Rattle Bag*.'

Morrow liked her honesty. 'Who in the family is called Bob?'

Sadiqa averted her gaze. 'No one: Billal, Omar and Aleesha.'

'No, Sadiqa,' said Morrow softly, 'I didn't say which of your children, I said who.'

Sadiqa nodded sadly at the floor, understanding that they knew already. 'Don't make ...' The conflict was unbearable. The fat on her cheeks began to tremble.

Morrow threw a hand out, cuffing her clumsily on the forearm, ''S OK.'

Sadiqa nodded at her arm and muttered, 'Thank you.'

''S OK,' she repeated and fell back a step, embarrassed in front of Bannerman at having bottled it and cut the moment off.

Sadiqa rubbed her nose and looked up. 'But where is my Aamir?'

'We don't know.' Bannerman took over.

'Is he alive, do you think?'

'We don't know that either. We're trying very hard to find him but we need your help,' said Bannerman who didn't seem to appreciate how much she had helped them already and how conflicted she was about it. Them and us. Typical cop. 'Omar is sometimes called Bob, isn't he?'

She bit her lip, couldn't look at them. 'I don't, well, I call him Omar. That's the name we chose ...'

Morrow would have thought less of her if she had given her son up happily. 'Sadiqa, how long have you been married?'

She had to think about it, moving her lips as she counted.

Aamir wasn't one for big anniversaries then. 'Twenty-eight years.'

'How old are you?'

'Forty-eight.' She didn't have to think about that.

'Aamir's older than you?'

'By twenty-two years. Met him when I was sixteen.' She glanced in at Aleesha. 'Her age.'

'Was it arranged?'

'God, no. I fell for him. My parents asked me to wait until after uni. We're not all that traditional, to be honest.'

'But Billal and Meeshra . . .'

'Yeah, Billal asked for an arranged marriage. That was his idea. Wanted his wife to come and live with us and all that whole . . . thing. That set-up. Young people nowadays, they're a bit disenchanted. Harking back to a past that isn't even really ours, you know? They think our generation are a bit slack.' She wrinkled her nose. 'Bit multicultural.'

'How's it working out with Meeshra?'

She cleared her throat, and focused on Aleesha. 'Good and bad. Meesh is nice enough but she's a stranger coming into a close family. Can be tricky. Still, the baby's in the house so we can see him all the time. And their room's far enough away from ours so we don't even get woken.' She smiled at her joke and Morrow smiled back.

'What did you do at uni?'

'English Literature. But I never did anything with it. Wanted to marry Aamir.' She sucked her cheeks in, a micro expression that Morrow couldn't read. Frustration maybe. Not a good thing anyway.

'A strong-willed girl,' said Morrow.

'Very. You don't understand until you're a parent yourself. Try to be firm but, you know . . . Because my parents didn't think he was good enough for me that made him especially beguiling.' She looked in at Aleesha again. 'Stubborn girls. Family trait.'

'She a bit of a handful too?'

'Aleesha?' Sadiqa looked adoringly in the window at her sleeping daughter. 'Thinks she knows everything.'

'Boy trouble?'

'Oh, no, I don't think so ...' she looked bewildered and a little hurt. 'Her major problem seems to be that I'm an idiot.'

'Aleesha doesn't wear traditional dress?'

'No.' Sadiqa smiled to herself, a little proud. 'No, she's ... No, she won't. She's an atheist.'

'What does her dad think about that?'

'Horrified. In front of her. Thrilled when she's out of the room.'

'He's not a disciplinarian, then?'

'Aamir?' She half giggled at the suggestion, remembered he was in mortal danger and became tearful. 'God, no, he's ... a nag, a worrier but not heavy handed. He's ...' She looked for a moment as if she might cry but caught herself, raised a hand to cover her face, hiding for a moment. 'Sorry.'

Morrow reached out a hand to her arm but didn't touch her. 'No, don't, it's awful ...'

Tired of being excluded by the women, Bannerman blurted, 'Why wasn't Aamir good enough for you?'

She took a breath, pulled herself upright. 'Poor Ugandan refugee. Had nothing but a strong work ethic.'

'And twenty-eight years later ...' Morrow left it open.

A happy woman would have grinned and nodded, smugly affirmed the rightness of her choice. Sadiqa smiled weakly. 'Yeah, it's a long time, right enough.' Absent-mindedly her hand strayed to the crusted blood on the front of her nightie and she looked down, suddenly distressed, taking her hand away and looking at it.

'Haven't the boys made it in yet?'

'No,' she said. 'No, they can't come because of the baby. I phoned them though. *I* phoned *them* because you can't even have a phone on in here. It interferes with the machines or something.'

The boys could have phoned the ward and been put through to their mother, Morrow knew that.

'Well, maybe it's best if they don't come up anyway.' Morrow touched her arm. 'It's bound to be quite frightening.'

She had given her an excuse and Sadiqa appreciated it. 'Yes.' She looked around. 'It is frightening. Very frightening. I'd actually rather they didn't ...'

'Would you like us to bring you some clothes from home?'

'No, no.' Sadiqa softened. 'No, I'll go home later in a cab, get some food. The food's disgusting here. They cook vegetables by boiling them for an hour ...'

'How's Aleesha doing?' asked Bannerman, shutting his notebook when he saw the coppers being let back into the ward by the nurse.

'She's not dying.' She raised her eyes in a silent prayer of thanks. 'Stable. Probably move her out of intensive care today. Half a foot to the left and she'd be—'

'Oh that's great,' he interrupted. 'Well, listen, we'll leave you with these officers and we'll go downstairs and make a phone call. When we come back in a minute we'll try to talk to her.'

They weren't coming back. He was keeping Sadiqa on point.

'OK.' Sadiqa nodded, watching uncertainly as Bannerman shuffled off to talk to one of the officers. She looked at Morrow.

'Thank you very much, Mrs Anwar.' Morrow nodded, letting her know she understood what she had done.

'*Please*,' said Sadiqa desperately. '*Please* find him.'

'We'll do our best.'

Sadiqa went back into the intensive-care room, resuming her purple seat, watching them anxiously through the window as she pulled her pink blanket up protectively over her chest.

Bannerman was muttering orders to the coppers. 'I don't want that woman using a phone until I give the say-so. Not talking on the ward phone, not using a mobile in the loo, not nipping downstairs to buy biscuits, understand?'

Through the intensive care window Morrow could see Sadiqa sitting tense, staring at her daughter, gnawing on a thumbnail.

20

When they opened the door to Shugie's bedroom the little man was sitting as they had left him, upright on the bed, but something was wrong: the corners of the pillowcase met his corners. He looked too tidy. He'd taken it off and put it back on again, which was bad, but his posture troubled them more: he sat confidently, shoulders down, head up, facing them, not cowering. His head swivelled as he looked from one to the other through the pillowcase, his bearing so upright they both felt inexplicably afraid, as if it was a rehearsal for meeting them in court. It was creepy because his bearing made him seem human.

Eddy looked at Pat, glanced at the crack in the curtains, looked back at the confident man. Pillowcase knew the police had been there. He had been at the window and seen them or heard them downstairs and thought they were coming to save him, banged on the floor deliberately to fuck them up.

Pat could feel Eddy's rage rise like a scream in a pitch too high to hear. Eddy stepped towards the bed, teeth bared, out of control and grabbed the man by the forearm, shaking him hard, toppling him face down into the mattress, twisting his arm up his back hard, the way the police did. The old man gave a squeal, 'no' or 'ah', but it was high anyway, shocked, not what he had expected. Pinning him face down on the bed, Eddy raised his other elbow high and jabbed a short punch into his kidney. The old man buckled and collapsed, groaning, the gush of air muffled in the mattress. Eddy punched again and again, hitting the soft skin on his back, missing the ribs deliberately, going for the soft tissue.

Pat looked away for part of the attack. Then he thought Eddy might see him looking elsewhere and forced his eyes on to the pillowcase. It twitched out a response to the blows.

Eddy stood unsteadily on the bed, over the body, saliva flecked on his chin, panting like a child on a bouncy castle. He was fighting off a smile. Pat watched as he wiped it away with the back of his hand. It was odd to enjoy it so much. A bit sadistic. You could kill a man doing that to him.

He looked down at the pillowcase, thinking vaguely about internal bleeding and the mysteries of the human body. If Eddy killed it he would have to sort out getting rid of the body, Pat wasn't going to do it, he hadn't laid a finger on him. But then Eddy would probably give a body to Shugie or some other arsehole and they'd get done for it.

As an afterthought the old man gave a twitch, raising his buttocks up in a futile attempt to get away, and he slumped back, face down on the bed.

Suddenly stern, Eddy gestured to the other side of the bed. Pat shuffled over and they took an arm each and dragged the pillowcase off the bed, trying to stand him up on his cloth legs. He buckled forwards. Twice more they tried to stand him up and both times his knees flopped hopelessly outwards. It was getting worrying. On the final try he took his weight, just one knee buckled, swinging a circle but coming back. Eddy nodded Pat to the door.

They dragged it on its toes out to the landing, through the mildew cloud at the bathroom door, yanking it, giving it contradictory signals about which way to go. By the time they reached the top of the stairs the pillowcase was crying and muttering, sputtering and gasping for air between sobs.

Eddy stopped, looked down to the front hall and back to Pat. Pat could feel warmth through the sleeve, human warmth, but he looked down at the hall carpet and thought of Aleesha, of the depth of her grief for her father, of slipping his arm around her shoulders and her silky hair sliding across his bare arm. His hand gliding around her shoulder, his fingertips memorising every hair, her sharp shoulder blades, vertebrae, the powdered softness of her skin. She would need him then. Desire made him peel his fingers away from the arm but as soon as he did he felt himself diminish and was ashamed.

Eddy took a step forward still holding the arm, yanking hard but the pillowcase stood firm, upright, looked at him angrily. It yanked its arm away indignantly. He knew there were stairs there.

A clatter of feet made them look down: Malki was running up towards them, lifting his knees high, smiling. 'Brought the car round the back,' he panted, stopping two steps down, holding the banister and swinging down a step again.

Eddy glared at him.

'Bloke's already heard my voice,' explained Malki, a hand on the wall and one on the banister, barring the way. 'I already spoke to him, when I give him the sweeties. He can't eat them 'cause they're not halal.'

Somehow the moment had passed. They couldn't do it in front of Malki. In front of Malki would risk a long conversation about right and wrong, a dispute; he would ask about their motives, talk about the pillowcase as a person. Foiled. Pat felt proud of his wee junkie cousin.

Eddy motioned for Pat to take the stairs ahead of him and followed him down, pinching the old man's elbow tight as he led him roughly down the steep steps.

Shugie was dozing on the damp settee. A second blue plastic bag was sitting open and next to him with three new cans in it. The previous bag of cans lay empty, the tins discarded on the floor.

'Dunno if three be enough,' said Malki. 'But it's all they had left in the shop.'

Pat shrugged. He didn't want to speak too much in front of the pillowcase. Carefully he reached around to his wallet and took out a twenty quid note. He looked at it, calculated that it was probably enough for an alki to buy drink but not enough for a really greedy drinker to spend a night in the pub with other people. He sat it on top of the cans in the bag.

They formed a strange parade, passing through the living room to the kitchen and out the back door: Malki ahead with his hurried junkie speed-walk, Pat behind him, the pillowcase puffing and jerking as he was prodded and shoved by Eddy following behind. Malki hesitated at the kitchen door, waiting for Eddy's signal. Eddy nodded and Malki opened it, letting fresh air into the festering corridor of bin bags.

They had been in the house for almost ten hours, breathing in every nuanced smell a human being can make without dying and the back garden seemed impossibly lush and fresh. Each in turn stopped on the back doorstep to take a grateful breath.

It was a jungle: grass grew long and dark here, an enclosing wall of deep green waxy hedges exploding upwards, bursting in every conceivable direction, swallowing the light. As the wind caressed the blades the grass winked its silver undersides.

The Lexus had been driven into the long grass so that the boot was facing the kitchen door and Malki had left a trail through the grass from the driver's door to the back step, from the boot to the passenger door as he emptied anything from it that might be used as a weapon. Pat followed the path to the boot, popped it and stepped back.

Eddy took his time, glancing spitefully at the old man. He

seemed unsatisfied that the pillowcase was walking stooped, that he was limping on one foot, flinching at the pain in his back. Swinging him by the elbow Eddy turned the pillowcase so that his back was to the boot and punched him in the groin, winding him so that he doubled up. Eddy stood up with a snigger and looked at Malki and Pat. Malki looked away. Pat smiled weakly. Oblivious to the animosity, Eddy smirked again and, as if telling a joke, put his hand flat on the old man's head and, with the smallest push, dropped him into the boot.

The excellent suspension echoed the fall of the old man's body. Eddy looked around for support, smiling, lips parted. Pat and Malki were from a wild sprawling family, composed mostly of ineffectually worried mothers and bad apples, a model of complex social problems, but it took a special kind of man not to empathise with a punch in the balls. They wouldn't meet his eye. Malki even tutted at the car.

Angry at having measured his violence wrong, yet again, Eddy picked up the feet in dirty slippers and dropped them into the boot, swinging the old man onto his side, and slammed it shut as if hoping to trap some small something between the metal lips.

Malki looked for Pat to say something. 'In the car, son,' said Pat and Malki obliged, shutting the door carefully behind him.

Eddy looked angrily at the back of Malki's head. 'Your Malki's a twat.' Pat glared at him. 'OK, I know he's your cousin, but he fucking *is* a twat.'

Pat's eyes were open wide in warning. The pillowcase could hear them. The wind hissed through the grass as Eddy looked away and blushed. He couldn't seem to stop fucking up. Pat turned away and walked around to the passenger door. The pillowcase knew two names now; Eddy had said them out loud and told him that two of them were cousins and so now Eddy couldn't let him walk, he'd have to kill him and leave Aleesha fatherless, rudderless, looking for love in all the wrong places. Pat could be one of those places.

As he opened the passenger door and slipped inside the car his chest was warm, full of thoughts of sunny places and hair on pillows.

21

Morrow and Bannerman were parked in Alison Street, looking across the road to two big shop windows.

The restaurant didn't have a name painted above the door, it wasn't listed in the phone book, but everyone knew it as Kasha's. It didn't even look like a restaurant; it looked more like a community centre because of the modest furnishings and utilitarian decor. The seats were moulded grey plastic, the tables wood effect tops with steel legs. Even the wallpaper was slightly grey, a dado rail hinted at a different pattern but mirrored the dull colours in the rest of the room. The food service area was a modest four-foot sandwich bar, a fridge full of cans of mango juice, bottles of water and glass jars of mango lassie.

Morrow knew that later in the evening it would be full of men eating, sipping coffees and drinking fresh lassie out of long glasses, but it was Ramadan and the men were sitting around empty tables, keeping each other company but not eating.

One table was conspicuously eating, though. The four men were sitting at a table away from the window near the dimly lit back of the shop, their table shamelessly strewn with plates of food. A fifth man stood in the doorway, dressed like the others. He stood with his hands crossed over his groin, watching the street. He wasn't the biggest of the men but Morrow knew him from his reputation. King Bo was a nasty, cold boy. He could break bones to order: one finger, two legs, even a thumb, which is a hard bone to break, did it without a flicker and he was fast too. But King

Bo was a sideshow, a soldier. The men at the table were the main event.

There were four of them, all big, all dressed in T-shirts and tracksuits, all frowning as they worked their way through their food. The Shields bosses, and at their centre was Ibby Ibrahim.

'Only be a minute,' said Morrow and got out. He let her go alone without a fight in the end. Ibby was a good contact, the sort of contact to boast about to other officers, a name to drop and he was letting her have it for the good of the case. It was big of him and she found that, reluctantly, despite herself, Morrow was starting to hate him a fraction less.

She shut the car door and stepped across the empty street, looking King Bo in the face as she approached. He reared his head back. His hair was cut short and gelled into a fin, the quiff tip matching his pointy chin. Afflicted with a slight squint he gave her his best mean look. She looked down to pull out her warrant card as she approached, and when she looked back she found him grinning.

'Nah,' drawled King Bo, 'that's not a pass in here, lady.'

She stopped four feet from him, her heels hanging off the edge of the pavement, and looked around. Ibby could see her standing in the street but she didn't look at him. He might tell her to fuck off. She hadn't seen him for twenty years, he might not even remember her.

She could just turn and leave, let the past be the past. Her Bob lead was already panning out and she was making herself vulnerable coming here. She was making herself traceable back to her maiden name, from there back to her family and she'd worked so hard to shed it all. But King Bo leaned backwards into the shop, listened to something and then bent towards her. 'OK, aye, you're in.' He stepped back in the dark, flicked his hand to send her to the table of men, avoided her eye as if they were letting her in against his advice.

Morrow was the only woman in the place and her top was low enough cut to show half an inch of cleavage. She walked in feeling like a stripper entering a monastery.

'Go.' King Bo pointed her towards Ibby.

She walked over but stopped a few feet short of the table and looked at him. 'Hello.'

Ibby looked up at her. He was a big man, brooding, wide shoulders, big fists. His nose had been broken many times, the bridge of it ruined. He was dressed in a tracksuit as if it was pyjamas, no attempt to make an impression or sway an audience. Everyone he met already knew about him. Ibby looked at her cheap work suit, looked at her face. 'Heard about you,' he said, chewing a mouthful of dark green sag aloo. Morrow could almost feel the mustard seeds popping on her tongue.

'How're you, Ibby?'

'No bad.' Ibby tore off a handful of virgin white flat bread from a plate in the middle of the table and used it to pinch a mouthful of spinach from his plate and put it in his mouth. 'How's Dimples?'

She shrugged, aware of Bannerman watching outside, hoping she looked professional through the window.

Ibby glanced at her cleavage and pointed, drawing the attention of the other men to it. 'Evening all,' he said. The boys sitting next to him laughed, not really understanding, she felt, but toadying to their boss none the less.

When the sycophantic laughter died down she spoke again. 'Your nose . . .'

'I was in a accident,' he said too loud, too flat.

'Some accident.'

He chewed the mouthful, smiling to himself and Morrow found herself smiling too. It was nice to see him again. It

204

was nice that he wasn't dead. Nice that neither of them were mad or in prison or jagging up.

Ibby grinned back, mustard seeds littering his teeth. 'Fuck, man, ye went polis?'

She shrugged. 'Couldn't handle the accident rate on the other side,' she said and looked out at Bannerman in the car. He wasn't looking at her; he seemed to be wiping the dust from the dashboard with a tissue.

Ibby picked up a paper napkin and rubbed his meaty fingers with it, ripping it into bits. He sat back and tipped his head at her. 'Go on, then. Say whatever.'

'OK, erm, you've heard about the hostage-taking last night?'

He nodded at his dinner.

'They were looking for Omar Anwar. For Bob.'

His face was blank, neither listening nor contradicting.

'*Bob*. You called him that.'

'I never called him Bob.'

'I don't mean you personally, Ibby, I mean *yous*.'

He felt for something in his teeth with his tongue, couldn't get it and picked at it with his pinkie fingernail. 'Hmm.'

'Bob?'

'Hmm.' He agreed. 'Some people call him Bob.'

'Only some people?'

Ibby looked up at her. 'No,' he said carefully.

She understood. 'OK. Anything you want to share about the events of last night?'

'Tell ye what, yous must be stuck to come here.'

'We could go to the community leaders but they'll just give us a load of, you know.'

'*Community* leaders? We're community leaders.' The men around him nodded smugly. 'Oh, *legitimate* community leaders, ye mean? Like MPs or councillors or whatever?'

The men were smiling, less at what he was saying than the tone of his voice. Ibby was enjoying himself. She wondered if he knew he was surrounded by arseholes. 'Well, *we're* a community, *we're* leaders, this table.' He pressed his finger down hard on the flat bread. 'This *table*'s a community.'

He was talking shit so she took her chance and interrupted him, 'Yeah, so anyway, you know anything about last night then or what?'

'Nothing,' he said flatly and meant it.

He looked to see if she doubted him. It was the angle as much as anything, him looking up at her. His face had broadened, darkened, but the eyes were the same. Deep brown, hooded. She couldn't see Ibby now. Instead she saw the child who sat next to her in first year of secondary school, the wee boy who scratched himself a lot, was small for his age. She was inexplicably fond of Ibby at the time, felt protective when he was asked anything by unthinking teachers, because he knew nothing. He was only in her school briefly. They sent him away after he nearly killed a boy.

The child was in their year and had a thing about Ibby's sister. He probably fancied the girl, Morrow thought in hindsight, but he'd got to that stage a month or so before everyone else, so that his chasing her seemed bizarre. Ibby thought it was a threat. Morrow could still see Ibby's fingers threaded through the boy's hair. His deep brown eyes were wet as he ground the boy's broken nose into the asphalt playground floor.

She understood him perfectly back then, the disproportionate wild quality of his violence. Social work got involved, she'd heard, and Ibby was taken away and never came back. They were all afraid of the social work, those children, the ones who stood, hands hanging by their sides and calmly watched Ibby do that, the ones whose parents didn't come up to the school after and demand answers. They kept their heads down because to get noticed was to disappear. When the teachers came to drag Ibby off, Alex was who he reached for. She managed to wriggle her way through the teachers' legs and touch his hand for a moment. Fingertips reaching for each other through a scuffle of legs. His knuckles were skinned raw.

Morrow said, 'Aamir Anwar's a nice man, isn't he?'

Ibby conceded that Aamir was OK with a dip of his head and a glance at the table top.

'No rumours you want to share?'

'White guys, Glasgow accents. Nothing to do with us.'

'You've got contacts.'

'So have you.' He smiled at his dinner as a plan formed in his mind. 'What station you working out of, then?'

The Young Shields were just head cases. They still had gang fights in the streets. It was all about territory still, they'd never gone professional or money-making. He might imply that he'd like a corrupt police officer on his payroll but Morrow was pretty sure Ibby didn't have a payroll.

'Here and there,' she said. 'Move about.'

He smirked. 'Might come and visit you at your work one day.' He wasn't really talking to her, just showing off to his pals.

'Yeah,' she said. 'Do that.'

'Tell Dimples hello from me.'

Morrow stopped. She hadn't noticed the first time he mentioned Danny because she'd been distracted by Bannerman outside but Ibby had name dropped Dimples twice now and each time he did the fat boy next to him pushed his chin out, proud. A protective familial reflex made her notice, wonder if they'd battered Danny or bettered him somehow. Instinct made her square up to the henchman, but she forced her eyes to the floor. She was being sucked back in, she should leave.

'Take care, Ibby,' she said. 'Try not to have any more accidents.'

She turned to the door when Ibby spoke again, under his breath, 'Hey, anyway, your da ... Sorry he's no well. In the infirmary ... ?'

Morrow read his face. The old man was such a has-been no one would have bothered to pass on the information. Danny must have told him. 'Aye,' she said gently. 'Fuck him, anyway.' She walked away.

King Bo stepped aside when she came to the door, lifting his arm away from her, as if being in the police was something you could catch from social contact.

'Bye bye,' she said pleasantly, and the big gangster sneered to show how hard he was.

She crossed the street back to the car. As she opened the door she looked through the window of Kasha's again. King Bo had a mean face on, arms crossed, looking down the road for invading hordes. Inside Ibby was stuffing bread into his face. She could see under the table that his belly was heavy. He was getting fat. They were all heading for old. She climbed into the car and Bannerman started the engine.

'Well, it wasn't the Shields,' she said.

'We knew that.'

'No. We suspected that. Now we know it definitely wasn't them.'

'You believe the word of a crim?'

'I believe Ibby Ibrahim,' she said as Bannerman pulled out into the road. 'He's too proud to lie.'

He smirked. 'If he's too proud to lie we should get him in for questioning. Clear up half the batterings that went down on the Southside last year.'

'Well, he's honest off the record. On the record he might just be willing to lower himself.'

They drove down Alison Street. Alex watching out of the window, glancing up every crumbling close but not seeing, wondering about Danny and Ibby. Thinking about family prompted her to ask: 'How's your mum?'

'Bad.'

She left it hanging for a moment. 'Sorry.'

'No, she's on the mend, she'll be fine really. She's going to be fine. She's on oxygen and massive doses of antibiotics but she's sitting up and everything.'

'Eating?'

'Eating a bit, yeah.'

'So you don't need compassionate leave?'

'No.'

Morrow slapped her leg. 'Damn!'

Bannerman grinned at the joke. 'You *are* as much of a bitch as they say you are.'

It stung a bit but she hid her hurt and took it in good part. 'Well, you know what they say, it's iceberg bitchiness with me: only ten per cent visible.'

They drove on, smiling away from each other, glad to have what lay between them acknowledged: he got her big case and she wasn't popular. Having ripped their plasters off they sat quietly, letting the air dry the wounds.

Bannerman suddenly veered the car, twitched his hips as if responding to a sudden itch. He pulled his crappy work phone out of his pocket and gave it to her. It was vibrating. Morrow pressed the green button and held it to her ear.

'Bannerman?' It was MacKechnie.

'No, sir, it's Morrow; Bannerman's driving.'

'We've found footage of the car at Harthill. It's a silver Lexus. Hired under a fictitious name. We're looking for it now.'

'Great—'

'The kidnappers called the Anwar house ten minutes ago. Go over on the pretext of picking up the tape, get another look at Bob.'

22

Even from inside the boot Aamir knew that where they were going was worse. The texture of the road beneath became rough. First they were bumping across broken asphalt then on grit, the wheels crunching over small stones, not factory-ground gravel but wild irregular stones.

The driver slowed, saving the car paint from being chipped. Aamir remembered it was a new car, he had smelled it last night. They crawled along the road for more than a mile until Aamir couldn't hear the sounds of any other cars, just the wind buffeting the side and the faint swish of grass, birds.

The car stopped. The engine died. The men in the cabin spoke in short sentences. They got out and opened the boot to the blinding daylight. Someone prodded him to get out, yanked him up by the neck and Aamir scrambled to his feet, felt the wind on his hands and neck, chill and damp on his legs and hands.

A British passport.

They couldn't read, those soldiers, just saw the navy blue cover and knew that they had official sanction to steal, to do whatever they wanted. It was on the way to the airport, one day before the ninety days ran out. His older brother had stayed behind to guard the house. They never saw or heard from him again. Aamir saw his mother sobbing by the roadside, the contents of their suitcase strewn across the red dust of the road, green shirts, photos of ancestors, her meagre jewellery taken.

They all disappeared behind the van and Aamir heard

them: her sobbing and the men laughing awkwardly, the way men do when they see a stripper or talk about sex, a different quality laugh, deep, embarrassed. And he knew before they came around to the road, adjusting their flies, before he saw the blood, that they had fucked his maman. Aamir sat very still in the taxi, staring forward, straight through the soldier sitting on the taxi bonnet smoking a cigarillo, knowing they would be killed.

She fell back into the taxi next to Aamir, sari pressed tight over her mouth and didn't look at him. One of the soldiers shut the door after her, hung in the window and touched her hair because he could, running it between his thumb and finger as if it was material he was thinking about buying for his wife.

Aamir felt the cold Scottish wind buffet him again and braced himself, cowering, his chin on his chest. Men like these men did not drive to the countryside for no reason. They were going to kill him. He shut his eyes to pray and, from a deep dark place, a small bubble of honest emotion rose to his chest, an old feeling, a puff of African dust and the smell of cigarillos. The feeling was urgent and fresh, unadulterated by memory. He had been running from this small bubble for thirty years, suppressing it with prayers and work and worry, with children and home improvements and food. A puff of dust from the November road to Entebbe airport. Under the pillowcase Aamir opened his eyes in shock. Facing death his last thought was honest and pure. It was relief.

In Scotland a hand pulled him roughly by the arm, so that he staggered wildly over the uneven road of shattered concrete, he tumbled forwards, over and over, around a big building that blocked the wind, through a high open door into shadows. Inside smelled damp and stale, of cold and mud and wet on the walls. It sounded like a tall, wide room.

They walked Aamir through the hall, deeper and deeper into the gathering darkness, away from the door and the sound of the wind. Leading him calmly now, across metal pathways with a pattern on it, nonslip, he could feel it through his slipper soles. Silent, they took him over wooden planks that were not fixed into the ground, rocking under his weight. Up a steep set of clanging metal steps, they kicked the back of his heels, making him lift his feet and step through a lipped doorway.

It wasn't a room. The air smelled of dusty iron. His footsteps were deadened. The sound of his own breathing echoed back at him like an ambush. Aamir tried to make sense of it: the floor was concave, he was standing in a big iron tube. Looking down at the ground beneath his pillowcase and in the light from the doorway, all he could see was a crumbling carpet of rust, red sheets that fell to dust under his feet, red like the road to Entebbe.

His arm was let go, the men backed away. Aamir shuffled around to face them, turned his palms up, lifting them in welcome to the coming close. The men shuffled on the metal steps, one of them going down, another dragging something. Something metal. A heavy metal door, rust resisting their efforts to pull it shut.

No. They had to kill him.

Aamir stepped towards them, hands out now, a beggar. They couldn't leave him with this acid desire to be gone.

'PLEA—' He stepped towards them but the door slammed shut. All was darkness. A bolt ground closed on the outside of the door. They meant to leave him in here.

Reckless, trying to force their hand, Aamir yanked the pillowcase off his head but it made no difference: the dark was absolute. He could hear the distant thump of feet on metal as the men outside walked away.

Young again, on the road to the airport, a hand on the

hot plastic of the taxi's back seat and the smell of indifferent cigarillos. He'd stayed in the taxi and let them have her, listened to them laughing as they watched one another fuck her, just so that he could live. Pointless. He could never touch her again, never forgave her, felt soiled and tired for every waking moment after that. He had traded her honour for a life he didn't want.

Aamir threw his head back and screamed, a strangled roar that echoed back, knocking him to his knees in the brutal inky dark.

23

He'd say he forgot if they caught him. Forgot to stay in. No big deal, but Shugie walked faster than usual along the road and he kept his head down too, as if he didn't have a distinctive puff of white hair and wasn't the only guy in an electric-blue leather bomber jacket shuffling down to Brian's Bar, as if he could make himself invisible through force of will.

Still, he felt relief as he stepped through the cordon of smokers gathered around the door and his fingers fell on the familiar grit of the dirty swing door. He stepped into Brian's, the metal sole protectors on his cowboy boots tip-tapping on the stone floor, and made his way to the bar. A free seat.

Senga was serving, her hands as soft as her eyes. She always dressed in T-shirts she got free, whether with cash and carry purchases or from the brewery. Today she was wearing one with a circle on it, advertising cancer. It clung to her hips, hung loose around her shoulders. She was eating cheese and onion crisps and slowly pulled her hand out of the crinkling bag, yawning her mouth open to get them in whole, her heavy eyes watching the bar for clients, for trouble, but never judging.

Without wasting the effort of walking down to greet Shugie she tipped her chin, asking if he wanted what she thought he wanted. Shugie blinked back a yes. She slopped over to the taps and drew a half of heavy, poured a cheap whisky, and sauntered over, used a sour cloth to moisten the stickiness on the bar in front of him and set the drinks up.

The twenty pound note impressed her and she didn't try to hide the fact. She gave the note a respectful nod and held it up to the light to make sure it was for real. She touched his hand when she gave him back the change. Senga didn't always do that.

Shugie looked at his drinks glittering in the glasses in front of him, like old times, glory days. He had change in one pocket, fags in the other. Sunshine filtered in through the dirty windows and Senga settled back into her packet of crisps. The whisky fired first his mouth and then his throat. Shugie Nirvana.

As he raised the beer chaser to his mouth, tipping his head back to receive his communion, his eyes fell on the silent television in the corner. Sky News. A red tickertape along the bottom of the screen. Glasgow businessman taken hostage. Police appeal for information. Shugie knew about that. He was still working scams, pulling strokes, keeping moody. He was still who he thought he was. Smiling to himself he put the glass on the bar, he caught Senga's eye, gave her a wink.

She couldn't have done it if she tried: in exactly the same moment, with perfect precision and without rehearsal, Senga simultaneously tutted flirtatiously and farted at him.

Billal had known that the police were coming. He opened the door solemnly, inviting them into the quiet house.

Bannerman muttered some pleasantries but Billal didn't respond. He shut the door behind them and they noticed how quiet the house was now, how comfy and warm. The hall carpet seemed softer than yesterday, thicker. The door to the bedroom was slightly ajar and they could hear Meeshra snoring softly, napping with her baby.

The only reminder of the night before was the bloody wall and clock. Someone had tried to wash the blood off but they had used hot water, Morrow could tell from the rusty brown smears. A man. Women knew how to wash blood. Never wash blood with hot water, she remembered her mother telling her over her underpants, because it cooks it into the material. It was the only useful bit of information she'd ever given her other than you won't meet your husband at a football match.

Billal gestured them into the front room. The Anwars' living room was a symphony in peach and white, everything ordered, white and silver ornaments carefully spaced along the mantelpiece and a big white-framed mirror above it. Morrow had the impression that no one came in here much. The kitchen was for standing in, the table too small for the whole family. They were not a family who ate together.

Billal waited until they were in and orderly before he spoke: 'The kidnappers actually spoke to my brother, so I'm not really sure what they said really.' He lowered his big square frame gingerly onto the edge of a flouncy settee, the arms and back curved outwards like lips. 'But I have the tape for you.' He held out a black mini cassette. Bannerman took it and dropped it into an evidence bag, fitting it into his pocket. He took out an evidence label and got Billal to sign it.

'What's this for?' he said, writing his name on the line. 'Not signing my life away, am I?'

'No, no,' Bannerman smiled affably, 'it's just so that if we use it in evidence we can say who's had access to the item.'

'I see.' He handed back the tag and looked uncertain. 'I don't know if my brother handled that. He was there ...'

'Did he take it out of the machine or anything?'

'Um, no, I don't think ... Uh, no.' Billal was in charge last night, ordering his brother into the car, telling Meeshra off for breastfeeding badly, but now he seemed quite passive.

'Is your brother here?'

217

'No. He's ...' Nervous, he brushed a non-existent speck from the cushion next to him. 'Omar's gone out.'

'What did the kidnappers ask for?' asked Bannerman, sitting back down carefully on the armchair, trying not to disturb anything.

'Two million by tonight.' Billal searched the glass coffee table in front of him for clues. 'I mean, where the hell do they think we're getting that from?'

'Why do you think they'd ask you for that much?'

He blew his lips out and shrugged hard. 'They must ...' He stopped to think. 'They *must* have the wrong house. I mean, they're looking for someone called "Rob" and two million quid, it must be the wrong house ...'

'*Bob*,' said Morrow.

Billal looked at her. 'Sorry?'

'Bob,' she said flatly. 'They were looking for Bob.'

He flinched, frowned at the tape in the bag, looked out of the window.

'Billal, why did you change it and say Rob?'

He struggled with his thoughts for a moment and when he finally spoke his voice was strained and raw. 'Bob's ... It's my brother's ... sometimes called Bob by some people. We thought it would be better if you ... we thought you'd concentrate on finding my dad.'

'If we weren't suspicious about the family?'

'Well, it's right though, isn't it?' He looked from one to another. 'You'd look harder for my dad if you thought it was a mistake and they'd taken the wrong guy, wouldn't you? We thought ... actually *I* thought, it was my idea to say Rob.' He laughed miserably. 'My idea. Am I in trouble?'

'See,' Bannerman leaned forward sympathetically, 'the prob-jylem now is that we *are* suspicious. Because you lied.'

Billal tried hard to smile but couldn't get his lips to work. 'Sorry,' he whispered. 'My brother's a good kid.'

'I'm sure he is.'

'No, he *is*,' he insisted, arguing with himself. 'He is a good wee guy ...'

'Do you know of anyone who'd target him?'

'No. No, no, no.'

Way too adamant, thought Morrow. 'What does your brother do for a living?' she asked.

Billal had paled slightly and rubbed his face with an open palm as if he wanted to wipe something off. 'Ah, um, well, he's just started a business. Just recently, past couple of months.'

'Doing what?'

'Import/export.'

Import. Export. The words clanged into the room, stunning Morrow. She looked at Bannerman. His mouth had fallen open, his face greying as the blood drained from him. Import/Export. Impossible prosecution.

Bannerman cleared his throat. 'He's importing and exporting what sort of goods?'

'I don't really understand the business myself,' said Billal, 'but it seems to be something to do with computer chips or something?' He looked at them as if they'd know. 'Silicone chips?'

Bannerman nodded at his shoes. 'I see.' He swallowed hard. 'Yes, yes, I see.'

Morrow felt the sudden urge to giggle hysterically. They had all attended the lecture about VAT fraud after the Halligan case collapsed but, unlike many of the presentations they were given, the facts stuck in everyone's mind because of the grotesque amounts of money: a single businessman committing a paper fraud had netted £15 million in a three-month period, a group of three in Birmingham got fifty million in ten months – £1.5 billion cost to taxpayers in one year alone. The numbers were staggering but even more amazing were the clear-up rates: two million recovered in the same period, a tiny portion of the theft.

Everyone hated the cases because the facts were so hard to present to a jury. There was hardly any evidence, the goods were either tiny silicone chips or phones or non-existent. The paper trail evidence was dull, companies and subsidiaries shut down and opened up, directors changed their names and worst of all, most of the perpetrators were small businessmen, shopkeepers, nice men, familiar types, not meaning to hurt anyone, just telling lies on forms. Juries couldn't stomach sending them to jail.

Two million pounds ransom was nothing to a VAT fraudster. Two million was two days' wages. Two million was exactly what unprofessional idiots with no firearms experience would ask a VAT fraudster for, a quick skim from a deep pool. Morrow saw that Bannerman understood and she felt for him suddenly. It was an important case. A clumsy resolution would colour his entire career.

'Hm hm.' Billal nodded at Morrow. 'Listen, thanks for last night, I meant to say, Meesh said you were great with the baby ...' He was thinking about Morrow's breasts, his eyes flickered down and up and he blushed, stumbling over what he was going to say. 'So ... thanks.'

'No problem.' She grinned, not caring, then looked at Bannerman to redirect the questioning.

Bannerman looked a little ill. 'Does your brother have an office? Where does he run the business from?'

'Out the back. There's a shed ...' He looked from one to the other. 'Do you want to ...?'

'Yes.' Bannerman sounded very tired. 'Please.'

Billal stood up and Bannerman and Morrow copied him, following him to the door and out into the hall. He tiptoed through the hall, past the soft call of Meeshra's snores, through the back hallway to the kitchen. There were a couple of other doors leading to other bedrooms but they were shut and the hallway was dark. As they passed through the kitchen Morrow noticed a fat green book on top of the microwave, and stood on her tiptoes to read the title: *The Rattle Bag.*

The back door was old, not replaced by a white plastic UPVC but an old wooden door with glass panels that looked original. Billal took a key from a tin on the worktop and opened it, leaving it wide as he stepped out into the garden. Paving slabs had settled unevenly, sticking up at the corners, sliding into the earth, a graveyard on judgement day. Billal stepped carefully, putting his hands out to steady himself as he walked across, and Bannerman stepped gingerly after him. Morrow hung back. They had looked out here when they searched the house but it was dark and they had all assumed the garden was more shallow than it was. The space was quite deep but a gnarled old tree in the foreground hid a section against the back fence.

Ahead of her Bannerman stood on the corner of a paving stone, tipping the slab down into a puddle of muddy water hidden underneath. A sudden spring of grey water engulfed his beige suede shoe. Bannerman stared at his foot, slowly raised it and shook it out, spitting curses. Morrow padded after him across the choppy garden.

'Bollocks,' he said to his foot.

''S a shit turn of events,' she said kindly. 'Sorry for ye.'

Billal was waiting behind the knobbly tree, in front of a brand new shed of orange wood with a tar paper roof. The same colour as the fence behind it, the shed was well hidden. The door was shut with a big padlock.

'Em, I don't have a key though.'

Bannerman had a wet foot but his shock had subsided. Morrow tried to lighten the mood: 'Know what that's called?' She pointed at the padlock.

Billal guessed, 'A padlock?'

'A homing device for heroin addicts.'

Billal laughed politely and looked at Bannerman. Bannerman wasn't smiling. By now he was not only disappointed at the direction of the case but livid. He snatched the padlock. 'Mr Anwar, we're cutting this off.'

Billal raised his hands and stepped away from the shed door. 'Fair enough,' he said, looking sorry. 'Absolutely fair enough. Wire in.'

Bannerman stepped down the side of the shed and looked in the high window. His mouth tightened miserably and he turned back to Morrow. 'Call and get some SOCOs down here. Tell them to bring evidence bags.'

Morrow didn't mind that he was talking to her like that, or that he was issuing orders. She did exactly as she was asked.

When the cops arrived Morrow and Bannerman stood to the side while they donned their latex gloves and got the metal cutters out of a bag.

'Fuck,' muttered Bannerman, almost to himself.

Morrow touched his forearm. 'I'm so sorry,' she said.

He looked grateful. 'Fuck.'

'It might not be . . .'

'It is,' he said, watching the cops clip the padlock open. 'It's a fucking VAT fraud and it's going to get taken over by the Fraud Squad. And like half their fucking cases it'll end in a ton of paperwork and a hung jury. My arse'll be in a sling.' They pulled their latex gloves on and went for a look in the shed.

Disappointing. No dead bodies or loaded shot guns. Just a small desk, a chair, a filing cabinet at the back and a small hard drive sitting on the floor and a long orange extension flex which presumably could be used to reach back to the house and provide power.

The shed was so new it still smelled of seasoning wood. Omar had left it fairly plain, furnishing it with a small Ikea white plastic desk, a chair and a single grey filing cabinet; second-hand, judging from the dents in the side. A month-by-month wall planner had been pinned to the wall but was devoid of appointments. A sheet of stickers was lying on the desk, event markers. The sheet was complete.

On the desk a Celtic mug with a broken handle was being used for two pencils and a biro. The desk had a thin layer of white dust on it, undisturbed. Even the chair had dust on it.

'Oh.' Billal stood in the doorway looking in, disappointed. 'I thought it would be busier. He spent a lot of time in here, I just thought ... I dunno.' He was looking at the filing cabinet, the only object of promise in the room other than the hard drive. Bannerman followed his gaze and went over to it, opening the top drawer and finding it empty. He opened the second drawer. A set of accounts books still in the sealed clear wrapper.

In the third drawer down by the floor he pulled out two cricket magazines and, rummaging at the back, a copy of *Asian Babes*. Billal saw it and seemed shocked.

Bannerman stood up and pointed at the hard drive. 'We're going to take this, OK?'

Billal shrugged. 'Sure.'

'Because it may have something on it.'

'Sure, sure.' He shrugged again. 'Take whatever you want.'

Everything was bagged and tagged and loaded into the van. Billal had finished his prayers and came out of the bedroom looking calmer, ready to see them out. He stood at the door and signed the evidence receipts for Bannerman. Morrow made a point of shaking his hand.

'Thanks,' he said. 'Bye.'

'Where does your brother do business with?' she asked.

'How do you mean?'

'Where does he import from? Does he ever have dealings with Arabic countries?' She was asking to find an anomaly in the pattern, to give Bannerman hope. VAT fraud was an EU crime.

'Like where?'

'Oh, you know, Saudi Arabia, those countries, maybe even Afghanistan?'

'No,' said Billal thoughtfully. 'Just Europe, I think. They don't make silicone chips in Afghanistan, do they?' He half smiled. 'They can't even make chips there, can they? Bit backward ...' Bannerman turned away.

She tried again. 'What makes you think he only deals with Europe, does he travel?'

'No, he just mentioned it.'

Morrow looked at him but found he was looking at Bannerman's back. 'Thank you for all your help, Mr Anwar. We'll listen to the tape and see what we can find out about your dad.'

'Thank you.' Billal was still watching Bannerman. 'Thank you very much.'

Behind him a bedraggled Meeshra appeared at the door of the bedroom, the baby crying behind her. 'Billal ...' she said plaintively.

'Coming,' said Billal over his shoulder. 'I'm coming.'

The atmosphere in the car was so tense that at one point she thought Bannerman might be on the verge of crying. He drove hunched over the wheel and his voice sounded changed.

'Before five o'clock I want you to go to the university and

see if you can find out more about him,' he said. 'If he's working this with anyone else. He could have made contacts there.'

'You going to liaise with Fraud?'

'Only if I have to.'

'Makes sense of the ransom demand though, doesn't it? Remember they shut the Cayman Island banks where everyone was laundering the VAT money?'

'Did they?'

'Yeah, in that lecture they said no major movement of money had happened for a year, since they clamped down on the Caymans. Said they must be keeping it all in cash, look out for lock-ups. Big boxes of readies, large cheques cashed.'

'So, Omar could have millions in boxes in a lock-up and he's let them keep his dad?'

'Could be.'

'What kind of prick does that?'

Morrow shrugged. 'A prick that doesn't want to get caught?' She smiled.

'You're fucking chuffed, aren't you?' He spat the words through a tense jaw, threatened, as if she'd orchestrated the whole thing to spite him.

'Well, I'm fucking delighted it's not my case.'

The frank admission broke the space between them and Bannerman smiled at the road ahead. 'Bastard.'

They drove on for a moment until Morrow spoke. 'Billal's not that bright, is he?'

'Hmm. Very into his family. Did you see him blushing when I found that scuddy mag?'

'Yeah,' she said. 'That's odd. You saw the rows of that stuff in his dad's shop. It's no worse than them and they're straight across from the counter. He'd have been looking right at it every day he worked there.'

'Maybe he doesn't use porn. Maybe he did once, and feels bad about it.'

She had the impression that it was Bannerman's own story. 'Maybe he's short-sighted,' she said to brush over it. 'Anyway, he just gave his brother up.'

Neither of them said anything but they were both thinking that Billal didn't seem all that sad about it.

Shugie stayed on the same bar stool all afternoon. Even when he went out for a smoke he came back and found that Senga had shooed squatters away from his perch. The money evaporated over six rounds or so, he found he only had enough for a whisky but he didn't want to ask her for that. Women knew when the money was running out. They could smell it, like loneliness.

Shugie stumbled off his stool, caught himself from falling by grabbing hold of the end of the bar, just had time to congratulate himself on his snake-like reflexes when his knees melted like butter in a pan and he dropped softly to the floor, sighed and fell asleep on the cold stone. A guy coming back from a smoke saw him go down and moved to yank him up again.

'Leave it!' ordered Senga protectively. '*Leave* it.'

The men in the bar looked at Shugie, lying on his side, cuddled into the brass foot rail. Senga might allow dozing on chairs but she forbade sleeping on the floor. There must be something between them.

24

The absolute dark took on a life. It was an animal, a gas, a liquid that filled Aamir's nose and suffocated him, coated his eyes, crept in through his ear canal and crossed membranes, seeping into capillaries, veins, arteries, catastrophically colonising.

There was nothing. No noise from outside, no chinks of light, nothing coming back. Nothing.

Aamir shook his head, opened his eyes wide, shut them, slapped his own face, tugged at the skin on his belly but nothing could stop it. He began to move, slowly at first, tentatively trying to get away from it. He shuffled his feet, chipping rust dust from the floor with his toes, scurrying back and forth along the lowest point of the drum, touching each end with his outstretched hands, slamming into the wall and pushing himself back. He did it several times before he realised that he wasn't outrunning it but running into it, deeper and deeper and now he was fathoms down into the dark and would never be able to swim out of it.

He doubled over, dropped messily to his knees. Face pressed tight to his knee, he bared his teeth and bit deep into the skin but felt nothing. His hands stretched slowly out in front of him. He could feel the rust flaking off in papery sheets, coming away at the merest nudge of his fingertips.

Through the blackness the deep red blood on his mother's sari seeped towards him and he was powerless to move away. He closed his eyes and felt the warm blood wash over his scalp, down his back, over his buttocks. Engulfed in the salt of her he continued to breathe. There was not a chink of mercy left in the world for him.

He could hear himself breathing loudly through his nose, panting like a dog. Rust crumbled to dust, he could smell it. Shards scratched at the material of his pyjamas, cutting into it and sticking into the soft skin on his knees.

His life had no meaning. It was intolerable. The last three decades had been a hollow waste of time.

Hands searched the floor in the oily darkness, fingertips jamming recklessly into rusting iron, pulling it up and crumbling it in his hands, feeling again and again, getting sharp splinters of it stuck under his nails, in his palms, until he found a shard of iron that was solid.

He held it, pressed the middle of it with his thumb, tried to bend it with both hands but it was hard. Like a fossil of a bone the earth fell away around it. He sat up and looked through the darkness imagining the object in his hand. With touch as his guide he cleaned it off, coming to know every speck of its surface, feeling for a flaw but failing. He spat on his hand and cleaned it, wiping it dry on his pyjama top.

As long as a pencil with a serrated edge and sharp tip. A knife.

Insistent pains nagged at his knees and fingers but he resisted the distraction. He extended his left hand into the molten dark and pulled the sleeve up. Slowly, as if in a ritual, he found the sinews of his wrist with his fingers and drew the metal hard across the skin.

Warm wet dripped from him into the void. He held his right hand below it and felt the welcome blood run over his fingers, drip through and drop, wetting the dusty Ugandan soil.

Aamir raised his face to the God who had suffered him to live through children and work and meals, a million bloody meals, sleep and changes of carpet and striving, endless pointless striving.

He turned his face up and muttered a final quiet prayer: 'You bloody nasty bastard.'

Mr Kaira had been looking at the screen for thirty seconds, a small smile frozen on his mouth, his forefinger tapping the completely empty desk like a slow pulse. He turned his smile to Omar and his eyes followed slowly. 'System is slow today,' he explained and turned back. The light on his face changed to pale blue and he exclaimed a little 'ah!' and frowned at the numbers on the screen.

Omar had been coming here since he was ten. The bank was in the west end of the city, past all the halal butchers and the sari and sweet shops, before the university on the hill, right in the middle of student pubs and cafes and second-hand book shops.

Every second week his daddy had brought him here to watch him make his deposits, to speak to Mr Kaira. Mr Kaira, whose oiled hairstyle never came or went from fashion, whose tiny collar stayed about his fat neck, whose smile was never more or less fixed; always a constant. The decor stayed the same: hessian moss-green walls, smoked glass between the counter and Mr Kaira's office. The chairs had been replaced but only by exact replicas. Before Omar's time there had been an open counter for service but they had replaced it with a bullet-proof window after a raid.

All their family money was in the Allied Bank of Pakistan, which was silly really because there was only one branch in Glasgow and it was on the other side of the city, but Aamir liked it. The small staff rarely changed and he could always talk to Mr Kaira about his affairs, create accounts for weddings and holidays without having to explain to a stranger. All his friends at mosque knew that he banked here and Omar thought his father drew a sense of authenticity from it. He was a Ugandan Asian, an African Asian, not an Asian Asian like everyone else in mosque. Aamir was always an outsider.

Mr Kaira frowned at the blue screen, jotted something on a notepad without looking at his hand and sat back. 'Mr Anwar, as I told you on the telephone this morning, in the collected accounts of your family is deposited this much.' He smiled and pushed the pad across to Omar – £43,193.33. 'Your father is a prudent man.'

Not prudent enough. They would need a loan for a huge amount, much more than the house was worth, more than all the cars. A ransom wasn't exactly a good investment. Their only hope was that Mr Kaira hadn't heard about the kidnapping already.

'Um, Mr Kaira.' Omar looked at him. Mr Kaira smiled encouragingly. 'Could I withdraw this money?'

He looked a little shocked. 'All this money?'

'It's for my father. He's away and he needs it.'

'I see.' Mr Kaira didn't see, the clouds in his eyes made that clear. 'I see, I see. Your brother would need to counter-sign for it. The accounts all require two signatories from the partnership.' Everyone trusted fine upstanding Billal. 'Would he be willing to do that?'

Omar heard him ask if he was planning to steal it. They all distrusted the next generation, those old guys, especially the youngest sons. 'Yes, he will sign. The thing is, my father needs a lot more than that. Would you be able to advance us a loan?'

Mr Kaira snorted as if that was impossible. 'For how much?'

Omar did the calculation, realised he wasn't going to get a loan for £1,950,000 and balked. 'Um. I'll talk to Billal, see what he thinks.'

'The withdrawals, we will need advance notice of your withdrawals—'

'No.' Panic rose from Omar's guts to his stomach to his throat, blocking his airway, making it hard to breathe. 'How much notice?' Omar stood up, gathering the bank papers he had brought with him and shoving them back in the brown envelope.

'A month on your sister's wedding fund, a week for the high interest account.'

'But I need it right away.'

'Ah, but then you'll lose all the interest on those accounts.'

'That's fine. I need it right away.' He hurried to the office door but Mr Kaira beat him to it.

'If your father is in trouble . . .'

'No. No.' Omar blinked hard, desperate to get out through the smoked-glass door Mr Kaira was blocking with his rotund body.

'Mr Anwar, I heard about last night. I cannot advance you the money but if I personally can be of any service . . . ?'

Red-eyed, Omar reached around behind him and grabbed the door handle. 'Thanks.' He slipped past Mr Kaira and made it to the door, threw it open and stepped out into the street. He felt the cold wind brush past his face, saw a cluster of school kids eating chips across the road.

Omar looked up the hill to the students' union building and wished, dearly, that he was back at uni, that it was any time but this time, this awful gut-wrenching time.

With a jolt, Omar realized that the bank staff could see him through the door, and Mr Kaira would be watching him, waiting to see what he did next. He turned stiffly and walked off uphill as if he knew where he was going, heading towards the university.

Afraid of meeting anyone he knew Omar took the back streets and lanes, dodging the streets around the mosque in Oakfield Avenue, looking for a place to hide. He passed the fence around Hillhead high school, saw kids inside hanging around the playground, kids dressed like poor gangster rappers, fat teenage girls wearing tight clothes and pixie boots, their conversations over-animated, posturing, attention-seeking. In the street fresh-faced first year students brushed past him, hurrying to classes.

He veered off down a road he knew was lined by houses used by the German department. No one he knew did German. The street was quiet and he dropped his head as he walked along, let his tired shoulders slump.

Aamir would know what to do. He'd have railed and shouted and then told him what to do. Whenever Omar thought about Aamir he imagined him as a small angry mouse in pyjamas. Small because he was small, angry because he was angry all the time, never spoke to any of them but to recriminate or correct, and wearing pyjamas because Aamir was rarely home unless it was time to go to bed. They didn't need to pay school fees any more, he didn't need to work a sixteen-hour day. He was avoiding them.

Omar saw his father looking at his spoiled, lucky children, sensed his bewilderment, his disappointment. They expected new clothes and cars and bedrooms of their own, they wanted shoes and food and holidays and iPods. Sadiqa wanted books and new clothes all the time because she was always getting fatter. They didn't want to pray in the night, they didn't want to walk anywhere, they didn't want to work shifts in the smelly wee shop with Johnny Lander telling the same stories over and over about his time in the army. They were private school kids and thought it was humiliating to sit behind a counter, taking shit from alkis and shoplifters and racist fuckwits out in their slippers looking for bottles of ginger and tea bags.

Aamir had been chased out of Uganda and came to

Glasgow with nothing behind him. He'd worked as a dustman for two years, taking abuse everyday from colleagues, passing school children, everyone. Finally he opened a shop where someone called him a black bastard at least once a day, where he hid from his frightening new wife and the children when they came. Omar knew these facts, he understood the hardships that had formed his father, but he had never felt the gross injustice of all that had happened to Aamir until now.

He had wandered into a back court surrounded by smelly bin sheds and overgrown gardens. He was one wall away from the university. A white cat skittered away through a hole in a fence. Purposefully, he stepped into a bin shed.

In the dark, dank smell of rotting nappies and mouldy veg, Omar covered his face and sobbed with worry for his hard-done-by daddy.

25

They were dawdling. Bannerman and Morrow strolled from the car park around the station house and along the road as if they had all the time in the world, as if every moment was not a timeframe during which an old man who had worked blamelessly every waking moment of the last thirty years could be killed.

If they had thought about it neither of them would have been quite sure why they lingered in one another's company. They didn't like each other, had fuck all in common, but they had achieved a sort of truce over the day. They were reluctant to lose that in the company of others.

Bannerman spotted the mini supermarket down the road. 'I need a paper . . .' he said.

'No.' Morrow pushed him towards the yard door. 'Come on . . .'

Miserably he punched the security code into the numbered pad. The door buzzed and they both stared at it until Morrow sighed and pushed it open. 'Fucking get in.'

The processing bar was busy with a couple of easy collars having a laugh with the guys on the desk. Morrow and Bannerman kept their heads down and went through to the duty seargeant's desk. The copper she'd been unkind to about the graffitti scowled when he saw her. For a moment she thought about apologising but decided it would be easier to scowl back.

She typed the code into the CID corridor and they sloped inside, both eyeing MacKechnie's office. The lights were on but the door shut, as if he was on a phone call or picking his nose. They stepped up the corridor and Morrow tried to peel off and go to their office but Bannerman pinched her sleeve and made her come with him.

MacKechnie called them to come. Bannerman opened the door wide into the corridor and tried to get Morrow to go in first but she held firm. MacKechnie looked up expectantly at Bannerman.

'Sir,' he said, 'Omar Anwar wasn't in ...'

MacKechnie looked up from his paperwork and saw the look on his face. 'What is it? Do you want me to guess?'

Bannerman slumped. 'Omar is Bob. He's got a business doing import/export to the EU.'

MacKechnie stiffened. 'Bugger. Carousel VAT fraud? Is that what you're saying?'

Bannerman shrugged. 'That would be my supposition ... We've taken his paperwork and his computer hard drive ... They're being processed now.'

'Right ... right. Do we have to call Fraud right now? Would you say it was that pressing?' MacKechnie could see the danger of it; the public perception of a department prosecuting a victim of violent crime, the endless paper trails and his officers spending weeks milling in High Court corridors, waiting to be called to give evidence.

'Well ... we could see what's on the hard drive first. It's just a suspicion, we haven't really got any evidence ...'

'OK,' he said vaguely. 'Lab reports are in, Morrow, go and check them out.'

Bannerman turned to her as she left, pleading for her to come back and save him. She grinned and slapped his back. She was glad to get outside the room and shut the door firmly behind her.

In her office someone had carefully stacked hard copies of lab reports, of the fingerprint evidence which had already been gone over with no anomalies found, over the lab reports on the van which turned up squat. She read them again. The tinfoil had opiate residue in it, cut solely with milk powder, no laxatives, no talc, just pure milk. It was unusual. She puzzled over it as she put the Anwars' answerphone tape into a tape recorder. She made a copy and played it.

Billal answered, they asked for Bob and he handed it over to his brother. The kidnapper asked after Aleesha's injuries and agreed to phone back at five to make an arrangement for a pick-up. He ended by saying he knew about Omar. She noted the interest in Aleesha, wondering if he knew her or was worried about the charges against him.

She took it into the incident room for transcription. DC Routher was prematurely balding and long overdue a promotion. He was good at paperwork though, efficient, and no one who got him ever wanted to let him go. She gave him the tape. 'Anyone got a picture of the M8 motor?'

'Aye.' He pointed her over to a board of images and notes that MacKechnie had been adding to. In the centre was a big photo of a car. It was grainy, taken from CCTV cameras, enlarged and printed onto copy paper.

Because the cameras were up high on the motorway lights the driver's face was obscured by the car roof. In the second picture the car was fuller, they could see a front passenger's thighs and a hand on a knee. A final picture of the car driving back towards the town showed that the chassis was sitting low.

She went back over to Routher. 'Where did it come off?'

'Town centre, Charing Cross.'

'Fuck.' Charing Cross had seven exits and three broken cameras. The car could have gone anywhere. 'Lost it?'

''Fraid so. The reg is out now anyway. Everyone in the city's looking for it. If they're not picked up in the next half-hour they must be sitting in a garage somewhere.'

'Did Bannerman drop in a bag of CCTV tapes from a shop?'

Routher pointed to a small office room across the corridor. She could see Harris in profile through the strip of glass on the door, sitting on a chair, arms crossed, watching the far wall intently. He didn't look happy.

She walked across the corridor and opened the door. 'Right?'

Harris didn't look up. 'It's because I said about the DVD, isn't it?'

'I don't know why Bannerman loves you enough to give you this, Harris, he just does.'

'Ma'am, it's days and days' worth.'

'You don't have to watch it in real time, you can speed it up.'

She looked at the image on the telly. A small man sitting on a stool behind the counter in Aamir's shop. She'd seen the publicity photo they were releasing to the news, a family snap shot of him three quarters side on, but this man looked smaller, angrier, less sympathetic.

Harris pressed fast forward on the remote and, suddenly, the wee man was wriggling this way and that, getting down, messing with the shelves behind him, sitting back up. Someone came in and bought fags. A figure came in around the counter, got up on the stool next to him, got down, disappeared, came back with two mugs. She squinted and saw that it was Lander. It was a bad-quality tape, a crap angle too.

'My eyes'll be bleeding in a minute,' said Harris.

'Harris, you're the only man we trust this with,' she said sarcastically, backing out of the room.

Bannerman shuffled miserably across her path.

'Is everything turning to shit in front of ye?'

He didn't answer but smirked at his shoes.

She filled him in on the kidnapper's call and then, 'Listen to this: the residue in the tinfoil wrap from the van? This heroin has been cut with milk powder, but only with milk powder. No talc, no ash, nothing extra. Just milk powder. It's very clean.'

'So?'

'Well, if they were only cutting it with a single substance the quantities needed would attract attention. Usually it's lots of different things.'

'Is he a cutter then?'

She shrugged. 'Unlikely because those guys are very undercover, paid for discretion, and they lose their job if they use. More likely he's got a long habit and gets a custom deal from someone—'

'I said that. Long-term habit, I said that before ...' He seemed desperate to have got something right so she let him have it.

'Maybe he lives with a dealer? Has a supply or gets it wholesale. Either way he's well in with dealers.'

'Cuts it himself?'

'For himself.'

He looked hopeful. 'Could this be traceable then?'

Morrow shrugged. 'Worth a try.'

At half past one Eddy and Pat were still cruising in the car, listening to the radio. Pat turned it up so loud that Eddy couldn't talk over it. A high-pitched alert signalled from Eddy's pocket and he pulled over to the side to read it.

Pat could see the text. It was from Eddy's ex-missus in Manchester. Their youngest daughter was six today. Phone or she'd cut his balls off.

Eddy's colour changed as he read it and Pat knew if he didn't get out of the car he'd get the brunt of it.

'I'll jump out here,' he said, throwing the door open to the street.

'She's fuckin'—' Eddy leaned over the seat. 'Pat, get back in.'

'No, no.' Pat backed away from the car, holding the edge of the door. 'Give ye privacy to call. Pick me up in half an hour.' And he slammed the door shut, instantly regretting that he'd left the paper with her picture inside. He looked in at Eddy. A nothing in Reactalite glasses. Small, fat, furious.

Eddy pointed straight down to the ground and mouthed angrily, 'Here?'

'In half an hour.' Pat turned away so that Eddy couldn't argue, walking quickly away down the road. He kept moving at the same pace until he saw the silver car draw past him, down the road and disappear around a corner.

Pat breathed out and looked up, actually excited at the prospect of a half-hour holiday from Eddy. When he saw where he was he almost choked. He was just around the corner from the Vicky. She was just around the corner.

He hurried up, breaking into a jog until he reached the junction and stopped. A low row of newsagents and chip shops on his right but to his left, across the road, loomed the Vicky Infirmary. He struggled to breathe in. He searched his conscience to see if it was true, if he really hadn't known where he was. He hadn't: it was as if it was meant.

Outside smokers were huddled in their coats, standing singly or in twos, gazing aimlessly out into the street. Pat stood with his toes over the edge of the pavement, straining, face first towards the passing traffic. He wanted to be there, just a little closer.

Suddenly aware that he might be acting strangely and attract attention, he veered right and went into a newsagent's shop. He bought the paper again, smiling to himself

239

as he picked a can of juice out of a fridge, and found himself asking for ten Marlboro reds, imagining that it was what she might smoke, if she smoked.

The man behind the counter tried to chat, asking if he had finished his work for the day, but Pat couldn't hear him. He nodded and paid and left the shop, hurried off across the road, dodging buses and cars, snaking between parked cars. He was grinning as he walked over to the Infirmary and took his place among the line-up under the smokers' shelter.

An old man in a green bunnet and tweed coat was standing next to him, watching Pat as he took out his packet of ten from his pocket and unwrapped the clear cellophane.

'You just starting again?' The old man's voice was low and rough, his nose a blistered mess of skin, but he stood upright.

'No.' Pat looked down at his packet and pulled out the silver foil, crumpling it into his palm and pulling a cigarette out. 'Just . . . sometimes. When I'm stressed. Have ye a light, faither?'

The old man reached into his pocket and brought out a dun tin lighter, flicked the wheel and held the flame to the tip.

Pat puffed, superficially, not really inhaling but getting a wild buzz off it none the less. He felt dizzy and reached back to steady himself against the building, smiling when the stone hit his palm. She was in there, on the other side of this wall, and he was touching it.

'Well, son, ye look pretty happy for someone under stress. Are ye visiting?'

'Aye, but she's getting out.'

'Oh, lucky, aye.' The man looked away. 'You're lucky.'

He wanted to be asked about the person he was visiting,

a wife or a son maybe, but Pat didn't want to talk. He opened his paper and pretended to read the front page, leaning his back on the wall, feeling cold from the smooth stone chill at his back. He forgot to smoke his cigarette. He let it burn out in his fingers as he looked at the picture and thought of her upstairs and him down here, just about to visit her with yet more flowers, with women's magazines and sweeties.

And she would sit up in the bed when she saw him walking towards her, and her face would open towards him and her hands would slide from the blanket over her knees to her sides, and he would walk, faster and faster, until he was inches from her face and he would hold her face in his big warm hands and he would kiss her.

It was counter-intuitive to trust Kevin Niven. He had greasy hair, wore trackies, had the bad skin and vague speech patterns of a junkie. In fact, he was a decorated officer with years of undercover experience. He sat alone in the canteen though, nibbling a poor homemade sandwich, looking shifty and attracting sidelong looks from the officers who didn't know him.

Morrow could imagine how uncomfortable he made them, like someone dressed in a Nazi uniform hanging about a synagogue: you might know he was dressed like that for some higher purpose but in absent-minded moments you'd still feel the urge to punch him.

'That's, like, no easy, like, to say ...' He trailed off, head jerking to the side. 'Know?'

One question in, he already had Bannerman's hackles up. 'Where could we find out?'

'Dunno ...' He seemed to suddenly absorb the information. 'That's not that usual, though, eh?'

'What isn't?'

'Someone with a supply or bulk-buying and moderating it, know? Using like a medicine.'

'What would normally happen if someone had a supply?'

He opened his arms wide and grinned. '*Gorge.*'

Morrow laughed but Bannerman was staring at him intently. 'Can you think of another reason for this, then, this chemical profile of the residue?'

Niven looked at the lab report, considered it, tipped his head one way at one possibility, the other way at another. 'Here.' He drew a meaningless mind map on the table, tapping with four fingers to the left. 'New supply from someone with a lot of milk powder.' His hand traced a long line. 'Pattern emerges later.'

Morrow smiled, getting it, but Bannerman looked angrily at the table.

'Here . . .' Kevin tapped another portion of the table. 'One off, bad mixing, milk powder clustered in one part of a mix.'

'Hm.' Morrow was disappointed. 'So it could mean nothing?'

'Or,' Kevin opened his eyes wide, 'holiday supply, bought elsewhere, used here.'

Morrow nodded. 'In short, fuck all use, then?'

'Aye.'

'Means nothing?'

'Nah, s'not evidence. Well, he mibbi knows someone, early stages. When ye find him he'll mibbi be someone's pal.'

'Part of a crew?'

'Nah. Unreliable.'

'So we can only use the connection for confirmation?'

'Yeah.'

Bannerman looked sadly at the table.

Kevin sucked his teeth noisily. 'Check for prints, but?'

'On the foil?' Bannerman looked up. 'Don't know.'

''Cause, know how ye go straight to one bit of the lab for residue, eh? Don't want to dust for prints in case they mess that up, understandable but see they check *inside* for prints, eh?'

'Right?'

'Oh aye,' said Kevin, looking at his empty hands, turning an invisible bit of foil around and around. ''Cause if there's prints they'll be good ones, man.' He looked up and smiled. 'They'll be fuck-off good y'uns.'

26

University Avenue felt like part of a different city. The buildings were pretty, architectural statements. The gothic main building with its high tower and quadrangles, the circular Reading Room, the new medical building. The students were well fed, tanned and tall, wearing clothes that were cleaner and better fitting than most of the people Morrow came into contact with.

As they locked up the car on the steep approach to the university gates Morrow overheard a girl who looked all of seventeen tell another that it was just *impossible* to get a parking space around here. These people weren't just better than the population they nicked, they were better than them: better starts in life, better homes, knew better people.

Morrow had brought Gobby with her, just for peace, but was regretting it already. He was so quiet it was creepy, as if he'd been jinxed. His defensive swagger was exaggerated, his expression sullen and intimidated by the strange poshness of the university students. Alex wasn't bothered; she spent her childhood being banned from friends' houses. Single parent families were frowned upon then, her mother was half mad with depression and the reputation of a connection to the McGraths never left her. She grew up knowing that everyone was better than her.

They got to the gate house and walked in, passing the porter's box, entering the uni grounds. The Law School was separate from the main building, around the side to the right, across a grassy square. A long terrace of thin town houses, high narrow windows and small black front doors emphasised the stern look of the place. The houses must have been university accommodation at one time: a blue plaque on a wall notified disinterested passersby about a long-dead famous resident.

The main entrance to Law was through one of the small front doors. They followed the numbers down and took the steps. The hallway was inauspicious. Electric blue carpet, blue wood-chip walls and white paint on the woodwork. Cork notice boards with bits of paper pinned to them, the same notice on all of them warning all students to check their email regularly. Morrow wasn't the only idiot, it seemed. The town houses were joined together through passages punched into the adjoining walls.

The hour must be turning: from the stairs and the door behind them students began to filter into the building.

On the right-hand side, just inside the front door, a glass cubicle was marked 'Enquiries' and a man in a blue shirt looked out at them expectantly.

'Hello, we're looking for the tutor of one of your students,' said Morrow amiably.

'And who might that be, young lady?' His eyes twinkled playfully, as if Morrow was in on the joke and knew she was neither a lady nor young.

'Omar Anwar.' She sounded cold. 'Graduated last June.'

The security guard took a deep breath, ready to reciprocate the rebuff. She pulled out her warrant card and slapped it on the window. He looked at it, nodding as he emptied his lungs, and turned back to the computer, asking her for spellings and telling her that Tormod MacLeòid was her man. He'd call up and see if he was in.

Professor Tormod MacLeòid fancied the arse off himself. His office and personal appearance spoke of a man who lived for pretentious obfuscation and all things dusty. He kept them waiting for ten minutes in his secretary's office and then came in, ordered the secretary to bring him Omar's student file before they began the interview. Once in his office he made them sit in a passive silence while he read the file. Happily it wasn't more than five paragraphs long but it gave Morrow a chance to look around the office.

Like the building itself the room was tall and narrow. Every bit of wall space was weighed down with books, most of which were old, battered and looked out of print. Layered in front of the books and on top of them were busts with missing noses, bits of stone and brick, mini reproduction Greek vases. On top of one of the shelves, rolled up into a cylinder, was a time-faded Fettes brown and pink tie. Morrow was sure that every single object had a story attached to it, and that every story would be long and ponderous.

She had taken the single seat in front of his messy desk, leaving Gobby to sit on a chair near the door, perching in front of a precarious stack of essays, silently wringing his hands and contemplating the nuances of his discomfort.

Finally the professor leaned back in his wooden throne, stroking his beard, adjusted his sports jacket and smiled a patronising yellow smile. 'I do recall him, certainly, yes. Where was he from?'

'Pollockshields,' said Morrow.

'Ah.' His eyes widened at the implied correction. 'Yes, the old colony of Pollockshields,' he smirked. '*Quite.*'

'He did honours in your class and got a first.' Morrow thickened her scummy southsider accent to challenge his Fettes drawl. 'So I kinda though you'd mibbi remember more about him than the shade of his tan.'

Tormod's face snapped into a mean squint. 'I did not mention his skin colour.'

She waited for a beat, letting him squirm. 'What sort of student was he?'

He cleared his throat testily and looked again at the file. 'Very good, able, hard working.'

'And your subject is . . . ?'

He blinked long and hard. 'Civil Law. Roman Law.'

'Why would he study Roman Law?'

Tormod drew a long breath, tipped his beard at them and launched into a stale speech he had given many times: 'Civil Law is studied at honours level for one of two reasons. Either the student is hoping to become an advocate and, potentially, a judge, or else they have an abiding interest in the history of Law. It is, as it were, a more arts-based approach to the study of Law. Less black letter Law, more interpretative. In . . .' he glanced at the file again, '*Omar*'s case, he wished to study with a view to advocacy. At least that was my understanding at the time of accepting him at the commencement of the course.'

'And yet he decided not to go into practice. Not even to be a solicitor.'

'Indeed.'

'Why?'

'No idea. You'd have to ask him.'

'Did you help organise any of the extra-curricular activities Omar was involved in?'

He looked blank and glanced at his sheet for a prompt. 'The mooting competition?'

'What's that?'

'The mooting competition is just a debating society really, but with a legal emphasis. Role play.' He sounded dismissive.

'Omar was involved in that?'

'Says so here.'

'You're not involved in it?'

247

'No.'

'Do they get credits for it?'

'Certainly not. Time consuming though.'

'Suggests he was keen when he started the course, doesn't it?' She kept her face neutral but he heared the veiled reproach. Slowly his lip curled with disdain.

Morrow stood up abruptly. 'Thank you very much,' and pulled her coat from the back of the chair. Gobby leapt to his feet.

Tormod almost stood up to see them out but then thought better of it and sat down again. 'I trust you can see yourselves out,' he said briskly.

Morrow pointed to the door Gobby was halfway through. 'D'ye mean ye trust us to find the door here, in the wall?'

He looked sulky and she realised he was just the sort to complain to someone senior at a golf club dinner, so she thanked him for his time and all the help he had been and then slammed the door behind her. If she had been an Asian kid studying under Tormod MacLeòid she'd have thought twice about going into practice too.

Gobby was sweating as they walked down the stairs. The building was overheated and he didn't feel comfortable enough to take his coat off. He couldn't wait to get outside but Morrow stopped him at the bottom of the stairs. 'No, wait.' She was looking at a group of students gathering around the fourth-year notice board. 'Come on over here . . .'

Gobby was almost moved to speak, but caught himself and followed her over. She picked the biggest, most confident-looking boy in the group and Gobby stood behind her, outside the cluster of students, sweating.

The boy was tall and as healthy-looking as any mother could wish, dressed in expensive casual clothes with brand names up and down the arms, a thick leather bag and sharp haircut.

'Excuse me?'

He smiled at Morrow through perfect teeth.

'I wonder if you could help me. We're looking for someone who knows Omar Anwar, he graduated last June. He was involved in the mooting competition?'

'Oh, yeah, yeah, Omar. Yeah, Omar, everyone knows Omar.'

'Do you know him?'

He frowned and touched his hair. 'Yeah. Why?'

'Are you involved in the mooting? What year are you?'

'You're the police, aren't you?'

'What are you, a fourth year?' she said quietly. 'We're trying to find out who knows Omar.'

'God, it *was* him. On the news, the kidnap? Did his wee sister get shot?'

She dropped her eyes. 'Look, could we go somewhere to talk?'

'Sure, come on.' He made sure she was following him as he walked off through a doorway to the next building. They took the stairs up to the second floor and he opened the door to a large room, flooded with light through two long windows. A coffee machine as tall as a man stood next to a small table with a bowl of loose change. By the wall a corridor of purple leather Chesterfield chairs sat looking at each other.

'This used to be the smoking room,' he said.

In front of the windows a ten-foot-long mahogany table was strewn with notepads and stacks of law books. All of the seats were empty, bagsied with jumpers and jackets. The students were all missing.

'Lecture?' asked Morrow.

'Lunch,' he said, dumping his bag behind the door. He pointed at the coffee machine. 'Drink?'

Gobby shook his head and Morrow wrinkled her nose.

'Got one of them at our work. Leaves your tongue all gritty.'

'Shall we sit then?' asked their host.

Morrow took a Chesterfield and the boy sat opposite her. Gobby slid into a chair next to her, still keeping his coat on, self-consciously yanking the edges of it out around his belly as she took her notebook out.

'OK, what's your name?'

'Lamont, James.'

'Lamont, like the judge?'

He tipped his head in embarrassment and looked away quickly. She smiled kindly at him. The two great sources of shame: privilege and penury.

'So, you know Omar?'

'Not a bad word to say about him. Brilliant bloke.'

'Who does he hang about with?'

'His best mate's Mo. He did Science, physics or something. Graduated at the same time. Those guys hung about together all the time.'

'No real friends in Law School?'

'Loads, but you know, towards the end of your degree everyone's thinking about the next step and Omar didn't want to go into practice—'

'Even though he got a first?'

'It's not for everyone.'

'What did he want to do?'

'He started a business, I think, went into business. You know, like his dad.'

'His dad owns a corner shop.'

He seemed surprised by that, and pleased as well, as if they had been a little competitive with each other and this was a point in James's favour. 'Really? I thought he had a few shops, that's what Omar said.'

'Hm, no, just one shop.'

'Still his dad must've done pretty well with it.' She could

see him struggle, overlaying his win with more noble thoughts. 'He saw the two boys through private school, didn't he?'

'Not his sister?'

James jerked his head sideways as if he'd just remembered. 'Um, no. The sister went to Shawlands Academy.'

'A comprehensive?'

'Yeah, but I always thought that wasn't about money. Omar thought it wasn't about money.'

'Was it because she was a girl?'

He shrugged, blushing a little at his implied membership of the patriarchy. She liked him more and more. 'I dunno, I think she was the brightest of them, Omar said, I never met her. Really sharp, he said. Said she was a bit wild. So wild he wouldn't introduce her to any of us.'

'Wild in what way? Bad boyfriends? Drinking?'

'No, no, just ... I dunno ... I got the impression she was contrary. He expected her to run off on her sixteenth birthday "like a greased rat", he said.' James smiled at that. 'I remembered because of the phrase.'

She nodded, made a note to enquire at Shawlands about Aleesha. 'Did Omar say his dad had a few shops?'

'No. No, now that I think about it, he just seemed to have money. His business had been doing well. Had cash. He's certainly got money now.'

'What sort of business?'

James looked as if he'd never really thought about it. 'I don't know, I don't think he said.'

She smiled warmly. 'But he's doing well?'

He reciprocated the smile. 'God yeah, he showed me a picture of this car he's buying. A fucking Lamborghini.'

'Right?'

'Yeah.'

'It's blue, isn't it?'

251

'Is it? I thought it was yellow.' He glanced at Gobby. 'Banana yellow, I think.'

'Oh yeah, where did he get it?'

'Um . . .' His brow had dropped. If Morrow had been the sort to give advice she'd have told him not to take up poker.

'From the place in Glasgow?'

'Out by the motorway . . .'

'So, you've met recently?'

'Yeah, we met a month ago.' He kept glancing at Gobby, troubled by the sight of him sweating so heavily in his overcoat.

Morrow could see James withdrawing. Gobby looked like a policeman straight from central casting: pudgy, big, out of place in his formal overcoat and ill-fitting suit. She saw James realising suddenly that this wasn't an innocent chat, that it was official.

A chasm opened up between them and James sat back in his armchair, crossing his legs. He caught her eye and smiled politely.

Warmth wouldn't work now, she knew that from experience. 'He told you about this car when you met a month ago?'

'Um, I dunno, I think so . . .' He was giving himself time to think.

'Where was that?'

'Um . . . where?'

She looked at her knees, straightening her skirt. She hadn't slept for thirty hours and felt suddenly weak and sick. 'Do you suspect Omar of something?'

'*What?*'

'You seem defensive. Do you suspect him of something?'

'God,' he spluttered, sitting forward. 'No, no, I don't *at all*. Not *at all*.'

252

'Hm.' she smiled. 'Right, well just tell us the truth, then. Where did you meet him a month ago?'

'At the Tunnel Club.'

'The Tunnel Club?'

'Outside, having a fag, he took out his wallet and showed us a photo of the car.'

'Did he tell you how much it cost?'

'No, but it was on the picture, the brochure, he'd cut it out so you could see the price. I thought it was weird, him leaving the price on. I mean, he'd cut it out, why leave that on? It was a hundred and forty grand, about.'

'About?'

'Well, you know, hundred and thirty-nine ninety-nine or something like that. About forty grand.'

'Have you ever known him by any name other than Omar?'

'Like what?'

'Does he go to the Tunnel Club often?'

'No.'

'Do you?'

'Sometimes.'

'But not recently?'

'Yeah, I was there last week.'

She stood up and James rose to meet her. He looked frightened.

'Omar's a good guy . . .' he said.

'You seem to suspect him of something.'

'Is he a suspect?'

'In what?'

They looked at each other for a moment.

'What do you suspect him of, James?'

'Nothing.'

'Why are you being careful with what you say about him, then?'

'Am I?'

Morrow let him squirm for a minute and then nodded sympathetically. 'It's a hell of a lot of money for a car.'

'It's shit loads of money for a car,' he agreed. 'I mean, if he already had a car and was getting a slightly better car I could understand that, but to go from no car to *that* car, I mean, you've come into a lot of money really quickly, haven't you? And you don't care who knows it either, I mean, you're not exactly being discreet buying a car like that, are you? Stands to reason you've got nothing to hide if you're buying a car like that ...'

'Yeah,' she said, picked up her coat and stood up.

His face was panicky. 'Sorry. For rambling.'

'This is my card.' She gave him one from her handbag. 'Would you ring me if you think of anything else?'

James's eyes skirted around the floor, retracing the conversation, trying, she thought, to work out where it had got away from him. She made him shake her hand, showed him her teeth. Gobby brushed past him without saying anything.

Gobby walked taller as they made their way back down the hill, back to the car. He kept his chin up now, meeting the curious look of students, taking up his space on the pavement without apologising.

'He was a bit of a prick, wasn't he?' he said, suddenly cocky now that it was over.

'You're fuck-all use, Gobby. You look so much like a polis, Jesus'd be cagey around you.'

Gobby seemed hurt. Her phone rang, denying him the right to even a silent appeal. Bannerman was a warm relief in her ear. 'They did the fingerprint analysis on the tinfoil in the trees, they've managed to get a match. A certain Malki Tait. They're calling his records down from central right now.'

Morrow grinned and checked her watch: 3.10. 'Back in ten.'

'OK,' she could hear that Bannerman was grinning too, 'but listen, hurry up. We need to go back to the Anwar house for five. Pick Omar up. D'you get anything?'

'Rumours that he's got money. We've got probable.'

She heard Bannerman give a long heartfelt sigh. 'Thanks,' he said quietly. 'Thank you.'

27

Aamir had been waiting for a change, a passage to somewhere else, for nothingness, nothingness would have done. He waited a long time in the dark, hearing no change and seeing no change.

Slowly, as the urgent pain in his wrist throbbed and the blood gathered in his cupped hand, drip-dripping between his fingers and soaking into the dusty rust on the floor, slowly, despite himself, he began to feel hope. He resisted, reminding himself of the betrayal, of the certainty he'd had a moment ago that nothing meant anything and he had wasted his efforts. But the absolute conviction that he should die had evaporated.

Suddenly the balance tipped and he could see it up ahead, like a pinpoint of light in the darkness, the moment when he would not be able to remember clearly why this was definitely a good idea.

Suicide should be sudden, he decided. Slow suicides could struggle, forget, change their minds. He saw himself in a misty plastic bag struggling wildly against the masking tape at his neck. He saw himself in a dark garage, jumping from a chair with a rope around his neck and fighting hard against it, scrabbling for purchase on a shelving unit. Too slow. Himself sleepy in an exhaust-filled car, slowly lifting a regretful hand to the lock. Too slow.

Slow. He wondered if he was hoping hard or the bleeding had slowed. He opened his fingers. Thick gummy blood fell softly onto the spongy rust below and he swept his hand beneath the cut on his wrist. It had stopped. A trickle was running down his arm but the flood of blood had stopped. He looked around the blackness, feeling ridiculous, embarrassed at his previous outburst. Ashamed before God. He imagined his sons watching him in the dark and cleared his throat authoritatively, holding his clean hand to his mouth, making the slash on his wrist gape. It hurt.

Slowly, for want of anything else to do, he stood up. He was aware suddenly of the pains in his scratched knees, of the awful slash of pain in his wrist and how sticky his right hand was.

What a mess to get yourself in, said Johnny Lander. He had said it to Aamir, but while looking at an alki who had come into the shop for fags. The man had a dead moth stuck to his jaw. What a mess to get yourself in.

Arms out to the side, shuffling his feet to orientate himself in the filthy dark, Aamir followed the camber to the end of the drum and found the door he had come in by, feeling along the rim with his sticky hand. He could feel the outline of the bottom of the door, no light or breeze, sealed tight.

In the absence of any other ideas he raised a bloody knuckle and knocked politely, three raps that clanged and swirled around the drum. He couldn't hear anything. There was no one out there.

Suddenly the drum quivered with a scratch of metal. A pause and another clang. The door opened two inches. The stab of light made Aamir stagger backwards, lifting his bloody hand to shield his eyes.

A disembodied voice spoke softly: 'Fuckin' hell.'

A figure in white, an angel, was in the doorway. A skinny angel. 'Man, what the fuck happened to you?'

Aamir shut his eyes against the blinding day and heard the voice clearly. Not an angel. A ned. The voice was nasal, high, indignant. A junkie voice, familiar somehow.

The door opened further, making Aamir cry out at the brutal light and the ned stepped into the drum. 'Wee man, you're all bloody. S'there rats bothering ye in here or something?'

It was the sudden realisation of what he had done that made shame and fury explode in Aamir's chest. He flailed his good hand out wildly and hit the man. It was awkward, less a punch, not even a slap, more of a clumsy glancing entanglement and Aamir turned away from the terrible light, baring his back to take the beating.

He waited. The emotion subsided. He became conscious of the small needling pains everywhere, in his wrist, in his knees, under his fingernails and the balls of his hands.

A small scuffle behind him. It sounded as if the ned was doing a dance, small, quick, delicate steps. Not dancing but shuffling on the platform at the top of the ladder, not shuffling but falling.

In the very moment that Aamir realised the man was struggling to stay upright, the ned toppled, crashing down into the drum. He landed heavily, flat, with a clang so loud it crashed over them in a cold wash. Aamir covered his head, expecting the man to jump to his feet, furiously swing his arms, punch, kick, a jab-jab-jab in his back. But he lay where he fell. The soft sound of a wet cough. Then a military beat, growing louder, faster, more insistent.

Still cringing Aamir stole a glance behind, towards the door. He could see a foot in a pristine white trainer, heel jerking off the floor, beating time, faster, tapping out a crazy beat, too fast to follow. It stopped. Aamir waited with his arms over his eyes, watching the foot below.

The sound of wet.

Keeping his eyes covered Aamir retreated to the shadows at the back of the drum, turned and finally managed to open his burning eyes.

A ned in white, his skip cap half covering his face. White legs, white wrists but the rest was as red as roses. Wet. Dark. And the blood was still coming. Aamir looked at his own hand. The slice of metal was still in it. He had thought it was bigger in the dark. It was sharp. Not where he had thought it was sharp, not along the ridge but on the end. And it was glinting.

Carefully Aamir stepped towards the white legs and looked down at the man's face. Blood gurgled from his neck like oil from the ground. The skin was drained to a ferocious blue-white marble, slowly clashing with the ginger of his hair, orange stubble on his face sprouting vivid. Eyes rolled up under the lids, irises coming to rest just below his upper eyelids. Blue as a vein under white skin.

He knew suddenly where he recognised the voice from. The boy in the bedroom offered him sweeties and apologised for the mess of the place. Aamir didn't take them in case they were poisoned but he'd been impressed that when he gave a religious objection it was understood and respected.

Aamir looked at the cut on his own wrist. Hardly bloody at all. No gash marks, just a dried dribble around his wrist like a drawing of a bangle.

Softly, slowly, Aamir sank to his knees. He stayed there for a long time until his knees were so stiff he could hardly stand to move them, until the pains shot into his hips and the bruises on his back throbbed. Even then he sat still.

Beyond the door the sun was going down, the dark creeping back in to swallow the day. It was time to pray but Aamir couldn't. He couldn't make himself known to God. Keeping his eyes shut, feeling his way with his feet and the sound of his whimper, Aamir shuffled back into the hateful dark at the end of the drum and awaited his fate.

They had a laugh at the mug shot, Morrow and Bannerman, sitting in their office looking at the record pulled from central, but it was partly relief that they were getting somewhere. The other part was how sorry for himself Malki Tait looked.

He was dressed for a really good night out. Though his colouring was very Scottish, pale skin, eyebrows and lashes brighter than a polished orange, Malki had dyed his hair black and carefully styled it in a bowl cut. The black was uniform and so lush and conditioned that it looked like a lady's wig. He was dressed in a grey jacket with epaulettes and what looked like a sort of cravat. According to the report he had been arrested outside of Rooftops nightclub with a pocket full of pills, too much to consume alone but not really enough to deal. But what really made them laugh was his expression. Malki's face was an eloquent expression of injustice. His mouth turned down, eyebrows raised over his brow, like a skinny child being picked on.

'Look.' She pointed out his previous: car theft and reset. He'd burnt out cars before, early in his career.

'And he's a Tait,' said Bannerman with a smile.

Morrow nodded. It couldn't be coincidence. It had to mean they were getting close to something. She stood up off the desk. 'I'll go tell MacKechnie—'

'No.' Bannerman stood up so fast he toppled his chair and had to reach back to catch it and stop it falling. 'No, I'll tell him.' He was determined to be the bearer of the developments. He wouldn't look at her as he yanked his jacket off the back of the chair and pulled it on, straightening his tie.

Morrow sat and watched him, stone faced, letting him sweat. She waited until he was dressed and standing in front of her.

'Good work today, Morrow.' He didn't want her to come with him and share the glory but couldn't say it outright.

She stayed where she was. 'Yeah, cheers.'

Uncomfortable, Bannerman looked at his watch. 'Four fifteen.'

'Yeah.' She stood up. 'We should go and pick Omar up.'

'No, I'll go with a squad.' Bannerman blinked and looked at his desk. When he looked at her again all the warmth was gone. 'If you could look through the hard drive from the shed, see if you can get anything else for probable on it.' He stood back, angling himself towards the door, telling her to get out and get on with the tasks he had allotted her.

Morrow curled her lip and stepped towards the door. She opened it, flinging him a dirty backward glance and left.

Bannerman was fixing his tie as he walked up the corridor, paused outside MacKechnie's office door to clear his throat and knocked twice. At the call to 'come' he opened it and stood in the door frame, just as she knew he would. He was in a hurry to do good work, couldn't stay, just passing on the good news about his discoveries. He didn't hear Morrow creep up behind him, or notice that she had put herself directly in MacKechnie's line of vision so that they looked as if they were together. With affected modesty he related the developments of the day, using the singular 'I' throughout. Morrow watched him, drawing MacKechnie's eye with big swoops of her eyebrows.

'The Taits?' MacKechnie was talking to her. 'Really?'

'Well,' answered Morrow, startling Bannerman with her presence, 'his name is Tait but we don't honestly know if he's any connection. Judging from his sheet,' Bannerman was staring at her, his neck jerking indignantly, 'he's just a junkie headcase and aspiring dealer. All his arrests are drugs-related or for joyriding. He lives in Cambuslang, so he could be a cousin.'

'I didn't—' Bannerman stopped himself.

'Anyway,' Morrow held up her hands, 'I've got things to get on with. I'll leave you to pick up Omar Anwar, Bannerman, OK?'

And she backed away, grinning at him.

Eddy was breathing through his nose, snorting like a bull, leaning forward in the seat, over the wheel, as if he wanted to jump someone.

Pat should ask, he knew, what happened with Eddy's daughter, how she was, what birthday it was or something. He could cue Eddy up for a vent about how his ex was responsible for him forgetting the wee lassie's birthday, but he knew of old that it would only make it worse. Once Eddy got going on his ex no good came of it. Pat had spent endless shifts trapped, listening to Eddy digging over her crimes, telling ridiculous lies about it all, trying to convince himself that everything was her fault.

Pat never liked the woman, even in the good times. She never fucking shut up talking, but he could see that Eddy was no picnic. And Malki was wrong; they weren't nice kids. They were half wild. Pat grew up around big families but until he met Eddy's kids he'd never known that children could make noise like that, for as long as that.

So he didn't ask and Eddy's arse was making buttons trying to get him to. 'Never trust a fucking woman, man,' he said, grinding his teeth.

Pat looked out of the window and thought of the cold of the Vicky's wall sinking into his hand, numbing his finger-tips. His hand was on his lap and he smiled at his fingers as he thought about it. 'Hope Malki's OK.'

'Cunt better be, the dough we're paying him.'

Pat wanted to say it wasn't that great a rate, not for what he was doing, not for the sentence he could be facing. He was good Malki, reliable. They didn't have to make sure he was too pissed to walk, like Shugie, so that he couldn't go to a pub and blurt something about it to a moody wide-o who'd go and tell someone. And you knew Malki wasn't going to get in a temper and kill the fucking guy. He wouldn't be blurting everyone's fucking names either, making it impossible to send the old guy home.

Pat could change his name. He imagined himself in a sunny country with Aleesha. His arm was resting on her shoulders, relaxed, and she was smiling away from him, at something, they were posing as if someone was taking their photo but taking ages about it and they couldn't be bothered standing still any more.

Aleesha and Roy. He smiled to himself. Roy? He laughed and pinched his nose. Who the fuck was called Roy?

Eddy stopped too fast and the seat belt bit into Pat's chest and waist. He looked and saw Eddy staring up at the sky through the windscreen, looking for cameras. They were in a street off Maryhill Road, it would have been a busy road once but everything around it was knocked down and the street was one way now. A lone phone box stood at a street corner.

Eddy undid his seat belt and Pat felt suddenly panicked and hurried to undo his. 'No worries mate, I'll do it.'

'Naw.' Eddy had that face on him, the let's-have-a-big-fucking-fight face. 'I'll do it.'

Pat stared him out and slid his belt buckle back into the clip. 'Go on then.'

Eddy's jaw jutted once, a small punctuation mark to the fight they hadn't had, and he turned and got out, slamming the door. Pat knew Eddy would be doing his hard-man swagger. As a petty act of spite he didn't watch Eddy stride across the road. He knew the walk well enough: shoulders up, head wheeling left and right, looking for the fates that defied him.

This was the sort of thing Morrow excelled at, looking, seeing, processing. She pulled her office door shut, set her chair at a good distance from the monitor and clicked on the first of Omar's files.

It was an Excel spreadsheet of meaningless figures, the years at the top, starting with the present, and in the columns below gradually increasing numbers following a starkly straight trajectory. She snorted a laugh when she saw that rounded figure of £80,000 in the final column. Not a penny less, no odd bits of change. It was a joke, a fiction, a bedtime story to himself.

Hurriedly she looked through the other files: badly scanned VAT forms. He didn't have any capital, or income, didn't even know how to fill out the form. It was as if he'd heard a rumour about the scam but hadn't listened properly.

'Malki Tait's ma says he was out till two last night.' Bannerman was smiling at the door, standing a little outside so that she wasn't really sure he was talking to her. She'd expected him to be annoyed at her for crashing his glory meet with MacKechnie but he seemed quite calm.

'Where is he now?'

'Doesn't know.'

'Did he just walk out of the house this morning?'

'Left the house in a minicab this morning. Gobby and Routher called around the local firms and found the cab that attended the address. They're tracking down the driver for a destination. Anyway,' he fell back into the corridor, 'move it. We've got Omar upstairs. His lawyer's with him. I want you with me.'

She looked at the thumbnail images on her screen. 'I don't think he's doing a VAT fraud, Grant, to be honest—'

'Yeah, let's go up and find out.' Bannerman wasn't looking at her. He was smiling down the corridor.

28

Omar didn't look up as his lawyer shepherded him down the corridor to the interview room. He didn't look worried so much as exhausted. His eyes were red, like someone who'd been eccied, up all night, and had just started coming down. Morrow saw him shut them tight a few times, as if trying to coax moisture across them. She felt a bit that way herself. She thought of home and hoped Omar's interview would drag on and on, that they'd uncover information that would spark an urgent new course of investigation. She was overtired now and felt too delicate to go home.

It was teatime, shift change at the station, and the interview rooms were all empty. Bannerman chose Four, a slightly larger room than Three, with a newer camera lower down on the wall so that their faces would be seen in the viewing room. The lawyer was aware of the camera and tried to get Omar a seat with his back to it. It was a sharp move. A video of even a slight inconsistency in evidence, a sarcastic remark, an unpleasant manner, could go a long way to conviction if it came down to a jury trial. Morrow wondered what Omar had told her.

Bannerman was aware of what they were doing, though, and insisted that they take the side of the table facing the camera. When the lawyer asked him slyly why, he said it was because he wanted them facing the camera and he was questioning them, not the other way around.

She conceded and they took their seats, the lawyer on the outside, unpacking her papers and pens, Omar by the wall, shifting about in his seat, wringing his hands under the table, getting them out again. Morrow watched him from the corner of her eye. He didn't seem unduly nervous, not guilty-nervous, just appropriately uncomfortable.

Lord of them all, Bannerman was the last to take his place at the table. He stood behind his chair and undid his jacket button, flapping the front panels back as if clearing the reach for his guns. He looked at Omar, who looked innocently back and grinned. Then Bannerman sat down.

He and Morrow busied themselves with cassette tapes, fitted them, turned the machine on and waited for the beep to notify them that the recording had begun. Bannerman told it who was here, the date and made the lawyer say her name.

The lawyer was young, a pretty blonde woman with an enormous amount of make-up on. Pearly pink blusher was drawn in thick stripes across her cheeks and eyelashes glued into black sticks.

Omar looked even thinner than yesterday but that was due to his clothes. They weren't baggy like the traditional dress he had worn the day before but western clothes, a black T-shirt of thick cotton, a yellow 'Diesel' slogan on it. It was fitted around his narrow waist and broad shoulders, and his baggy jeans sat halfway down his hips with white underpants showing above them. He looked like a model, not cut-glass handsome but one of those daring models who straddled the ugly/handsome boundary.

When they were all settled he looked up and recognised Morrow from the night before. 'Oh, hi again,' he said, eyes open and hopeful, pleased to see her, not at all like an accused.

Both Bannerman and the lawyer put their hands on the table in front of him to stay the conversation. 'Let's do the formalities,' prompted the lawyer nodding at Bannerman who cleared his throat.

'Omar, in the course of our investigations we have un-covered some facts that we would like to ask you about. In relation to that you're being detained here and I'm going to read you this caution, OK?'

Omar answered at the same time as his lawyer's formal response that he was willing to cooperate in any way: 'Oh, 'course, aye, yeah. Fine.'

Bannerman held the laminated sheet up and read the formal caution slowly. He looked at the lawyer at the end to make sure she'd witnessed it. She gave him a noncommittal nod. Bannerman asked Omar, 'Do you understand?'

'Yeah, yeah, I do,' said Omar, whose attention seemed to have wandered a little during the recitation.

'Well, Omar, first of all, you said in the interview last night that the gunmen were looking for—'

'Rob, I know.' Omar covered his eyes with his willowy hand and cringed. 'I know, sorry. I spoke to Billal and he said you knew it was Bob. Sorry about that.'

'. . . not be flippant,' muttered the lawyer.

Omar straightened his face and opened his giant hands towards them in appeal. 'No, I know, I *am* sorry. I am. We just, you know, thought it would be better if you were looking for those guys instead of thinking it was something to do with me.'

'When did you decide to lie?'

Omar frowned as if he thought Bannerman was being rather rude dwelling on it. They didn't need to know the details but Morrow knew Bannerman was taking charge, drumming home that he was the man and Omar shouldn't fuck with him.

Coldly Bannerman repeated, 'At what point in the evening did you decide to tell us a lie?'

Omar dropped his gaze. 'Well, um, after we called 999.

When the ambulance came, just before the ambulance came.'

'How did you decide?'

Omar's mouth flapped once. 'Wha'?'

'Did you all get together and agree a version of what happened?'

'No,' he was adamant, 'no, no, no, listen we were, Mum was, tying a tea towel to Aleesha's arm, and we just sort of said, you know, might be best if we said Rob instead of Bob.'

'You said it?'

'I dunno, no, I think Bill said it. Said, you know, best just say Rob instead, since some folk call me Bob.' He looked confused. 'Is it that big a deal?'

'So your family know you're called Bob by some people?'

'Yeah, yeah, they know.'

'Your dad knows you're called Bob?'

It was a good move, Morrow had to give it to him, a good build to the point and a good crash. Omar frowned at the table.

'What do you suppose your dad's thinking now? They came looking for you and you didn't own up so they took him. What do you think he's thinking now?'

Tearful, Omar shrugged.

Bannerman leaned in, spoke softly: 'Do you get on with your dad?'

Omar's voice was soft, childlike. 'Not ... great. Better recently.'

'Better recently?'

He shrugged again, a small gesture, shameful. 'Been trying harder.'

'Why?' asked Morrow.

He sucked his teeth, looked as if he was thinking about telling a lie, looked at Bannerman and Morrow in turn. 'He's loaning me the capital to start a business. The condition is that I abide by his rules.'

'Capital for a business?'

'Yeah.' He seemed quite happy to talk about it but Bannerman brushed it aside for the moment.

You lied to us and said 'Rob' so that it didn't look as if it was about you?'

Omar nodded at the table.

'But it *was* about you.'

'No, no, no, it wasn't anything to do with me—'

'They came looking for you. Gunmen were after you and you just stood back and let them take your dad.'

The force of indignation brought him to his feet. 'No!' but his lawyer slid her hand over the table again, a flat hand that commanded him to sit back down. She had coached him well because he did.

Bannerman opened his mouth to speak but Omar burst in: 'As I told you last night I was sitting in that car and ran in when the gun went off. I was stunned. My wee sister was shot up! There was blood every fucking where, I could hardly hear what they were saying but if you see guys wi' guns and there's blood everywhere, you know whatever they ask you to do isn't going to be good, is it? You can't hardly hear what anyone's saying in a situation like that either, I didn't think they'd grab him.'

'OK,' said Bannerman, sounding reasonable. 'Fair enough.'

'You wouldn't put your hand up to it. S'counter intuitive.'

'OK.' Bannerman looked at his notes and Morrow caught his eye, asking permission. He blinked a yes.

She spoke softly. 'Why were you and Mo sitting outside in the car?'

He sucked a hiss through his teeth, thinking about the consequences. 'OK: Nugget's well religious—'

'*Nugget?*'

'My da.' He scowled at her. 'His name in the family. Nugget.'

'How come?'

'It's what Aleesha calls him – Naggy Uganda Guts.'

Morrow smiled. 'She's got quite a strong character, Aleesha?'

Omar nodded admiringly. 'If that's what you call it.'

'What would you call it?'

'Mental. Scared of none of them. Told Meeshra to fuck off and shut up when she was in labour.'

'Someone told us you expected her to run away when she turned sixteen.'

'I'm amazed she hasn't. They treat her like shit.'

'Your mum treats her like shit?'

'Nah, Mum admires her. I think she wishes she was her. They sent us to private school and sent her to a comprehensive, did you know that?'

'Did they run out of money?'

'No. Girls don't need an education, according to him. What is this, the eighteen-fifties?'

'You don't agree with that?'

'She reads all my books on her own, my uni text books. Didn't go in for the last three months of school and still got top grades in her GCSEs. School don't want her to leave. She's upping the entire year's average.'

'Has she got a boyfriend, friends who could have done this?'

'No.' He was certain. 'Stays in her room working, reading mostly, only comes out to watch telly when no one else is around.'

'Doesn't go to mosque?'

'*She's an atheist.*' He was so impressed by her he could only whisper it.

'But she doesn't get on with your dad?'

'Naggy Uganda Guts.'

'Is he a nag?'

'Non-stop. Calls from the shop, on the hour, to find out what we're doing and tell us to stop it and do something else.' Omar didn't sound bitter but fond, wistful, as if he was missing it.

'So he's very religious?'

'Um, yeah, he is now. Never used to be much, sent us to Catholic school and that, but Billal got big into religion and Nugget sort of started going mad for it as well. I think, well . . .'

'Well what?'

He shrugged. 'Getting older, eh? Sort of feel your family move away from you. Religion's something to have in common. Now I have to go along with it, condition of getting help wi' my business.'

Whenever he mentioned the business she could feel Bannerman thrill next to her. It was to be his finale with Omar but the fact that Omar kept bringing it up was as significant to Morrow as the silly numbers in the income columns. It meant the business was a nothing. Something to talk about.

'Why did Billal get religious?'

'Dunno.' Omar avoided her eye. 'Just did.'

'When?'

'Couple of years ago.'

'Nothing to do with 9/11 or anything, the backlash to that?'

'Nah.' Omar was sure. 'Long after that. To be honest I've taken less religious abuse *since* 9/11, but, I suppose, I'm not making my way to school everyday in a green and gold uniform any more.'

Green and gold, Catholic colours. The school would be

just as well sending the kids home with a 'kick me' sign on their backs.

Morrow smiled. 'Did you take abuse for that?'

'Fuck aye, non-stop. Boys on the train used to chuck lit matches at us.'

'So, a couple of years ago Billal got religion and then your dad got into it?'

'Yeah and he's mad for it. Thinks it'll bring us together as a family but, well ...' And suddenly here before them was the terrified son, bent, tremble-chinned, afraid for his daddy and horrified by his part in all of it. His spine bent slowly until his nose was an inch from the tabletop, hiding his face in his hands. He clutched the hair on his crown, holding his head off the table as he choked out spluttering tears.

Bannerman adjusted his collar. The lawyer fingered her notes. Only Morrow watched the boy as his back heaved and he managed to draw in a breath. He couldn't look at any of them. His hands swiped the wet away, first right, then left. The lawyer held out a tissue between two fingers, not looking at him. Her manner told him to stop it, stop embarrassing all of them by bringing this turmoil into their work.

Omar took the hankie. 'I'm not that ... You know ... committed. I was outside in the car when the gunmen ... because me and Mo left Ramadan prayers early. I knew if I went in to the house early Nugget'd be mad ... I was just waiting ... till it was the right time, so he'd think ...'

Morrow asked, 'Was Billal converted by someone?'

'No, no.'

'Just spontaneously got very religious?'

'Uh huh.' Omar wouldn't look at her, swallowed as if he was trying to stop himself saying something and brought it back to himself: 'I'm not that committed.'

Bannerman took a breath as if he was going to speak but Morrow cut him off – 'Your dad wanted you to be a lawyer?'

Omar looked surprised, but it was hardly a difficult deduction. 'Aye, he does.'

'But you never even went for interviews?'

'Nah. Not for me.'

'We met Tormod MacLeòid.' Morrow raised an eyebrow.

'Yeah, you might understand what put me off, then.'

'So, you'll defy your dad on that issue, but not on the matter of religion?'

'Well, different thing, eh?'

'How?'

'Well, it's about being part of something for him. Nugget's not part of much, he's had a hard life ... I want to please him, he's my da, he's financing my business but I mean, Ramadan's two hours prayers every night—'

Bannerman couldn't resist any longer. 'Omar, what is the business you've just set up?'

'Importing cars.'

'*Cars?*'

'Yeah, classic cars. They don't last here because of the weather. You can import them from, like, Spain and Italy and that. Fraction of the price. If you can get them here you can make a big margin selling them on.'

'How much does shipment cost?'

'I don't know. Shipping companies won't really tell ye until you've got an actual thing to import but on the Internet I noticed the differential in the market and the prices between, like, here and there. Could be making like three, four thou on every single car ...'

Bannerman smirked. 'What if it cost that much to ship them?'

This had clearly never ever occurred to Omar. He shrugged, exhausted. 'It can't.'

Morrow butt in. 'Can't?'

'Yeah. It can't cost that.'

'Why not?'

He shrugged. 'Just . . . can't cost that much.'

She thought about Billal. 'Why did you tell your brother you were importing silicone chips?'

Omar snorted a laugh. '*Silicone* chips?'

'He thought it was chips you were importing.'

'Billal's . . . we don't talk about business.' He seemed a bit annoyed about it.

'Why did you have VAT forms scanned onto your computer?'

'Oh, well, I know there's loads of admin, running a business, I was just playing around. Got like a spreadsheet package, payroll, tax forms and stuff came free with it. Just messing about.' He frowned. 'Why?'

'Did your dad buy the shed?' Bannerman glanced at Morrow.

'Aye. He took me to PC World and bought the small business package as well.'

It was the most ill-considered business plan she'd ever heard but Omar seemed certain it would work. It occurred to her that Omar was not quite the criminal mastermind they had supposed and yet he was clearly very bright.

Morrow stepped in. 'Omar, how come you can afford a Lamborghini?'

The lawyer jerked her head around to face him and Omar panicked. 'Lamborghini?'

'The Lamborghini,' said Morrow, calm and enjoying it. 'How can you afford it if you need your dad to buy a shed for you?'

'Well,' he coughed, 'the Lamborghini . . .' he scratched his face. 'See, with that, the thing is—'

The lawyer leaned across him to Morrow. 'We need a comfort break.'

'You've just come in.'

'We need one *now*.'

'OK. Let's take ten minutes, then.' Bannerman noted the time, that they were stopping for a short break and switched off the tape recorder.

The lawyer stood up. 'Omar and I are going out to the corridor for a moment.'

'Are we?'

'Yes,' she ordered. Omar got up and trotted out after her. He looked scared.

Bannerman and Morrow sat at the table, feeling distinctly like the winning side as Omar and his lawyer whispered in the corridor. Morrow checked her buttons and make-up, flattened her hair and then Bannerman gave her a comradely smile. They knew better than to speak within earshot of the person they were questioning but Morrow shrugged and mouthed 'Not VAT?' Bannerman beamed.

The lawyer came back in with her jaw clenched and sat down on the inside this time. Omar followed her sheepishly and sat down where she pointed him to sit.

'Mr Anwar wants to tell you about the Lamborghini now.'

'OK,' said Bannerman slowly, putting the tape back on, getting the details on it and sitting back smugly. 'So, Omar, you wanted to tell us about the Lamborghini?'

Omar cleared his throat. 'Yes,' he said formally, 'I *do* want to tell you about it. I have been thinking about ordering a Lamborghini from the Stark-McClure garage in Rosevale Road.'

'*Thinking?*'

'Well, I've done a couple of test drives and I put down a deposit, my dad put it down, as a present for getting a first in my degree.'

276

'Deposit?'

'Aye.'

'Much?'

'Two grand.'

'Is that all?'

'Yeah, but when the order goes through you have to pay the full amount.'

Bannerman tried not to smirk. 'And I suppose you have documentation to the effect that your dad put the deposit down for you?'

Omar looked at his lawyer who nodded angrily at him to tell Bannerman.

'The receipt is in his name and the credit card payment is his. Both receipts are in the strong box my dad keeps on top of the fridge in the kitchen.'

Not sure where to run with the ball Bannerman got angry. 'They came looking for you, for Bob, who knows you as Bob?'

'Loads of people. Half the Southside calls me Bob.'

'Did people at uni call you Bob?'

'No.'

'You were in the Young Shields?'

'Well, I hung about with them a bit. As I said, I was getting battered on my way home from school ... St Al's uniform was a bit of a beacon.'

'How did you leave the Shields?'

'My dad found out I was hanging about with them and grounded me for six months.' He looked angry about it and then talked himself round. 'He was right, he was right to do that actually. I started working hard then, 'cause I was stuck in all the time anyway and that's when I started doing well at school ...' Thinking about his father, his eyes welled up again. He looked at the three adults around the table. Again Morrow was the only one who didn't look away. 'Do you think he'll be OK?'

She wasn't one for doling out cheap comfort. 'We're doing our utmost,' she said. 'Omar, who do you think did this?'

'I have absolutely no idea. Who has a gun? Isn't that the big thing? Who could even get a gun like that?'

Bannerman made a play of looking at his notes and then put them down. 'What else have you lied about?'

Omar opened his hands wide. 'Nothing, man, swear.'

Bannerman stared at him. 'Omar,' he said softly, 'what else have you lied about?'

Omar looked concerned and turned to his lawyer. 'I haven't lied about anything else. I dunno what to say . . .'

'Yes,' she said, 'I think we've done all we can here.'

Suddenly furious, Bannerman slapped his hand loudly on the table. 'We are questioning you, Mr Anwar. This isn't a game. We're attempting to find your dad and you're supposed to be helping us, not impeding our work.' Bannerman had judged it wrong, he was too angry, too loud, and everyone sat still around the table. Morrow watched a bubbled fleck of Bannerman's spit that had landed on the tabletop. The skin thinned and the bubble burst.

Bannerman looked at his notes again, holding them up as if he wanted to hide behind them. He dropped them angrily on the table. 'The kidnappers called again this evening?'

'Yes they did,' said Omar obediently.

'You offered them forty thousand pounds.'

'I did.' Omar seemed afraid to look up. 'I offered them that, yes.'

'How did you arrive at that figure?'

'I went to the bank this afternoon. That's all the money we have in our bank accounts.'

'All the money your dad has in his accounts?'

'They're family accounts, one's under the name of his business.'

'What did the kidnappers say to that?'

'Said fuck off.'

'Meaning that's not enough to get him back?'

'Yeah.'

Bannerman sat still. 'Omar, what would you say about a man who had the money to get his father back like that,' he clicked his fingers, 'and didn't pay up?'

Omar frowned at Bannerman's fingers. 'Had the money?'

'A man who had the money sitting in a shoebox in the back room, had plenty of money just sitting about but refused to hand it over.'

'Why would anyone do that?'

Bannerman shrugged. 'You tell me. Maybe he hates his dad.'

'He's still his dad though.'

'Maybe he got the money doing something he shouldn't. Maybe he knows he'll get in a lot of trouble if he hands the money over. What would you say about someone like that?'

Omar looked up into a corner of the room, considering the scenario, and brought a steady gaze down to Bannerman. 'I'd say he was a total bastard,' he said simply.

29

They both knew it. Of all the grim fucking nights they had spent together in the past ten years, this would be the longest.

Pat couldn't bring himself to ask about the birthday Eddy had forgotten, or nod that it was the wife's fault because she didn't remind Eddy in time. That he hadn't asked about it meant that a fight was brewing. They'd had fights before, when they were drunk, over money, but they were both angry those times. Only Eddy was angry now. Without discussion, without warning, Pat had shifted away.

Eddy ground his teeth as he drove, his nostrils flared, a distant look on his face, as if he was daydreaming about hurting someone. Pat wondered if Eddy had his gun with him. His own was still down the back of the bin in Shugie's kitchen.

The Lexus pulled slowly through the moat of gravel around Breslin's, crossed a grassy bank and onto the concrete runway. Eddy stopped in front of the loading bay entrance. It was open, big enough for three lorries to back up for loading at the same time. Eddy pulled on the handbrake, leaned over the wheel, snorted at the dark mouth of the door, and looked at Pat expectantly.

Pat blinked. The plastic bag on his lap was burning the skin on his thighs. It was a Chinese takeaway. Oil had leaked out of a bag of spring rolls and puddled in a corner of the blue plastic, burning into his lap. Even though they hadn't eaten since their morning roll and the cabin was saturated with the delicious aroma, Pat didn't want to eat.

He stared hard at the door, blinked, looked out of the passenger window. He wanted to throw the passenger door open and run, to run away across the dark fields, run through the knee-deep marshes, away to the fast road and hitch a lift back to the city.

'Malki'll be hungry,' said Pat, blinking faster now, as if he could wipe the night away. Eddy opened his door and Pat did the same. They stepped out into the dark.

Breslin's had been shut down twenty or so years ago and the building was disintegrating. The cantilevered lintel above the loading bay door had snapped off and now barred the doorway, the metal struts sticking out of the concrete, twisted and rotted orange. The whole of the building had been colonised by defiant vegetation, bursting through the cracks, easing the slabs apart in geological time.

Leading the way ahead of Eddy Pat carried the takeaway reverentially, as if he was leading an offertory procession. He ducked under the collapsed lintel, stepping into the wall of blackness inside. His footsteps sounded dead as he took the stairs up to the loading platform, and through the door into the packing hall. He stopped, waiting for his eyes to adjust to the dark, but it was too thick.

Eddy stepped in front of him, holding up his mobile phone high for the light from its face. The blue gleam barely made a dent in the dark, the phone was old, so he supplemented it with a pen torch he kept on his keyring.

Holding the mobile high and the pen torch low, they picked their steps into the room. Pat followed Eddy, clutching the takeaway to his chest for warmth. It seemed very quiet. They expected Malki to have a wee radio on or something, to have a wee light on, they'd left him a couple of candles and knew he'd be off his nuts anyway. Junkies were like cats or foxes, they could make themselves comfortable anywhere.

Silently, Pat and Eddy made excuses to themselves all the way through the packing bay, but at the mouth of the works room they could see that there was no light on, no whispery radio, no bed made of newspaper, no snoring. Pat stuck his face through the doorway, into the absolute dark, listening.

The works room had a metal floor, metal tables bolted to it, some of the legs bent where someone had tried to lever them off the ground but failed. Metal steps at the back led up to the big circular boiler where they had left the pillowcase. The whole room was metal, a leaf couldn't pass through without making a noise. But they heard nothing.

Malki wasn't sitting where they'd left him. The candles weren't lit, there wasn't even a sound of him hiding from them, if he thought they were the police or something. Malki had fucked off. It was going to make everything worse.

Pat whispered before he even realised he was going to, 'Malki?'

Eddy muscled in the doorway next to him, held the torch up. The pinpoint pierced the room, dimming twenty feet away, casting a narrow canal of glow, helping hardly at all.

'Malki?' Pat spoke louder, telling himself he'd feel foolish when Malki walked in at the back of him. 'Where are ye?'

Holding the mobile and torch in one hand Eddy reached into his pocket and took out a bag of five tea light candles, bursting the plastic with his teeth, taking out a lighter and bending down, emptying the candles on the floor. He set them up right, lit the lighter but it was draughty. The first couple of times he tried the wind blew the flame out. Purposefully he crab-walked into the room, his feet clanking on the metal floor, the sound booming around the empty space. He set the candles up at the base of the wall inside, in a line, each dropping to the ground with a little 'pup' that echoed around the metal room. His lighter took, successfully catching the wicks with the flame.

Pat watched Eddy crouching, rolling forward rhythmically over and back, over and back, like a man up to his waist in rough seas, and he knew then that Eddy was so angry he was on the brink of going absolutely fucking mental.

Pat put the takeaway down on the floor and looked around. The candles tried but failed, their poor light struggling against the blackness, seeping into it and being swallowed, deepening the shadows. Pat looked up to the boiler. The steps were empty, the platform at the top of the ladder beyond the thin reach of the light, a black void. He stepped towards it, calling softly for his wee cousin, pleading with him to come out, hoping to Christ that Eddy didn't have a gun in his pocket, certain that he would be looking for an excuse to use it. Pat couldn't let Eddy shoot him. Malki wouldn't fight back. Like his long gone father Malki was a rogue, but a gent. He wasn't even a fast runner.

'I'm going to look outside,' snarled Eddy, the glow from his mobile phone lighting his chin, making him resemble a Halloween ghoul.

'No!' Pat's voice snapped back from the cold metal floor. 'Just,' he held a hand up, 'just wait a minute. Give us the fucking pen torch.'

He took the keys from Eddy, holding the torch steady, not looking at his hurried hands as he fitted the spokes of the keys on it through his fingers to make a weapon in case Eddy went for Malki.

He headed to the ladder, hoping to find warm foil or a burnt spoon on the landing. Maybe Malki was outside pissing; he was like that, had nice manners, ideas about how to do things, keeping things clean. He put his foot on the first step and pulled himself up.

The narrow beam of torchlight spilled over the landing

step to the boiler door and Pat saw that it was open. Thinking Malki had let the pillowcase go and had run off himself, he took the next step and the light swept into the round belly of the boiler. A white leg, a blue cap, squinty, a blue stripe, wet. Red.

Pat dropped his hands to the dusty step, scrambling up the remaining steps, across the landing, into the black dark of the boiler.

Still as a waxwork. Malki was lying flat on his back, arms out-stretched like Jesus, one knee pulled up to his side, a dancer in mid flight. Pat reached forward and took his hand as if he was going to shake it. Rigid, skin cold. The mouth was open, lips pulled tight across his teeth. Dry. The teeth were dry.

A crash from behind heralded Eddy running towards him, jumping up the steps, pointing his phone, the dull gleam whipping around the inside of the boiler, then steady. Eddy stood in the doorway, shining the brutal light at Malki's face. Scarlet freckles were splattered all over his face. It came from his neck, at the side, a ragged mess of skin, like something had burst out of it, a cut like lips, only an inch or so long, but the redness came from it. A puddle had formed underneath Malki and soaked into his white tracksuit, it was working its way up through the material. He looked old, skullish, but Pat knew he was just a wee boy.

Eddy: 'How did the cunt get overpowered by a midget Paki?'

Slowly, Pat stood up. He stared straight into the beam of light, an expression on his face that made Eddy's feet falter. 'My phone . . .' said Pat flatly.

Eddy tipped his head quizzically, as though he had never seen Pat's face before. Pat pushed past him, down the ladder. His steps fell loud as cannons as he crossed to the door.

'Um, Pat?' Eddy called after him, his voice small, 'are ye off to phone his ma?'

With wide purposeful strides Pat passed through the packing room to the light at the loading bay door. Eddy's voice was thin and far away.

'I'll wait here then, eh?'

Through the loading bay, under the lintel, into the broad concrete road, Pat burst into a run, faster and faster until he got to the car and then a sudden burst of adrenalin made it impossible to stop. He sprinted the three hundred yards to the end of the concrete strip, dropped to touch the edge for reasons he would later find bewildering, and bolted back to the car. He was by the door, jogging on the spot, knees up to his chest, faster and faster and faster, trying to keep time with his heart, lifting his fists in time, punching his chest. He panted like a woman in labour, trying to breathe the pain out, trying to burn it up.

Twenty-three years ago Pat had sat on a settee with his feet not reaching the end of the seat. Auntie Annie sat next to him, her hands hovering beneath the baby's back and head, and Pat holding the baby for a photo. Pat grinning, the baby turning away from him, secretly making an ugly face that no one knew about until they got the picture back from the chemist's. They'd ordered two sets.

Malki once had a girlfriend who looked like a monkey. Big jaw. She chucked him and he cried for a week.

A car door, blue, new, swinging open in a street in Shettleston as Pat yomped the five miles home in shitting icy rain one Hogmanay night and Malki's gleeful face grinning out from the driver's seat. 'Lift?' He was thirteen.

Pat kept running on the spot until his lungs felt like they might burst. The energy left him as fast as it had come. He slumped over the roof of the car, pressing hard against the cold metal. Pat pushed his face into the roof, pushed until the bridge of his nose clicked.

Standing up, he drew in a breath and held it. The marsh smelled of rotting things, of dead grass melting into the water. Without a thought in his head Pat pressed the button on the car key in his hand, opened the door and climbed into the driver's seat. He shut the door and locked it, adjusted the seat to fit him, pulled the seat belt over himself.

He flicked the headlights on just as Eddy's face appeared under the lintel. Eddy's mouth was open, eyes wide as the headlights crossed him. Swinging the car in a wide circle on the concrete, Pat turned around and drove away.

30

Morrow drove home through the calm traffic, wishing it was heavier, hoping someone not far in front would have an accident. No one did.

Blair Avenue was settling in front of the television after a heavy dinner, curtains were being pulled, lights were on upstairs as families spread out and children steeled themselves to do their homework. A man coaxed an old dog along the road, touching its back to remind it of the direction. Three teenage boys eyed two girls chatting showily on a far corner.

Her curtains were drawn open, the light was on in the living room but she couldn't see the flicker from the TV. They had a security timer on the lights. He might not even be in there.

Taking her courage in both hands she reach forward, took the car key from the engine and opened the door to the street. She put one foot on the road, made the other one follow it, slammed the door, locked it and kept her head down as she walked up the path to the house. He'd done some tidying in the garden since this morning. Weeds pulled up and the loose soil brushed back off the tiled path. He'd brushed the steps as well.

Her key was in and the door half open before she heard the radio from the kitchen. Her chin crumpled, a hot red flush rose to her eyes, making her stop on the step to take a deep shuddering breath. Dread of home. Not tonight. Not him and not tonight.

Being stuck on her own doorstep made her angry and

she used the feeling to open the door and step in. Shutting it carefully behind her, she dropped her shoulders and let the coat slide down her back and into her hands. She threw the coat on the end of the banister, dropped her bag so that it would be in the way and marched into the kitchen.

Perched at the end of the kitchen table, Brian was doing some work on his laptop. He had heard her coming in, was already looking up at her, the resentment smothered by his pursed lips. White light from the computer screen glinted off his glasses, turning his eyes into harsh silver razor blades.

'Alex . . . ?'

'Hi.' She meant to sound light but it came out leaden. She dropped her keys on the counter. 'Big case, didn't get back last night. Haven't slept for about forty hours.'

'Hm. You must be tired.'

She almost laughed at the banality of the observation. He sat back, one of his broad shoulders turning a circle as if his neck was sore. He looked at her, his mouth twitched softly. He was waiting patiently for her to answer. 'Yes,' she responded in the same bland tone. 'I am. How are you?'

'Fine. Neck's a bit sore again. The plumber came, sorted out that drain in the garden.'

She flicked through the gathered letters on the table to give herself something to do. 'Good. Did he find the blockage?'

'Newspaper, he said.' Brian was trying to catch her eye, ducking his head to meet her, missing every time. 'He said someone in the street has been using newspaper instead of toilet paper. It doesn't dissolve in the same way.' She didn't speak. He waited for a beat. 'I think it's the students farther down, probably, in the Bianci house. They probably ran out of paper and were improvising.' He forced his mouth to smile, half closing his eyes, keeping them shut when the

288

smile was gone, trying to mask his hurt. 'Can I run a bath for you?'

Morrow no longer loved the texture of skin on his neck, no longer loved the way he held his mug or the steadiness of his gaze. 'Think I'll have some herbal tea. Want some?'

'I'm on the beer tonight.' He held his bottle up, as if guilty. 'Needed a beer ...'

She turned away and flicked on the kettle, biting her bottom lip hard to stop herself shouting.

Brian was skirting it, getting around to talking about *things*. Losing her breath she turned away to the crockery cupboard and issued a warning: 'God, I'm absolutely exhausted.' She took out a mug and watched the kettle rumble to its high C. *Don't say that, Brian. Don't fucking say it.*

Brian watched her back for a moment, she could feel him reaching for her and finding her gone. 'Well, you know what they say.' *Don't Brian, don't say that.* 'A watched kettle never ... well, you know.' He sniggered to cover his embarrassment.

Morrow kept her face to the kettle and brought her index finger to her mouth. She bit the knuckle so hard she could taste blood.

In the dark the artexed ceiling of the bedroom was a jagged mountain range. Morrow stared hard at it, angrily wishing herself asleep, making her way from one side of the room to the other, through the passes, sticking to the low ground. It calmed her, a big job, and the ceiling was broad and dark, hard to keep track of all the ridges. She had been doing it for almost an hour when she heard movement downstairs, a light snapping off, a door shutting. She listened, mapping the movements of Brian's slow, inexorable approach.

He had finished working, had pushed his chair back on

the stone floor with the backs of his knees. She heard him slap his laptop shut. He moved to the hall to put the laptop into the protective foam zip bag and then into his bag for the morning. He'd say it in his head because she wasn't there to say it to: *sorting things out, ready for the morning.*

Brain stayed safe in routine, in cliches. He ate the same lunch every day, ham and cheese on brown bread and an apple. Regular in his habits, predictable. Safe.

She was halfway along the ceiling, almost dead centre, when Brian had a quiet moment and she wasn't sure where he was, but then the dishwasher began its evening churn. Hall lights snapped off and then the steady thud of his feet up the carpeted stairs heading to the bathroom for his routine. Tooth brushing, flossing, examining the floss. Face washed and then dried, three pats of a towel – cheek, cheek, neck.

But Brian didn't go into the bathroom. At the top of the stairs he left the grid of predictability. He had stopped outside the nursery. She listened for him to move but he didn't. Brian stopped too long for it to mean he'd forgotten something, remembered something, was lost in an extraneous thought. He thought she was asleep, that he was alone, and out there in the lonely dark she heard him keening softly.

Separated by the splinters of the door, Brian cried quietly for the lost axis of his world and Morrow lost her way among the mountains.

31

His legs were numb, his hands were numb, his face, chest and heart were numb. Aamir stood in the tall grass with the sea behind him, looking back over the marsh he had waded through.

In the dark the water was black and still, a solid glass floor over an underworld. Aamir had no memory of passing through it. His clothes were wet and freezing around him, his skin tight, his muscles twitching but he looked back at the black and all he could recall was the loss of warmth. She was in there, lost.

He had cowered inside the metal tube for an infinity, staring at the brightness at the door, aware of the boy's body and then not aware. He thought he saw the tracksuit melt into the red dusty road. Quite suddenly, the wind was on his face, birds were in the air above him and his feet became wet, cold, his shins, his knees, his genitals. Pulling his knees up to walk became a Herculean task but he did it, holding her hand the whole time, dragging her behind him like a doll, like a heavy, dead doll.

In the black water, somewhere, at some point, his mother's hand slipped from his and took the heat of his body with her. She was in the water but he hadn't the courage to go back for her.

The sandy bank he was standing on slowly began to give way beneath his bare foot and he stepped away from the edge. He looked down. He had a slipper on. Just one. It had soaked up water and that was what had made his foot so cold. Remedying the problem of biting cold on his foot he slipped his foot out and stood in the dark, watching the damp dark sand rise up between his toes.

Around him the air began to lighten. A bird rose from the ground a hundred feet away. Aamir raised his face to it and saw a light, a bulb, swinging hypnotically in the dark. He lifted his right knee, took one step and then another.

Eddy watched as the sun rose over the wetlands, a sluggish October haze of dirty yellow behind nasty clouds. He sat on a concrete block at the end of the road burning-eyed, spent, and watched as birds rose from nests near the water and seagulls swooped over the far estuary, shrieking like indignant women. He was deep down cold. His head ached from grinding his jaw all night.

He turned, looking down the road. Apart from the security issue, he couldn't call a cab because he'd no fucking money to pay the fucker. Four miles to the nearest service station and he had £2.43. He came out with twenty on him, leaving his cards at home for security purposes, and he'd spent a good bit of that on the chinkie.

As the meagre sun came up he looked at his hands. Greasy from the chinkie food. Dirty. He rubbed his thumb and forefinger together. The dirt came off in a paste, rolled into greasy cigars. Brown. He looked at it closer, rubbing his fingertips into the bowl of his palm. It was blood. Junkie blood with Chinese grease over it. He'd been eating that. His stomach turned over: disgusting. Might have Hep B or Aids in it or something. He looked up at the sun as if it was responsible. Revolting. He said it aloud for company: 'Revoltin'.

The sun struggled into the heavy sky and he looked around at the rubble of Breslin's forecourt. Weans had been here, smashed every window, wrote on big blank walls with house paint. They'd written dirty words: shit, cunt, then run out of ideas and thrown it at a wall in a big splash. The tin was still there. Magnolia gloss.

Eddy sucked his teeth, reliving the bloody meal. If he left the takeaway empties in the building rats would come, maybe eat the face. The thought turned his stomach but he tried to pretend it didn't by frowning. They always ate a person's face in films but maybe that wasn't true. If they did it would be good. Unrecognisable.

He sighed, shifted his buttocks and pulled out his phone. The battery symbol was blinking. He'd been using it for light in the night, when the candles ran out, checking the floor for firewood but failing to find a single combustible item in the whole fucking factory.

He checked the time on the phone's face: 6.50. Too early. He'd be annoyed but Eddy couldn't wait any longer. He held the mobile to his forehead and shut his eyes, rerunning the facts in head, what to say and what not to say. Then he looked at the keypad and stabbed the number in with his blood-greasy finger.

The phone was answered with a deep silence.

'Me,' said Eddy, feeling suddenly overwhelmed and tearful.

'Let me guess,' said the Irish, 'you got nothing last night?'

'Correct.' Eddy had meant to plough on through the awkwardness of recriminations at the beginning but he lost his breath slightly and didn't trust his voice.

'What's happening?'

'Lost . . . a man.'

'*Lost?*' Irish seemed to be sitting up, paying attention suddenly.

'Aye. *Lost.*'

'The subject?'

'No, one of ours . . .'

'Where's the subject?'

293

'Hm.' Eddy looked around the grass in front of him as if expecting Aamir to pop up out of it and wave. 'Location unclear.'

'Unclear? *Unclear?*'

'Kind of . . .'

Irish was sitting bolt upright now, Eddy could tell, and he was leaning hard into the receiver. 'Son, just so we're clear about this: one of your guys is dead and the hostage got away, is that right?'

Eddy didn't like them talking normally; it made it all seem stupid and hopeless. He faltered, kind of groaning from inside his throat and managed a faltering, 'Uh huh.'

'You owe me for them guns anyway,' said Irish, sounding less cool and professional now, sounding worried and fretful. 'Right? I'm not letting you off wi' that, right?'

Eddy looked at the phone angrily. Irish was supposed to be a professional for fuck's sake, he was supposed to be unshakeable, the training was supposed to kick in when things went tits up. Eddy could do frightened-to-fucking-death himself. He listened to a hard breath on the other end and Irish spoke again. 'He got away. Has he arrived home, do you know?'

Eddy looked around the wetlands. 'No.'

'Will he?'

Eddy shut his eyes hard. He didn't want to talk about this. 'No.'

'Good. What did they offer you?'

'Forty grand.'

'Is that all?'

'Aye.' Eddy felt tearful at the thought of forty grand. 'Look, are you sure these people are pulling strokes?'

'Intel is rock solid. Intel is local, gave us the layout of the house, everything.'

Eddy wondered at that, at the Irishman having the layout

and not telling them about it. 'Just, they seem kind of normal, the house isn't all that big and there's a million of them living in it.'

'Pakis do that. Intel is solid. They're playing hard ball. Accept the forty. Arrange a pick-up this morning.'

'But forty grand's fuck all—'

'Cut and run, son. Call, accept, arrange for immediate pick-up.'

'Then disappear?' said Eddy hopefully, liking the fact that it all sounded like a training exercise, like a set of movements that guaranteed a successful mission.

Irish faltered. 'Well ... OK ...?'

Eddy frowned at the non sequitur.

'OK, look, I'll tell ye what. Call, accept, arrange for pick-up this evening at seven o'clock, right?'

'Why?'

A bluster of a sigh tickled Eddy's eardrum. 'Son, we do this all the time, never a hint of a worry, right? This one's ... complicated. Your first time, not a lot of ... guidance. But I'll say this for ye, son, you've shown real promise ... *Real* promise.'

Eddy wasn't stupid. He didn't really think he had shown promise; he'd made a couple of mistakes, but he wondered how it looked from that side of the Irish Channel. He'd lied a lot. Maybe it looked better there than it did from here.

'That's to be encouraged. Need good men. Call, accept and arrange pick-up for seven, I'll be off the ferry at five tonight. Meet me at the place at six—' The voice stopped, the phone light went out and Eddy looked at it. His phone had run out of juice.

Aamir lifted a knee and took the next step and the next and the next, heading for the light. The water was there, moving water, a sea. He walked along a rough path, stumbling, lifting knee after knee until he got to the light. A torch. It was on the ground, flat, the precious light spilling wastefully over a patch of concrete. Behind it stood a figure wearing a good warm winter coat, hood up, facing out to sea. Aamir blinked and saw that he was holding a fishing rod.

He turned his face to Aamir, his hood unmoving, his face sliced in half. The man was Aamir's age, Aamir's height, a Scottish man.

'Dear heavens,' he said, 'what in the name of God happened to you?'

32

Morrow's eyes opened a fraction, searching for the red numbers on the alarm clock radio, but she woke up facing the wrong way, towards Brian's side of the bed. The duvet was still tucked in, his pillow unflattened. She blinked again and rolled over towards the window. Morning scowled behind the curtains.

The alarm said 7.18. She could reasonably get up. Normally she would. She'd get up and leave him sleeping here for another forty minutes. She'd have the house to herself, listen to crap on the radio, eat toast, be alone, leave before he got up, but he was up already, out there, somewhere in the house.

She sat up, the duvet peeling off her, the warmth evaporating from it into the cold room. The heating was timed for 7.50. She liked the cold of the mornings, liked the prickle of chill on her face as she drank warm tea.

She sat up and looked at the closed bedroom door hatefully. She couldn't stay in here. She needed a pee. Aware that she'd just opened her eyes and was already angry, she threw the rest of the warmth off herself and stood up, going to the wardrobe and pulling out clothes for herself, clean shirt, fresh suit wrapped in thin plastic from the dry cleaners. Brown, her safe suit, the one she wore for assessment interviews. Pulling on the trousers and jacket made her feel stronger, smarter, armoured. She put on socks and shoes and stopped behind the door, warning herself just to get ready and out, don't engage, don't respond.

In the bathroom she found herself listening for him,

hypervigilant, like a house sweep. She washed her face and put on some mascara from the shelf behind the sink, tipping her head back, avoiding her own eye by staring at the lashes. The toilet flush sounded unreasonably loud and she stood watching the whirlpool in the bowl. Wherever he was in the house now he could hear her, knew where she was.

There was no radio on as she stepped down to the hall. His computer bag was still there, propped carefully against the wall, his jacket was hung up on the peg by the door. She passed the table and saw his keys in the bowl but he wasn't in the kitchen eating a neat breakfast or standing at the worktop organising his packed lunch.

Surreptitiously, pretending to look for something in her bag, she ducked back into the hall and glanced into the living room but he wasn't there either. Frowning, she flicked the kettle on, pulled some bread out of the bread bin and dropped it into the toaster and turned to look around. Brian was in the garden, wearing his dressing gown and propped up in a stained and faded deckchair they'd inherited from his parents. The wood had rotted and she'd wanted to chuck it but he insisted. Next to the deck chair, lying willy nilly in the wet grass, were three empty beer bottles.

She stood, frowning at him. Slowly his hand slipped down to the side, towards the bottles, limp, as if he was unconscious, as if he was dead. Overdose.

Morrow leapt across the kitchen, grabbed the handle for the French door and threw it open, not frightened but glad almost, glad there was an action to be performed. She stepped in front of the deckchair.

Brian was wearing sunglasses and a jumper under his dressing gown. He had walking boots on and a blanket over his knees. The other hand wasn't limp. The other hand was clutching a mug of cold tea. He looked up at her, over his glasses, tried to smile, but his gaze faltered and fell to her knees, as if he couldn't bear to look at her.

Morrow crouched down next to him, held his forearm, spoke with a professional voice. 'Brian, have you taken anything?'

Sluggishly he looked down at her fingers on his arm. It was the first time she had touched him in the five months since their son died. She looked up. His eyes were raw and broken but Brian wasn't sad or coping, wasn't smug or irritated, all those small nuanced things he always was. This was a Brian she didn't know, and he was looking at her neutrally, one eyebrow arched, protesting the impertinence of her touch.

Her fingers slowly retracted but their eyes were locked. He opened his mouth and whispered, 'Can't do this any more.'

She tried to deflect him. 'You need to get ready for your work—'

'Alex,' he said, his voice quiet and measured, as if he'd been thinking about this one sentence all night, 'I hate who you make me.'

The fisherman had laid newspaper on the car seat, ripped open a plastic shopping bag to protect it and then sat Aamir in the passenger seat. He was very kind. He turned his good winter coat inside out, because of the mud, and threaded Aamir's arms in, one at a time, pulled the cord on the waist tight to do it up. He even gave Aamir his socks to put on his numb feet.

Aamir sat in the haze of warmth from the car heater and looked at the socks as his feet thawed. Grey socks, red toes. They were thermal, the man said. Thermal.

He was alone in the car. The man busied himself outside,

packing up, folding a chair, pulling his fishing rod into bits and slipping them into socks of their own.

You think about that and I'll pack up, he had said.

Aamir was to think. His job, set by the man, was to think: where do you want to go?

It was off the motorway, on the edge of a large roundabout and would, she imagined, be a serious draw for people who cared about that sort of thing. In the window the luxury cars were polished to a wink, lined up on the diagonal against the glass wall so that the sun glinted off them, drawing the eye of covetous drivers.

The building was a glass box, two storeys high, with a canary-yellow Lamborghini hanging on a wired shelf, five feet off the ground, tilted towards the window like the display in a jeweller's.

The garage wasn't suppose to open until ten o'clock but two cars were parked up around the back, a small blue-grey BMW sports car with sharky gills along the side next to a dirty, unloved shit car, like hers.

Finding a plain door in the wall marked 'Deliveries' she knocked and waited an eternity. Again and again she knocked but no one answered. Finally she took out her mobile, thinking she should get the number and phone them, when a voice crackled over an intercom above her head.

'Whit?' A woman's voice, rough and nasal.

Morrow looked up at the source of the voice. A grey cone with a red ball on the end of it was attached to the wall above her head. A camera with an intercom system on it. She stepped back and looked up at it. 'I'm a police officer,' she said, finding her voice high and pleading. 'I want the manager.'

Another silence followed and a man's voice came on the

intercom, creamy smooth. 'Hello, may I help you today?'

Morrow got out her wallet, flipped it open and held it up to the camera. 'DS Alex Morrow, Strathclyde CID.'

She thought the voice said 'For fucksa—' and then the door buzzed and clicked and fell open. She pushed it, into a cold concrete corridor, took two steps and heard the door shut firmly behind her. She took another door ten feet away and stepped out into the plush showroom.

The glass walls were smoked and lent the room an evening air, like a smart hotel in a foreign locale frequented by wealthy businessmen. The cars were even shinier inside, their lines beguiling and the colours bright, like perfect children lined up for adoption.

An army of identical plug-in heaters littered the room, rumbling heat out into the ridiculous space, losing the battle against the faint smell of mouldering damp. In the distance, silhouetted against the window, a dumpy woman in track-suit bottoms and T-shirt vacuumed the dark carpet under a car.

A man her own age and height stepped in front of her, smiling politely. He wasn't good-looking, wasn't tall but was very carefully groomed. Even the grey fleck around the temples of his black hair looked like a deliberate design. His grey suit hung beautifully from his shoulders. He smiled, showing her an army of capped teeth. 'May I see your warrant card again, please?'

She got it out and gave it to him, noting that he knew a warrant card was called a warrant card and finding that interesting. He handed it back, letting off exactly the same smile. 'Many thanks.'

She couldn't look at the row of enamels without imagining a dentist going at his real teeth with a hammer and chisel.

'We have to be very careful,' he explained, 'because of the

value of the merchandise. So, what can I do for you today?'

'You had a car on order for a Mr Omar Anwar?'

'Hm, what brand?' He was smiling, not picking up on the air of menace she was trying to exude. Morrow felt a bit insulted.

'Lamborghini.'

'Ah, Lamborghini ...' He rolled his eyes towards the ceiling and she noticed that his bottom teeth were yellow and crooked, as if they were from a different mouth altogether. 'The bad boy. The King.'

'Aye, well you can cut the shite with me, I just want to see your records.'

He faltered at that. She shouldn't have said it. It wasn't just who she made Brian be, it was everyone. She was turning everyone she saw into an arsehole. It didn't used to be like that. She thought of Brian in his mum's old deckchair and her anger abated. 'I'm sorry, I shouldn't have said ... that was rude.'

The man showed her his teeth again. 'Yes, there's no need for language.'

She looked around the showroom again. 'Damp?'

He sighed. 'Smells, doesn't it? Wouldn't mind but we actually own the building so we can't threaten to move or anything. There's a stream.' He drew a line along the floor. 'We're suing the architect.'

'Good,' she said, trying to be friendly.

'Listen, I can't just show you someone's records of purchase without a warrant or anything. I have to protect my clients. Would be bad for business if people thought they couldn't trust us to be discreet.'

'Purchaser is more than happy for us to have a look at your records. Could bring him here or you can call him.'

'I think the latter would be more suitable.' He beamed again, better this time, as if his face was warming up. 'You have to appreciate, a lot of the people we sell to . . .' He gave her a knowing nod, smiled and walked away.

In Morrow's head she asked him if his clients were crooks, drug dealers, buying his cars with stolen money. In her head she threatened to look at all his records, pull the fuckers in and say she'd got it from him, give them his photo and let slip his name and address but she shut up. Gerald had died. It was the first time she'd thought the words since they left the hospital. Gerald has died. She hadn't said it to anyone because she couldn't even think it. Gerald died, but this, the carnage afterwards, this was her creation.

She followed him across the damp-smelling floor, blinking back small tears, wishing her hand was on Brian's forearm, before he looked at her, the scratch of the soft wood on her wrist.

The man's office was really just a large circular desk in the corner of the room, big enough to look fancy but up close just four curved tables shoved next to each other. He took his jacket off and hung it on a hanger, sat down in a wheeled office chair and walked himself across to the computer monitor, flicking on the hard drive. He sat, with his eyes on the screen, hands poised above the keyboard, a concert pianist waiting for the maestro's signal.

It took a long time. Behind Morrow the vacuum hummed and the fan heaters grumbled to one another. She'd been turning away from Brian since they left the hospital, since the lift down in the hospital in fact, insisting that she would carry both the plastic bags of Gerald's belongings, refusing to even let him take the SpongeBob doll from under her arm. She'd never felt it was a choice until now.

The monitor flicked bright suddenly and made them both jump. He smiled up at her. 'Oh,' he stood up formally and held his hand out, 'I'm Bill Prescott.'

Morrow shook the hand, wondering why she hadn't asked his name, worrying that she hadn't.

He sat back down, the smile lingering on his face, adding, 'General manager.'

Morrow nodded, shifted her weight, cleared her throat softly. It was suddenly getting warm in the showroom. She felt a prickle of sweat in her oxters.

'Here we go.' He used the mouse to choose a file, and picked up the phone next to him, dialling the number on the screen. Holding the receiver to his ear he smiled up at her, waiting, and suddenly his face brightened. 'Ah, hello, is this Mr Omar Anwar?' He nodded. 'This is Stark-McClure over on Rosevale, yeah, sure yeah uh, brilliant, OK, well listen, Mr Anwar, I have a police officer with—' He listened, looked at Morrow as if she was being discussed, smiled the million dollar smile, 'Great. That's OK with you, then? All and any documentation, Mr Anwar? Great.' Looking suddenly worried he nodded and tried to interrupt, 'I see. It is refundable. The full deposit isn't refundable but that deposit is. OK, will – will do. Fine, as I said before, sir, that's absolutely – OK, OK? Well, if you wanted to come in and look for any— OK, straight back to the account, OK. Great. Great. Bye. Bye.'

Bowing obsequiously he leaned forward, following the receiver down to the port, and hung up. He sat up and managed a faltering smile and spread his hands. 'Cancelled the order. Wants a refund. And he said you can have anything.'

Alex sat in her car in the car park and looked at the photocopies. The deposit had been paid in the name of Aamir Anwar. Bill Prescott explained at length that it was a deposit to secure a place on the Lamborghini waiting list, not actually a deposit for the car. Omar had cancelled it and wanted a full refund into Aamir's account.

Two grand was hardly evidence of massive international fraud. He could have saved it up himself from a bar job.

The receipts were confirmation of everything Omar had said the night before. It bothered her though. Three kids, a religious father and he was helping his unemployed youngest son to buy a Lamborghini. Not even the oldest son. And the father was frugal. He had a cheap white van parked in front of the house. That level of flash didn't sound consistent. She looked at the receipt again.

Aamir Anwar's account details had been blanked out by Bill Prescott but his name was there. Omar said yesterday that he could empty these accounts to pay for his father's return. He had access to those accounts. There was nothing to stop him paying for a car out of them as long as he repaid the money.

She realised what it meant: Omar was a fantasist, he didn't have money or a rich father, or a fraud scam. He was, at worst, optimistic about a bad business idea.

They had nothing but Malki Tait's fingerprints and the chances were they were from an old foil.

33

The office seemed unnaturally quiet when she got there. She went into her office, shed her bag and jacket and looked at Bannerman's desk. His computer was turned off and there was no coffee cup. She looked out into the corridor. MacKechnie's office was shut and dark too. They were off together somewhere. They were off to see the Fraud Squad. She should have phoned ahead about the garage.

The incident room was busy, DCs following up on leads and scraps, making notes, phoning. She didn't go in but turned and saw Harris sitting on his own in the small office, staring hard at a screen and looking even more pissed off than yesterday. She leaned into him. 'Ye right?'

He groaned. 'Up half the night with a blinding headache from watching this shite.'

'Poor you. Where's Bannerman?'

'Have you not heard?' He leaned forward and pressed the pause button. 'Bannerman's taken compassionate. His mum's got pneumonia apparently. She's in hospital.'

'*Compassionate?*'

'Yeah, doesn't know when he'll be back.'

She bit the dirtiest word she knew back, chewing on her inner lip until she got back into her office and closed the door. Morrow sat down. The cunt was ducking the cunting fucking case because he was a cunt and he was using his stinking fucking mother's pneumonia to do it. Killer fucking instinct, right enough. Cunt.

*

MacKechnie was fully aware of the situation Bannerman had put her in, but it was important for everyone to pull together and support him at this difficult time.

'So,' he said carefully, patting the desk in front of her chair, 'it falls to you to take his place as the SIO.'

Morrow sat back in the office chair by his desk and read his face. If he knew his protégé was dodging the job because it wasn't panning out, MacKechnie wasn't letting on. They looked at each other for a long while until MacKechnie broke off. 'You called me a racist a few days ago. You wanted this case so much you actually said that to me.'

She could see just how intensely he disliked her at that moment. Everything about her was wrong. It wasn't just that she was a woman, wasn't her habit of swearing or her brisk manner, her poor southsider accent, her lack of allies. What he disliked about her most was that she didn't really give a fuck, because wherever she was, whatever was going on in the gentle heave and sway of office politics, all she really cared about in the world was gone. MacKechnie could sense that dark belligerent void and knew that he couldn't touch her.

'This case is a great opportunity for you—'

'This case is big fat bollocks and you know it. The family are lying out of their arses. Thirty-six hours since he was taken and every minute that passes makes it less likely that we'll find the man alive—'

MacKechnie couldn't take it any more. He stood up and hissed at her, 'Do your job. Get out.'

Harris pulled the car up carefully to the curb. He needn't have been careful, there weren't many other cars in the street and they were mostly tucked away in bricked-over gardens at the front of the houses, but he was delighted to be out of the office and away from the videos and enjoying kicking the facts of the briefing about.

'Toryglen?'

'Yeah, dropped him off at the main road, he said.'

'Any Taits there?'

'No.'

'Didn't you find anything on the shop's CCTV tapes?' she said.

'Well, there are a couple of oddities but nothing major. I've highlighted them and asked Gobby to have a look at them, see if I was just going blind or what.'

'Show them to me when we get back.'

'Yeah. But boss, you know, even if it is VAT fraud it's a bit irrelevant. Even if the family are screwing millions out of the VAT office that only tells us how they became targets, it doesn't help us find the old man or get him out alive, does it?'

Morrow nodded. 'Yeah, but finding out how they were targeted'll lead us to the kidnappers. And when it comes to trial any defence lawyer's going to bring it up to discredit them. Makes the whole case harder.'

'S'pose.' Harris opened his door and stopped with one foot in the road. 'D'you reckon Bannerman's bunking off?'

It would be breaking rank to say so. 'DC Harris, whatever makes you say that?' As they stood on either side of the car looking down the road, getting the measure of the place, she asked him: 'Really, what makes you say that?'

He shrugged, still unsure of her. 'Rumour.'

'Oh.' He wasn't prepared to go into it. She liked that.

'What's the rumours about me?'

'There aren't any rumours about you, boss.'

She looked at him, worried they were skating close to sincerity and felt uncomfortable about it. 'Shame. I started a couple of good 'uns.'

'Except that you're getting the squeeze.'

She almost choked, she'd never expected sympathy and it touched her deeply. She looked away, hiding her face.

They were poor houses. A long curving street of flat-fronted council houses with telephone and electrical wires slung across them, grey plaster facades that had blackened into the architectural equivalent of a skin complaint. A lot of the houses had been bought by the tenants though: incongruous wooden porches were built around a couple of doors. One of the houses had mock Tudor windows, all lead strips and flouncy nets behind. The gardens were well kept too, carefully organised gravel and flower baskets hanging from walls, garden pots too big to pick up and walk away with, and hedges carefully trimmed where they grew. She wouldn't have chosen to live here but the people who did clearly liked it. Pink plastic toys littered the grass in one garden and a deflated football was resting by the curb in the street. Morrow noticed that the street was a dead end. It was a nice safe playground for kids. The street was empty though; all the children off at school, all the parents tending house or out working. At the end of the street a modern chapel loomed on a hillock like a village jail.

Malki Tait's address was number twelve. It looked like a pensioner's house from the outside. Modest china ornaments were lined up along the window sill; an Alsatian dog, a tiny China bouquet of flowers, a mouse holding a bit of cheese. The front step had just been washed, was damp but drying, the sweep of the wet handbrush lingering grey on the concrete.

The door was council, flat panelled and painted a jaunty cornflower blue, not a bought house, no money here, but the door hadn't been changed since the seventies. The tenant had been here since then. The council stripped out older fittings when new tenants moved in. They offered

309

new doors and windows to existing tenants too but the older ones usually wanted to keep things the same, being members of a generation who liked what they liked and didn't believe decor was subject to yearly fashions.

'Old lady,' guessed Morrow, pressing the doorbell.

'A quid,' bet Harris.

Shuffling steps, a weak call of 'hello' in an old lady's voice. Morrow smiled at the step. 'Mrs Tait?'

'Hello?'

Harris and Morrow looked at each other. Either she hadn't heard Morrow or she was working for time. Malcolm Tait could be walking out of the back door right now.

Suddenly animated, Morrow raised her fist to bang on the door and Harris backed away to the street, looking for a lane to the back garden. The door opened suddenly and a thin woman looked out at them, tipping her head back to see them through the bottom portion of red plastic bifocal glasses.

Annie Tait was wearing a pair of baggy red joggers and a white vest with bra straps showing. She had the arms of a much younger woman. She'd once had red hair like her son, but had dyed it blonde, two inch roots of red and grey mingled at her scalp. It was wild frizzy hair, the tips not helped by the drying effect of the hair dye. It looked like a rain-flattened afro. Embarrassed by her appearance she raised her hand to it. 'Who are you?'

Morrow stepped forward. 'I'm DS Morrow, this is DC Harris. We're here about Malcolm.'

'What about him? He's not been arrested?'

'No, Mrs Tait, we're just really keen to talk to him.'

Annie pulled the door shut so that she blocked the view of the house with her body. 'Keep the heat in ...' she explained to Harris and turned back to Morrow, as if she was the natural leader. 'I'm looking for Malki too. I'm always looking for bloody Malki. Did you get the taxi firm number?'

'We did, aye, that's what we wanted to talk to you about.'

'How?' Annie tipped her chin down, trying to see better through the top portion of the bifocals. Unsatisfied she went back to the bottom portion. The lenses were warping Morrow's view of her eyes, it was making her feel a bit sick.

'Can we come in, Mrs Tait? Would that be OK?'

Annie looked across the street, then up the road to the chapel, as if checking that Jesus wasn't watching and opened the door. 'Aye,' she wrinkled her nose as if she was letting a wet stray in for a drink of water, 'come in.'

Harris followed behind Morrow, closing the door behind himself. The hall was narrow and plain, painted green with matching carpet. To the left was a front room, as neat in its way as the Anwars' but with older, cheaper furnishings. A set of stairs led up the right-hand wall to the bedrooms. Along the wall by the stairs were click-frame collages of family photos, all of Malcolm and ginger Annie in different fashions, in the front garden here, in ugly halls at weddings, never abroad, never on a beach. There didn't seem to be any pictures of a dad.

Malcolm making his first communion, standing stiff as a board in a shirt and tie, solemn-faced, hair watered flat, rosary beads strapped around his prayer-clasped hands like a parlour Houdini. It was outside the chapel down the road, Morrow realised, she could just see this house in the far background.

Annie saw her looking at the photo. 'That's him, when he was cute. He's still cute now, just not in the same way. So, did ye find the taxi cab? He's never phoned home and he usually does if he's staying out and can remember, if he's gageing off his nuts.'

'Gageing?' repeated Harris, thinking he had misheard.

Annie crossed her arms. 'D'ye not know? Malki's a heroin addict.' She pointed at a pile of photocopied leaflets sitting on the floor by the door. 'M.A.D.: Mothers Against Dealers.' She touched her chest. 'Founder member,' she said proudly.

'Good for you,' said Harris.

'It's a family disease,' she said, as if that explained it.

'Is it?' Harris looked genuinely perplexed and interested. Morrow was impressed. 'What do you do about it?'

'Oooh,' Annie rolled her eyes back into her head, 'talk about it.'

'Hm.' Harris didn't know what else to ask so he tipped his head in sympathy.

Annie seemed appeased by this, she led them into the front room, offering them the threadbare brown settee. They sat down side by side. A large sacred heart picture of Jesus was on the wall, the colours blue and red, Disney-ish. The television was boxy and old, the carpet worn.

'You'll notice that the ornaments in here are shite,' she said proudly. 'That's what it's like to live with an addict. Ye have to watch the fuckers every minute or they'll rob the eyes out your head, swear to God.'

'Must be hell,' said Harris lightly.

'It is.' Annie hung her head. 'It's especially hard on the mothers. That's why we set up M.A.D.'

'So it's a support group?' asked Morrow.

'Oh, more than that.' Annie was suddenly animated. 'We're activists. Chased two of the fuckers out of this scheme last year.'

'Chased?' asked Harris mildly.

Smirking, Annie mimed lighting a match and throwing it. Morrow did remember something in the papers about houses on that scheme being firebombed. 'Ye firebombed their houses?' she said. 'That's illegal, Annie, someone could get killed.'

'Never said that, did I?' She stuck her tongue deep into her cheek defiantly, almost flirtatiously, daring them to prove it.

'If you know of dealing on the scheme you should phone us.'

Annie wasn't used to being disagreed with. 'Well, we can hardly call the polis on them, can we? Ye never appear. Half of ye are on the take anyway.'

Morrow gave her a warning look, flicking her eyes to Harris, suggesting that though she herself was tolerant he'd be liable to lift her. Aware that she'd said the wrong thing, Annie looked penitent. 'Sorry,' she said to Harris. 'God forgive me. I know a lot of ye are on the level.'

'Did you firebomb someone?'

'Naw, we never really,' she said, but she was smirking. 'Just kidding.'

'Look.' Morrow took charge. 'Malcolm took a taxi from here to Toryglen yesterday morning. We think he might be in a lot of bother.' It was a lie but she could live with it. 'Could ye tell us who he knows there?'

She was stunned at the news. 'In Toryglen?'

'Toryglen, yeah, on the Southside.'

'Doesn't know anyone there. *Toryglen*, are ye sure?'

'Yeah.'

'Toryglen's twenty quid away.'

'Yeah.' Morrow looked at her notes. 'The fare was ... eighteen thirty.'

'Well,' Annie was furious, 'that wee fucker better be in a lot of trouble, somebody else better have paid that for him, I can tell ye, if he had money like that and wasn't hiding it in the house. He owes me a lot of dough.' She looked hopefully at Morrow's notes. 'Did someone else pay it?'

'No, he pulled out a twenty and took the change.'

'I'll fucking kill him.'

'Who's he been spending time with recently? Is he working? Do you know who he's been hanging about with, say, over the past couple of days?'

Annie was too angry to think. 'I'll fucking kill him. God for-fucking-give me, so fucking help me ...' Leaning back she glanced out of the front window and froze. As they watched she seemed to be nodding a wild signal at the picture window. Harris and Morrow stood up to see what she was looking at. Nothing there but a silver car. Morrow looked at Annie and realised that she wasn't nodding but peering into the street alternately through the bottom and top half of her glasses, trying to get focus.

'Mrs Tait? Who's Malcolm been spending time with?'

Keeping her eyes on the road Annie seemed suddenly very calm. 'Just his usual pals. Dealer over in Shettleston. James Kairn, lives near the Tower Bar. Might want to check that out. Could ye excuse me?' She hurried out into the hall, opened the door and ushered them out into the street. Despite still having her slippers on she grabbed a set of keys from the sill inside and shut and locked the door, bid them a perfunctory goodbye, and scurried across the road.

They watched as Annie opened a neighbour's garden gate and hurried up the path to concrete steps leading up to the front door. The other side of the road was on a slight hill and the steps were steep. Standing at the top, turning to greet Annie, was a blond man.

He was handsome, square-jawed, slim, dressed in clean jeans and a white T-shirt, no coat. He didn't look like a local, he looked healthy, had muscled arms and a flat stomach, but he did have a broken nose. Outside the house a brand new silver Lexus was parked at the gate.

'Have you got the plate of the Lexus we were looking for?' asked Morrow.

Harris looked at his notebook. 'VF1 7LJ.'

It wasn't a match. 'Unusual car out here, I would have thought. Run that plate anyway. We'll wait.'

Harris scribbled it down and went back to the car to radio, leaving Morrow to watch. The blond man seemed pleased and surprised to see Annie. He turned to her and kissed her cheek, gave her a chaste cuddle. Clearly fond of the guy Annie couldn't stop herself smiling up at him, but tried to affect annoyance by frowning hard and putting her hands on her hips, elbows jutting angrily out to the side.

Harris came back to her side.

'Not that worried about Malcolm, is she?' observed Morrow.

'More worried about the twenty quid he had.'

Across the street the door opened and they disappeared inside. Harris was opening his car door but Morrow stopped him. 'Look.'

The house was bought, the front door had been exchanged for a solid oak thing with vicious bolts studded on it on a Castilian pattern. The windows all had alarm wiring threaded along the glass and cameras were dotted along the wall. But what was bizarre was that Annie was standing at a window in the next-door house, two windows along, as if the houses had been knocked into one another.

'Fortress Tait,' said Harris. 'I knew it was here somewhere, just never got the actual address.'

'You call that number plate in?'

'Yeah, boss, they're checking it out now. Probably bogus, though.'

'Yeah. What d'ye think she's doing in there?'

Harris watched and shrugged. 'Visiting family? Maybe she's in there setting a firebomb.'

34

Annie was the one person in the world Pat wanted to see less than Eddy at the moment but she wouldn't be shaken off and she wouldn't shut up about Malki's twenty quid.

She stood too close to Pat, so close he couldn't focus on her face without hurting his eyes. And she wasn't standing still either, she was reeling towards and away from Pat, peering at him top and bottom through ridiculously thick glasses.

'I mean if he's getting money from somewhere it should come through me,' said Annie, a grasping smile at the corner of her mouth. 'I pay for everything, he owes me about seven hundred quid or nine hundred quid anyway.'

'I dunno anything about it, Auntie Annie, honest.'

Pat was waiting to be told the Big Man wouldn't see him, waiting to be told he should deal with Parki, who was reading a newspaper at the far end of the room and ignoring him. They always made you wait.

Pat didn't want to see the Big Man really, it was too complicated, too much bowing and scraping. He had knocked them back for job after job, for security positions in the family firm, for one-off muscle shifts. Worse than that, Pat wouldn't let them use his name on any of the legal papers for the security firm. Relations with his relatives were cold to say the least. That's how they got everyone involved, freezing them out if they didn't comply. Pat had been pretty straight his whole life until now, until this. Loyalty to Eddy had made him go along with it.

'Where'd he get it from?' Annie persisted. 'From you? For what?'

Pat shrugged and looked away. He hated this cold house. They'd knocked two into one, knocked down a wall to make a living room that was double the size. It was all wrong, the shape was wrong, ceilings too low to fit with the room, four big windows from the front and back, like a waiting room or something. Impossible to heat. Stupid. The big man had money but no taste, he'd bought expensive stuff, desks and antiques and that, but the stuff was all dotted around the room like a garage sale.

'Never came from me, Annie, I dunno why he's got money.'

Big Man wouldn't let anyone clean it now either, not since his wife died, and everything looked sticky and dirty. Pat focused his eye on a glass display cabinet. It looked like something that should be in a shop, a glass box with three shelves in it and a dead bulb at the top, hanging slightly out of its socket. Inside were three sculptures of Chinese women, one sitting under a brolly, one leaning against a tree, one sitting on a bench. They all had the same face.

'Mean, everb'y knows I handle his money. If they've got anything else to give him they should gae it tae me.'

This was what he had to get away from. All of this. Mothers chiselling money from weans, cold rooms, waiting for knock-backs. He wanted toast and warm and pink and hair on pillows. He wanted family members who cried when one of them was taken away. Kindness.

'See, Pat, son—'

'Auntie Annie, he never got that money from me. I don't know where he got it.'

She crossed her arms and looked him up and down. 'He's been hanging about Toryglen. Who lives in Toryglen?' She was threatening him.

Pat stared at her. 'Did he tell ye he was going to Toryglen?'

'Nut,' she glanced out of the window, 'polis are looking for him.' She was looking at a couple in a black Ford outside. 'He got a cab yesterday and they found out he'd went there.'

The police were sitting in a car outside the house right now looking for Malki. Pat felt suddenly violently sick. He shrugged awkwardly. 'I dunno anyone in Toryglen.'

'Shugie Wilson,' said Annie, flatly.

She was so fucking fly. Pat always forgot. 'I don't know Shugie.'

'Aye, ye do,' she said, looking at him through the bottom of the lenses. 'Alki. Drinks in Brian's. Used to run wi' the Bankshead buoys.'

Parki coughed a dry bark and turned the page of his newspaper noisily. He was telling Annie to shut up, that Pat was an outsider and not to be trusted. He had been a knife-fighter when he was young. He had a scar across his face, a slash that took his bottom lip apart. They mismatched the slit when they put it together. It still made Pat flinch to look at it.

Annie was standing close to Pat, smiling over at Parki as if they were together. 'Auntie Annie, do you mind?'

'What, son?'

'I want to talk to Parki in private.'

She looked at Parki to overrule Pat but he didn't say anything, his face didn't flicker. They both stared at her.

'Oh that's fucking nice.' She stepped back along the room. 'Tell your old auntie to go fuck herself.' She stopped, waiting for them to insist on her coming back but they didn't. Sulking, she sloped off. Gordon, the Big Man's other heavy, let her out of the front door.

Pat and Parki looked at each other across the football pitch of a room. ''S a wonder Malki's such a nice wee guy, innit?' said Parki.

318

Gordon came in from the door. He'd been a body builder in his day. Took steroids but hadn't worked out since his back injury. All the muscle had turned to fat. Even his fingers were fat now. Rumour was his dick was the size of a cigarette. 'The big man'll see ye now, Pat.'

Dumb with surprise Pat followed Gordon out of the room and up the stairs. Gordon's back was so fat that his neck wasn't visible from one step down. At the top of the stairs Gordon turned to Pat and smiled. 'Nice to see you here, by the way,' he said. It struck Pat as strange that he said it like that, warm, as if Pat was back with them. He motioned to the door, knocked twice on Pat's behalf and swung it open into a small living room.

The Big Man probably didn't recognise it himself and Pat only saw it because he'd been away for so long, but the pokey upstairs living room was a recreation of the house he used to live in. A brown armchair faced its twin, empty now that the wife was dead. A small telly sat on top of a lacy doily over a wee chest of dark wood drawers that they'd had in the old house. The sideboard was even running away from the door the way it did in the old room, before he bought the next house and had the wall knocked down. On the walls and dotted around the room were the symbols of his tribe, a big wooden crucifix with a brass Christ writhing on it, novenas propped up against devotional candles, a framed picture of Padre Pio on the wall. School photos of his daughter, smiling, gap-toothed.

The Big Man wasn't big but he was square, like professional footballers in another age, a terrier of a man. He looked up at Pat from his armchair and seemed old but still vital, still threatening. 'Son.' He nodded, almost smiled, and Pat wondered if he'd been missed. It seemed unlikely. The Big Man had a lot of nephews and Pat's mother had been dead a long time. 'What's your business?'

'Um.' Pat stood awkwardly by the door, his hands in his pockets, wanting to leave. 'I'm sorry to come here ...'

The Big Man waved his hand, telling him to get on with it.

'I've got a hire car outside, need to get rid of it and get another motor. I didn't know who else to come to ...'

'Hired in your name?'

'No.'

'Model?'

'Lexus.'

The Big Man nodded. 'OK. Tell Parki I said it's OK and you've to get a few grand as well.' He looked at Pat expectantly.

'Oh. Um, thanks very much.'

'Yes?'

Bewildered by the non sequitur Pat glanced behind him. 'No ... ?' prompted the Big Man, turning his ear, wanting to hear something. Pat frowned, he couldn't guess what that was.

'Sorry?'

Bizarrely, the Big Man chortled to himself and said Pat's name a few times. He sighed and looked at him. 'I knew it.' He stood up and walked over to the sideboard, reached down and took out a bottle of Johnny Walker Black Label. He unscrewed the lid and poured two shots into crystal glasses that looked dusty, smiling all the while.

It hit Pat like a slap on the back of the head. The Big Man knew. He knew about the van, the guns and the pillowcase, and he thought Pat understood or he'd have dragged it out, made him guess.

He handed Pat a glass, and lifted the other to his mouth. 'How's it going?'

'Going?'

'The thing. With Eddy, how's it going?'

320

Pat held the glass to his mouth and breathed in a cloud of bitter whisky.

'Aye,' said the Big Man. 'Ye can see me after – square up then.'

They owed him money. Eddy owed the Big Man money. That's how they got the van, the guns, the brand new clothes, the fucking face paint Eddy had asked him to put on in the bedsit before. Pat had struggled to stay out of all this and it turned out now that Eddy had gone to the Big Man for capital and betrayed him from the off.

'Still attending to your devotions?' He was frowning up at Pat, serious, nodding, as if this was what really mattered to him.

Pat downed the whisky in a oner, gasping, 'No. I'm not religious.'

The Big Man held his glass but didn't drink. 'That's a shame,' he said into the glass. 'That's a shame. Our faith is what holds us together. Used to be a culture, a family, what kept us together. Now folk go sometimes, don't do confession, only pray sometimes. It's not a finger buffet. Ye can't just pick and choose bits of it to please yourself.'

Pat put the glass down on the sideboard. 'I better get going.'

'Aye, tell Eddy I'll expect him.'

Gordon let him out and leaned in for a silent order from his boss, trotted after Pat down the stairs, into the barn-sized living room and overtook him, whispering to Parki. Parki nodded and put down his paper on the Victorian card table. It was open at a picture of a topless bird. She looked very pleased with herself. He stood up slowly and made his way over to the window, peering out into the street. Pat hoped he didn't spot the police.

'The Kia's a bird's car but it's reliable.'

It was a kind offer and Pat appreciated it. 'That's good of ye, Parki.'

But Parki brushed it aside. 'What the Big Man says, goes.' He reached into an antique wall cupboard sitting on the floor and pulled out a set of keys. 'Go out the back. Round to the lock-ups, third door in.'

Pat blinked hard as he took the car key. 'Thanks, man.'

'How ye keeping anyway?'

Pat shrugged.

Parki pulled a wad of notes out of his back pocket, peeled ten one-hundred notes off and handed them to Pat. 'How's your Malki? Never seen him for ages.'

Pat took the keys out of his pocket, the pen torch and Eddy's house keys were on it, and handed them to Parki, backing away across the room. 'Ye off now?' said Parki, still trying to work out what was going on.

'Have tae, man,' said Pat quietly. 'Got somewhere I have to be.'

Morrow was sitting in the car outside Annie Tait's house with Harris when the call came. The registration was bogus, belonged to another make, another year, another car altogether.

She picked up the radio mike and gave her first order on the case: two squads to come and follow the car, see where it went when it left here. It was a long shot but they didn't have any short shots so it would have to do.

They waited until they knew the unmarked cars were in position, marking both entrances to the scheme before Harris started the engine and pulled out.

35

Gobby had looked through them as well and agreed with Harris that there was something to see. They left the tapes for Morrow in her office but it was hard for her to concentrate on the screen, resentful thoughts about Bannerman kept piercing her concentration. Phrases she would like to say to him if it came to a fight, which it never would, pointless articulations of the exact nature of his wrongs; selfish, careerist, self-important, coward, twat, arse, fucking arse. She knew from long past experience that rehearsing a fight that would never happen was a short-lived luxury. Initially intoxicating, it didn't help any, just wound her up even more.

She forced her eyes to the screen but couldn't focus because the image was blurry anyway. Mr Anwar's videos had been used over and over again and the magnetic tapes had been stretched at the top sometimes, cutting out important bits of the picture with hyperactive diagonal lines. Intermittent waves of snow descended across the image as well and she found herself leaning this way and that, as if she could see past the obstacle. In the faded grey colours of the shop nothing seemed interesting except the extent of Mr Anwar's concern with tidying up the sweet shelves.

Every time someone bought a chocolate bar or a bag of crisps he'd wait until they had left and then, slightly guiltily, skirt around the counter to straighten the shelves. Johnny Lander was there a lot, sitting silently on the stool next to him. He'd nip around and straighten the shelves without being asked.

Twat.

Another snow-front shimmied down the screen and she stood up quickly, almost over-balancing her chair, stepping over to the door and flinging it open. 'Harris!' she shouted out into the corridor, 'come in here and tell me what I'm supposed to be looking at. My head's bursting looking at this.'

Harris appeared at the door, pleased finally to have his pain acknowledged and pulled over a chair. She sat down next to him and mumbled a clumsy apology. He ignored it and she appreciated it.

'Right.' He held a hand out to the back of her chair and together they shuffled back ten feet from the screen and watched. 'Sit back from the screen or you'll get a migraine and shut your eyes a bit.'

He sped the tape on a little, reeling through hours of Lander and Anwar's relationship in minutes. The two old men hurried around the shop Keystone style, Johnny Lander energetic, disappearing from view often, stacking shelves, bringing tea, Aamir still. The men had a curious intimacy, rarely speaking but sitting a little closer to each other than most men would, never really looking at each other, preferring to face the counter when they were sitting.

A series of customers shifted in and out, commuters, absent as they bought fags or snacks or papers, hardly noticing the shop or the men as they daydreamed their way to work.

'Here,' said Harris, changing the speed and shuffling his chair towards the screen.

The woman caught the attention because of how present she was. Tall, she definitely looked tall, and slim. Middle-class hair, no flashes of colour or inappropriate blonde streaks but shiny brown hair, long and brushed. She wore white trousers with brown boots underneath and a shirt that was waisted to show off her figure. As soon as the door opened and the top of her head appeared in the frame Aamir Anwar warmed and stepped off his stool to greet her. Johnny Lander dropped off his chair and disappeared towards the back door.

The woman at the door was bent down as she came to the counter, holding a child's hand. A small brown-haired boy, a toddler turning into a child. He pulled his hand away and ran over to the break at the side of the counter, chubby arms pumping at his sides, head down.

'Watch this,' said Harris, licking his lips.

Aamir Anwar bent towards the child, hands on his knees, craning indulgently towards the child who gave him a reluctant kiss on the beard. Anwar stood up, holding his hand over the kiss, delighted with the boy and then with a flick of his fingers waved the boy to the sweetie rack.

The mother was facing the camera now and didn't look too pleased about it. Her arms were crossed but she didn't interfere as the boy grabbed two packets of Skittles, a Milky Way, small packets of jelly sweeties, cradling them in his arms, looking at the old man to check that it was OK. Aamir raised his hands in mock-shock, said something the child didn't understand and then chortled happily to himself.

And then the visit was over. The woman took the sweets from the child, put them on the counter where he couldn't see them, edited the pile by pushing some of the packets over to the side, and spoke briefly but seriously to Aamir before unwrapping and giving the boy the Milky Way bar and putting the rest in her handbag. Nice bag, thought Morrow, plain beige leather, big shoulder bag, lots of pockets.

'Now watch this,' said Harris.

Aamir kissed the child's head and followed them to the

door of the shop, standing in the opened doorway to wave them off, smiling to himself when he got back behind the counter and climbed back onto his chair. Johnny Lander came back and they sat silently, the smile lingering on Aamir's face.

'Is he not allowed friends?' asked Morrow.

Harris looked at her. 'They never paid for the sweeties.'

She scratched her chin. Harris was right. The woman pocketed the sweets and left. 'So ...?'

'Boss, d'ye know the profit margins these shops work on? *They never paid for the sweeties.* If that's not his grand wean, it's his wean.'

Johnny Lander assumed his customary position at the top of the stairs, leaning over the banister to watch them coming up. He was dressed as before but noted the rush in their steps and waited for them in the close, stiff as if awaiting news. He looked anxiously from Morrow to Harris. 'You've not found him?'

'No,' said Morrow.

Lander held his chest and slumped. 'For Pete's sake, the way ye came bombing up the stairs there ...'

'No, Mr Lander, we haven't found Mr Anwar.'

'What are you thinking then ...?'

'No, we've every reason to believe he's alive and well.'

'Thank God for that, anyway.' Relief seemed to have made him forget his manners and they stood for a moment looking blankly at each other in the cold close.

Morrow stepped towards the door. 'Can we come in for a minute?'

'Oh, aye, sorry.' He jumped in front of her, holding the door open for her to come into the hallway. ''Scuse me.'

She stepped in and walked into the orderly living room. Lander had been reading the local paper when the door buzzed, drinking a mug of tea and eating three biscuits set out on a side plate, everything orderly, and arranged around his armchair. The electric fire had a bar on as well and the room was cosy.

He shut the front door behind them. 'This is a hell of a thing, this waiting, isn't it?' he said.

Morrow reached into her bag and brought out the clumsy video camera that belonged to the department. 'Mr Lander, can you tell me who this is?'

He stood close to her as she played the video of the woman in the shop. To save time Harris had just filmed the tape from the TV screen and the definition was even worse than before. Lander watched to the end.

'Who is this woman?'

'Lily. That's Lily.'

Morrow looked at him. 'Who is Lily to Mr Anwar?'

She could see it was awkward for him. He wanted to help in any way he could but his loyalty was in the way. He looked out of the window and hummed for a moment before taking a sharp breath. The conflict made him cringe. 'Can I give you her address and you can ask her yourself?'

'Sure.'

He gave them the address, knew it off the top of his head and he gave them good directions too. It wasn't five minutes away by car, he said.

As they were leaving, as an afterthought before she put her notebook away, Morrow asked for Lily's surname.

'Tait,' said Lander. 'Lily Tait.'

The house was less than half a mile from the shop, straight along the road headed away from the city. Morrow noted that almost any journey to the town would have meant driving past the shop.

They pulled up in the street behind a black and silver

Range Rover with stick-on window shades and a 'Baby on Board' sign hanging in the back window, and looked up a steep path to a grand, semi-detached house. In front of it, the garden was carefully planted with seasonal flowers and shrubs.

Morrow and Harris took the path up to the front door. Though the house was elegant blond sandstone someone had added a wooden porch which had worn badly. Brown paint was weathered and peeling, the door on the outside flimsy glass. They could see shoes inside and a child's blue and red trike. Lined up along the rotting windowsills someone was growing herbs and small bedding trays were set out on a trestle table near the back, making use of the sunlight.

Harris couldn't find a bell so he tried the door and found it open. They walked up to the front door proper, a grand Victorian window with the outline of an urn etched on the glass.

Lily Tait opened the door. Both Morrow and Harris knew the Taits. No one in Glasgow could fail to know the father; he was pictured in the local papers every time a gangster was found murdered, but Lily didn't look like one of them at all. She was tall and slender, dressed in a huge mustard jumper with moth holes on the arm, and cut-off denim shorts. She looked gorgeous. Morrow could see Harris ogling her spectacular brown legs and painted toe nails. And yet there, in the roundness of the eyes, in the square set of the shoulders, she could see some small echo of Lily's background. It was the curse of aspiration, the next generation were better fed, educated beyond the grasp of their own parents.

Behind Lily in the pale grey hall a sulky three-year-old peered out at them, hanging off the waxed balustrade of the staircase. Beyond him the hallway led through to a bright, cheerful kitchen.

'Lily?'

She smiled out at them. 'Yeah, can I help you?'

The child, seeing their dark suits and formal stance, lost interest and ran off into the kitchen.

Morrow introduced herself and Harris. 'We're investigating the kidnap of Mr Aamir Anwar. Can we come in and talk to you?'

'Oh, gosh, yes of course.' She swung the door open and welcomed them into the house. 'Have you heard anything about Aamir? Is he home?'

'Not yet, I'm afraid.'

'Come in, come in.' She led them through to the kitchen and offered them seats at a pine table littered with cups and children's drawings and bills. 'Bit chaotic before the cleaner gets here,' she said, sweeping the rubble over to one end. The boy was sitting in a miniature red armchair in the corner, drinking from a sipper cup, watching them and looking cross.

Lily slipped into a kitchen chair across from them. 'So, how can I help?'

'Well,' Morrow took her notebook out for show, 'your name came up a couple of times and we wondered if we could talk to you about your relationship with Mr Anwar.'

She looked a little uncomfortable and glanced at the little prince in the armchair. 'OK.'

'How did you meet?'

She shrugged. 'At school.'

Morrow looked at her, 'You were at school . . .'

'Omar and Billal, yeah. Same year as Billal.'

'Right.' She wrote it in her notebook, giving herself time to think. 'OK, and what is your relationship?'

'Well, Billal is Oliver's father . . .'

The child looked furiously back and forth, knowing he was being talked about and not pleased about it.

'And how old is Oliver?'

'Three years and four months,' she said, as if it was a triumph.

Morrow wrote it in longhand in her notebook. Her pencil tip ripped the paper. 'But you're not with Billal?'

'No.' Lily was looking at the paper, at the rip, frowning her gorgeous forehead.

'And,' said Morrow, 'you know he's just had another baby with his wife.'

'Hm,' she looked from the rip to Morrow, knowing the woman was trying to upset her. 'Fine by me.'

'You'd split up anyway?'

Lily took her thick hair in her hand and leaned on her elbow. 'Billal's ...' a glance at the child, 'hard work, to be honest. Not for me.'

'What do you mean hard work?'

She hesitated and dropped her voice. 'He's very into family.'

'Your family?'

Lily looked hard at her and avoided the question. 'I split up with him shortly after Mr Nutkins arrived,' she nodded to the boy, 'but he didn't split up with me until quite a long time afterwards.'

'You mean he's been hassling you?'

Clearing her throat Lily sat up and looked at the wall clock. 'Look, um, my nanny's going to come in very soon, could we wait and talk about this then? I'm not that comfortable ...'

'No,' said Morrow flatly, 'this is urgent.'

She wasn't pleased. She looked from Morrow to the rip in the notebook and back again, chewed her cheek and turned to the child. 'Nutkins, how about putting on a play jersey and going into the garden for a run around?'

The kid shrugged and stood up, dropping his cup

carelessly. She went over, pulled a pale blue jersey from the floor over his head and checked his laces and opened the back door, shoving him out. 'Stay away from the nettles.'

She left the door open and came back to the table, suddenly looking much harder. 'OK, I don't know what that fucker told you – I'm mental probably, I'm a grasping bitch probably—'

'Is Billal involved with your family business?'

'*Right.*' She raised a furious finger in Morrow's face. 'First off, it's not *my family business*. We can none of us help where we come from. I haven't seen my father for five years. Two: Bill and I knew each other from school. Nothing I can do about that. He met my dad then. If they're going on fucking holiday together now it's nothing to do with me. I'm nothing to do with either of them, nothing. I never see him. He gets supervised visitation once a month and I'm not even there—'

Her fury was losing momentum and Morrow used it as an opportunity to take charge. 'Did you start going out at school?'

'No. It was at a friend's wedding. He was fine at first but I got pregnant, fine, OK, still together but then suddenly, out of fucking *nowhere*, he gets all wrapped up in business and suddenly he's got religion – big time.'

'He join any groups, start hanging about with anyone?'

'No, he's not ... it's not that sort of religion. It's not political.'

'What then? Spiritual awakening?'

'Spiritual? God, no.' She laughed, shook her head. 'Spiritual? No. You're not from religious people are you?'

Morrow shook her head. Harris gave a sideways nod that suggested he was, if anyone was interested. No one was.

'It's not just about ... you know, Jesus or whoever. It's about ... you know ...' Lily seemed puzzled, struggled to

331

find the words. '*Belonging* to people, you know?'

She looked to them for understanding. Morrow nodded. 'Go on.'

'Billal wanted me to convert, go and live with his mother. Don't get me wrong, I love Sadiqa, she's gorgeous, but I'm Catholic, I'm Scottish, I'm not going to move in with total strangers and cover my head with a fucking scarf for the rest of my life.'

'That would be a shame.'

The women looked at Harris who started, as if he hadn't realised he'd said it out loud.

Morrow brought her back. 'But Billal didn't take it well?'

She snorted. 'Under-fucking statement.' Hurt eyes skirted the table, weaving through a thousand arguments and midnight calls. 'I mean if it wasn't for Aamir and Sadiqa insisting he wouldn't even pay the support.'

'Why? Does he think you make enough yourself?'

'Oh, I don't work.' She seemed surprised at the suggestion. 'Oliver's only three and a bit.'

'I see.' Morrow looked around the big kitchen. 'What about your family?'

'No,' she was indignant, thinking Morrow didn't understand, 'I wouldn't take money, no way.' It seemed to be a point of pride for her that she wouldn't take cash from her dad. The irony that she'd just found someone else to squeeze seemed lost on her. 'Bill thought I'd marry him if he stopped paying the mortgage. He even stopped paying for the nanny at one point. Then he got even more into being a Muslim and married that girl from bloody Newcastle or wherever. Arranged, for fucksake, like it was the middle ages or something. I mean, I know Sadiqa was shocked. Hers and Aamir's was a love match. She doesn't like subservient women.' She shook her thick hair off her shoulders, implying that Sadiqa preferred her over Meeshra. 'I don't either.'

'Lily, what does Billal do for a living?'

Lily stopped, confused as to why the conversation had diverted from a thorough exploration of her complaints. 'For a living? Bill's in the motor business.'

'Bill?'

'Specialist cars.'

Morrow thought about the Lamborghini, smelled the damp, saw a set of ludicrously white teeth. 'I see, I see,' she said, trying to slow her mind down by talking slowly. 'Where's his garage?'

'No, he hasn't got a garage.'

'No garage?'

'No, no,' Lily waved a hand dismissively, 'he's just a middle man. Import/export.'

36

Pat's heart beat a bossa nova rhythm, a joyful tat tat tat at the thought of her being in there, through those locked wooden doors, sitting upright in bed bathed in yellow sunshine, a bride awaiting her groom, facing the corridor with the beginning of a smile on her lips. It was almost forty-eight hours since they had seen each other but it felt much longer.

He had been hanging about by the lifts, uncertain that this was the right floor, when he saw the mother waddle towards him, still wearing her nightie and overcoat. He turned away, covered his face and read the signs on the wall until she was past. There were orders posted all over the walls in the corridor: no mobiles, no visitors other than family before a certain time, no hot drinks, no this, no that. He swung behind her and made his way to the ward doors.

He saw through the glass panel that the corridor ahead of him was empty, buffed, glinting like a river. Acutely aware of every sensation, of his head tipping, of his heels leading the step of his feet, he reached forward and pushed the door.

Locked. He pushed lightly with his fingertips. Really locked, not stuck. He looked in through the window but couldn't see anyone in there. It was definitely the right ward if the mother had just been there.

'No one there?'

A woman standing behind him, slim, fifty, suited, glasses on a gold chain, carrying a sheaf of papers wrapped in a glossy yellow envelope. He gave her his best smile and shrugged. She smiled back, shifted the folders to balance on her raised knee and stabbed zero on the keypad five times. The door dropped open and he touched it with his fingertips, pushed, opening the passage into the river.

Pat held the door open for the woman and her folders and she thanked him with a simpering smile and a glance at his torso. 'Not many gentlemen left, these days,' she said as if everyone else had let her down.

Pat smiled again. He had held the door so that she would go ahead of him, so she wouldn't be watching as he looked around. She walked down the corridor, standing straight and swaying her hips, certain of his attention.

But Pat wasn't watching. He looked from left to right, into single rooms with yellow curtains half drawn across dark windows. Quiet ward. An old woman in a bed watching a wall-mounted television tuned to a chat show. A fat woman with both legs in plaster, sleeping, a teenage daughter next to her reading a celebrity magazine. Acute surgical.

The corridor snaked around a dog leg turn and each of the rooms had four beds in them, curtain partitions running on rails above them, many half pulled or yanked open incompletely. He could see who was in which room but he couldn't stop for a good look in case anyone asked him who he was and what he was doing there.

As he approached the far end of the ward his courage began to fail him. Two toilet doors marked the end of the corridor and he had made up his mind to go into one, sit in it and decide what to do. It was then that he saw her.

He stood, staring in through the window at an old woman lying flat on a bed alone in the room. She had an oxygen mask on over her nose and mouth and he knew the grey look. She was dying, like Malki, alone, deserted.

'Sorry ...?' A fat student nurse was ten feet away, wondering who he was.

Pat pointed at the window. 'How long ...?'

He meant how long until she dies but the nurse misunderstood. 'Mrs Welbeck has been here for five days. Are you her ...?'

Pat turned back to the window and whispered, 'Nephew?'

'Oh dear.' She tilted her head. 'So sorry. They did try to find family ...'

He shook his head sadly, 'No worries.'

Not knowing what to say now, he turned back to the window. The woman was in her seventies, eighties, balding like a baby bird, grey hair on a skull. She was propped up on pristine pillows but hadn't moved. As she exhaled a barely perceptible skin of condensation formed on the mask. She was hardly breathing at all.

The nurse put a kindly hand on his arm. 'Would you like to go in and see her?'

Pat nodded sadly and she took him by the hand, led him through the door into the room. A silent heart monitor blinked an orange eye at him. The room smelled of diluting orange tempered with talc. The sympathetic nurse led him to the bedside and brought a plastic chair over for him to sit on, which he did.

Grey flesh on a skull. Hands covered in paper-thin skin, veins you could see the pulse bump through. A thin wedding band, a miserly engagement ring, hanging loose on thin fingers. He could see a sticking plaster rolled around the back of the engagement ring to stop it falling off.

'I'll leave you alone.' She walked around to the far side of the bed and began to pull the curtain between the window and the corridor.

'No, no, no, please – it's better to have the light ...'

It sounded stupid. There was a window behind him,

336

there wasn't any light coming out of the corridor, but the nurse was used to dealing with grieving people making stupid comments and she went along with it. 'Of course,' she said and backed off out of the room, leaving Pat alone.

A sign above the bed said her name was Minnie Welbeck. In case the nurse was looking back into the room Pat took her right hand in both of his and found the fingertips cold, the palm warm, as if she was dying from the extremities inwards.

He had come here to cheer himself up, see the beautiful girl sitting in a bed, bathed in sunshine. He had thought about nothing but seeing her since he got in the car and drove away from Breslin's, but there was something about Minnie that he couldn't tear himself away from. She'd been married, maybe widowed. And now she was dying, alone, tucked out of everyone's way, next to the toilets.

Slowly, like a tall flower dying on a fast exposure film, Pat wilted over his knees towards the little hand held between both of his. Gentle as air, he held Minnie's knuckles to his forehead and wept.

They weren't selling Lamborghinis here, that was for sure. The Lexus had been driven there by an unknown male, young, neddy-looking, clearly not the owner, certainly not Edward Morrison, the holder of the driver's licence who'd hired the car and left a photocopy of his photo ID at the Avis office. The boy stopped outside the chicken wire fence, made a phone call and was let through the gates by an old guy. Morrow and Harris drew up across the road, and heard the FAU report over the radio that there was an Audi drawing up and an unidentified male, big, broad, letting himself through the gates, locking the two padlocks after himself and driving into the building.

'Saw an Audi outside the Anwars' the night the old man got taken,' she said to Harris.

'Reckon it's Billal?'

'Could be.'

It had been purpose built as a garage but a long time ago. The forecourt lay empty, weeds growing out of the cracks. Sun and rain had bleached the cheerful bunting clinging to the rusting chicken wire. It was on an industrial estate two miles out of town, visible from nowhere. It had probably failed under a couple of owners and been sold on cheap. The company that owned it now was a shell company, according to Routher's investigations. They were still registered at Companies House but did business with no one and had filed a tax return that suggested they were still waiting to go into business. No known names on the list of directors. Billal was smart.

For a sleeping company they were taking a hell of a lot of precautions. Two padlocks on the gates, new automatic doors on the workshop, fresh bars on the windows and an elaborate CCTV system, a fish eye camera on every corner. The building itself was low slung, solid grey, unremarkable apart from the security measures. There wasn't even a name on the door that she could see.

'D'you think he's in there?' asked Harris.

'Yeah, but we won't get anywhere near him until FAU've had all their toys out.'

FAU were around the back, their van hidden a street away, crouching, working out a path in.

'Think it was spite?' asked Harris.

She kept her eyes on the door. 'What?'

'Going after Billal, because he'd hassled Lily? Think it was the Taits?'

'Nah.' She thought of the boy scowling at them from the armchair, of his thick brown hair and the perfect roundness

338

of his chin, his fingers, his eyelashes. She imagined the softness of his cheek meeting her lips. 'Grandad Tait must be desperate to see that boy. He wouldn't risk it. Might pass the intel on to someone else but he'd never risk that, I don't think. His wife died . . .'

'How would he know about Billal having a VAT scam, though?'

'Suppose he'd keep his ear to the ground, wonder where the money for Lily was coming from, dig about.'

'Aye, dirt sees dirt, eh?'

Morrow smiled at that. 'Yeah, dirt sees dirt right enough.'

The radio crackled to life, the FAU officer notified her that they were ready to go in around the back and Morrow and Harris looked at each other, excited as children.

They saw nothing. Watching the bland front of the garage they heard a crash, some shouting, another crash, someone shouting back and then silence. A long silence. When the FAU officer came back on the radio he sounded out of breath and angry. 'We've got three guys. No firearms. A room full of . . .' he broke off to ask someone what the room was full of, and then came back onto the radio, 'broken-up cars. No papers to verify the ownership. Seems like . . . um . . . not, eh, legitimate.'

Morrow and Harris threw the car doors open and ran around to the back of the building. FAU had clipped a big hole through the chicken wire and battered the back door flat so it lay in the back entrance like a bridge. It led straight into the workshop.

It was so much colder inside that Morrow found herself shivering as she looked around at the engines and car doors stacked up against the wall. She was smiling as she looked up at the big FAUs in their protective gear and the three men they had nicked. Two wee guys and the big broad man in the Audi. The only one not wearing a cheap gaudy tracksuit. Danny McGrath looked at Morrow coldly, as if he'd never seen his sister in his life before.

She had skated straight into the path of the train.

37

The heavy metal doors opened with a clang and the passengers poured onto the car deck, snaking their way between the vans and cars lined up neatly in rows, facing the green ramp wall of the ferry. An overhead announcement ordered them in prissy estuary English not to start their engines before the ferry docked and the ramp was lowered. And to not even think of lighting a cigarette on the car deck.

An unexceptional white-haired man in a navy golfing jersey, belly like a plain-clothed Santa, made his way past cars of families going or coming from holidays or visits to family, past vans heading for work in Glasgow or London, to a green Peugeot estate car. He unlocked it, climbed in, did his seat belt up, slid the keys in but did not turn them and waited patiently, keeping his eyes down, remaining unremarkable. The ferrymen, in dayglo yellow jackets and big wellies, stood by the doors, staring at the passengers insolently, waiting.

The roar of the ferry engines suddenly changed gear, churning backwards, slowing the ferry's approach to the pier and the boat lurched sideways, coming to a stop. The prow was lowered slowly in front of them, letting the bright grey day into the bowel of the ship.

The first row of cars fired up their engines and the ferrymen signalled to them to drive on, herding them over the ramp and into Scotland.

Even in his maddest dreams of blood-soaked glory Eddy had never imagined himself sitting in a car with an actual ex-paramilitary terrorist, cruising along the streets of Glasgow after a roast beef dinner at a Beefeater all-you-can-eat buffet. Eddy was, in short, creaming it. He was trying to act cool but observe as much as he possibly could about the guy. He liked the calm manner, and the shoulder swagger when he walked. Liked the way the guy seemed to be watching all the time, never really making eye contact with him much but watching over his shoulder. And he loved that when they went to the Beefeater, after the man had piled a small plate with meat and gravy and a single potato, that he had chosen a seat in the corner, away from the door and windows. Careful. A pro.

Looking out of the passenger window of the Peugeot Eddy reflected that this would have gone very differently if the Irishman had been there all along, that he must have been very high up when he was in the Provos because he had such natural authority, and that Eddy would have followed him into battle.

'There.' The white-haired man, who had asked Eddy just to call him T, pulled the car over to the pavement and nodded at a phone box in the street up ahead.

'But,' Eddy didn't know whether to say it or not, 'place is polluted with cameras.'

The man looked out through the windscreen at the grey box attached to a street light. 'Not a problem,' he drawled in his throaty accent. 'Ye know just to keep your cap on and chin down, don't ye, boy?'

Eddy didn't know that but noted it for future escapades. 'Um, I haven't got my cap with me, but—' T reached over the back of his chair into the footwell behind him and pulled out two identical England Cricket Team navy-blue skip caps, handing one to Eddy.

Eddy chanced a little camaraderie, pointing at the logo. 'I hope that's a fucking joke,' he said.

'What do you think yourself, son?' He had a twinkle in his eye. Eddy was starting to think T liked him.

'T, man, what's to stop them picking us up at the drop? What if they have phoned the polis?'

T smirked at him, keeping his mouth shut tight. 'Done this a hundred times, son, don't you worry about that.' He pulled his cap low over his face and Eddy copied him.

Caps donned, they exited the vehicle and walked over to the phone box in sharp formation. Both getting into the box was a squeeze, though, because the Irish was a bit fat around the middle and Eddy was none too slender himself, having done a lot of work on himself in the gym. They managed to get the door almost shut behind them though, blocking out the background sounds of traffic and high beep of the pedestrian crossing a hundred yards away.

The Irish had one latex glove on and picked up the receiver, holding it between his shoulder and chin as he pulled a pound coin out of his pocket and dropped it into the phone. 'Right,' he said, 'you dial then, son.'

Eddy nodded, pulled out the Tesco's receipt with the Anwars' home number scribbled on it in pencil and started to stab it into the keypad, using his knuckles in a manner he hoped looked professional and fingerprint savvy.

'You've got it written on a scrap of paper in your pocket? What if ye get picked up? That's the case against ye right there.'

Eddy flinched. 'Aye, but just, my mate was calling them and so I didn't know it off by heart and then, well,' he could see the dismay in the man's face, 'I'm going to ... eat it after we call now.'

'Right?' T's disappointment turned to surprise. 'You're going to eat a Tesco's receipt?'

'To get rid, like.' Embarrassed at his gaffe, Eddy stabbed in the final numbers on the receipt and put it in his mouth, wishing it wasn't such a long receipt because it tasted of ink and newspapers.

T watched him, curious and a little disgusted. 'Ye should maybe have waited until we were sure it was the right number before ye—' His attention was suddenly drawn by someone on the other end. 'Anwar?'

Eddy couldn't hear the answer on the other end but the ambivalence was gone from T's face. 'I've a matter of business to discuss with you,' he said firmly, his brow coming down over his eyes.

Carefully, T reached over and opened the door to the phone box, gently but firmly shoving Eddy out into the street and closing the door behind him. Eddy stood in the street, chewing the paper dutifully as the rain flecked the lenses of his Reactalite glasses until he couldn't see any more.

Sadiqa, Omar and Billal stared at the phone as it rang, jittery as flies. Apologetically Omar reached for the receiver. The voice on the other end claimed he had a matter of business to discuss. It was a different voice, Northern Irish, more nasal, deeper.

'Who is this?' asked Omar.

'The Boss. Who's this?'

'Omar.'

'Anwar?'

'Anwar's the family name, my first name's Omar.'

'But that's not what they call ye, is it?'

Omar sighed, saw Billal glaring at him and shut his eyes so he didn't have to look at him.

'You've a nickname, haven't ye?' The man was smiling on the other end of the phone. He could hear the crocodile mouth, open wide, ready to snap him in half. 'They call ye Bill, don't they?'

'Bob.'

'Eh?'

'They call me Bob.'

'Nah,' he laughed humourlessly. 'Nah, don't try games wi' me, son. Bill, they call ye.'

Omar opened his eyes. Billal had heard it too. He looked at Omar, looked at the phone.

'Well, Bill, we happen to know a wee bit about what you're up to—'

Shocked, Billal crouched suddenly, punching at the tape recorder as if it was a spider on his dinner, switching it off.

'With the old VAT fraud and that, so you'd better cough up pronto or your wee daddy's getting it, understand?'

Billal stayed where he was, crouched down in front of the telephone table, his head slumped forward.

'Where and when?'

'In an hour. Drop the bag on the AI at the first emergency phone box past the services. Understand?'

'Yes. I can't get what you asked for, I've got forty grand.'

'That'll have to do.'

'Then will you release my dad?'

'Soon as they pick-up he'll be let go in the city with money for a taxi home. Clear?'

'First emergency phone box past the services. Got it.'

'And if it's not a Paki driving that car I'll know you've called the police. You know what'll happen then, don't ye?'

Omar could hardly speak, the threat and the racial slur together were too much.

'In fact,' said the voice, 'in fact, can your mammy drive?'

'Uh, aye.'

'Send her with the bag. Send her alone.'

Omar managed three words. 'In an hour.'

'In one hour.'

He was holding the receiver so tight to his ear that

345

the hang-up click hurt his ear drum. Slowly, with shallow breath, Omar took the receiver away, raised it above his head and clubbed Billal as hard as he could on the back of the head.

Harris looked up at the Anwars' house. The low garden wall was still staved in but all the evidence cards and tape were gone from the garden and the bungalow looked as unremarkable as any of its neighbours.

'Wouldn't look twice,' he said. 'Much do you think he's got stashed away?'

'Companies House has a trail of failed companies going back eighteen months. VAT can pull in millions a month. Must have storage somewhere.'

'And he's living in one bedroom with his new missus?'

'He'll be spending a fortune on Lady and Master Nutkins though.'

'Much do ye reckon? Thousands a month?'

Morrow shrugged. 'He's still got boxes and boxes of cash somewhere.' She could see someone moving through the mottled glass on the Anwars' front door, a mad lurch from one side of the hall to the other. She was imagining scenarios that would make sense of it: a leap for a phone, a jumping game among family members, someone falling forwards to catch a falling vase, when a giant body crashed into the glass pane, making it shudder outwards.

Harris and Morrow were out of the car and up the path, just as the body got up and fell away from the door. Harris tried the door, shouted, 'Police! Police! Let us in!'

The door was flung open by Sadiqa. She gestured down the hall like a frightened magician's assistant.

Omar was sitting on his brother's chest, trying to club him with the weighted base of the phone. Billal was bloodied, held both arms over his face and cycled, kneeing

346

his wee brother in the back with each of his knees alternately. Omar's face didn't register the blows to his kidneys. Omar didn't even hear Harris coming across the hall towards him. Intent on what he was doing he brought the weighted receiver of the phone down and up, down and up on his brother, an angry child breaking a toy he had come to hate.

Harris grabbed the phone from his hand, put a throttle hold on Omar, yanking him off his brother, pulling him to his feet.

Suddenly free, Billal looked up, his nose was a bloody mess but he saw Morrow looking at him and waited a beat pause before he started shouting, 'Oh god, my god!' He rolled away from her, his eyes still trained on her, willing her to come and look to make sure he was OK. That's what made her look away.

Dead-eyed with shock, Meeshra was in the bedroom doorway, her hands out, holding either side of the door jamb. Morrow took a step towards her and was surprised to see her jump a little. 'Meeshra?' Behind her the baby gave a squeak but Meeshra's eye didn't waver. She wasn't blocking the doorway to protect the baby. Meeshra was protecting something else.

Keeping eye contact, Morrow walked towards her, took the woman's right hand from the frame and saw the horror on her face as she realised she'd given them away. Morrow walked over to the only piece of furniture in the room large enough. She allowed herself a lick of the lips, bent down and took the edge of the divan bed in both hands. The mattress slid to the ground on the far side and the wooden frame lifted easily. She held it over her head and looked down.

Shrink-wrapped blocks of pink and purple bank notes, solid as bricks, so many she had to estimate in feet: five feet by four feet, one yard high.

Aware of the hush in the hall she looked out. Beyond Meeshra, Sadiqa, Harris and Omar saw the money and stopped, stunned, until Sadiqa fell forward from the waist, picked up the telephone from the floor and, with remarkable grace for a woman of her size, smashed her eldest son in the bollocks with it.

Here was the nurse, back to ask him if he wanted to go down to the cafeteria for a cup of tea; she could change his auntie and have her nice and ready for the doctors' round. He could come back then and speak to them.

Pat sat up, looking at Minnie's hand, finding her middle knuckle white from the pressure of his forehead. Carefully, he placed the hand back on top of the covers and sat up. His back was aching. His face was wet, his eyes puffed from crying and being bent over double for so long. He suddenly felt very foolish.

'Aye, I mibbi will now,' Pat stood up slowly, hiding his face from the nurse. She handed him a clutch of tissues. He dried his face.

'Just you take your time,' she said softly, and left again.

Pat went out into the corridor and locked himself in the toilet. He turned on the tap and leaned over the basin, cupping cold water in his hands and throwing it at his face. He tried to look at himself in the mirror, to check that he looked OK, but he couldn't find the courage to do it. He dabbed his face dry with rough green paper and left.

A different nurse watched him walking down the corridor towards her, an older woman, navy uniform and trousers. Seeing his red eyes she smiled, head tilted in sympathy. 'Mr Welbeck?'

Pat tried to skirt past her. 'Just going for a cup of tea,' he mumbled.

'Well, the doctors won't be down to see your auntie for

at least half an hour, so just you take your time, there's no hurry.'

He tried to get past but she stepped towards him and touched his elbow, dipping at the knees to get him to look up at her. He stopped, caught her eye, found he hadn't the strength to resist.

'She has been very comfortable,' she said. 'You mustn't worry about that.'

He nodded, dragged a breath into his chest to quell more tears and, in doing so, tipped his head back.

She was a small woman. Beyond her, over her shoulder, was a wire mesh window into a room, the glass marked with the yellowed flaking residue of old sellotape. Yellow curtains with pink triangles on them. And there she was, sitting up in bed, an oil slick of hair pulled over one shoulder, hands on the bed sheets in front of her, the light behind her. She was looking at him.

'. . . Although she does have some bedsores, they are very clean and the saline baths seem to be helping.'

Pat could not rip his gaze from Aleesha, nor she from him. He thought he saw her eyes widen, as if in recognition, but then wondered if maybe it was his own eyes that had opened wider, as if he was trying to take in more of her.

The woman in front of him talked on about bedsores, about the home Minnie had come from, about a report and a test for something but he couldn't hear her properly, just disjointed words swimming towards him, over him, by his ears.

Without breaking eye contact, without seeming even to move her head, Aleesha threw the covers back, swung her feet in perfect point to the floor and stood up. One of her hands was bandaged, white padded. She kept it high and held his eye as she walked to him. Even at the door frame, even when they couldn't see each other for the woodchip

349

wall, they held one another's gaze. She lingered at the door, waiting for the nurse to go.

'Sorry,' the nurse touched her chest, 'I'm Staff Nurse Sarah, what's your name?'

Aleesha stepped back so that one of her eyes was hidden behind the door frame, she seemed to be unsure that coming to talk to the stranger was a good idea, bottled it a bit and looked at her bandaged hand, back curved as if she was going to step back into the room, as if a force in there was sucking her backwards.

'Roy.' He stepped to the side, past the nurse and reached out to Aleesha with a flat hand, palm outwards, not offering a shake but gesturing to take her hand, lead her away. 'Hello.'

Aleesha looked at his hand, raised an eyebrow at the impertinence, looked at him, read the desperate need the man had for her.

He was gorgeous. Tall. Dirty blond hair so thick it stood up, not, like, with gel, not uniform spikes that made boys look as if they cared so much they'd spent hours styling it. A jaw speckled with stubble of a hundred different colours, a flat nose, like he'd been in a car accident, and shoulders broader than the door almost. He raised his eyebrows at her, sad smiling eyes, pale blue.

She didn't take the hand. She sloped back into her room, turning so that her face was hidden from him.

'Sorry,' the nurse said, looking slightly resentfully at Aleesha's foot, 'do you two know each other?'

'Yeah,' said Pat, 'I'm pretty sure we do, but I can't think where from.'

Aleesha swung back at the door. 'You go to St Al's?'

Pat snorted a tired laugh. 'I'm twenty-eight, it's a long time since I was at school and I never went there, no.'

'I thought you went to St Al's,' she said. Her voice was

higher than he had thought it would be, sweeter.

He looked at her and saw a girl, not the goddess of his imagination. He liked the girl better. 'My, um,' he looked back down the corridor to the toilets, 'my auntie's getting ready for the doctors' round. I was, um ...' He looked at the ward doors and was struck by the impossibility of this happening. 'I'm going for a cuppa ...'

She saw how tired he was and how sad and how handsome. 'You've been crying.' He nodded. 'Why?'

The nurse tutted at the girl and crossed her arms, siding with him against her. Pat pulled one of his ears, gulped, tried hard not to cry again. 'Sad,' he whispered and thumbed behind him.

They looked each other in the eye again, stuck again for too long, inappropriate. He saw her feel it, saw her eyes melt into his mood. With her good hand she held out the bundle of bandages and dressings to show him. 'I'm acting weird,' she said, ''cause I'm on shit loads of painkillers.'

He pointed at the hand with a limp index finger, wanted to ask what happened, act surprised, but he couldn't bring himself to start the thing with a lie. They both watched as Aleesha fingered a fray on the bandage.

The nurse was cross at finding herself a spectator. She stepped between them but, with superhuman grace, Aleesha stepped to the side, back into Pat's line of vision.

'If my mum phones,' she said, 'tell her I'll be back in twenty minutes.'

38

They had the Lexus and seventeen other stolen cars, or bits of them, and they couldn't tie a thing to Danny McGrath. His prints were on nothing, his name was on nothing but he had come in voluntarily to help them with their questioning, as a courtesy to the police.

Danny had never been a threat to her before; they'd left each other alone always. That he was here now meant he believed that Morrow had broken the ceasefire. And she knew that even if she got him alone and explained what had happened, it would never be all right again.

She couldn't let anyone else question him in case he gave her up but to do it herself would mean people seeing them together, seeing the similarities; they'd know where she came from. She didn't want to leave the disabled toilet ever again. She almost wished there was a window she could crawl out of, that she had a lighter and could set off the fire alarm. A gentle rap on the door was followed by Harris's voice: 'Are ye stuck in there?'

She made a sound like a laugh at the door, straightened her clothes, managed a light, 'Just coming,' opened the door quite suddenly and found Harris standing a little too close to the door. 'Fuck's sake,' she said. 'Behave yourself.'

'You've been in there for twenty minutes, boss. He's about to go home. He's in voluntary, you know? He can leave.'

She nodded back at CID. 'Where's himself?'

'MacKechnie's gone home.'

She looked at her watch, 'It's only half four.'

352

'Had a meeting and then went home. Be back in for the pick-up, he said. Going out in the Obs van with you.'

'Fuck.' It was a relief. At least he wouldn't see her and Danny together. 'Fuck.'

'You feeling sick?'

'Wee bit. Do I look sick?'

'Wee bit.'

She was talking very fast, she realised, dead giveaway. She stared helplessly at the wall until Harris prompted her. 'Clock's ticking, he's within his rights—'

'What room's he in?'

'Four.'

'Get Gobby up to the corridor outside Three. I want a word with him before we go in. If he's not there in two minutes I'll kick his bollocks in.'

Danny was sitting across from her next to his lawyer. The lawyer didn't look like a criminal lawyer at all, Morrow had never met him or even heard his name. He dealt mostly with corporate, he said, when she remarked on it, and he smiled charmingly.

Danny looked cheap and angry. He slumped in the chair, one arm flung over the back as if he was the most relaxed guy in the world. Their father used to sit like that. She'd seen him swing a punch at a man from that stance. And he was wearing his duck-down puffa jacket, more expensive than most suits, but it placed him as a poor man who'd done well.

His lawyer in contrast wore a genuinely expensive suit, wool, and carried a briefcase of exquisite leather. He pulled from it a notepad and a tortoiseshell pen, a small glasses case containing gold-rimmed half-moon glasses and a packet of chewing gun, which he offered to Danny. Morrow sat as still as she could.

The door opened flat against the wall and Gobby sauntered in with a strange expression on his face, half haughty, half indigestion. Morrow stood up respectfully and the lawyer followed her lead, holding his hand out. 'DSI MacKechnie?'

Gobby took the hand and shook it, looked at Morrow a little unkindly, she thought, and took his jacket off, shaking it out the way Bannerman had done with Omar. He sat down, clenched his hands in front of himself on the table and cleared his throat. Everyone waited for him to speak. Gobby cleared his throat again and glanced reproachfully at Morrow.

'Right,' she said. 'Sorry, OK, I'm DS Morrow, this is D – well, you've met. I don't know if you know why you're here, do you?'

Danny clenched his jaw at her and his eyes promised her that he would never forget this.

'Basically,' she continued, 'a hostage has been taken by gunmen and we're trying to find them. A car used in that crime was followed to the garage you were, um, apprehended in. Can you tell me how you came to be in there?'

'Buying parts,' said Danny.

'Car parts?'

He blinked yes.

'Who were you buying them from?'

'Guys that was there.'

'The two other men we apprehended in the garage itself?'

He shrugged.

'What parts were you buying?'

'Spark plugs.' He sounded contemptuous.

'Spark plugs?'

He sucked a hiss between his teeth. 'Just says that, didn't I?'

'Why were you buying them there?'

354

He gave a careless one shoulder shrug. 'Good as anywhere.'

'They're not an expensive item are they?'

He snorted and sat back.

'Why buy them there if you can buy them just as cheaply elsewhere?'

He muttered something at the table.

'Pardon?'

'You've got some fucking cheek,' he said quietly.

'Have I?'

'Making me fucking sit here and listen tae this shit.' He was looking at Gobby but talking to her. He nodded towards her. 'See her?'

Gobby looked at Morrow.

Danny grinned. His dimples were already sagging into slashes, she realised, his charm already going south, bitterness already setting in. 'But, d'ye *see* her?'

The lawyer was looking at them, back and forth. Seeing the similarities. The dimpled cheeks, the high brow.

Danny and Morrow looked at each other for a moment, and for a moment she could see herself in him utterly, deep-rooted fear making him angry, wanting to control the desperate, craven desire to belong.

'I'd like to speak to you alone,' he said smugly.

Morrow hesitated. 'To me?'

'To him.' He reached into his pocket and took out a chewing gum packet, flipped two small white rectangles into his palm and threw them into his mouth like headache pills. He bit down on them, the crunch of the coating audible in the quiet room.

Gobby sat forward. 'To me? Why?'

'Got something to tell ye.'

He wouldn't, she was sure he wouldn't, but he was threatening her, letting her know it was possible, that he could.

355

'Mr McGrath,' Gobby leaned back, copying Danny's posture, 'we only ever talk to criminals when there is another police officer present. For the purposes of corroborating evidence.'

The lawyer butted in, 'I'm afraid—'

Danny silenced him with a hand. 'I've got information that would interest you.'

'Oh.' Gobby sounded surprised. 'You want to be an informant?'

'No.'

'DCI MacKechnie,' the lawyer sounded ridiculously well spoken, 'I'm very much afraid that I don't really know what my client is suggesting, could we have a moment alone?'

Gobby took charge. 'No. Why did you come here? Are you willing to tell us about the cars?'

Danny seemed a lot less certain now. 'Or what?'

'Or nothing,' said Morrow.

'Or you'll arrest me for buying a spark plug?'

'Mr McGrath,' she said, 'why did you come in here voluntarily? Why are you paying to have your lawyer with you to be here?'

Danny sat back, threw both arms behind his chair back, baring his chest at her, his chin out. 'How come, Alex, how come I know where you live? How come I know,' he hesitated at the next threat, 'where your wean goes to nursery?'

Morrow sat back and looked at him. He thought he knew her, had picked up details about her life from gossip but he didn't know the big stuff. He didn't know anything about Gerald and that was all that mattered. Danny was not her family. She looked at him for a long time and when she finally spoke she was calm. 'Mr McGrath, you know nothing about me.'

Gobby stood up. 'Come in here again,' he said sternly to the lawyer, 'and it'll be wasting police time.'

The lawyer nodded at his briefcase and packed up. It was only then that Danny took the trouble to look up at the video camera and saw the wire and the jack dangling loose.

Morrow hurried downstairs ahead of all of them and met Routher in reception. 'Ma'am, your husband's outside in the yard. Wants to see you.'

Aleesha was on medication, that was true. Paracetamol. The operation had gone well, it was two days ago and they'd taken her off the morphine fourteen hours ago. But she pretended to be slightly out of it, walking as if she was a little unsteady, stepping slow, picking things up and putting them down again as if she'd forgotten they already had a tray on the rails at the self-service canteen, they already had a spoon, sugar portions. She was doing it for a reason. She was doing it as a test.

Roy seemed protective, stepped to the side when a trolley hurried past, shielding her. He gently put the second tray back, the sugar back, spoke softly to her. As he paid for the bottle of water for her and mug of tea for himself she watched his face. He was grieving, the sorrow so deep behind his eyes that it wasn't shaken by superficial expressions like smiles to tea ladies and remembering the spoon.

When he took the change of his fiver she saw him glance at the charity box for the hospital, look at his change, knowing he should put some of it in and then decide not to. She saw the micro-expression on his face as he felt bad about it. She liked that.

He led her carefully over to a corner seat, away from the bustle near the corridor, sat her in the chair least likely to be jostled and took the opposite for himself. He sat down, put the bottle of water on the table in front of her, set the tea by his elbow and put the tray on the floor resting on the table leg. He looked up at her, his eyes starting at her chin, weaving up past her lips, the bridge of her nose, luxuriating over her eyebrows and finally meeting her eyes. She saw all the grief evaporate, the hurt lift from him and was aware that she was doing that.

'Roy?'

'Yeah, I'm Roy.'

'Um, Roy, why are you sad?'

He shrugged, eyes slid to the side, sinking again into grief. 'I've lost ...' He seemed to forget what he was saying.

Aleesha peeled the label off the water bottle with her good hand, struggling to keep the bottle upright. He was looking at her.

'What's your story?'

She smiled.

'Seriously,' he insisted. 'What's the deal with you?'

'The deal?'

'Why are you pretending to be off your tits?'

She squared up to him, picked up the water bottle, pointed the nozzle at him in a warning. But he was smiling. 'I know what medicated looks like.'

She smiled back. 'You really like me, don't you?'

'Yeah.' He meant it so much he could hardly say it.

'Why do you like me?'

She was expecting a compliment, a cheesy list of good points: nice eyes, good hair, fit figure. Roy leaned back in his chair, pinched the handle to the mug and dropped his hand to the table and said the only thing in the world that would make her trust him: 'I've no idea. But I really, really do.'

Struggling to drink the water through a wide grin Aleesha looked at him. He sat watching her, eyes narrowed in appreciation, mapping her arms, her shoulders, loving her. Her

358

heart rate was increasing, her breaths deepening, as she looked at him across the plastic bottle. She swallowed, felt the narrow nozzle suck on her lip as she took the bottle from her mouth.

'Roy?'

He smiled just hearing her say the name.

'Roy, do you have a car?'

Morrow didn't recognise the car. It wasn't their car but she looked into it because it was the only civilian car in the yard that she didn't recognise immediately. A lumbering pale blue Honda Accord. The gesture was so unexpected it took the breath from her. She stopped on the ramp, holding the handrail for support.

He was in the driver's seat, hands resting on his thighs, looking out at her. Brian had bought a car without asking her. A second-hand car. Not a remarkable car, bit of a shit car actually, but an exact replica of the car he'd owned when they met.

He had stopped at the bus stop outside the Battlefield Rest Rotunda at the Vicky and offered her a lift home when they were both at Langside College. They weren't friends but had sat near each other in history a few times, were aware of each other, had coffee with the same people once or twice.

Now, with a jaundiced policewoman's knowledge of the world, now, she would never get into a car with a man she didn't know. Now she would have leaned down, the rain pattering on her hood and her ankles freezing, and said thanks but no, she was fine to get the bus, she'd see him tomorrow, did he know he was parked in a yellow square? Now she'd never get in the car with Brian. But back then she'd felt the warmth billowing out of the passenger window and climbed in from the cold bus stop on the exposed road and pulled her hood down and he drove her to her door. They talked about music and the weather and the history teacher and how Brian liked hill walking and would she like to come sometime.

He had the car for two years and sold it for scrap before they got married. At her insistence they went together and bought a new car, more modest but fresh, new, with a promise of no problems.

At the bottom of the ramp the wind swirled around the floor of the police yard, ushering leaves under cars. The station door slapped shut behind her and some coppers squeezed past down the narrow ramp. She let them by and then hurried down to the pale blue car, standing in front of the bonnet, looking in at him. Brian looked back through the windscreen, reached up, took his glasses off. The bridge of his nose had two red oval indents, his eyes looked raw without glass over them. He looked younger.

Morrow wanted to fly through the windscreen and engulf him then, smother him with her body, swallow him. Instead she dropped her chin to her chest, hiding her face in case anyone saw her on the many cameras that were dotted around the yard, and stomped around to the passenger door. She opened it, the handle mechanism so much like a physical memory that she felt her hand cup her own younger trusting hand, felt the warmth from her smooth skin.

Heat billowed out from the cabin. Brian had the heater up full, just as he had the day at the bus stop. Later he'd told her it was so that she'd feel it when he wound the window down and asked her in, so she'd be tempted to come into the warm.

She dropped into the seat and slammed the door behind her. Raising a hand she flipped the sun shield down so that her wet eyes couldn't be seen from outside, not by the cameras or passersby coming on shift or going out in cars.

Morrow looked out of the side window, searching for a phrase or a line or a thing to say, but there were no words for this. Her eyes skirted over the bonnets of the cars lined up with theirs, over to the shit-brick wall around the yard, and she began to trace a journey through the mortar to the building. Next to her, far away, she was aware of Brian sighing.

A wrist touching her wrist. For the first time since Gerald died she didn't draw away from him, didn't flinch at the touch. It was so warm in the car she'd hardly noticed the movement of his hand as it flattened against the back of her hand.

Hand against hand, his wrist slipped up until it was on top of hers, edge to edge. His pinkie moved a millimetre, stroking her pinkie, and then, quick as a landslide, their fingertips found each other, working through and over in the secret language of lovers, saying things there were no words for.

Morrow's face was wet, her breath short, her eyes smarting bitterly, but she kept working her way across the wall, through the rough dips and dark valleys as she struggled for breath, remembering her place in the maze even when she shut her eyes to shed the shuddering veil of tears. She kept going until, quite suddenly, she found herself at the far wall with no further to go.

Out of the blue Brian said, 'I got sacked.'

She looked at the hand wound tightly around hers. A fine hand. Tiny hairs. The fingers loosened on hers, the tips stroking her fingertips. 'Haven't been in since ...'

She looked out of the window at the wall. People were moving outside, blurred uniforms, getting in cars, pulling out. 'We in trouble? Financially?'

'Might need to sell that house.' His fingers were moving quickly over hers, anxious, nervous, waiting for the warmth to turn.

She turned to look and found him turned away, face to the window, fat tears dripping off his chin. 'Oh, Brian. I hate that fucking house.'

Fingers through fingers, tight, tight and unmoving, Morrow raised Brian's hand to her lips and there it stayed.

39

Her belly touching the steering wheel, Sadiqa looked up apologetically at Morrow and MacKechnie. 'I'm fat ...' she said simply.

It didn't look very safe. 'Can't you push the seat back a bit?' asked McKechnie.

'My legs are short,' she said, looking around the cabin as if she might find something there to lengthen them.

Morrow leaned down to the open window. 'Can you drive it though?'

Drawing her stomach in Sadiqa made a determined face, nodded at the wheel. 'Yes. Yes, I can drive. I'm not really confident about motorway driving though.'

'Will you be OK?'

She looked at the dashboard, uncertain, as if she had been asked to fly a plane and decided, 'Yes.'

'Now, the officers are there already, you know where you're going?'

'Yeah.'

'You get out, put the bag behind the emergency telephone, get back in and rejoin the motorway, OK?'

'Then come back here?'

'Then come back here.'

It was freezing in the Obs van. Gobby was crouching on a small foldaway stool by the back doors. There was no room for him on the bench; MacKechnie and Morrow were perched there, giving them the best vantage point to watch the boxy grey screens.

The motorway cameras were high up and the images angled, one of four grey lanes, crash barrier in the middle. It was a long stretch of straight road, good for reading the number plate on any car, and the camera was angled so that the drivers' faces could be clearly seen, well lit by the street lights. They could go back over any one of them and still and print it. Great in court.

It was a main artery, a busy bit of road for the time of night. A steady parade of cars and vans and lorries came towards the camera, drove under it, front seat faces talking, silent, singing, picking noses or slack, hypnotised by the blandness of the road. Another boxy screen showed a lay-by with an emergency phone in the foreground. The image was still apart from passing lights licking the edge of the image. They had two other screens, both trained on junctions, in case the kidnappers got that far before they were intercepted.

'Everybody where they should be?' asked MacKechnie, not actually knowing where they should be.

'Sorted, sir,' said Morrow.

MacKechnie was delighted with her but it only highlighted how poorly he had thought of her before. He was imagining the glory before them, she felt, and points at which to siphon it off. His respectfulness made her uncomfortable. Morrow was born on the back foot and only ever felt easy as an underdog.

They sat in silence for ten tense minutes, watching the grey shapes shifting in front of them, their eyes flicking from screen to screen. She had ordered radio silence; if the kidnappers were at all professional they'd be listening to the police frequencies. She rang Harris on his mobile. He was where he was supposed to be and nothing had happened.

''Kay,' she said. 'Be ready.'

The bench was small and there wasn't a lot of room to move. MacKechnie looked at her casually and it felt like a prelude to an awkward kiss. Morrow checked her watch – they were almost ten minutes late for the one-hour deadline.

'There!' she said pointing to the four-lane screen.

They could see Sadiqa trundling slowly towards them, saw another driver change lanes to avoid her. Then, on monitor two, a lorry hurried past and frightened her into slowing down even more. Unused to motorway driving, Sadiqa took the outside lane, drawing attention to herself by driving at the speed limit and verging slowly to the right every time she checked her rear mirror. She disappeared off camera for a moment, should have been pulling into the drop point.

On another monitor, in grainy black and white, reverse lights flashed on the emergency phone as Sadiqa backed up in the lay-by. MacKechnie breathed a curse, watching as she missed the emergency phone post by inches.

Sadiqa stopped, pulled on the handbrake so hard the car seemed to be taking a deep breath. The door opened and she got out. Stagily, she looked at the cars passing, standing at the open door, and waddled around to the boot, opened it and pulled out the black holdall. Sadiqa then dropped it heavily onto the road, tried to pick it up again and seemed defeated. She bent down, inelegantly bending her little legs out to the side, taking one of the handles, dragging it over behind the emergency post. She stood up, looking at it. She seemed to be talking to the bag. She turned and went back to the car, opened the door, sat down and shut the door. The engine restarted,

'I can hardly bear to watch her pull back out,' said Mac-Kechnie to no one.

A couple of stalls, and she finally made it back onto the

road, reappearing in a further screen a good bit further down the road. But they weren't watching Sadiqa. They were watching the bag.

Car headlights strobed past, oblivious to the forty grand in the bag. A lorry rumbled past. A ragged plastic bag floated by. Morrow's eyes strayed to the other screens. Steady, no special driving, no strange vans with too many men in the front seat for the time of night.

'There!' MacKechnie was on his feet, watching as a car pulled into the lay-by, hazards flashing, pulling in too far along, just the front half of the vehicle in shot.

'Shit,' said Morrow who was on her feet too. 'I asked them to broaden the shot. Shit!'

A bald man got out of the car, a saloon, came around to the boot, bent down to look at his tail lights. He stood up, stroked his head as if he was trying to comfort himself, looked around. Cars flashed past him as he stood and watched. Gobby scribbled down the number plate and called it in for a check.

The man got back in his car and went away. Gobby hung up his mobile and looked at Morrow. 'Random?'

She shrugged. Even if it all went tits up, if Aamir died and the money was lost, she had Brian, had held his hand and a future felt possible.

The change was so slow that the apparent movement seemed at first to be a feature of the weak light in the empty lay by. The bag was moving.

MacKechnie squinted. An arm, from off-camera, coming out of the dark hillside out of shot, a foot just visible getting purchase to pull the heavy load up the steep incline. Two hands on the handle, suddenly moving fast, swinging it up the hill and disappearing. MacKechnie panicked and stood up. 'Shit, shit! The other side, they've come from the other side of the motorway!' He turned on Morrow, blocking her view of the monitors. 'What's on the other side of the motorway?'

Morrow didn't get to her feet. She sat still, watching all the screens intently. Gobby looked down at her and spoke: 'They never came on the motorway, ma'am.'

She reached forward and touched MacKechnie's hip, pushing him out of the way of her view. 'OK,' she said slowly. 'OK.'

Eddy hardly had a breath in him. As well as having to negotiate the steepness of the hillside he had to pick his steps. The slope was covered in wide netting to stop stones tumbling down onto the motorway and he caught his toes, almost falling over, almost dropping the bag. At the crest of the hill he stopped for a gasp and lunged forward, leaving the bright lights from the motorway and tumbling into the dark field.

Stubs of cut straw crumpled beneath his heavy boots. Two hundred yards to the dark Peugeot, T had the wit to turn the lights off but Eddy could see his outline in the driver's seat, his puff of silver hair a beacon in the dark.

Eddy had forty grand in his hand, forty grand in readies, but more than that, better than that, he had done it. Not Malki, not Pat, none of them. He had successfully organised and done it. A surge of energy made him lurch forward, his feet in the flat boots stumbling after him, the heavy bag swinging at his knees, dragging him back and forth off centre. His heart was bursting in his chest.

T didn't look up when Eddy arrived and ran around the back, popping the boot, chucking the bag carelessly in and skipping around to the passenger side. He opened the door and T leaned across, blocking his seat. 'Check the money for trackers? Check for paint bombs?'

Eddy's lungs were burnt. He'd run too long without

drawing breath, but he staggered back to the boot and pulled the bag onto the road as T had told him to. He tugged at the zip until it came open all the way.

Bundles of twenties held together with red elastic bands, messy, like someone had done it at home. Bricks in the bottom to weigh the bag, in case it had been blown away, but no tracker boxes, no paint bombs in amongst it all. Eddy ran his hand over the money and found that he was salivating.

'Well?' T was calling to him from the front seat.

'Nothing.'

'Hurry, then.'

He threw the bag back in, slammed the boot and lunged for the passenger door, aware that his knees were aching and strained from running in unwieldy boots. He was too old for this, for the excitement and the physical strains. Next time he'd mastermind it and sit in a car while someone else ran half a mile to the roadside and climbed up a steep hill. He could feel the hot scorch of the cold night air in his windpipe, felt the dull pain in his knees and his heart battering in his chest. He threw himself into the passenger seat and slammed the door after him.

'Well done, son,' said T. 'Very well done,' and he drove off at a regular speed, as if they were out for a late-night dawdle, lights still off, a small smile on his face.

'Now, you know, Eddy, you can just give me back the guns and we'll call it even. Have ye them on ye now?'

Eddy looked at him and it occurred to him suddenly that maybe T didn't really think he had done well, that maybe T was planning to shoot him in the face.

The outside world suddenly flashed, bright white light flooding in through every window, scorching Eddy's retina so he couldn't see T but he could hear him: a gasp and gargle, a kind of mad hissing groan in response to the blinding light. It seemed an odd thing to say.

Slowly the Peugeot rolled off the road and veered into a shallow ditch with a small, harmless bump. Eddy couldn't open his eyes but heard the horn groan loudly, mournfully. He threw his hands over his face and peered under his elbow.

T was facing him, his cheek pressed into the centre of the wheel, eyes rolled back. His top set of dentures had slipped to a diagonal in his mouth and Eddy knew that he wasn't breathing, saw the special quality of the stillness about him.

'Wake up!' He was whimpering, not talking. 'Wake up!'

The car settled into the ditch, the bright white lights began to dim around them as a series of search lights were switched off. The car was surrounded and T's body tipped forward, taking the weight of his head off the horn.

Eddy dropped his hands from his face.

In front of him, around the bonnet, by both doors were the black silhouettes of men in flack vests, heavily armed, all with weapons trained on him.

Standing outside Morrow knew it would take a month to preserve the scene properly. A square half-mile of drab concrete littered with rubble, dust and fibres. A marsh beyond it made the place damp, meaning everyone who had been here in the past five years would have left a detectable trace of themselves.

Stunned that his co-conspirator was dead of a heart attack, Eddy Morrison had confessed and given them a map of Breslin's machine works, a crude drawing of a loading bay opening with a lintel dropped over the doorway and a pathway cut through a couple of big halls into the very back of the dark building. This was the last place they had seen Aamir, in a boiler at the back Aamir had killed his guard, Eddy claimed, and run off. Morrow didn't believe it. It made Eddy sound too innocent. Those stories were rarely true.

Harris sidled up next to her. 'What ye thinking, ma'am?'

They could preserve the scene for evidence or plough straight in and find out what happened. She looked at the split lintel over the door. 'OK, let's call it life and limb. Harris, you're coming with me.'

'Thank you, ma'am,' He sounded obsequious and immediately blushed and regretted it.

They got torches out of the boot, issue searchlights with handles and batteries that weighed four pounds. Harris used his weight to lift one and Morrow lugged the other one through the doorway, carefully picking a roundabout path that no one else would choose, skirting around the obvious way in order to preserve the evidence. The place was crumbling in on itself. As her torch beam licked up the walls she could see layers of the walls collapsing down to the floor, dust thick as snowdrifts, a great bubbled mess on the floor. Harris spotted the trails of footsteps back and forth from one room and silently made her aware of it by circling his torch over it. As they approached the back room the footsteps took on a darker colour; Morrow thought at first it was a quality of the dust, that it was just darker underneath, until Harris stopped swinging his light and she saw the smears on the bare concrete. Brown, like the Anwars' wall in the hall. Blood.

Eddy had told them about Malki but Morrow wouldn't have believed how pitiful he looked. A skinny boy, much too thin, not like Omar, not all muscle and sinew waiting to put on weight when his mouth finally caught up with his metabolism, but sickly thin, ill-fed thin, the bones of his skinny knees showing through his white tracksuit. And his brand new trainers, a shock of white against the black darkness of the boiler.

She stood on the metal ladder and swept the torch across the belly of the boiler. Aamir Anwar was gone.

They called it off. At seven in the morning the fingertip search around Breslin's was called off and all the officers were bussed back to the station to sign up for their overtime claims. The helicopter veered across the bay, taking its searchlight with it, the dinghys on the marshes found mooring and their passengers disembarked. The diving teams packed up and went home. Not a trace had been found of Aamir Anwar.

Morrow stood by the metal steps as SOC officers sorted around Malki Tait's body, picking through the detritus of a building crumbling in on itself. It was freezing here and smelled of metal and dust. The SOCs had rigged up bright spotlights, pointing them at the ceiling for the soft, deflected light. Thick flexes from the portable generator were strung across the dirty floor. Morrow felt the cold, shuddered at the strange way sound moved around the room and thought of poor Aamir and how terrified he must have been alone here with a dead body, and how frightened he would have been for his daughter, how frightened and cold and lonely.

She pulled her coat tight around her middle, thought warm thoughts of Brian, how still he was, how he could let her be and sit quiet in her company.

Morrow smiled to herself. She knew exactly where Aamir was.

40

Towards Leadhills the M74 broadens into three lanes of perfect tarmac that snake gracefully through big soft hills. Great feats of engineering lift the road across the uneven ground so that it remains perfectly level while the land around it dips and rolls, making the road separate from the land, of it, but steadier, more perfect.

Through a cleft of massive hills the road slopes down to the right for three miles and then rights itself to the left, rolling clockwise around a hill moulded by time and rain into a colossal green bowling ball. On the vale below a narrow silver river snakes deep through mossy green fields like a wire through cheese.

Aleesha had chosen the music, Glasvegas, which she insisted Roy should love or not be regarded seriously as a person. It wasn't the sort of music he was used to listening to, in the nightclubs he'd worked in the music was older, more dance tunes, everything she liked was a bit guitary.

She was looking out of the window at the vale, her bare feet resting on the dashboard, a red enamelled ring on her big toe. She didn't want a seat belt on. Said they scratched her neck.

'Wow.'

'Ever done this drive before?'

'No.'

'Beautiful.'

'Hm.'

He was coming up to the curve, going fast because that

was how she liked it, in the inside lane. Aleesha was in a hurry to get away.

'Can I have my hand back?' he said.

She looked at the big meaty hand beneath her good one, resting on the gearstick. She held it up by the index finger. 'This old thing? What do you need this for?'

Roy smiled. 'I need it to drive, to steer the car we're driving in at seventy miles an hour.'

She flipped around in the seat so that she was kneeling facing him, still holding his hand by the finger. 'You know, Roy, if you loved me really, if you really, really loved me, as a sign of how much you loved me, I think you could do everything with one hand too.'

'Like a love token thing?'

'Like a sign of how incredibly close and alike we are, you could do that.' She was leaning towards him, breathing on his ear in a way she knew was distracting, one of her lips touched the rim of his ear. He felt a shudder in his cock.

Behind them an articulated lorry was nudging up the middle lane, and Roy was vaguely aware that the lorry was going too fast for the curve they were coming up to, too fast and in the wrong lane, boxing them in. Behind him, a hundred feet away but closing, was a pale blue sports car.

Aleesha worked her warm tongue around the folds on his ear.

Morrow and Harris, Gobby and Routher ran up the cold concrete stairs, the sound of their steps following them, echo catching the echo so that they sounded like a squadron running in formation.

There he was, standing outside the door, sentry-stiff on the mat, his cardigan buttoned up to his neck, hands flat by his thighs. Honour may have dampened his eyes but his training allowed him to do hard things, bad things.

373

Morrow gave him a look that ordered him back into the hall. As she followed him in Lander stumbled backwards into the living room, followed by Morrow and the three men. She raised a finger as if she might slap him. 'Where is he?'

He hesitated, ran his tongue along the stubbled line of his moustache and looked at them again. His hand came up slowly to a door at the back of the living room. For no reason other than annoyance, Morrow kicked the door open.

The bed was army made, blankets and sheet, the corners folded as neatly as an envelope. It was his feet she saw first, gnarled old man's feet, yellowed hard skin with a white tinge, like bracken, over brown skin. He was dressed in purple and gold striped pyjamas, Lander's probably; they were too short for him. He had a cut on his ankle and a plaster on his wrist. His hands were limp by his side, his mouth hanging open, teeth worn down through to the pulp, like a sheep's.

Aamir Anwar was flat on his back, the pillow to Lander's single bed sat neatly on a nearby chair. They had slipped off, the headphones tuned to the AM radio sat crazily so that one small disc of grey foam was on his cheek, the other tucked behind his head.

Behind them Lander whispered, 'He needs to sleep. He's taken a pill.'

Morrow spun to meet him. 'How the fuck did he even get here?'

'I dunno. He chapped my door. Said he needed a rest. I wanted to call ye but he said to give him a minute and could he have one of my sleeping pills.' He pointed to the headphones. 'Australia are getting gubbed.' He smiled as if that was news that would please everyone.

'His family are frantic!' she said, knowing it was a lie,

knowing she was really talking about herself.

Lander looked at his old friend, at the soft rise and fall of his chest, and he grinned so wide that all of his own stubby worn old teeth were showing. 'Aye,' he said, 'but Aamir's all right. As for the rest, I don't really give a hoot.'

A crowd had gathered at the service station, an elderly coach party from Newcastle on their way to the Highlands. They were buying nice Marks and Spencer's sandwiches to eat on the long journey north and standing in an orderly queue for the checkout along the window looking out over the motorway.

Across the forecourt they were standing close, he holding the petrol pump, she leaning her forehead on his free shoulder. Aleesha and Roy were filling the car up for a long drive.

The petrol hummed, the gauge clicked and she whispered into his side, 'Roy?'

'Aye?'

'Roy.'

He gave a deep contented sigh. 'Aye.'

She cleared her throat. 'Roy? When we ... you know ... first ...'

Roy wrapped his free arm around her waist and drew her tiny frame towards him. 'When we first what?'

She didn't answer.

He smiled down at her and tried to rock her from foot to foot. She clung to him, head down, not looking at him, feet planted. She seemed a little afraid.

He used his chin to rock her face up to his. 'Doll, nothing's wrong, nothing can be wrong, I'm here with you. Everything, anything ... if you don't want ... you know, for *years*, that's fine by me, either way, just as long as we're together, anything. Anything you want.'

'Not first *that*, I'm not ... it's not that.'

'When we first what, then?'

She pulled away from him, looked at the window of old people staring at them, drinking in how young and lithe and in love they were. 'When we first *met* ...'

Roy frowned and shook the petrol gun in the hole, shaking off the drips. His jaw was clenched as he hung the gun on the petrol tank.

They could make it a lie, all he had to do was say 'at the hospital' – 'When we met at the hospital?' She was young, biddable, he could make her say they met at the hospital. And if they said it enough, after a while, the lie would seem true, between them, would be the story they told the children. But he was Roy now and Roy couldn't make himself tell Aleesha that lie.

Panic tightened in his chest. She was moving away from him, he could feel the light dying and soon he would be alone in the darkness again. 'When ...?'

'I's thinking, you know that, like, really, that's one worry we don't have.' She drew in a breath so deep it arched her back and, staring at the old people in the window, spun on one foot and dropped an arm around his neck. 'I mean, it's good in a way,' she whispered. 'I mean, 'cause, you've kind of already met my parents.' Holding onto his neck she lifted her legs, wrapping them around his waist.

A sob caught his throat, sounding like a hiccup and he pulled her flat against him, burying his face in her soft neck, tears wetting the perfect skin.

Despite the odds Roy and Aleesha clung tight to each other for a long, long time, until her legs were stiff and he felt very, very old.

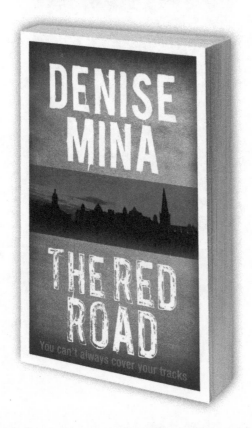

I

1997

Rose Wilson was fourteen but looked sixteen. Sammy said it was a shame.

She was alone in his car, in a dark city centre street of shuttered pubs and clubs. Outside, the soft summer breeze stirred the silt of a Saturday night, lifting paper wrappers, rolling empty cans. Rose watched a yellow burger box crab-scuttle from the mouth of a dark alley and tentatively make its way across the pavement to the kerb.

She was waiting for Sammy to drive her back. It had been a long night. A sore night. Three parties in different flats. She used to think she was lucky she wasn't freezing on the streets but she wasn't sure tonight. He was off arranging next week. Lots of dough, he said with a twinkle in his eye.

Rose leaned her head on the window. Sammy was full of shit – they weren't making a lot of money. She shut her eyes. They weren't even doing it for the money. He was doing it to make other men like him, so he had something they wanted. She was making them pay for what they were taking anyway. But they went through this pretence, like it was a big moneymaker, her being underage. He said the money was lower than he promised because she did look sixteen, but never mind, eh? She still had a good long time to make her money. The men weren't interested in her age. They weren't perverts. Rose knew all too well that those men just befriended some daft junkie cow with six weans and took it for free. The men Sammy fed her to were just normal men. They liked that she was young because they knew no one would believe her. Nothing easier than making a wean shut up.

But Sammy needed to lie to himself, pretending he was a businessman or something. He'd save the money, he said, and they'd live together when she was legal. It was about the money and he loved her, they loved each other. Whenever he said that he looked deep into her eyes, like a stage hypnotist she once saw at the Pavilion.

Before her mum died, Rose never went out. She hardly even went to school. She couldn't leave her mum alone with the young kids because she was always nodding out and dropping lit cigarettes, letting anyone into the house. But she went out that one time because she didn't want to let Ida down. Ida T. was their neighbour back in the flats. Ida was decent. She knew there were problems, more than normal. Thinking Rose's mum was like herself, but with loads of kids, Ida thought she'd feel better if she got more fun out of life, had a laugh. She bought two tickets for the late-night hypnotism show. By the time Ida came to collect her Rose's mum was asleep and looked like staying that way, so Rose pulled her coat on and went instead.

When the lights went down and the show started the hypnotist got everyone in the audience to press both hands together as if they were praying, and then told them that their hands were stuck.

In the dark theatre Rose's tiny hands came apart easily. So did Ida's. They both thought the trick hadn't worked until people began to stand up, lifting prayerful hands, laughing, baffled. They kept their hands together as they clambered over knees and bags, making their way to the aisle, and assembled on the stage, prayer-stuck, beseeching the Almighty for a bit of naughty fun.

The hypnotist gave them orders, stupid things to do, and the rest of the audience laughed at them. Some of the people on stage were having sex with chairs, taking their tops off, snogging invisible movie stars; some of them weren't hypnotised. Rose

2

could tell. They were pretending, so they could get up on stage and act stupid and get attention or something. It was a lie they all agreed to tell each other.

When Sammy looked deep into her eyes and said they were doing it for the money she pretended like she was hypnotised. Love you too. But Rose's hands came apart in the dark. She was waiting until she could get away from him, until she could find someone else, someone that she didn't need to lie to. You did need somebody to cling to, she knew that.

She looked out at the street of pubs and clubs, where pals and cousins and sisters and workmates had met and spent the evening together. Her brothers and sisters had been scattered all over, adopted into different families down in England. It wasn't even that long ago but she couldn't remember all of their faces properly. She didn't miss the responsibility, the weight of them all. She watched them leave, relieved. They wouldn't miss her, she was sure. Wherever they went would be better than where they'd been. They might do all right, in a new place. She let them go. Rose had been twelve and a half, too old for adoption, she knew that. People wanted to adopt fresh kids, and she wasn't that.

Everyone else had someone. They weren't even grateful. Mostly they complained about who they had. Rose hated kids at school whining about their folks. Moaning because someone demanded to know where they'd been all night, angry if they came home covered in bruises, smelling of sick and spunk.

Sorry for herself, she felt that familiar plummet in mood. She couldn't control the drop, or slow it, because she was so tired, it was morning, and she was heading back for a fight with the care-home staff because she had been out all night. She ran through the night staff rota in her head: that new woman was on, the tall one, so Rose wouldn't even be able to fall back on the old trick to get out of a grilling: she couldn't pull her clothes off and force the male support worker to leave the room. The staff were always calm, she hated that. They never raised their voices or got

3

excited or screamed because they loved you. Sammy screamed and shouted. Sammy's mood rose and fell, swooped and dived from extreme to extreme. That's what first made her notice him. He stopped her on her way to school and said she was beautiful and she got embarrassed and told him to fuck off. The next day he was there, waiting to see her, but now he was angry and told her she was full of herself, wake up, hen, you've got an arse the size of Partick. Then the next day he was sorry, he looked sorry too. He just wanted to talk. He felt this connection between them, that's why he came back. Rose had kept her eyes down since her mother died. The first time she looked up it was for Sammy's bullshit.

Her mood was shifting now, swooping low, low, low, below angry. Random memories that echoed her mood came to mind: taking her pants off in a hallway stacked with bin bags; a grubby avocado-coloured bath with yellow fag burns; four men looking up at her from a living room.

She'd never admit it to her psychologist, but she did use some of his techniques: she shut her eyes, breathed deeply and summoned Pinkie Brown.

Pinkie holding her hand, his big hand over her small hand. Pinkie stirring a pot of food. Pinkie in their clean, wee flat. Pinkie holding a baby, their baby, maybe.

It worked. The breathing and the images shifted the tar-black mood. The psychologist said you could only hold one thought in your head at a time and she could choose that thought. It wasn't easy, he said, but she could choose.

Pinkie sitting on a settee watching a football match on telly, wearing joggers and no top. Pinkie's hand brushing his buzz cut.

The truth was that she didn't really know Pinkie Brown. She'd spotted him a couple of times when they fought with Cleveden, the other kids' home nearby. She saw him standing at the back, a head taller than everyone else. He was different. He was in charge. She noticed him cup the elbow of a crying child, his wee brother Michael, as it turned out. He'd be good with kids, she knew he would. He caught her eye twice, once in the street, once outside school. A girl at school said Pinkie had asked about Rose.

Pinkie Brown got stuck in her head and she made up stories about him: Pinkie was her childhood sweetheart. Sure, they both grew up in care, but they understood family, like those wee girls in the home with bad teeth: their mum walked all the way across the city to visit so she could spend her bus fare on sweeties for them.

In Rose's story she and Pinkie grew up together. They stayed true to each other. When they were old enough they got a wee clean house, had a baby. They wore matching rings from Argos. He never cared what she'd done in her early life either. He understood and she made good money. Maybe she'd stop it when she got older and could. Maybe she'd go to college and become a social worker, not like her social worker but a really good one, one who actually knew what went on, and could stop stuff happening to kids like her.

Better. A warm lift took the black edge off her. She felt the mood subside. Getting dozy, she sat up and bit her cheek to keep herself awake. She had to stay on guard because when she got in the staff would take her in the office and quiz her about where she had been all night. She must not say anything about Sammy or the parties or the men. They'd kill her. They never threatened her but she heard them talk. Easiest thing in the world, getting rid of a girl no one was looking for. And the staff: she didn't want them to know about this other world. The kids all said they hated the staff but there was something sweet about some of them, hoping they could help. She didn't want to spoil things for them.

So she opened her burning eyes, sat up and found herself looking straight at Pinkie Brown.

He stepped out of a dark alley, side-wall to ChipsPakoraKebab. He was looking straight back at her. Her pulse throbbed in her throat. He had come, as if her yearning had conjured him from the filthy dark.

Stepping out of the shadows, he kept his eyes locked on hers as he walked fast towards the car. Street lights hit him and she saw his dark T-shirt was ripped at the hem, wet all down the front.

He reached forward, pulled the passenger door open. 'Rosie fae Turnberry.' He was breathless, skin glistening with sweat and panic. 'Come on.'

Elated, Rosie stepped out to meet him, and then she saw the red splatter on his neck, on his forearm. His T-shirt was soaked in blood.

He shut the car door behind her and pulled her deep into the alley. Heavy chip-fat air was cut through with the sharp smell of piss.

''S that your blood?' she asked, aware that it was the first thing she had ever said to him in real life.

'Nut.' The alley was dark. 'Guys frae the Drum jumped us. Battered our Michael.' The kid he'd comforted: his brother – he cared about that kid. 'I'd tae get them off him.'

'Was it another home?'

'Nut.' He looked at her then, to see if she understood, and she did. When not-in-care gangs came, they were after all of you. Cleveden or Turnberry meant nothing to them. To them you were all care-home scum. They knew you'd get the blame for everything.

'Rose.' Pinkie lifted a hand between them. 'Take this?'

Not a ring from Argos. Instead, in his open palm, sat a Rambo knife, curved blade, ragged teeth. The handle was gaffer-taped silver, spongy with blood.

'Put it down your sock and I'll come for it later?' He raised the hand towards her face. 'Gonnae hide it for me? The polis'll search Cleveden for sure. I need it but I can't keep a hold of it.'

The bloody knife was inches from her nose.

He watched her expectantly but Rose didn't move. Her eyes

6

brimmed with stinging tears. She kept staring at the blurry knife. She blinked and behind her lids saw yellow burns on a green bath. She opened them and a tear fell, landing on the dirty blade: a clean silver splash on the red.

'Don't be scared,' he said, but Rose wasn't crying because she was scared. 'You like me, don't you?'

Rose lifted her hand slowly and took the knife by the handle. It was wet and sticky. It didn't matter. She had touched worse.

Pinkie smiled, whispered, 'Your prints are on that now.'

A trap. Eight men in a flat, not Sammy's one friend. Drunk men, dirty bed, vodka to wash her mouth clean. Her hold tightened on the handle and blood oozed from the gaffer tape, like mud through toes.

He sensed the change in her and tried to soften it. 'I like you too, Rose.' But he said it flat, like 'nice to meet you', like 'it's for your own good', like 'we're only trying to help'.

Pinkie Brown had clocked her like she clocked punters with cash and a conscience. She could read compunction like other kids read crisp flavours and Pinkie Brown had read her. He would never hold her hand or stir a pot or coo at a baby. There was no one in the wee clean house. There was no house. When she made up those stories about him, she had been pressing her hands together, convincing herself they were stuck. Well, they were unstuck now.

This was all there was. Dirt and piss smells and Sammy and filth. She shut her eyes tight.

'Rose, I've see ye at school—' Pinkie's shadow was over her, his breath in her face.

Hope exhausted, she shoved him away.

Except she didn't.

She meant to shove him, slap his shoulder in a flat cold rage. But he had moved and she'd forgotten the Rambo knife in her hand. The sensations registered in her elbow: teeth catching in meat. Warm wet flecked on her cheek. Disgust and panic made her jerk her hand down fast, sawing through whatever she was caught on. Down and down, the knife ground free. She dropped it, heard the chink of cutlery on stone. She shut her eyes tighter, pressing her lips together so that nothing splashed into her mouth.

A suck of air signalled the weight of him dropping to the ground. She heard him land, heard him grunt with surprise. She heard a splash on cobbles. The rubber sole of his trainers shrieked as he scrabbled against the floor. Then he was still.

She couldn't look. The wet on her face began to cool.

Wary, she opened the eye closest to the wall. Normal. Dark, smelly, night. The stench of piss and fat. She looked down. The cobbles were molten.

Pinkie was on the ground and next to him lay the knife. He had fallen sideways, arms out, eyes half open. He lay completely still except for something moving under his neck, a brief throb that caught the silver light.

Rose watched the beat slow. She stood, barely breathing, looking sixteen, feeling twelve. A slow dawning realisation: a door had shut. She would never get away. They'd cut her up and leave her in a bag.

Keeping her hands on the wall behind her, she bent down, picked up the knife and tucked it into her sock like Pinkie said to. She slid upright against the wall, fingers sticky because her jeans and socks were covered with blood.

Rose blinked and turned off all her physical sensations, she knew how to do that. Then she clung onto the wall, edging backwards out of the alley, smearing bloody prints as she edged away.

She crossed the pavement to the car, not even looking to see if there was anyone there. Back inside the car she locked the door, pulled on the seat belt and sat still, looking blankly out of the window.

As soon as Sammy saw what she had done she was dead. Like her mum. A man on top of her. A fat, smothering man on top

8

of her mum in the dark kitchen, heels kicking the floor, a fat man on top of her. She kept kicking, as if it would help. Kicking against air, looking for a thing to kick against. Rose closed the bedroom door and stood against it, watching the wee ones, praying that none of them would move or wake or make a noise. She stood behind the door until the man left. A drunk, fat, clumsy man, brushing against walls on the way out, never seen again, never found. Her mum had tried suicide many times, failed and was sorry she'd failed and yet she died kicking against air.

Rose sat in Sammy's car and thought about that for an hour or a day or a minute, she couldn't tell. Finally Sammy sauntered along the street. He walked up to the car, not looking in the alley. As he put the key in the door his plump belly flattened against the window. He would kill her. Or take her to the men who would kill her. Soon as he saw the blood on her she was dead, but he climbed back in without looking at her.

Sammy was bald at only twenty-four. He was fat too. He looked about fifty to her. She looked sixteen but he looked fucking fifty or something, disgusting.

'Fucking hell, guess what?' he said, looking out of the windscreen, his voice normal and loud and cheerful.

'What?' Rose asked, numb.

'Princess Diana's dead.' He huffed a small laugh. ''Magine! Died in a car crash in Paris.'

Rose couldn't see how that was relevant. 'Fuck off,' she said, mechanically.

He smiled at that and started the engine. 'Aye. In a car crash.'

''King hell,' said Rose.

Sammy flicked the lights on and pulled out into the deserted street.

'Wow,' he said as he drove. 'Makes you think.' He seemed excited about the whole thing. 'She was young to die. And those boys. What d'ye think Charles'll have to say about it?'

Rose wasn't used to discussing current events with Sammy, or

9

anything with Sammy. It made the night feel even more strange, him being chummy, like they always talked about stuff like this.

He nudged her with his fat elbow as they drove down Bath Street. 'What d'you think? Charles: what'll he be feeling?'

'Dunno.' She had to say something. 'Gutted?'

'Nah.' He smiled as he took a turn at some lights. 'Not gutted. He's free to marry that other one now.'

He gibbered on about it, about the Queen and Prince Charles. Rose tuned out. She didn't know about politics. She was so deep-down tired that she forgot Pinkie Brown. All she could remember was that she was dead and there was blood. Death filled her consciousness like an ache.

They were drawing up into the mouth of Turnberry Avenue. She reached down to absent-mindedly scratch away an itch from her ankle. As dampness registered on her fingertips she remembered: it was itchy because it was covered in Pinkie Brown's blood and she had killed him. She froze, bent double, her fingers touching the car floor like a sprinter on the blocks.

The kids' home was in a big Victorian villa at the heart of the posh West End. Sammy's eyes flicked around the street, checking for staff or witnesses.

'Good girl,' he said, seeing her bent down, thinking she was hiding for him.

He parked two hundred yards further up the road, in the deep shadow under a big old tree. A branch sagged down in front of them under the weight of leaves, heavy, swaying, leaves flipping over and back in the breeze, silver, black. Orange street lights winked through but dawn was already bleeding into the night. Rose stayed down.

Sammy was chatting away now, she thought he'd had a smoke or something while he was out of the car.

He said, 'One day you'll grow out of me, hen, you know? You'll move on in your young life, but I hope you'll remember me kindly. I think the world of you, you know.'

He waited for the responsorial lie – I'll never move on from you, Sammy, you're the only one in the world who gives a fuck about me – but Rose didn't say anything. She was thinking about air and kicking air and felt that same urge rise up in her.

Her eye fell on the posh flats outside, dark with curtains drawn. Sleeping in those flats were lawyers and students and dentists, refreshing themselves with warm, comfy sleeps. They'd wake up in a few hours, have calm breakfasts and then settle into Sunday. They'd get dressed and start writing letters to the council, complaining about the children's home bringing down property prices.

'What do you want for yourself, Rose?' he said, repeating the tone, changing the sentiment. 'From life, what do you want?' And then he pulled on the handbrake as if he was planning to settle in for a long conversation.

'Dough,' she told the floor. She couldn't get up. He'd see the blood.

'Well, you're going the right way about that, hen.' He laughed softly. 'What ye doing down there?' He was looking at her now, his big stupid face kind of gawping.

What was she doing down here? The question howled through her. What was she doing all the way down here? Why was *she* all the way down here? The injustice of it struck her so suddenly and completely that she had to blink to warm her eyes. Why were other girls asleep? Why were they wearing ironed clothes and worried about the size of their thighs and learning piano and painting their fingernails and she was down here?

Rose looked back at him, her fingers creeping up her leg, drawing the jeans up with them until she felt the gaffer tape.

'You're in a strange mood – what's down there—'

She bolted up against the air, swung the knife at his neck, in and out. She'd kicked and now she shut her eyes, curled up knees to chin, cowering into the passenger door.

Wet gasps and thrashing. Rain in the car. Sammy kicking, feet scrabbling against the pedals. He grabbed her hair and yanked her down to the side.

Slowly, his fingers relented, slid down her wet arm and disappeared. Rose waited as the thrashing slowed. Like her mum, Sammy's legs were the last thing to still. The only sound in the car was a wet gurgle.

Sammy deflated, wilting onto the steering wheel, and the horn eased out a long droning blare.

Rose couldn't hide indoors, she was covered in blood.

She couldn't run away. When the police found the body of Sammy the Perv the first place they'd look was the children's home; the first thing they'd notice was that she was missing. Even if she got away from the police the men would find her.

She'd never get away.

She opened her eyes and looked out of a window filigreed with blood, deaf to the skirl of the horn.

Outside the car lights burst on in flats. Curtains drew back. Angry faces looking for the car horn ripping their Sunday morning. Rose watched the street lights deferring to the dawn, flicking off, one by one.

She sat inside the bloody car and waited for the police to come.